PRAISE

"Clipston (*With This Ring*) .... the idyllic backdrop of Coral Cove, N.C. . . . . Clipston builds the chemistry between gruff Cade and chipper, can-do Everleigh through a satisfying mix of flirty exchanges and revealing conversations as the two work to untangle their problems and, with the aid of their faith, find their way to one another. Readers won't be able to resist this."

—*Publishers Weekly* for *Second Chance at Sunshine Inn*

"Amy Clipston's *Second Chance at Sunshine Inn* is like a warm hug on a rainy day. With relatable characters, tender emotions, and a charming seaside setting, this story of two strangers brought together by an unexpected inheritance will tug at your heartstrings. It's a beautiful reminder that love and second chances often appear when you least expect them."

—Rachel Hanna, *USA TODAY* bestseller of *The Inn at Seagrove*

"Amy Clipston masterfully weaves the grumpy-sunshine trope with a setting so charming you'll want to book a stay yourself. Readers will fall for Cade and Everleigh's undeniable chemistry, their emotional journey, and the delightful nod to Sweet Home Alabama. *Second Chance at Sunshine Inn* is a feel-good, swoonworthy story that will leave you smiling long after the last page."

—Heidi McCahan, Bestselling author of *Her Alaskan Family*

"Say 'I do' to *With This Ring*, a warm and fuzzy second-chance romance filled with family, forgiveness, and fairy-tale wedding feels. I loved the charming town of Flowering Grove, especially Dakota's bridal shop, and I was cheering for her and Hudson to make their own trip down the aisle from the very first chapter."

—Teri Wilson, *New York Times* and *USA TODAY* bestselling author

"Once again, Amy Clipston delivers a heartwarming book about love and second chances. *With This Ring* is like a warm hug and a perfect feel-good read about the beauty of family, friends, and reconnecting with your first love."

—Rachel Magee, author of *It's All Relative*

"Clipston's latest is a sweet read of finding love and family."

—Rachel Hauck, *New York Times* bestselling author, on *Finding You*

"Amy Clipston delivers swoon-worthy romance while addressing realistic issues of fame and long-distance relationships. Heather is a heroine to root for, and when she meets her opposite in Alex, humor and growth are the result. A thoroughly enjoyable love story."

—Lee Tobin McClain, *New York Times* bestselling author, on *Starstruck*

"*Starstruck* is a lovely story filled with wonderfully drawn, fully relatable characters and a charming community. Amy Clipston writes with warmth and heart."

—RaeAnne Thayne, *New York Times* bestselling author

"Music, love, and dreams all combine in perfect harmony in this sweet romance."

—Sheila Roberts, *USA TODAY* bestselling author, on *Starstruck*

"A rockstar and his 'Baker Girl' will warm your heart in this sweet, small-town, slow-burn romance!"

—Jennifer Snow, *USA TODAY* bestselling author, on *Starstruck*

"Applause for *Starstruck*! Amy Clipston has masterfully crafted an endearing story of hope and taking chances. Readers will be instantly captivated by the charm of Bookish Brownies and Chocolate Chunk Novel cookies! A definite must-read for those looking for a feel-good romance."

—Lacey Baker, *USA TODAY* bestselling author of *Snow Place Like Home*

"Hometown charm and swoon-worthy second chances make this a must-read."

—Kristen McKanagh, author of *Snowball's Christmas*, on *Something Old, Something New*

"Amy Clipston writes a sweet and tender romance filled with a beautiful look at how love brings healing to broken hearts. This small-town romance, with an adorable little girl and cat to boot, is a great addition to your TBR list."

—Pepper Basham, author of *Authentically, Izzy*, on *The View from Coral Cove*

"Grieving and brokenhearted, novelist Maya Reynolds moves to Coral Cove, the place where she felt happiest as a child. An old family secret upends Maya's plan for a fresh start, as does her longing to love and be loved. *The View from Coral Cove* is Amy Clipston at her best—a tender story of hope, healing, and a love that's meant to be."

—Suzanne Woods Fisher, bestselling author of *On a Summer Tide*

"*The Heart of Splendid Lake* offers a welcome escape in the form of a sympathetic heroine and her struggling lakeside resort. Clipston proficiently explores love and loss, family and friendship in a touching, small-town romance that I devoured in a single day!"

—Denise Hunter, bestselling author of the Bluebell Inn series

"A touching story of grief, love, and life carrying on, *The Heart of Splendid Lake* engaged my heart from the very first page. Sometimes the feelings we run from lead us to the hope we can't escape, and that's a beautiful thing to see through the eyes of these winning characters. Amy Clipston deftly guides readers on an emotionally satisfying journey that will appeal to fans of Denise Hunter and Becky Wade."

—Bethany Turner, award-winning author of *Plot Twist*

"Amy Clipston's characters are always so endearing and well-developed."

—Shelley Shepard Gray, *New York Times* and *USA TODAY* bestselling author

"Revealing the underbelly of main characters, a trademark talent of Amy Clipston, makes them relatable and endearing."

—Suzanne Woods Fisher, bestselling author of *On a Summer Tide*

"Clipston's heartfelt writing and engaging characters make her a fan favorite."

—*Library Journal* on *The Cherished Quilt*

SECOND CHANCE
at Sunshine Inn

OTHER BOOKS BY AMY CLIPSTON

CONTEMPORARY ROMANCE
The Heart of Splendid Lake
The View from Coral Cove
Something Old, Something New
Starstruck
Finding You
With This Ring

THE AMISH LEGACY SERIES
Foundation of Love
Building a Future
Breaking New Ground
The Heart's Shelter

THE AMISH MARKETPLACE SERIES
The Bake Shop
The Farm Stand
The Coffee Corner
The Jam and Jelly Nook

THE AMISH HOMESTEAD SERIES
A Place at Our Table
Room on the Porch Swing
A Seat by the Hearth
A Welcome at Our Door

THE AMISH HEIRLOOM SERIES
The Forgotten Recipe
The Courtship Basket
The Cherished Quilt
The Beloved Hope Chest

THE HEARTS OF THE LANCASTER GRAND HOTEL SERIES
A Hopeful Heart
A Mother's Secret
A Dream of Home
A Simple Prayer

THE KAUFFMAN AMISH BAKERY SERIES
A Gift of Grace
A Promise of Hope

A Place of Peace
A Life of Joy
A Season of Love

YOUNG ADULT
Roadside Assistance
Reckless Heart
Destination Unknown
Miles from Nowhere

STORY COLLECTIONS
Amish Sweethearts
Seasons of an Amish Garden
An Amish Singing

STORIES
A Plain and Simple Christmas
Naomi's Gift included in *An Amish Christmas Gift*
A Spoonful of Love included in *An Amish Kitchen*
Love Birds included in *An Amish Market*
Love and Buggy Rides included in *An Amish Harvest*
Summer Storms included in *An Amish Summer*
The Christmas Cat included in *An Amish Christmas Love*
Home Sweet Home included in *An Amish Winter*
A Son for Always included in *An Amish Spring*
A Legacy of Love included in *An Amish Heirloom*
No Place Like Home included in *An Amish Homecoming*
Their True Home included in *An Amish Reunion*
Cookies and Cheer included in *An Amish Christmas Bakery*
Baskets of Sunshine included in *An Amish Picnic*
Evergreen Love included in *An Amish Christmas Wedding*
Bundles of Blessings included in *Amish Midwives*
Building a Dream included in *An Amish Barn Raising*
A Class for Laurel included in *An Amish Schoolroom*
Patchwork Promises included in *An Amish Quilting Bee*
A Perfectly Splendid Christmas included in *On the Way to Christmas*

NONFICTION
The Gift of Love

Second Chance at Sunshine Inn

AMY CLIPSTON

Second Chance at Sunshine Inn

Copyright © 2025 by Amy Clipston

All rights reserved. No portion of this book may be reproduced, stored in a retrieval system, or transmitted in any form or by any means—electronic, mechanical, photocopy, recording, scanning, or other—except for brief quotations in critical reviews or articles, without the prior written permission of the publisher.

Published in Nashville, Tennessee, by Thomas Nelson. Thomas Nelson is a registered trademark of HarperCollins Christian Publishing, Inc.

Thomas Nelson titles may be purchased in bulk for educational, business, fundraising, or sales promotional use. For information, please email SpecialMarkets@ThomasNelson.com.

Publisher's Note: This novel is a work of fiction. Names, characters, places, and incidents are either products of the author's imagination or used fictitiously. All characters are fictional, and any similarity to people living or dead is purely coincidental.

Any internet addresses (websites, blogs, etc.) in this book are offered as a resource. They are not intended in any way to be or imply an endorsement by Thomas Nelson, nor does Thomas Nelson vouch for the content of these sites for the life of this book.

Library of Congress Cataloging-in-Publication Data

Names: Clipston, Amy, author.
Title: Second chance at Sunshine Inn / Amy Clipston.
Description: Nashville, Tennessee : Thomas Nelson, 2025. | Summary: "Welcome to the Sunshine Inn, a picturesque coastal inn with sweeping views and two new owners who couldn't be more opposite. From bestselling author Amy Clipston comes a no spice grumpy/sunshine romance perfect for fans of Anne-Marie Meyer and RaeAnne Thayne"—Provided by publisher.
Identifiers: LCCN 2024060273 (print) | LCCN 2024060274 (ebook) | ISBN 9780840716354 (TP) | ISBN 9780840716422 (IE) | ISBN 9780840716439
Subjects: LCGFT: Christian fiction. | Romance fiction. | Novels.
Classification: LCC PS3603.L58 S46 2025 (print) | LCC PS3603.L58 (ebook) | DDC 813/.6—dc23/eng/20241223
LC record available at https://lccn.loc.gov/2024060273
LC ebook record available at https://lccn.loc.gov/2024060274

Printed in the United States of America

25 26 27 28 29 LBC 5 4 3 2 1

*In loving memory of Trudy—my aunt, my godmother, my friend.
You will always be remembered as a blessing to our family.
We miss you every day.*

CHAPTER 1

EVERLEIGH GRIPPED THE door handle in the back seat of the gray Tahoe and consulted her phone: 4:18 P.M. Thunder rumbled, then rain began pattering on the SUV's roof. Nineties alternative rock sang softly through the speakers while the wipers began their rhythmic humming.

She took in the line of traffic in front of her and forced a smile despite the tightening in her belly.

It's okay. I'm only eighteen minutes late. It's not like it's an hour. Surely the attorney will understand. And if not, Mom will explain it to him.

Her flight from Atlanta had been delayed, and now there was a rush-hour rainstorm—but surely she'd be there soon. This Uber driver seemed experienced. She could trust him to get her there safely and promptly.

Her phone buzzed with a text message:

Mom: Are you close?

The traffic picked up speed, rolling closer to twenty-five miles per hour now as the Welcome to Coral Cove sign came into view. They were making progress. Everything was going to be just fine!

Everleigh: Getting closer. A few more blocks.

Mom: The receptionist said they'll give you another ten minutes. If you don't make it, then we'll have to reschedule with the lawyer.

Everleigh's leg bounced as she typed: Be there in five.

Scenery that had been the backdrop of her childhood came into view—her elementary, middle, and high schools sat in a cluster not far from the library, main fire station, and town hall—and her head began to pound. It had been more than a year and a half since she'd been home. In fact, two Christmases ago was when she'd last seen her parents and her two siblings.

And it had been more than a year since she'd hugged Alana—her godmother, favorite "aunt," and confidante.

But now Alana was gone.

Everleigh tried to swallow the lump of grief that expanded in her throat. She and Alana had spoken just two weeks ago. Or was it a month ago?

Why couldn't she remember?

Their last conversation came into focus in her mind: a discussion about the nonprofit they wanted to start together. As a traveling neonatal intensive care unit nurse, Everleigh had met plenty of parents who struggled to make ends meet while their children stayed in the NICU. For a long time, she'd dreamed of starting a charity to help parents of critically ill children. Some of those children needed care for several months, and the parents needed assistance with not only the cost of care but also their household expenses.

When Everleigh first shared these stories with Alana, her godmother immediately volunteered to help, and they began putting together a business plan. They had named their nonprofit Helping Angels. Everleigh had spent the past three years searching for financial backers, and during her last conversation with Alana, she'd told her she wasn't giving up. Their dream, Everleigh insisted, *would* come to fruition.

But she'd run out of time. Alana was gone.

And Everleigh had let her down.

Her eyes felt wet, and she swiped the back of her hand over her face. Alana had shown up for every milestone—every birthday party, every dance recital, every graduation—all the way through nursing school. Everleigh couldn't think of a holiday or event that Alana hadn't attended.

She held her breath to choke back a sob.

What would her Uber driver think if she started bawling in the back seat?

Keep it together, Everleigh! You have to be strong—especially for Mom.

One of Alana's favorite sayings echoed through her mind: *"Smile through your tears,"* she often said. Yes, Everleigh could smile through her tears. She *had* to.

The rain came down harder, and large drops dotted the windshield as the SUV splashed through puddles. The Tahoe motored to an intersection and stopped at a red light. She checked her phone: now four twenty-four.

She stared at the traffic light, willing it to change, and nibbled her lower lip. She even considered pretending to blow the traffic light out, just like the game her mom had taught her when she was little. But if she did that, then the driver would *really* think she was nuts!

Come on. Come on! Turn green already! We can make it!

Seconds ticked by.

At four twenty-six, she had four minutes before the lawyer would insist they reschedule. She rubbed her eyes. She was going to get there on time.

The light turned green, and the driver steered down the street before pulling up in front of a large glass window with Buford, Buford & Gallagher etched across the front in fancy script.

The middle-aged man slipped the SUV into park, then angled himself in the seat so his dark, deep-set eyes were focused on Everleigh. "Here we are."

Just in time!

"Thank you," Everleigh said, the sound of the rain permeating the vehicle.

The driver hit a button, and the locks popped. "Trunk's unlocked," he mumbled before turning his attention back to the windshield.

She turned toward the front of the lawyers' office, realizing she didn't have a jacket or an umbrella. Surely Mom had seen her pull up and would run out with an umbrella.

"You gettin' out?" the driver barked.

"Uh . . . yeah." Everleigh slipped her crossbody purse over her head and shouldered her backpack, then pushed open the door and jumped out into the pouring rain. Her black Converse high tops sloshed through the standing water as she pushed on the tailgate trunk lever. It didn't want to budge, so she yanked on it. Then smacked it.

Nothing happened.

"Ugh!" she yelled. The downpour was soaking her hair, along with her black T-shirt and jeans.

Everleigh spotted the driver's reflection in the side mirror. His head was bent as if studying his phone. She huffed out a frustrated noise and hit the tailgate button again. She'd taken many Ubers since she started working as a traveling nurse, but this was the first driver she'd encountered who hadn't bothered to open the trunk for her.

"Need some help?"

Everleigh jumped with a start and spun toward the deep voice: a man now holding a large umbrella over both of them.

Oh, hello, blue eyes!

The stranger was tall—at least five or six inches taller than her own five-foot-seven height—and his sandy-brown hair was cut short and had a natural wave. But those azure eyes . . . They were focused on *her*. She guessed he was in his late twenties or possibly early thirties, but no matter. The man was handsome, and he'd arrived just in time!

Relief slid through her. "Yes!"

"Here, hold this." The stranger handed her the umbrella before pushing the lever on the tailgate, which lifted with a *whoosh*, as if by magic.

"I guess there are some gentlemen left in this world," Everleigh declared as he grabbed the handle on her black-and-white houndstooth suitcase and yanked it from the trunk with a grunt.

"Brought your rock collection?" he grumbled, heaving the ginormous suitcase onto the sidewalk.

She gave him a sheepish expression and pointed to the lawyers' office across the sidewalk from them. "Thanks. I'll take it from here."

"I got it."

Confusion overtook her. How did this guy know where she was going?

He slammed the tailgate, then made a sweeping gesture toward the office. "Go."

"But how did you—" she started.

"It's pouring," he said, interrupting her. Now he *pointed* toward the office. "Go," he repeated.

Everleigh hustled through the rain, doing her best to hold the large umbrella over herself and the stranger. When they reached the door, she wrenched it open and held it for him.

"Everleigh!" Mom crossed the room and pulled her in for a hug. "You finally made it."

Ignoring her own questions about the stranger, Everleigh leaned down and held on to her mother. Nearly a decade ago, Everleigh had sprouted up taller than both her mother and her older sister. She breathed in the comforting scent of Mom's perfume—White Diamonds—an aroma that always took her back to her childhood. And thoughts of her childhood always brought with them memories of Alana.

"Oh, sweetie." Mom pulled a wad of tissues from her pocket and placed it in her hand. The dark circles under Mom's deep-brown eyes were signs she'd been struggling to sleep, just like Everleigh had since she'd gotten the news. Mom's eyes welled with tears, and Everleigh touched her hand. "I can't grasp that my best friend since college is gone." Her voice was rough.

Everleigh sniffed. *Don't cry! Be strong for Mom!*

Motion out of the corner of Everleigh's eye drew her attention back to the stranger. He had set her suitcase and his umbrella beside her, then sat on a chair in the corner of the reception area before pulling out his phone and staring at it.

"Ms. Hartnett?" A young woman with flawless dark skin, tight curls, and bright-red lipstick held a clipboard. Her navy-blue pantsuit appeared expensive and appropriate for the office.

Everleigh took in her own soaked attire and felt like a drowned rat, especially since she was certain her drenched red hair was molded to her head. *It's okay,* she told herself. *Everyone will understand that I traveled all day from Texas to be here.*

Mom turned at the sound of her name. "Yes?"

But the woman focused on Everleigh. "Are you Everleigh Hartnett?"

She nodded.

"You're just in time. I was afraid I was going to have to reschedule you for next week." She scanned the room. "I believe we're all here now." She turned toward the handsome stranger. "Mr. Witherspoon."

He stood and pocketed the phone in his jeans, which hugged him in all the right places.

"And Mrs. Caroline Hartnett," the woman said, referring to Mom. "Mr. Buford is ready for you all." The young woman backed through the doorway. "Please, follow me." Then she started down the hallway, her heels clacking on the hardwoods.

"Wait." Everleigh turned to her mother. "What about Harlowe and Landon?"

Mom shook her head. "Alana apparently didn't include them in her will."

"Why only us?" Everleigh turned to the stranger—Mr. Witherspoon?—who watched her with a hesitant expression. Who was he? And why was he here?

"I don't know why she left your siblings out, but Alana included us and Cade, who worked for her." She smiled at the man.

He replied with a stoic nod.

This guy worked for Alana? Her godmother had never mentioned him before. More questions swirled in Everleigh's mind.

"We need to go in now," Mom said. "Mr. Buford has another appointment at five, so we're almost out of time." She picked up the umbrella and then took off after the woman with the clipboard.

But Everleigh didn't move. Instead, she traced her fingers over the handle of her suitcase and tried to make sense of the chaos.

Nothing had made sense since Mom told her nearly two weeks ago that Alana had passed. The news had knocked the wind out of her, but when Mr. Buford had called her last week and told her she was in the will, she'd been shocked. Never had she expected Alana to—

The man cleared his throat.

Everleigh realized the handsome stranger was now staring at her.

"You going?" Those striking blue eyes watched her, his expression grim.

Heat crawled up her neck. "Yeah." She shook her head. "Sorry."

The wheels on her suitcase scraped across the floor on her way to the large office at the end of the hallway. She left her bags at the back of the room and sat beside her mother in an armchair across from a large desk, where a tall man with a handlebar mustache and thinning gray hair sat with his hands folded atop a pile of paperwork.

The woman, whom Everleigh assumed was his assistant, sat in a chair adjacent to the desk. Then Mr. Witherspoon—Cade?—took a seat on the other side of Everleigh.

"We're here for the reading of Ms. Alana Elizabeth McFadden's will." The lawyer's beady eyes flicked over Mom, Everleigh, and Cade. "I see we're all here, so I'll proceed with the reading." He set his glasses on his large nose and began to read aloud. "I, Alana Elizabeth McFadden, a resident of Brunswick County, North Carolina, and a citizen of the United States of America, declare this to be my Last Will and Testament. I hereby revoke . . ."

Everleigh stared down at her wet jeans and lost herself in memories of Alana as the lawyer read the will. The memories played like a movie through her mind. Playing at the beach with Alana. Watching movies together and eating popcorn. Crying in Alana's arms after her first boyfriend dumped her.

She recalled dancing in the kitchen of Alana's bed-and-breakfast, the Sunshine Inn, where Everleigh had worked part-time until she graduated from high school and went to college to study nursing. Alana had helped her with her college expenses, always sending her care packages full of snacks and supplies with an envelope of cash strategically placed at the bottom of each box.

And she'd never forget the night when Alana insisted on staying on the phone with her to make sure she didn't fall asleep while Everleigh drove from Colorado to Texas for her next nursing position. They had discussed everything from their favorite movies to Everleigh's nonexistent love life, to the nonprofit they'd dreamed of and the parents and children they hoped to help.

But now Alana was gone, and so were those late-night phone calls and hugs and . . . everything.

Suddenly, the tears she'd kept at bay during her trip from Texas to North Carolina welled up. She'd been trying all day to hold the tears back and stay strong.

She sucked in a breath, hoping to stop the display.

Oh no.

Then the tears poured from her eyes.

She felt like a fool for losing it in the middle of a lawyer's office—especially in front of Mr. Buford and the mysterious Cade. She yanked a tissue from her pocket and wiped her eyes and nose.

A hand touched her arm. She turned toward Mom, who was staring at her. "Did you hear that, Everleigh?" she asked, pinning her with a serious expression.

She shook her head. "I'm sorry. I was lost in thought. What did I miss?"

Mr. Buford pressed his thin lips together. "I'll read it again, Ms. Hartnett." He gave his throat a dramatic clearing. "I hereby bequeath fifty percent each of my said property, real, personal, or mixed, to Everleigh Alana Hartnett and Benjamin Cade Witherspoon III."

Everleigh blinked and tried to comprehend what the lawyer had said. She listened intently while he continued reciting the document, but her mind was buzzing with confusion. What did it all mean?

When the lawyer stopped reading, Everleigh took a shuddering breath. "Mr. Buford, can you please explain what you just read?"

He took off his glasses and set them down on the desk before refolding his hands. "Ms. McFadden left you and Mr. Witherspoon each fifty percent of everything—her bed-and-breakfast and the contents therein, as well as any funds. She'd also like you and your mother to go through her personal items and decide what to do with them."

"Sh-she left me the bed-and-breakfast?" Everleigh whispered as her eyes brimmed with tears once again. Alana had left her everything—*everything*. Her shock spilled down her cheeks.

Her godmother's generosity was too much to comprehend. She was so grateful. Alana had always been thoughtful and giving, but leaving Everleigh everything was above and beyond.

But wait—Alana *hadn't* left her everything.

Everleigh had to share the B&B with a *stranger*.

She turned to the man sitting next to her. He appeared just as stunned as she felt as he pushed his hand through his thick, golden-brown hair.

Who was he anyway? And why did Alana want her to share the B&B with him, a man she'd never heard of? Alana had lost her parents years ago and never had any siblings or children of her own. In fact, she'd never married. And her last name was McFadden, not Witherspoon, which meant they couldn't be related.

Or could they?

Had she found a long-lost cousin during the eighteen months since Everleigh had been home? And if so, why hadn't Alana mentioned him when they'd spoken? Everleigh always told Alana everything about her life—even secrets she hadn't shared with her mother. So, wouldn't Alana have done the same?

Everleigh knew the answer to that question: Alana *hadn't* told her everything. In fact, she hadn't even told her she was sick, which made Everleigh's heart hurt.

"Now, we have some documents you'll need to sign, and then you can be on your way," Mr. Buford announced, standing. "Rhiannon will help you with those since I need to get to my next appointment."

After the paperwork was complete, Everleigh and her mother walked out to the lobby. She felt as if she were walking in a dream. She was now half owner of the Sunshine Inn. How was any of this possible? Was she stuck in an alternate universe? Would she suddenly wake up and find everything back to normal?

"Oh, good," Mom announced, pulling her keys from her designer purse. "It stopped raining. I'm parked right out front."

Everleigh turned to Benjamin Cade Witherspoon III. Such a fancy name. She held her hand out and smiled. "Is it Cade or Ben?"

"Cade." He gave her hand a quick shake, but his expression remained glum.

My, my—that five o'clock shadow!

"I guess we're business partners now, huh?" She had so many questions for him, but it didn't seem like the appropriate place to delve into them.

"We should talk." His voice was distinct—deep and smooth, reminding her of butter. But his face was so serious.

"Absolutely."

Mom's cell phone started to ring, and she fished it out of her purse. "Hi, Dave." She rubbed her forehead. "Yeah, we just finished up. We're on our way now. See you there." She disconnected the phone and sighed. "Everleigh, your dad's going to meet us at the restaurant." She gave Cade a stiff smile. "Good to see you." Then she turned her focus back to Everleigh. "Let's go." Mom pushed open the office door and headed toward the car.

Everleigh waved to Cade. "We'll get together soon."

He nodded, stuffed his hands in his pockets, and pressed his lips into a flat line.

Everleigh headed out into the humid air, pulling her enormous, damp suitcase behind her.

CHAPTER 2

THAT EVENING, CADE grabbed the handful of mail from the mailbox and then sauntered up the driveway toward the Sunshine Inn. The late-August air felt heavy from the earlier rain. The sky above him was a kaleidoscope of colors as the sun began to set, and the cicadas began their nightly song. He looked out toward Coral Cove Bay, where a chorus of frogs sang the day into night. Soon, the stars would be reflecting off the water. He breathed in the salty air.

Sighing, he faced the inn. The yellow two-story colonial stood before him in all its glory, haloed by the waning light. The sprawling inn featured eight bedrooms for guests—six upstairs and two downstairs, plus a suite where Alana had lived. This time of day, the golden hour, was when the Sunshine Inn looked its best.

Grief rained down on him as a vision of Alana McFadden filled his mind. She'd been gone for twelve days now, but it seemed like only a few days since their last conversation. He'd been grateful to Alana when she'd hired him eighteen months ago. Working as a handyman wasn't his forte, but he'd relied on YouTube, learning how to fix things while he settled into the job. The best part, though, was how the position came with a studio apartment for him above the detached three-car garage.

He headed into the kitchen and dropped the stack of letters on the island. He grumbled as he sifted the bills and postcards from Realtors wanting to buy the place. As if he would sell. He'd promised Alana to keep the inn running, and that was what he intended to do.

His cell phone rang, and his best friend's name popped up on the screen. "Hey," he answered.

"How'd it go with the lawyer today?" Roger asked.

"Fine." Cade poured himself a glass of sweet tea, then leaned against the counter while he took a long draw.

"Could you be a bit more specific?"

"Alana left me half of everything." Cade set the glass down on the counter.

Silence permeated the line for a few beats. "How long have you worked for her?" Roger finally asked.

"Almost two years."

"And she left you half of *everything*? Wow," Roger said. "Who got the other half?"

"Her goddaughter."

"Was she at the reading of the will too?"

"Yup."

"Is she going to help you run the inn?"

"Not sure. We didn't get to talk." He'd hoped to set up a meeting to discuss everything with her after the reading of the will, but she'd flittered away, saying they'd get together. She hadn't even bothered to give him her number. Not a great start to their partnership.

He frowned. He was done with worthless business partners, and he wasn't about to allow another one to ruin his livelihood. He was responsible for this inn, and he refused to let an irresponsible person run it into the ground.

"I'm sure she'll be at the memorial service on Saturday," Roger said. "You can talk to her then."

"Right." He'd do his best to get his new "partner" to set up a time to hash out how this partnership was going to work.

"It's getting late," said Roger. "I'll let you go."

Cade said good night, pushed his phone into the back pocket of his jeans, then slipped his empty glass into the dishwasher. He scanned the pile of mail and shook his head. Just another task he'd deal with later, he thought as he walked out to the path leading to the detached garage.

As he walked, a large fluffy gray cat brushed against his leg and meowed.

"Hey, Bryant." Cade leaned down and scratched the cat's head.

Bryant, the inn's resident feline, blinked up at him, and his purr rumbled low.

"Hungry?" Cade asked, and the cat meowed again. "Come on, boy."

Bryant trotted beside him on the path, chattering along the way.

When they reached the apartment, Cade unlocked the door with the noisy gray cat underfoot. Together they climbed the steep steps to Cade's home. He appreciated the place with its large den, galley kitchen, bathroom, and moderate-sized bedroom. It was only a fraction of the size of the home he had rented in Tuscaloosa, but it was all he needed.

Cade opened a can of cat food. He got a whiff of fish and groaned. "You'll love it."

The cat continued to sing his song and weave between his feet. Cade set the bowl down and stowed the can before sitting on the sofa and opening his laptop. As he found the inn's webpage and studied it, his last conversation with Alana echoed in his mind. She'd been admitted to the hospital, and while he sat beside her, she'd managed to say, "Make me a promise, Cade."

Cade took her hand in his. "Anything."

"Promise me you'll find your sunshine. Don't keep your heart closed forever."

Cade's heart had seized. Such a big promise, but Alana had always seen the best in him. He owed it to Alana to look for the best in himself. He nodded.

"Promise me." Her voice was a weak whisper.

"I promise."

Tears stung his eyes, and he swiped them away while he perused the website. Alana had plenty of visitors who came to the Sunshine Inn every year, and he'd already received several emails asking if the inn would reopen soon so they could come back before the summer ended. Since Alana had made him promise to care for the inn, wasn't it his duty to open the reservations again? Cade held his finger over the button to set the reservations to open.

But he paused. Shouldn't he discuss it with his partner first? The one who couldn't be bothered to give him her phone number?

He glowered.

Bryant hopped up on the sofa beside him and began bathing himself, and Cade stroked the cat's fuzzy head. "Guess I need to consult my business partner before I reopen the place. Right, Bryant?"

The cat continued licking between his toes.

Alana had told Cade that Everleigh worked as a traveling nurse. Best-case scenario, she would allow Cade to run the inn while she returned to her job. If so, she'd be a silent business partner, only sharing in the profits instead of the day-to-day operations.

And that was the best kind of business partner to have.

✦ ✦ ✦

Everleigh breathed in the warm, salty air and scanned the neighborhood where she'd grown up. The sky was dark and showed no sign of the earlier rainstorm, and the stars twinkled above her. The brightly colored beach homes sat quietly along the street, illuminated by the golden streetlights lining the sidewalks. Each home was a different shape and style—no two were alike—and each house sported a cute and creative name like Rock 'N' Reel, Catch 'N' Relax, or Absolute Beach. The neighborhood felt warm and welcoming, and even though she'd been gone for nearly two years, everything looked the same.

She studied her parents' blue clapboard home, taking in the name her mother had given it when her parents had purchased it years before she'd been born—The Endless Summer—and she hugged her arms to her middle. The day had been surreal, from her long trip from Houston to the North Carolina coast to the appointment with the lawyer. She felt as if she were stuck in a fog.

After leaving the meeting with the lawyer, she and her mother had met Dad at Little Italy, the Italian restaurant in Coral Cove. It had always been one of her favorites, and Everleigh welcomed the warm comfort of her favorite pasta dish. She'd let the zesty sauce and good company heal her heartache. Soon enough, she was sharing stories about her work in Houston, about her precious patients and her friends at the hospital, before catching up on how her father was enjoying his retirement from the Coral Cove Police Department.

"Everleigh?"

She spun to face her mother, who was standing on the small front porch. "Yeah?"

"Are you going to come inside or stay in the driveway all night?" she asked gently. "Your dad already took your suitcase to your room, sweetie. Let's get you settled."

Instead of joining her mother on the porch, she leaned against the front bumper of her mother's late-model Subaru Outback. The questions she'd been holding deep inside were starting to bubble up to the surface.

"Why didn't she tell us she was sick?" Everleigh said, her words shaking as she locked eyes with her mother.

Mom came down the steps and took her hand. "I wish I knew. I only just found out too. I didn't even have a chance to tell you before . . ." Her voice trailed off.

"But we're her family—her *only* family. That's what she always told me."

"I know." Mom sniffed. "I imagine she didn't want us to worry."

Mom wiped at her tears, and seeing her mom cry tore up Everleigh even more. She hadn't meant to make her cry. She pulled her in for a hug and tried to hold back her own emotion.

When Everleigh released her, Mom pulled a tissue from her pocket and mopped up her eyes.

"I'm so confused, Mom. She left me half of the inn, but she also gave half to that guy Cade. Who is he?"

"He's been working for her for a while now. Maybe two years?" Mom leaned against the bumper beside her.

"Why didn't you tell me she hired someone?"

She shrugged. "I thought you knew."

"She never told me." Everleigh considered the man. He was so quiet, and he had never smiled once they were in the attorney's office. Odd. "What do you know about him?"

"He's originally from here, but he was gone a long time. I think he joined the military after high school and then moved around a bit. He came home and needed a job, so Alana hired him. You know how she always wanted to help people."

Everleigh nodded.

"She really admired him and said he did good work."

Everleigh considered that. Alana *had* been a good judge of character.

But this man was a stranger. Why would Alana leave half of her inn to a *stranger*?

She felt her mother watching her. "I can tell when you're really concentrating on something. Your brow wrinkles." Mom touched her shoulder. "Talk to me, Evie. What's on your mind?"

"I just can't figure out why Alana would want a stranger to have half of her everything . . . including the business she worked so hard to build and preserve!"

"Because he wasn't a stranger to her."

The truth smacked Everleigh in the face. "And if I had come home last year instead of going straight to the job in Texas, I might have met him and possibly gotten to know him before she passed away." Guilt burrowed deep in her gut at the thought.

The door opened, and Dad appeared on the porch. "Am I missing something out here?"

"Nope." Everleigh stood up, smiled, and patted her mother's back. "We were just coming in. Right, Mom?"

"That's right."

"I managed to maneuver your one-ton suitcase into your room," Dad joked.

"With my rock collection, right?" Everleigh shook her head, recalling Cade's snarky comment.

"Rock collection?" Mom asked.

"Never mind." Everleigh joined her father on the porch, and he pulled her into his arms for a tight hug.

"I'm so glad you're home." His deep voice held a hint of grief.

"Thanks, Dad." She stepped out of his arms and into the house, where she was greeted by the aroma of vanilla—her mother's favorite scented plug-in, which she kept in each room of the house. She wandered through the den, still decorated with the same furniture she remembered—a worn but comfortable brown sofa and two matching recliners, along with a dark wooden coffee table and end tables.

Once she reached the kitchen, she found a bottle of water in the refrigerator and took a long drink.

"You haven't told us how long we'll get to have you this time." Dad's expression was hopeful as he came to stand beside her. "Possibly longer than a few weeks?"

She nodded. "I finished my last contract, and I haven't signed a new one yet. I thought I'd give it at least a month. Now I guess I should see what happens with Alana's inn."

"Good." It had been almost two years since she'd last seen her parents, and more wrinkles outlined Dad's hazel eyes. She noted more flecks of gray in his brown hair too. "Where'd you leave your car?"

Everleigh set the half-full bottle on the counter beside her. "I didn't want to make the drive, so I paid a service to bring it here for me. And since they're running behind, it will be a few weeks before I have it."

"That was smart. No one should drive all that way after receiving such terrible news." Dad started for the doorway. "It's late, and you look worn out. You should get some sleep."

Mom appeared behind him. "Your dad is right. Tomorrow I'll need you to help me with the last-minute details for the memorial service on Saturday."

"Okay." Everleigh hugged each of them. "Good night."

She padded past the bathroom, her parents' room, and her older brother's former room, which had been transformed into Mom's craft room soon after Landon left for college.

She finally came to what was now the guest room at the end of the hallway. It seemed like only yesterday that she and her older sister, Harlowe, had shared this bedroom, until Harlowe also went to college. Their single beds positioned on either side of the room had been replaced with a double bed set in the center. Nine years ago, when Everleigh was eighteen, she had finally moved out herself.

She sighed and plopped down onto the edge of the bed. She scanned the room, taking in the clusters of family photos on the walls, along with the tall dresser and matching triple dresser. Exhaustion weighed heavily on her shoulders.

After reaching into her backpack, she pulled out her latest coloring book and a box of colored pencils. Then she kicked off her Converse high tops and scooted down the bed until her back hit the headboard. She turned to the next page and smiled—a sunset over a beach. Perfect. She'd found that enjoying a soothing coloring book was the best way to decompress after a long shift in the NICU.

Tomorrow she would help her mother finish planning Alana's memorial service. Then Saturday, she'd have to formally say goodbye to her godmother. She didn't know how she'd get through it all. She wanted so badly to be strong for Alana.

But right now, she'd lose herself in a colorful sunset—and hopefully get a break from her grief.

CHAPTER 3

EVERLEIGH SMOOTHED HER hands down her plain black dress and pushed her long, thick red braid over her shoulder. As her parents made their way up the cobblestone path to the chapel Saturday morning, she trailed behind. She felt ridiculous sporting more makeup than usual and wearing black high heels, adding at least two inches to her height and making her almost the same height as her father. Although she was much more comfortable in jeans, a T-shirt, a hoodie, and her sneakers, or even scrubs, she felt she needed to dress up today for Alana.

The sky above them was Carolina blue, and the sun was bright. The late-August air was hot and humid, and the seagulls called to each other. A murmur of conversation and the sweet smell of flowers greeted Everleigh when she entered the chapel. Her eyes quickly adjusted to the low light, and she smiled as she took in the spray of flowers on the altar that included hyacinth, bluebells, and carnations, along with Alana's favorite, gerbera daisies.

"Evie!"

She spun at the sound of her nickname, the one her family members insisted on calling her, just as her brother pulled her in for a tight hug. "Landon!" she exclaimed.

"It's been forever, baby sis." When he gave her a glum smile, he reminded her so much of Dad with his medium-brown hair, bright hazel eyes, and fit stature. His hair was high and tight, typical for a police officer. He had followed in Dad's footsteps and joined the Coral Cove Police Department right after college. "I'm so glad you're here."

She turned to Amber, his long-term girlfriend who stood beside him, and hugged her too.

Amber sniffed and pushed her short blond hair behind her ears. "It's such a shock that Alana is gone."

Everleigh nodded, and Landon looped his arm around his girlfriend's shoulder.

A moment later, Mom joined them. "Let's get a seat up front before the service begins."

Everleigh sat between Landon and Dad at the front of the chapel as the pews behind them began to fill up. When Everleigh's older sister and brother-in-law appeared at the back of the sanctuary, Mom stood and waved them to the front. Then she guided Harlowe and Branson to sit beside her, and Dad, Everleigh, Landon, and Amber scooted down to make room.

Mom whispered something to Harlowe, who gave Everleigh a half wave before returning her attention to Mom.

Everleigh smiled and waved back vigorously.

Although Harlowe rarely responded to her texts, Everleigh still reached out periodically, hoping her sister would reply. Harlowe looked just as she remembered, with her light-brown hair parted on the side and perfectly straightened. Everleigh had always longed to have beautiful light-brown hair like Harlowe and Mom, but she'd somehow managed to inherit Dad's great-aunt Margaret's red mane. But Harlowe's beauty didn't end there. She also resembled Mom with her high cheekbones, thin nose, and tiny chin, while Everleigh resembled Dad's sister, Gina.

Branson, Harlowe's husband of six years, greeted Amber and shook Landon's hand before addressing Everleigh. Then he nodded to Dad and turned back toward Harlowe.

"Is Harlowe okay?" Everleigh whispered to her brother.

He lifted one shoulder in a half shrug. "You know how moody she is."

She wanted to ask if something was wrong, but she was cut off when the organ rang out the first chords of the opening hymn.

She turned to the corresponding page in her hymnal and tried to concentrate on the words to "Beautiful Savior," Alana's favorite hymn, but her mind continued to wander from her grief for Alana to her disappointment with Harlowe. Her older sister always seemed annoyed with her about something, no matter how hard Everleigh tried to have a relationship with her. Still, she was determined to be close to her older sister someday. She'd never give up on her.

She felt someone watching her, and she turned to her left and scanned the second pew. There, her eyes found Cade sitting with a middle-aged couple and another man who appeared to be around his age. Cade was handsome in a dark-blue suit with a light-blue shirt and tie, his face clean-shaven, boasting a strong jaw that could have been molded from fine granite. He looked completely different from when he'd attended the reading of the will clad in jeans and a plain T-shirt, and Everleigh couldn't help but think that, while attractive and properly somber for the occasion, he seemed less comfortable and less himself right now. Even if his facial features were the same.

Maybe she was starting to get a feel for Cade Witherspoon, and it'd only taken two meetings to get there.

Or maybe not.

Their eyes met, and he studied her with a grim expression. Her brow crinkled, and she tried to imagine what he would look like if he smiled. She tipped her lips up and nodded, but instead of responding, he studied his hymnal.

Huh. Maybe he'd never learned how to smile. Did he miss that day in kindergarten? She almost laughed at the thought.

Although she tried to focus on the pastor's words during the memorial service, her mind kept replaying her best memories of Alana. The sanctuary was packed, and the crowded room filled with Alana's friends and loved ones warmed Everleigh's heart. Alana had always participated in community events—sponsoring school functions and contributing to the local charities. She'd been loved by the Coral Cove community.

When the service was over, the Hartnett family filed out of the pew and started across the parking lot to the main church building and fellowship hall. When she felt a strong hand on her arm, she turned and found her father.

His face was full of concern. "I saw you fidgeting during the service. You okay, Everleigh?"

"Yeah." She tried her best to smile. "Just a tough day."

"You've always tried to smile through the toughest days, but I know you, sweetie. You can talk to me. I get the feeling that something else is bothering you."

Well, my sister is blowing me off, and Alana left half of everything to a stranger, but I'm great, Dad. "Everything's fine." She hooked her arm through her father's. "Let's go to the reception."

In the large reception hall, folks were filling plates with food provided by the church's women's group.

"Dave!" a middle-aged man called before sidling up to Dad. "What are you doing to keep yourself busy during retirement?"

Dad shook the man's hand. "Larry, you know how it is. Caroline always has a honey-do list for me. How about you?"

Everleigh excused herself before continuing to the food tables. She picked up a plate and piled on macaroni and cheese, a piece of fried chicken, some kind of mystery casserole, pasta salad, a roll, and a piece of coconut cake. She moved past the cluster of tables and vaguely familiar faces until she found her siblings and their significant others. Her mother stood nearby, talking to a woman who had once been Mom's Sunday school co-teacher when Everleigh was little.

Everleigh set down her plate and then sat between Amber and Branson before turning her attention to her sister. "It's good to see you, Harlowe."

"I'm *so* glad you could join us, Evie." Her sister lifted her cup of lemonade, her smile bordering on surly.

Everleigh kept a pleasant expression on her face despite the barb. She wasn't going to allow Harlowe to get to her today. "I haven't heard from you in a while. How've you been?"

After swallowing a bite of cookie, Harlowe shrugged. "Fine."

"So, Everleigh," Branson began, "how's Texas?"

"Hot," Everleigh said, and everyone except for Harlowe chuckled. While she nibbled on her lunch, she shared stories about working in the NICU in Texas as Amber, Branson, and Landon asked questions. Harlowe, however, said nothing—and her reticence was eating away at Everleigh. She couldn't stand the distance between them. She suddenly felt like she was eleven again, fighting to get her fifteen-year-old sister's attention and acceptance.

When Harlowe stood, Everleigh turned toward her. "Are you leaving?"

"Just going to the restroom."

Everleigh popped up from her seat. "I'll come with you."

"Suit yourself," Harlowe muttered.

When they reached the hallway, Everleigh touched her sister's arm and tried to pull her in for a hug, but Harlowe stepped away from her. "I haven't heard from you in months," Everleigh said. "And when I text you, you either send one-word answers or don't respond at all. Is everything okay?"

"Why didn't you come home for Dad's sixtieth birthday party?" Harlowe asked, her eyes narrowing.

Everleigh looked as members of the congregation walked in and out of the reception hall. "You know the answer to that." Her stomach dropped as she took in the anger in her sister's face. "I sent you money for the party, and I made the video you asked me to make for Dad. Landon said he loved it. The party was in May, Harlowe. I thought you understood."

"You said you couldn't take off, but you're here now." She gestured around the hallway. "Why's that?"

"My contract ended yesterday, and I got on the first flight out. I needed to get here in time for the meeting with the lawyer and the memorial."

Harlowe studied her as if she were a pesky piece of gum stuck to the bottom of her shoe, and Everleigh's posture drooped. "How come only you and Mom were invited to the reading of the will?"

"Uh, well, um . . ." Everleigh stammered. *Things are about to get even more tense.* "We were in the will."

Her sister took a step toward her. "What do you mean?"

Everleigh peeked past her sister to where a few acquaintances she recognized from youth group milled around the hallway. "Alana named Mom as her executrix, and she wants Mom and me to go through her personal items."

"Is that all?" Harlowe's eyes locked on hers.

Everleigh hesitated. She didn't want to lie to her sister, but she also didn't want to cause more of a rift between them. Even if she omitted the truth, though, Harlowe would eventually find out. "I got fifty percent of the inn. Isn't that crazy?" She tried to laugh, but it sounded more like a squeak.

Harlowe's mouth opened and then closed before her eyes bugged out. "What?" she exclaimed. "You got half of the B&B?"

"Yeah, I did." Everleigh shifted her weight on her feet.

"Who got the other half?"

"Cade Witherspoon. He's been working for Alana for a while, but I hadn't met—"

"What about Landon and me?" Harlowe demanded, jamming her finger at her chest. "Why did you get it? Is it because Mom named you after her? How's that even fair?"

Everleigh turned toward the end of the hallway, where a group of folks watched them. "Harlowe, can we calm down, please?" she said, her words measured. "People are staring."

"I don't care!" her sister exclaimed. "Why did you get the inn while Landon and I got nothing?"

Everleigh pulled a deep breath in through her nose. "I-I don't know. Maybe because I worked there every summer from when I was eleven until I left for college?"

"Or maybe because you've always been her favorite for some ridiculous reason." Harlowe nearly spat the words at her before marching toward the ladies' room and leaving Everleigh standing alone.

Everleigh rested against the wall and rubbed her forehead. Why did she even bother trying to be closer to Harlowe, who snubbed her every chance she could? Why couldn't they work out whatever continued to fester between them?

But Everleigh could change her sister's mind. She'd keep working on her, and someday they'd have the close relationship she craved.

She glimpsed back down the hallway, and her gaze locked with Cade's. He stood with the older couple and the man she'd seen beside him in the pew. His expression was closed off, even cold, and she bit back a groan as embarrassment seized her.

Oh no. Had he witnessed her contentious exchange with her sister? She hoped not. Her lips formed a tight smile, and she waved as if Harlowe hadn't just ripped her apart in public.

Cade faced the woman who was talking.

"Everleigh!"

At the sound of her name, Everleigh turned. Quinn Evans had appeared and was reaching out to pull her into a tight hug. "I haven't seen you in a million years."

Relief flooded Everleigh. A friendly face was just what she needed, and Quinn Evans had been a dear friend to her when she was growing up.

"Quinn, you look amazing." She smiled. "Actually, you look exactly the same as you did in high school." Which was true—with her dark hair styled in the same pixie cut that had become her trademark, Everleigh's petite friend was still the five-foot-one dynamo she remembered. "What are you up to these days?"

"I'll have you know I'm the head librarian at the Coral Cove Library." She rested her hands on her small hips.

"Good for you."

"Thanks. I tried real estate for a while, but it didn't work out. I always loved libraries, so I decided to go back to school and make a career change." Her smile dipped downward. "I'm so sorry about Alana. I remember how close you were to her. You spent all of your free time with her, and I loved going with you and helping out at the inn." Her blue eyes studied Everleigh. "How are you holding up?"

"I'm fine," Everleigh said, hoping to shift gears. "Do you have a special guy in your life?"

"Nope. Still single. You?"

"Same. I'm going to be in town for a while. We should get together."

"Yes! Give me your phone." Quinn took Everleigh's phone and sent herself a text.

Everleigh saved her number and then rubbed her hands together. "Now. Give me all of the juicy town updates I've missed since high school."

Quinn lifted her eyebrows. "All of them?" she asked, and Everleigh nodded. "Well, did you know that the president of our senior class is now the president of a bank?"

"No way!" Everleigh laughed, relaxing a bit as Quinn began to fill her in on the latest gossip.

✦ ✦ ✦

"The service was lovely." Cade's mom sniffed and dabbed her eyes with a tissue while they stood in the hallway outside the reception hall. "Alana was such a sweet woman and only fifty-seven years old. I just can't believe it."

Cade swallowed the last sip from his cup of weak coffee. The pastor had done a good job of highlighting how special Alana had been and everything she'd done for the community. But Cade was done with the tears, sad looks, and expressions of condolence. He was itching to get back to the solitude of the inn as soon as possible, so he could spend the afternoon tinkering with his motorcycle.

He was grateful his best friend, Roger, had offered to come with him today. It was a relief to have his buddy to help deflect some of the idle conversation with people who'd barely known Alana.

"You just never know," Mom continued. "Right, Ben?"

Dad massaged her shoulder. "That's right. But we should get going, Trisha." He nodded at Cade and Roger. "Take care."

"See ya, Dad," Cade said before hugging Mom.

Cade tossed his empty cup into a nearby trash can and then turned toward the end of the hallway, where Everleigh stood with a short woman who was vaguely familiar. He was almost certain he'd seen her at the library. The woman spoke animatedly, waving her arms around, and Everleigh's dark eyes sparkled as she listened.

He'd witnessed a different scene earlier involving a woman he recognized from Alana's multiple photos of the Hartnett family. It seemed Everleigh and her older sister, whose name escaped him—Harper? Hope? Hallie?—were having a bit of a tiff. After her sister had stomped away from her, Everleigh had nearly collapsed against the wall. When she saw Cade, she'd looked like she was trying to recover—but he could tell it was all for show. For a moment, he wondered what had gone on between the sisters. But it was none of his business.

"So the redhead's your new business partner, huh?" Roger commented.

Cade nodded.

"She's pretty." Roger lifted his eyebrows.

Cade shrugged. He'd noticed that her black dress made the most of her slim figure and long legs. But he wasn't interested. He was done with love and relationships and all of that garbage.

"What do you know about her?" Roger asked.

"She's a traveling nurse."

"Will she be an easy business partner?"

"Hopefully a silent one." He pulled on his cuffs to straighten his suit jacket. "But I need to talk to her to find out."

When Cade started toward her, Roger grinned and followed. "I'll join you. Her friend is cute too."

Cade squelched the urge to roll his eyes. Roger was always ready to flirt with an attractive woman, but he had yet to find a lasting relationship. Cade approached Everleigh, and when her eyes met his, she stood up straight and brushed her hands down her dress. Her smile was bright.

"Cade, hi." She turned to her friend. "Quinn Evans, this is Cade Witherspoon, and . . ."

"Roger Hale." Roger held his hand out to her, and Everleigh shook it before he also shook Quinn's.

Cade focused all of his attention on Everleigh.

"It was a nice service, right?" Everleigh clasped her hands in front of her.

He was so tired of small talk. He folded his arms over his chest.

They stared at each other, and an awkward moment ticked by.

"We need some time to talk about the inn," he finally said. He had to get this conversation going.

"Oh, yes." She nodded with enthusiasm. "Also, my mom and I have to go through Alana's things. How about Monday?"

"Sure."

"All right then. I'll see you Monday." Her smile seemed to shine even brighter, if that was humanly possible. Then she waved at Roger. "Nice to meet you."

Cade and Roger headed for the exit, and Roger patted Cade's shoulder. "Keep me posted on how your first meeting with your hot new partner goes."

This time, Cade couldn't have stopped the eye roll if he'd tried.

CHAPTER 4

"I HAVE TO call your sister to see if she's feeling better today," Mom said while driving her Subaru Monday morning. "I was surprised she didn't come to supper last night."

Everleigh took in familiar landmarks whizzing past the window—the Coral Cove Veterinary Clinic, the pet store, the Surf Shop, Carolina Beachwear, and CeCe's Toy Chest. Landon and Amber had joined Everleigh, Mom, and Dad for a barbecue last night. Dad had grilled hot dogs and hamburgers, and Mom served her delicious potato salad, along with baked beans and chips. They'd shared some laughs and reminisced about Alana, and their time together had soothed Everleigh's soul.

Harlowe and Branson had been absent, which wasn't at all surprising.

"I know why Harlowe ditched the family supper last night." It was obvious to Everleigh, though Harlowe had cooked up some sob story about having a sour stomach. Everleigh had come to expect nothing less from her older sister, unfortunately.

But she would win her over—somehow.

Mom seemed surprised. "What do you mean?"

"She's upset with me."

"She hasn't seen you for almost two years. Why on earth would she be upset with you?"

"For starters, I didn't come to Dad's surprise sixtieth birthday party."

"But you had a good reason for that. If you *had* come, you would've been in breach of contract and then gotten blackballed by that healthcare system. Your dad understood why you couldn't make it, and he loved the video you made for him."

"Thanks, but Harlowe's still upset." Everleigh shrugged as if it didn't still sting. "And she's angry she wasn't in Alana's will." She gave an abbreviated summary of what her sister had said at the memorial service. "She hasn't spoken to me since."

Mom patted her hand. "I'm sure she didn't mean it," she said. "And I bet she'll apologize."

Everleigh nodded, conceding that everyone in her family was probably a little emotional at the moment. Then, as Mom steered them down the road leading to the Sunshine Inn, Everleigh's pulse began to pound. It would be the first time coming to the inn without Alana being there.

Keep it together, Everleigh told herself. *Do what it takes to cope.*

The sprawling historic colonial sported bright-yellow siding with white trim, along with a tower and a wraparound porch where Alana had taught Everleigh to roller-skate. Window boxes bursting with colorful flowers greeted them. The house overlooked Coral Cove Bay, where Everleigh and her siblings used to play in the summer. Alana had also added a detached three-car garage with an apartment above it, where Everleigh used to dream of living when she grew up one day and helped Alana run the inn.

Everleigh's chest tightened, and for one second, she wished she'd stayed home in bed. She wasn't ready to face the bittersweetness this special place now held. But even though it hurt, Sunshine Inn had been the backdrop to some of her fondest memories. She'd grown up coloring on this porch, and her first middle school crush had been on the son of one of Alana's repeat summer guests. Then, over cups of hot chocolate in the kitchen, she and Alana had gone over the plans for their next big project. Despite her loss, Everleigh still planned to keep her godmother's dreams alive. She had promised to get their nonprofit off the ground—and she would find a way to do it in memory of Alana.

Mom parked the car in front of the inn and pushed the door open. Then she turned and gave Everleigh a hesitant expression. "Ready?"

Everleigh took Mom's hand in hers. "We'll get through this together."

"Okay," she whispered.

Mom started up the front steps, her flip-flops lightly rapping against the wooden boards, but Everleigh hung back and took in the scenery. The early September morning air was humid, and the sky was bright blue. The songs of the seagulls drifted over her, and a warm breeze brought with it the scent of salt water. She hugged her arms against her bright-orange tank top and walked up the path until she came to the fake rock with the hide-a-key.

"It's still here?" she whispered before picking up the rock and removing the key. She laughed softly to herself and sank down on the bottom step, recalling the many summers she spent at the inn working for her godmother. Those were some of her happiest days, as Alana taught her goddaughter to take reservations and payments. They also cleaned rooms and cooked together. That is, *Alana* had done the cooking since Everleigh was never much of a cook. She could burn water without trying.

She looked up toward the porch and saw Mom staring at the front door. Everleigh could feel her mother's grief coming off her in waves, and her heart squeezed. She bolted up the steps and took her hand. "Mom? You okay?"

Mom nodded, but tears reflected in her eyes.

"You want to sit together for a moment?" She pointed toward the porch swing.

Mom sniffed, and then her lips tipped up. "No, thanks. I'll be fine."

"You sure?"

Mom lifted her chin. "Yeah." She started toward the door. "You coming?"

"I'm going to sit out here for a minute—if you're sure you're okay."

"I am. I'll see you in Alana's suite."

Everleigh blew her a kiss before Mom disappeared into the house.

Everleigh set her backpack purse on the step beside her and hugged her knees to her chest. She closed her eyes and let more memories soak through her.

Breathe, Everleigh. Breathe.

She took in deep breaths, inhaling the fresh, salty air.

She jumped with a start as something soft brushed against her back. Behind her, a fluffy gray cat blinked up at her. He bumped his head against her arm before blinking again and meowing.

When the cat sat down, Everleigh noticed how huge he was— bigger than any cat she'd ever met.

"Hi! What's your name?" She stroked his fuzzy head, and he purred loudly, reminding her of a car engine.

"Bryant."

Everleigh angled her body toward the driveway and saw Cade strolling toward her. She tried not to stare at him, but it was impossible. He wore a faded gray T-shirt and athletic shorts that boasted his fit and tanned legs.

Oh my goodness!

"Bryant, huh?" she asked, hoping she sounded casual.

Cade nodded.

"Nice to make your acquaintance, Bryant," she told the cat, who continued to purr. "Is he a Maine coon?"

Cade sat down beside her. "Maybe?" He rubbed the cat's ear, and the cat tilted his head toward Cade.

The cat's purrs rumbled even louder, and Everleigh laughed. "I think he likes that."

While rubbing the cat's ear, Cade pointed toward the hide-a-key. "Where was that?"

"Alana left it for me in case I came over after school and she was out." She smiled as the tender memories of those days overtook her. "I had my own key, but I lost it enough times for Alana to suggest a hide-a-key." She picked up the fake rock, turned it over in her hand, and held the secret key out to Cade.

"Keep it. All the doors have keypads now."

Bored with the attention, Bryant yawned and then sauntered down the porch steps before collapsing on the sidewalk and rolling onto his back.

Everleigh pocketed the key as Cade stood. She studied him. Tall, tanned, and grumpy, but she was sure that under his frown there must be a good guy. If not, why would Alana *and* Bryant be so fond of him?

"Going inside?" he asked.

She nodded. "Yeah." She jumped up, ready to tackle Alana's closet, when her foot caught on the step. For one second she was weightless, sure she was about to fall on her face. But then two warm hands caught her shoulders. Warm, strong hands belonging to a cool, almost cold face. But those sky-blue eyes were captivating, and for a moment she was certain they were masking a kindness he was determined not to share. But why?

He was watching her, and heat rose to her cheeks.

"Ah! Um, thanks for the catch," she sputtered as he helped her get her footing.

Cade just nodded and held the door open for her, and Everleigh decided then and there: She was going to befriend Cade if it was the last thing she did.

When she entered the foyer, she was immediately transported back in time as she took in the antique table and mirror on the wall, the expensive oriental rugs lining the entryway, and the polished wooden banister leading up to the guest rooms. The sitting room still featured its elegant love seat and wing chair, along with matching end tables and colorful Tiffany lamps.

Beyond it was the large kitchen and formal dining room, where she'd helped Alana set the table for guests. It seemed like only yesterday she was folding napkins and arranging the fancy china for visitors.

Everleigh hooked her thumbs through the belt loops of her denim shorts and pivoted to face Cade, who was still wearing a grim expression. "Are any guests here now?"

"No, I canceled all of the reservations when Alana took a turn for the worse." He propped his forearms on the island in the center of the kitchen. "I focused on taking care of her."

"You took care of her?" The news took Everleigh aback.

He nodded. "Drove her to appointments, picked up her medicine, all that."

Everleigh stood silently as surprise—soon followed by guilt—filled her heart. Had Alana told her she was ill, she would have broken her contract with the hospital in Houston. Why *hadn't* Alana asked her to come home? Oh, how Everleigh wished she had. She would have jumped at the chance.

Everleigh tried to push past her feelings by forcing her lips to curl into a smile. "Do you live here on the grounds?"

He pointed toward the large picture window at the far end of the dining room. "In the apartment above the garage."

"Huh." She nodded.

An awkward silence expanded between them.

Finally, Cade stood up straight and folded his arms over his wide chest. "You going through Alana's things?"

"Right." She'd almost forgotten the purpose of her visit. She started across the kitchen, her Birkenstocks slapping the hardwoods. "My mom's already in her suite."

Cade only nodded. "I'll be around then," he said, stepping backward toward the entry. "We can talk later."

"Okay." Once he was out of sight, she walked down the hallway, passing two guest rooms, the laundry room, and an office, until she reached the doorway leading to Alana's suite. Everleigh rested her hand on the doorknob and took a deep breath.

She pulled the door open and entered the suite. It was just as she remembered: a sitting area decorated with the same lumpy gray sofa, worn coffee table, and flat-screen TV. Beyond it was the door to the bathroom and the bedroom. Everleigh ran her hand over the back of the sofa and recalled the nights she'd slept on it after watching movies and eating popcorn and ice cream with Alana. They were some of her best childhood memories.

She padded to the bedroom doorway and stopped. Mom sat on Alana's double bed, wiping her eyes with her fingers as she flipped through a photo album. Everleigh jumped into action, hoping to ignore the sadness blooming inside her. She sat beside her mother and looped her arm around her shoulders. "What are you looking at?"

"Do you remember the time we went on vacation with Alana?"

"You mean the time we drove to Florida and ran out of gas on I-95?" Everleigh asked.

"Right." A smile broke out on Mom's face, and relief tumbled through Everleigh. Mom pointed to a photo of her, Alana, Everleigh, and her siblings standing by their broken-down SUV.

Everleigh took in Alana's bright smile in the photo. She'd always thought she was lovely and larger than life with her dark hair, petite nose, and contagious laugh.

"We spent hours waiting for a tow truck, and it was so hot. We sang Dolly Parton songs trying to keep our minds off how humid it was. And Landon kept whining that he wanted to go to SeaWorld."

Everleigh laughed. "I had forgotten about that."

They spent the next half hour going through the photo album and reminiscing, but they finally had to pull themselves away. They had a job to do, after all. Everleigh located a few empty plastic containers in Alana's walk-in closet, and they started packing them with Alana's mementos.

Everleigh chose a spot on the floor, opened one of Alana's desk drawers, and found it full of folders. She flipped through file after file full of artwork Everleigh had given her, beginning in preschool. She pulled out drawings of stick figures at the beach and stories Everleigh had composed in messy handwriting.

She found another folder that held the detailed business plan for their nonprofit, Helping Angels. Everleigh had emailed it to Alana, and her godmother's comments and suggestions were written in the margins in her beautiful script.

"An angel always finds its way to you, even in your darkest moments."

Even though Alana was gone, their dream could live on. And one day, whenever she opened an office for the nonprofit, Everleigh was going to have an artist paint her godmother's words onto the entry wall to remind people that hope can always find you, even when you are lost.

At the sound of a jingling keychain, Everleigh spun toward her mother on the other side of the room and smiled.

"I think these are her car keys. You should drive Alana's car until yours is delivered." She tossed the keys, and Everleigh caught them.

She recognized the little metal keychain with the words "I Heart U." Everleigh had bought it for Alana years ago, and she still used it. The sweetness was almost too much. Alana had held on to every drawing and gift, yet Everleigh hadn't even bothered to come home to see her for almost two years. Guilt moved in and set up camp.

She set the keys on the dresser and then stood. "I'm going to get a glass of water. Would you like one?"

Mom shook her head. "I'm fine."

"You sure?"

"Positive. Go ahead."

Everleigh jogged out to the kitchen and poured herself a glass of water, then took a long drink. She rested her arms on the sink and dipped her chin. This day was turning out to be even more difficult than she'd imagined. Part of her wanted to respond to the constant calls she was receiving from the agency recruiter, take the first hospital position she could, and get as far away from Coral Cove as possible—but she knew that was a coward's move. She had to stay until Alana's affairs were settled.

She pressed the water glass to her forehead, enjoying the feel of the cool condensation against her warm skin. As she set the empty glass in the dishwasher, her eyes landed on a stack of letters pushed to the corner of the island.

Curiosity got the better of her, and she picked up the stack. Riffling through it, she found a couple of utility bills, along with a handful of postcards and letters from Realtors offering to buy the inn. She flipped a postcard over, and she gasped when she found a suggested listing price of more than seven figures—almost three million dollars!

Her hands trembled slightly as her brain grappled with the numbers.

Even though she and Cade would have to split that amount, they would each walk away with well over a million dollars.

A *million dollars.*

The business plan she and Alana had been working on filled her mind. She'd applied for grants and tried to find backers for Helping Angels, but she'd come up empty-handed over and over. Since the plan had begun to feel more impossible than ever, Everleigh hadn't even told her family about it.

But if they could sell the inn . . .

An angel always finds its way to you.

Excitement whipped through her, and the postcard vibrated in her hand. Was this the miracle she'd been looking for? Was this why Alana had left her half the inn?

She felt someone watching her and flicked her eyes upward. Cade was leaning against the doorway, a small frown on his face. Everleigh wondered if this was his "concerned face." She'd have to start making a list if she was going to crack the code and figure out his various grumpy expressions.

She stood up straight and flashed a winning smile. "Hi." She hopped onto a stool. "Want to talk now?"

"Sure." He started toward her.

"What did you want to talk about?"

Cade gestured around the B&B. "Everything."

She held up a postcard. "Have you spoken to any of the Realtors?"

"No." He scoffed.

"Why not?"

He cleared his throat. "Because I'm not selling the inn."

She nodded slowly.

"You want to?" he asked, eyes narrowing.

"Well, this is a tempting price." She pointed to the postcard.

His face seemed to flash with something like anger. "This is about money?"

"No." She shook her head and considered what to tell him. The nonprofit idea still felt too personal. "I just think we should consider the option of a sale." She worked to keep her expression bright. "I love my job, and I can't imagine giving it up."

"Good. You can be a silent partner."

She hesitated. "But have you seen what the inn is worth?"

He shrugged. "I'm not selling. I'll keep it running, and you don't have to be here for me to do that," he said. "Let's discuss reopening. I've heard from several regulars who want to come back before the weather gets cold."

Everleigh worked hard to keep her smile from faltering. "But we both own it, so we have to agree on our plan going forward."

Those radiant eyes studied her as his entire face twisted with a glower. She shifted uncomfortably on the stool. This was *not* an "are you okay?" kind of frown.

"Right. We're *equal* partners," he said. "That means my opinion matters just as much as yours."

They stared at each other, and the tension tightened between them. The exact opposite of what Everleigh wanted.

She lifted her hands, hoping to calm him down. "I do respect your opinion, Cade. But please, just for a moment, hear me out. If we sold the inn, we could split the money and do something meaningful with it."

His face remained stony, and his eyes never left hers. "Do you honestly believe that's what Alana would want?"

"Yes," she said. "She would understand why I want to sell."

He was silent for a moment. "When was the last time you worked here, Everleigh?"

"Right before I left for college."

"How long ago?"

"Almost ten years ago."

"I've been here almost two years." He held up two fingers. "I know for a fact she wanted this place to stay open. In fact, she talked about leveling it up—adding a lunch and possibly a dinner menu."

Everleigh's mouth worked while she tried to come up with a reply. Alana had never mentioned to her about adding more dining options or expanding the inn. Maybe Everleigh *needed* to tell Cade about the nonprofit so he could understand how important it was to her and Alana. And surely he would, since Alana had trusted him enough to leave him half of her life's work.

She moved her fingers over the edge of the island. "Alana and I wanted to start a nonprofit. We'd been putting together a business plan, and for the past three years, I've been working on making it happen. But my major obstacle was financial backing."

"She never mentioned anything like that to me," he said.

Everleigh pointed to the doorway. "I can show you the business plan, if you'd like."

His face remained frigid.

That was definitely a no.

"If we sell the inn, I could start the nonprofit in her memory. I know that would make her happy." Everleigh snapped her fingers. "We can sell to someone who will keep her spirit alive—a buyer who promises to keep the inn going." She sat up taller, and her smile returned. "That way, the inn will stay intact, and I can start the nonprofit she and I dreamed up. Two birds, one stone."

He shook his head, clearly unimpressed. "No."

"What if—" she began.

"Everleigh?" Mom appeared in the doorway, cutting off her words. "I think I've done enough for the day. Could you help me put the containers in the back of the car?"

Cade continued to stare at Everleigh. "I'll help you, Mrs. Hartnett." Then he whirled around and set off toward Mom.

CHAPTER 5

CADE WAS SO angry, his body vibrated as he carried Mrs. Hartnett's plastic containers outside and loaded them into the back of her Subaru. He had never imagined that Everleigh—Alana's favorite person on the planet, the one she talked about incessantly, and the one whose smile graced nearly every framed photo in Alana's suite—would want to sell the inn. He had expected her to tell him she was leaving for her next traveling nurse adventure by the end of the month—not that she wanted to sell the place, split the profits, and go merrily on her way.

If Alana had truly wanted to start some nonprofit, then why hadn't she ever mentioned it to him? He'd sat with her for hours when she was in the hospital, and she'd shared endless stories about Everleigh, but she'd never once talked about a nonprofit. She had, however, implied that she wanted him to keep the inn open—so he would do everything in his power to prevent Everleigh's ridiculous plan from coming to pass, no matter what the redhead said.

"Thank you so much, Cade." Mrs. Hartnett pulled open the

driver's door. "I'll be back again tomorrow, but I've had enough of the emotional trip down memory lane today."

Cade slipped his hands into the pockets of his shorts and nodded.

"By the way, how many times now have I told you to call me Caroline?" She gave him a sad smile.

"Right," he relented. "Caroline."

Everleigh had trotted out of the inn as well, but rather than climbing into the car, she pulled her mom into a hug. "I'll see you at home, Mom."

Cade pressed his lips together. "You're not going with her?"

"No." She pulled out Alana's keychain. "I was hoping to borrow her Jeep since my car hasn't been delivered yet."

Most likely, she was staying so they could continue their heated discussion.

Great. Just great.

Well, Cade had had his fill of her, just as Caroline had had her fill of going through Alana's personal effects. He would keep their discussion short and sweet.

Caroline climbed into the car, and Everleigh waved goodbye.

Once Caroline's Subaru was gone, the redhead spun toward him. "Cade," she began, her smile bright, "we can work this out."

"I'm not selling. End of discussion." He started toward the front door. "You can take the Jeep."

"Just wait a minute, okay?" She pulled a folded postcard from her pocket with a Realtor's name on it, and he stopped moving. "Surely we can find a buyer we agree on."

A muscle ticked along his jaw. She needed to leave. "I'll open the garage for you." Without waiting for her response, he stalked toward the front door, and her shoes flapped as she chased after him.

"Wait, Cade. I didn't mean to offend you."

"Could've fooled me," he muttered, continuing out the back door and down the sidewalk.

She caught up to him, and they walked side by side down the path leading to the three-car garage.

"When are you going back to work?" he finally asked her.

"Not until Alana's affairs are settled."

"Fantastic." Was he going to be stuck with her for weeks or even months? He would have to convince her he was not going to sell the inn, then hopefully they could stay out of each other's way until she left.

He noticed her smile never faltered. Didn't her face hurt from smiling so much?

"Tonight I'll start researching, and I'll find us the best Realtor."

"Knock yourself out, but I'm not selling." He punched in the code on the keypad. The double garage door hummed as it lifted.

"Is the code 0325?" Everleigh's eyes widened.

He nodded.

"That's my birthday."

"Not surprised," he commented.

"What do you mean?" she asked.

He gave her a look of disbelief. "Alana talked about you all the time."

"Oh." She gave him a solemn expression, then turned toward Alana's gray late-model Jeep Grand Cherokee. "She loved her Jeeps." She scanned the garage, her eyes roving across his workbench and woodworking tools as she pulled the keychain from her pocket. But then she made a beeline for his bike. "Is this your motorcycle?"

"Yup." He remained by the door while she circled his black Harley-Davidson.

"It's really pretty." She turned toward him. "What kind is it?"

"A Harley."

She pointed to it. "Is it a certain model?"

"A bobber." When her brow creased, he explained, "I took off the front fender and shortened the rear fender. That's what 'bobbed' means." He made air quotes with his fingers. "Like a bobtail cat."

She continued to look confused. "Why would you do that?"

"Makes it lighter and faster."

"Oh." She studied the black bike with its orange and silver pinstripes and whitewall tires. "How long have you had it?"

"Few years."

"Do you ride it much?"

"Every once in a while."

"It's beautiful." She pushed a lock of thick, red hair behind her ear. "Well, thanks for opening the garage. I'd better get going." She returned to the Jeep and climbed in before lowering the window. "Bye, partner. We'll talk again soon, okay?"

He bit back a stinging retort as she put the Jeep in gear and drove off.

Once she was out of sight, he closed the garage door and stood in the driveway, looking out toward the bay. His anger boiled inside him, and he wondered how he was going to keep himself sane during the next few months while Everleigh Hartnett was in town.

As Cade stalked toward the main house, Bryant loped over to him. Cade rubbed the cat's head before opening the back door and allowing the cat to skip inside ahead of him.

If only there were a way to buy the inn from her. Buying her out would solve everything, but the option was impossible since he didn't have the funds. Plus, his parents had suffered a bankruptcy, so they wouldn't be able to cosign for him.

Cade scowled. He was thirty-three years old and couldn't qualify for a loan. He had to get his life together! He'd hoped coming home to Coral Cove would help him get back on track, but now he was in danger of losing his livelihood—*again*.

The idea of selling the place made him sick to his stomach. He was certain that if they put the inn up for sale, a developer would swoop in, buy the land, knock down the inn, and build overpriced townhomes or apartments in its place—and he couldn't allow that to happen.

No matter what.

✦ ✦ ✦

"How'd it go at the inn today?" Dad asked, looking from Everleigh to Mom.

Everleigh added cheese, sour cream, and lettuce to her taco, then took a big bite in order to avoid her father's curious expression. She'd arrived home from the inn, helped her mother unload the containers of Alana's things, and stored them in the garage before insisting on making supper.

Putting together a taco kit from a box was about the extent of Everleigh's cooking skills, but the task kept her busy while she contemplated her quandary: Cade Witherspoon and his complete refusal to entertain the idea of selling the inn.

"Everleigh?"

"Huh?" She peeked up at her parents, who were watching her with concerned expressions. She plastered a smile on her face. "I'm sorry. Did you say something?"

Dad set his taco down. "Your mom said it was an emotional day at the inn."

Everleigh nodded and took another bite of her taco.

"You never said how it went with Cade after I left." Mom built another taco while she spoke.

Everleigh shrugged. "It was fine."

"Really?" Mom seemed unconvinced. "You two looked like you were having an intense conversation when I came in and asked for help packing the car."

So she *had* overheard their disagreement. Everleigh had hoped she hadn't. She did her best to appear unaffected. "We talked a little bit longer, and then I drove the Jeep home."

Mom sipped her glass of Diet Coke. "Your conversation wasn't . . . heated?"

"No." Everleigh tried to laugh. "Why would you think that?"

"From where I was standing, Cade looked irritated when he offered to help me."

"Doesn't he always look that way?" Everleigh asked. "I haven't known him very long, but I haven't seen him smile yet." She leaned toward her mom. "Is he okay?"

"I think so. Alana once mentioned he was a serious guy, but she admired him." Mom's expression remained concerned for a moment, but then she turned to Dad. "How was your day?"

"The usual." Dad shrugged. "I mowed the lawn and then played a round of golf."

While Dad and Mom chitchatted, Everleigh returned to her predicament. She was stunned by how Cade insisted he knew what Alana wanted because he'd worked for her for almost two years. But Everleigh had to admit, there seemed to be a lot about her godmother she didn't know.

Cade . . . her illness . . . plans for the future of the inn . . .

For a moment, everything had seemed so clear to Everleigh. Alana had left her the inn as a way to help her jump-start the next phase of Helping Angels. Everleigh knew Alana's heart. Her godmother had supported her dream, even going so far as to help form her business plan. Surely Alana would be honored if Everleigh started it in her memory.

She pushed aside the little voice in her head that reminded her that Alana had only left her half of the inn, and that for some reason, she'd left the other half to Cade—the one who'd cared for Alana when she was sick, who had been there every day keeping the inn running, who was her *actual* partner in business.

No, her godmother must have had a reason for wanting her and Cade to come together. Maybe he needed the money for something too. Alana was their guardian angel—and while Cade hadn't been swayed yet, Everleigh would find a way to convince him.

"Okay, Everleigh," Dad began, "you've been silent long enough. You normally talk our ears off when you're home. What's on your mind?"

Her parents' determined stares finally broke her down. It was time to tell them exactly what she and Cade had discussed.

"I want to sell the inn, but Cade doesn't." Everleigh lifted one shoulder in a half shrug, but never let her smile drop.

"You want to sell the inn?" Dad asked.

Mom gasped. "What makes you think Alana would want you to sell it?"

Everleigh's finger absently drew shapes in the condensation on her glass of Diet Coke. "Alana and I often discussed starting a nonprofit to help parents of critically ill children. We've talked about it for a few years, but I haven't been able to make it happen yet. If I sell the inn, I can continue that dream in her memory."

Mom shook her head. "I remember when she inherited money from her parents to buy that inn. She was so excited. It was Alana's lifelong dream to own a place that made her visitors happy."

Everleigh swallowed.

Dad's expression was serious. "Cade's your equal partner. You need to respect his opinion."

"I know," Everleigh said. "I plan to talk to him about it some more and explain how the nonprofit can help so many people."

Dad's expression was grave. "Don't ruin your working relationship with him over this. My brother's insurance agency went under when he and his partner had a feud. This is serious."

Everleigh nodded but decided it was time to change the subject. "So, what's new around Coral Cove?" she asked brightly. "I haven't been home in a while."

"The boardwalk has changed a bit," Mom said.

"Really?" she asked. "How?"

"We have some new stores out there. Let's check it out sometime."

"Absolutely," Everleigh said.

After they finished supper and cleaned up the kitchen, Everleigh disappeared into her room and pulled out the postcards she'd stuffed in her pocket earlier. She found her laptop and began searching websites for local Realtors. A couple of them appeared friendly—but were they trustworthy? They couldn't leave the inn's future in the hands of just anyone.

Her mom's words echoed in her mind: *"It was Alana's lifelong dream to own a place that made her visitors happy."*

Everleigh slouched in her desk chair and swiveled back and forth. She'd never do anything to hurt Alana's memory. In fact, she was convinced Alana had left her half of the inn *for the purpose* of making the nonprofit a reality.

An idea hit her like a bolt of lightning. The best way to get through to Cade was to *be* there, on-site. If he got to know her, he'd see her intentions were sincere. Upon realizing that, surely he'd agree to sign with an agent and sell it to the right buyer. Then he could use his half to do something meaningful too.

And to make him see that, she needed to move into Alana's suite.

Excitement buzzed through her. Jumping up from the chair, Everleigh yanked her large suitcase from the closet and began filling it with her clothes.

"Going somewhere?"

Everleigh turned to her mother, who was standing in the doorway. "I'm moving into Alana's suite until her affairs are in order."

"Really?" Mom sat in Everleigh's desk chair and frowned.

Everleigh dropped a pair of socks in the suitcase, then took Mom's hand in hers. "What's wrong? Do you not want me to stay at the inn?"

"Oh no, it's not that. Staying there might be a good idea. But being there and going through Alana's stuff was just too much for me today. Do you think you can finish the job while you're there? I trust you to decide what you think we should keep."

"Sure." Everleigh gave her hand a gentle squeeze. "Are you okay, Mom?"

She wiped her eyes. "I just miss her."

"I do too." She smiled as a funny story from Alana made its way through her mind. "You know, Alana told me about that disastrous double blind date you two had when you were in college."

A burst of laughter escaped Mom's mouth, sending a happy glow through Everleigh. "I can't believe she told you that story."

"She explained how you went to meet these guys for dinner, and after you took one look at them, you wanted to escape out the back door."

Mom continued to laugh. "That's true. They weren't what we expected, but one of the guys recognized Alana and called us over to the table. We didn't want to be rude, so we had a couple of Cokes with them. But then the boys turned out to be a bit rude themselves."

"So you fled the scene?"

"We sure did!" She snickered. "We excused ourselves and went to the ladies' room. Then we crawled out a window, got into Alana's old Volvo station wagon, and hightailed it out of there!"

Mom's laughter was music to Everleigh's ears.

"I wish I had been a fly on the wall for that," Everleigh said.

"It was a sight." Mom wiped her eyes. "I was never very athletic. I half jumped, half fell out the window and landed in a puddle."

Everleigh grinned and rested her elbows on her thighs. She loved hearing stories about when Mom and Alana were young.

"We had some wonderful adventures together."

Then Mom's laughter faded, and her expression became serious again. "Please think long and hard before you sell the inn, okay?"

"I will." Everleigh paused for a beat. "But you need to trust me on this. I wouldn't do anything to hurt Alana." Leaning over, she hugged her mother.

"I know." Mom stood. "We still need to go shopping at the boardwalk."

"We will. I promise."

After Mom left the room, Everleigh continued packing. She would show everyone how she was going to make Alana proud. She just needed to start by convincing Cade that to best honor Alana's legacy, they needed to sell the Sunshine Inn.

CHAPTER 6

THE FOLLOWING MORNING, the sound of a vehicle driving toward the inn drew Cade's attention from the foyer to the front of the house. He finished tightening a new bulb into the elegant brass fixture above the door and then climbed down the ladder. Once out on the porch, he found Alana's Jeep parked with the trunk open.

What in the world?

Everleigh's grunts and groans floated through the air as he jogged down the steps to the back of the SUV, where she struggled to pull her enormous suitcase out of the trunk.

He grabbed the suitcase before it fell on her and set it on the driveway. "What are you doing?"

"Moving in!" Her smile was nearly as bright as the September morning sun.

"You're kidding."

"Nope." She held her head high. "I'm going to stay in Alana's suite so we can get to know each other better and work out a plan for the inn, partner."

"Fantastic," he grumbled. Now he wouldn't be able to get away from her.

She pointed to her suitcase and grinned. "Would you mind carrying my rock collection up the stairs for me?"

He lifted the hefty suitcase and carried it up the porch steps. Behind him, she closed the trunk and then followed with a couple of tote bags and a backpack. He sure hoped she wasn't planning to stay through the winter with all the stuff she was bringing.

He dragged the suitcase into the foyer, and she examined the ladder. "What are you doing here?" she asked.

"Changing light bulbs." He didn't bother to wait—just pulled the suitcase toward the hallway. Then he opened the door leading to Alana's suite and set the suitcase inside the den area, leaving Everleigh standing in the suite while he walked back to the foyer.

He moved the ladder to the dining room and began replacing the dead bulbs in the chandelier over the long table. His mouth sagged downward as he imagined how irritating it would be to have to see Everleigh every day, continually arguing with her about selling the place. There had to be a way to change her mind and end this debate.

He turned toward the row of windows overlooking the back of the inn's property and the beautiful bay. How could anyone want to sell this place? Once Everleigh dropped her ridiculous idea about a sale, she'd go back to working as a traveling nurse. Then his life could go back to some sense of normalcy—as normal as it could now be without Alana.

✦ ✦ ✦

Everleigh spent the next couple of hours going through Alana's clothes and making piles of items to donate and a few to keep for herself and her mother. Once the closet was nearly empty, she stowed her clothes inside. Needing a break, she retrieved a bottle of water from the refrigerator in the kitchen and then padded out to the large sunroom Alana had added onto the inn when Everleigh was around ten.

The room sat on the other side of the wall from Alana's suite, and the same wicker patio furniture she remembered was scattered throughout the room, the chairs waiting for someone to sit and enjoy the hot summer day. The humidity closed in on her, and her T-shirt began to stick to her back. She flipped the switch for the ceiling fans, and the four of them began to hum and swish and spin. She opened the bottle of water and stood by the wall screens, taking in the large oak tree reaching its branches over the room.

She surveyed the porch and the light-gray walls, and was almost certain it was the same shade of gray for every room downstairs. Why would Alana have ever chosen that? She tried to imagine brighter walls—maybe rubber duck yellow or lemonade. Excitement surged through her at the idea.

"Meow!"

Everleigh pivoted toward the door and found Bryant on the steps. "Hey, Bryant."

The cat meowed again and rubbed his big, fluffy gray face on the screen.

"Wanna come in?" She pushed open the creaky door, but instead of walking inside, the cat just waited. "Okay then. I'll join you instead."

She knelt down and rubbed the cat's head while he purred. At the other end of the driveway, the detached garage door was open, revealing Cade walking back and forth. Maybe he was working on his motorcycle or the old pickup truck parked beside it. Or maybe he was creating something with the woodworking tools she had spotted on his bench.

Everleigh basked in the view of the glorious bay. She'd spent many holidays at the inn, and especially had loved coming to see

Alana on the Fourth of July. They'd cook out, and her father would set off fireworks over the water. Life had been so simple back then. She thought fondly of all the hours she'd enjoyed, laughing and chasing her brother and sister.

Her thoughts turned to Harlowe. Everleigh had always been envious of friends who were close to their sisters, and she longed to open up to Harlowe and share her secrets, hopes, and dreams with her—like she had with Alana.

Grief packed around her heart, and she studied the cat. "Should I call my sister, Bryant?"

The cat yawned and hopped down the steps before flopping onto the concrete and stretching out his long body.

"I'll take that as a yes." She pulled her phone from her pocket. It was midmorning on a Tuesday, which meant Harlowe would be at work in the human resources office for the City of Coral Cove. She unlocked her phone, found her sister's number, and poised her thumb over it.

And then she stopped.

Why was she hesitating? Harlowe was her sister. A simple phone call shouldn't be so stressful. Maybe her sister would be happy to hear from her. What if this was the phone call that could change their relationship for the better? Hope swelled within her as she hit the button.

While the line rang, her attention moved back to the garage, where Cade stood in the doorway. He took a long drink from a bottle of water, then pushed his hand through his thick golden hair. When his eyes found hers, she waved. Instead of waving he walked back into the garage. *So that must be his "I'm really busy right now" frown.*

Harlowe's voicemail picked up, and Everleigh's hope dissolved. Maybe she was busy with an employee or in a meeting.

Or maybe she was avoiding Everleigh.

Stay positive! Everleigh told herself. *Harlowe and I will work this out!*

After the beep sounded, Everleigh began speaking. "Hey, Harlowe. This is your sister," she said, her voice sounding chipper. "I've been thinking of you and wanted to chat. Give me a call sometime, okay? Bye." Then she disconnected the call and pushed the phone into her pocket.

When she looked up again, she found Cade sauntering toward her. The cat jumped up and trotted toward him, meeting him by the driveway.

"Hey, bud." He leaned down and stroked the cat's ear.

Everleigh drank from her bottle of water and took in the sight of him in his athletic shorts and white T-shirt. The unremarkable clothing somehow did wonders for his muscular legs, arms, and chest. He was gorgeous.

She pulled herself away from the thought. She wasn't interested in a relationship anyhow. And if she were, starting one with Cade Witherspoon would make things even more complicated . . .

"How's unpacking?" he asked, still walking toward her.

The tone in his voice seemed different, so she was silent for a moment as she tried to read his face. Why was he suddenly being friendly? This expression seemed to be his "curious frown," and it was more approachable than the ones she'd encountered so far. Were they making progress toward something?

He lifted an eyebrow, and she realized she hadn't responded to his question.

"Fine." She rested her hands on her lap and smiled. "I went through Alana's clothes, and now I have a few bags to take to the donation place in town. My mom asked me to finish going through her stuff since yesterday was difficult for her."

"Understandable," Cade said. The cat appeared at his feet and started walking circles around them. He crouched down and brushed his hand over the kitty's back.

She nodded toward the garage. "Are you working on your bike?"

"Yeah." He set the bottle of water on the ground beside the cat.

"What are you doing to it?"

"Tune-up."

She studied him, and all at once, she wanted to know everything about him. "Where are you from?" she asked, resting her back on the step behind her.

"Here."

"You grew up here? Went to school here?"

"Yup."

"How old are you?"

"Is this an interrogation?"

She laughed, but he continued to watch her with the same expression. "No, I'm just curious."

"Thirty-three."

"Then you're two years older than my sister," she said. "Do you remember her from school?"

"Can't say I do." He dropped to the ground and folded his long legs under him. When Bryant came to sit in his lap, Cade continued massaging the cat's back. Tenderness flickered over his features so quickly that she almost missed it. Still, his affection for the cat was apparent, and it seemed mutual. The scene warmed her heart.

"And you've lived here all your life?" she asked. She was surprised she hadn't run into him, but she'd left for college and then hadn't returned. Also, he was six years older, and Mom had mentioned something about him joining the military.

He shook his head.

"Where have you lived?"

"Here and there."

For a moment she'd believed he was going to open up to her, but clearly she was wrong. She tried to mask her disappointment by fidgeting with her water bottle.

"I joined the military right out of high school."

She set the bottle down. "Which branch?"

"Army." He kept those dazzling eyes focused on the cat. "College wasn't an option. So the military made sense."

"What did you do in the army?"

"This and that." A cloud of cat hair floated away from him, and he brushed his hands over his shorts. "I was stationed all over—the West Coast, Europe, the Middle East—and then I landed in Alabama. Lived there for a while and came home a couple years ago."

"How'd you wind up working here?" she asked, hoping to keep him talking.

"Alana came into my mom's store one day, and Mom mentioned how I needed a job. Then she invited me for an interview."

"Your mom owns a store?"

"Crafty Creations."

"She owns the art supply store in town?" she asked. "I had no idea."

He nodded. "Been there for years."

"And I've been in there at least a hundred times." If all of this was true, then he really *was* a local. Now she yearned to know even more about him. "What did you do in Alabama?"

"Owned a business."

"What kind?"

"It didn't work out."

A long pause suffused the air, and her posture drooped. Just like that, he was reticent again. She pointed toward the sliding glass door. "Did you paint the sunroom?"

Suspicion flooded his features. "Why?"

"What if I brightened it a bit?"

"Why? It's too hot to sit out there between May and October."

"How about yellow?" she offered. "I love bright colors. They make me so happy."

"Whatever knocks your socks off, partner." He pushed himself up from the ground and stood up to his full height. "I should finish the tune-up," he muttered.

"See you later." She wished he'd chat for longer, but at least she was finally starting to get to know him—sort of. Surely that was a step in the right direction for their partnership and maybe even a friendship.

He started toward the garage. "Come on, Bryant," he called to the cat, and the feline loped after him.

Everleigh rested her chin on her palm while he made his way back to the garage.

✦ ✦ ✦

Cade sat on Roger's porch later that evening. After finishing the tune-up on his bike, he had taken it for a test drive and wound up near Roger's house. When he saw his buddy's truck in his driveway, Cade parked and knocked on the door.

Roger handed him a cold bottle of Coke, and the sound of waves crashing in the distance and the smell of the salt air floated over Cade. He would never get tired of living on the coast.

Roger opened his Coke, and the bottle fizzed. "How's it going with your partner?"

Cade groaned. "Terrible. She wants to sell the inn." He twisted off the bottle cap and let a *hiss* escape. "Oh, and she moved in today. Now she can bug me about it all day long."

Roger held his hand up like a traffic cop. "Whoa. Why does she want to sell it?"

"To start a nonprofit she insists Alana wanted."

Roger's brow wrinkled. "A nonprofit?"

Cade shrugged and took a sip of Coke.

"What are you going to do?"

"Stand my ground." He rested the bottle on the arm of the Adirondack chair. "She needs to go back on the road and let me run the inn. We could split the profits, and I'd only have to deal with her when she comes to visit, which hopefully would be rare."

Roger nodded.

"I wish I had enough to buy her out, but thanks to my ex, the only thing I have left is my bike." He pointed his bottle of soda toward the motorcycle sitting on the gravel driveway. "And the truck Alana gave me."

Roger was silent as he took a long drink of Coke. Then he angled his body toward Cade and grinned. "What if you tried another approach?"

"I'm listening."

"Humor her."

"How?"

"Tell her you'll sell," he began. When Cade opened his mouth to protest, Roger said, "Hold on. But you'll only agree with certain conditions."

"Rog, I don't want to sell."

"But if you make the conditions impossible, it won't sell anyway. Tell her she has to advertise it for sale by owner. That way, she won't have the help of an agent. And put a ridiculous deadline on her. Like two months. Then tell her if the inn doesn't sell by the deadline, she needs to go back to her job and let you run it."

Cade let the idea roll around in his head. "I don't know . . ."

"Just an idea." Roger shrugged and took a sip.

Cade contemplated Roger's suggestion while he looked out toward the street. At the very least, the plan might get her off his back.

He turned his focus back to his best friend. "You think that might work?"

"I do."

"But what if she gets an offer?"

Roger's grin was back. "She can't sell it without your signature, right?"

"Right."

"Then just refuse. She'll get frustrated and leave, and then it will be over. You'll have your sanity back too."

Cade nodded.

Roger patted his shoulder. "If nothing else, having an attractive partner ain't bad, right?"

Cade shook his head. "Right now, all I care about is getting her out of the inn and getting some visitors back. I'm ready to open up reservations whether she likes it or not."

"Good call, man."

Cade took another drink of soda and wondered if Roger's idea might just work. He wanted nothing more than to hang on to the inn—but maybe the easiest way to do that was to push Everleigh Hartnett out of his life for good.

CHAPTER 7

EVERLEIGH FLITTED AROUND the kitchen at the inn. It was Thursday evening, and she had tilapia on baking sheets and ready to go in the oven. The table in the dining room was set for two with Alana's best china. Everything was falling into place. She just had to finish the meal and then call for Cade. The last time she'd checked, the garage door was still open. She assumed he was tinkering on his motorcycle or his truck.

She'd spent the past week going through the last of Alana's things and settling in at the bed-and-breakfast. She and Cade had only spoken in passing since their conversation over a week ago when they'd sat outside the sunroom with Bryant. Cade had kept to himself while he took care of the grounds and rarely came inside the house. And even though she hadn't mentioned selling the inn again, she'd been busy researching Realtors. Tonight she'd planned a special meal so she could tell him what she'd found out.

Everleigh brushed melted butter on the fish and then sprinkled salt and pepper over it. When she opened the oven doors, smoke poured out, and soon the smoke detectors began shrieking.

Oh no! She'd forgotten to set the timer for the french fries!

Cade appeared in front of her. "Move," he ordered before yanking the baking pan from the oven and dropping it in the sink. He hissed and shook his injured hand.

She gasped. "Cade! Are you okay?" She took his hand in hers. "You should have used a hot pad instead of just grabbing the pan." Her eyes lingered on his rough skin, examining the red spots. But when she looked up at him, his sky-blue eyes were focused on hers. The look was intense and something she couldn't quite decipher, and an unexpected shiver moved through her body.

"Cold water will help." She turned on the faucet and angled his hand under it. "I'll make you an ice pack." She started searching through cabinets and drawers for zippered storage bags.

"Nurse Everleigh," he called over the screaming smoke detectors, "I'm okay, but the french fries aren't." When she turned back toward him, he pointed to the blackened fries in the sink. His lips twitched and curled upward. Then, suddenly, he finally graced her with a real smile for the first time since she'd met him. For a moment she was mesmerized. He was even more handsome this way, and the smile was more magnificent than she'd ever imagined. In fact, she couldn't take her eyes off him.

She realized she was staring, and she chuckled as heat invaded her cheeks.

He turned off the water and wiped his hands with a paper towel. Then he opened the kitchen windows while she flipped on the ceiling fan. After a couple of minutes, the smoke detectors finally stopped, and she propped herself against the counter and sighed. So much for surprising Cade with a nice meal.

He studied the baking sheet. "What are you attempting to make? Tilapia?"

She nodded.

"Marinated?"

She hesitated, sensing his disapproval. "Salt and pepper and a little bit of butter." His expression told her he wasn't that impressed. "Not good?"

"Hardly." He chuckled and washed his hands again, then he went to work in the pantry. He retrieved olive oil, garlic, dried parsley and oregano, pepper, and tabasco sauce, then placed the items on the counter. "I don't have a lemon, but there should be lemon juice in the fridge," he mumbled to himself.

Everleigh leaned on the kitchen island and watched in awe while he used the ingredients to whip up a quick marinade. He looked so at ease as he doused the pieces of fish, and he appeared almost . . . well, *happy* was the only word that came to Everleigh's mind. He seemed to belong in the kitchen somehow. She soaked in his positive energy while enjoying this side of Cade—a new one he was finally sharing with her.

"Technically, it should sit in the marinade for about ten minutes and then cook another ten or fifteen."

Who was this guy? She tilted her head. "Are you a chef or something?"

"In another lifetime." He pointed to the burned fries. "I'm guessing you're not."

"I make a mean bowl of cereal." She lifted her chin, pretending to brag.

He laughed, and she enjoyed the deep, rich sound. It was something she wanted to hear more often—perhaps all the time. He was even more attractive, if that was even possible. *So very hot!*

"What are you serving with the fish?" he asked. When she pointed to the scorched fries, he laughed again before returning to the pantry. "How about rice?"

"Sure. And I picked up a bagged salad yesterday."

He stopped and faced her, and his expression turned embarrassed. "Do you have guests coming?"

"Just you." She pointed at him. "I was making this for us."

A strange look fell over his face, and then he nodded. "I'll start on the rice if you want to make the salad."

They worked side by side, and soon the salad, fish, and rice were ready. They then seated themselves across from each other at the table.

Everleigh took a bite of fish and moaned. "This is delicious."

He smiled and ate a forkful.

"Where did you learn to cook like this?" she asked.

He swallowed some salad. "The army."

"Really?" she asked, and he nodded. "Have you ever considered working as a chef?"

He shrugged, but she noticed something in his eyes that told her there was more to the story he wasn't willing to share. Disappointment nipped at her. This man was so fascinating—and every secret revealed made him seem even more so.

"Do you cook for the guests here?"

He nodded. "Alana let me make breakfast. Before we shut down, we talked about offering suppers too. We wanted to make the inn more than a B&B. I created a menu, but it wasn't the right time." His expression seemed to light up when he talked about cooking.

"What kind of breakfasts did you make?"

"Hmm." He studied the ceiling as if the menus were projected there. "Eggs Benedict, pancakes, French toast, crepes . . . things like that."

"Did you ever cook with Alana?"

"Often." He pointed his fork at Everleigh. "But it looks like you didn't."

"And you'd be right." She laughed. "Have you ever considered owning a restaurant?"

"I did."

"And . . . ?" she prodded.

He took a sip from his glass of sweet iced tea. "Didn't work out."

"What happened?"

He took a bite of fish and swallowed it. "Why'd you become a nurse?"

She thought she might get whiplash from the subject change, but she decided to let it go. Cade didn't want to talk about himself. But she'd get the entire story out of him someday. He would open up to her.

"When I was a kid, my nana fell and broke her leg," she said. "Shattered it, really."

Cade winced. "Ouch."

"Yeah," she agreed. "She was in the hospital and then in rehab while she learned how to walk again. I remember going to visit her, and I was in awe of the nurses who took care of her. They would swoop in and bring her medication, transport her safely to the bathroom, and help her get dressed. They were the angels who made sure she had what she needed." She rested her fork on the edge of her plate. "They made a real impression on me. I was about eight when I decided I was going to be a nurse. I've always loved helping people, making them happy, making their day better."

He appeared impressed. "Do you work with the elderly?"

"No, the opposite. I work in the NICU."

"Nick-you?" he asked.

She smiled. "It stands for neonatal intensive care unit. It's where newborn babies go when they need special care."

"Oh." He nodded. "Why babies?"

"When I did my clinicals, I spent time in the NICU. I had to examine the babies, take their vitals, give them medication, and feed them." She sighed as memories flashed through her mind. "It was such a blessing to hold these little miracles in my arms." She picked up her fork and moved it around on the plate.

"I went on to other clinicals, but I couldn't stop thinking about the babies. When I finished school and found out about the traveling nurse program, I signed up for NICU positions so I could go to hospitals that need me. And that's how I became a traveler. The hours are long, and the shifts are unpredictable, but I love what I do. I was out in Iowa and then West Virginia and then Colorado." She rested her chin on her palm while she focused on the small pile of rice on her plate. "Some days are rough, but they're rewarding too. And there's nothing better than when a baby I've taken care of finally gets to go home. Just seeing the joy in the parents' faces is the most incredible feeling. It's such a gift to be a part of something so important."

She sighed. "I took a month off a couple years ago, and it was the last time I came home. I thought maybe it was time to move on and do something else. But I found I missed the cry of the babies and sound of the monitors going off." She snickered at herself. "That's when I accepted that being in the NICU is my calling."

She looked up and found him staring at her. And the intensity in his dazzling eyes stole her breath for a moment. She tried to decipher this expression, and wondered if he was intrigued. Was he as fascinated with her as she was with him?

The silence stretched between them, so she pushed back her chair. "How about some dessert? I was sure I'd mess up cookies if I tried to make them myself, so I picked up a box instead. I hope you like chocolate chip."

"Sure," he said softly.

The warmth in his expression caught her by surprise, and she hurried to the kitchen to collect the box of cookies. When she sat back down, her phone began to sing, but she turned off the ringer and pushed the phone to the pocket of her jean shorts.

"Friend of yours?" he asked while choosing a cookie from the box.

"One of the recruiters." When his brow puckered, she added, "I registered with a couple of agencies for nursing jobs, and the recruiters call me nonstop trying to offer me new positions. So many hospitals are short-staffed that I can pretty much choose where in the country I want to go. I can even apply to work abroad."

"Sounds like you're in high demand."

She chuckled. "Well, I wouldn't say that. I've told them I'm taking some time off to handle some family issues, but that doesn't deter them from constantly calling."

They each ate a cookie, and then Cade relaxed into the chair. "Delicious." He rested his hands on his flat abdomen. "What was the occasion?"

She sat up straight and took a deep breath. "I was hoping we could talk." She reached behind her and grabbed her business plan from the buffet. "I wanted to show you something."

He studied the document she handed him. When his face transformed, disappointment filled her. All the strides they'd seemed to make toward friendship seemed to disappear in that one moment. He held up the pieces of paper. "What's this?"

"The business plan for the nonprofit." She pointed to the script in the margins. "You'll recognize Alana's handwriting. We were working on this together, Cade. I'm telling you the truth."

He glanced at the document and dropped it onto the table beside his plate. His face filled with a frown, and she was certain this one said, *I've heard enough.*

"Please just listen, okay?" she asked, but he continued to look irked. "I would never do anything to hurt Alana's memory."

"Me neither."

"Great." She smiled. "We agree on that."

He watched her with suspicion.

"I spent the week interviewing Realtors, and I think you're going to like the one I chose."

At this, his features turned sour. "Should've known you had an ulterior motive." He pushed back his chair and stood.

"Wait!" she exclaimed. "Please, Cade. Let me finish. We can get a good price for this place, and the Realtor said we can interview the buyers to make sure we approve of their plans for the inn."

He scoffed. "Are you that naïve, Everleigh? You can't control what someone will do with a property once it's theirs. A developer would love to knock down the place, build a cookie-cutter neighborhood, and charge exorbitant prices for waterfront homes."

"We can't control that, but the Realtor said we can insist that we don't want the inn knocked down."

"Right," he snapped. "If we're going to get a few million for this place, the Realtor will tell you exactly what you want to hear, Everleigh." He shook his head. "And that's what you truly believe Alana would want us to do?"

She blinked and then nodded. "Yes, I'm convinced she left me half so I could help people with the nonprofit she and I designed." She pointed to the business plan. "I'd love to share it with you, Cade. Please take a look at it."

Cade's eyes were cool, sending a shiver through her. He clearly was upset and angry, and she longed to convince him she didn't have bad intentions.

"Please, Cade," she begged. "Just read through it, and you'll understand."

His lips worked for a moment, and she held her breath, waiting for him to speak. But then he stacked their plates, put their utensils on top, marched to the kitchen, and began filling the dishwasher.

She followed him through the doorway, and her stomach twisted. "Cade?"

He kept working, his movements rigid and jerky.

She carried their glasses over, along with the bowl with leftover salad, and set them on the counter. But he continued to arrange the dishes, ignoring her. The hostility between them began to gnaw at her.

"Cade," she pleaded. "Talk to me. Please."

"There's nothing more to say," he muttered.

She rubbed her forehead. "I'll clean up since you cooked."

"I got it." He added the dishes to the dishwasher.

"Cade, I know you're upset with me, but I—"

"We'll never agree about the inn." He slipped a dish detergent packet into the dispenser, pushed the door closed, and started the machine before facing her. He was silent for a moment, but then his glower relaxed, slightly. "Fine. You win," he said. "I'll make a deal with you."

Her breath hitched in surprise. "Really?"

"I'll let you put the inn on the market, but only with certain conditions." He held up his pointer finger. "First, no Realtor. You have to sell it by yourself."

"By myself?"

"Yup. For sale by owner *only*. No contract with a Realtor at all."

She blanched slightly. How on earth would she manage that?

"No entertaining offers from developers—only families or people interested in keeping the inn. And I want you to be the one showing it. You loved Alana, and she loved this place. I won't sell to someone who doesn't love it too. And we *both* have veto power. If someone makes an offer and I don't like it, I can turn it down, and you can do the same."

She nodded. "That's fair."

"My next condition is that you've got two months. If it's not sold by Thanksgiving, then we keep it." He nodded toward her.

"You go back on the road." Then he pointed at himself. "And I run it. You'll be my silent partner and leave the day-to-day business to me."

"Is that it?" she asked. *Please, no more conditions!*

"Nope. I'm opening up reservations tonight. Every day that goes by without visitors is a day we're losing money. After I leave here, I'm heading up to my apartment, logging on, and opening the calendar. I'll accept reservations through Thanksgiving for now."

"Okay." She clasped and unclasped her hands. "Anything else?"

"Lastly, you have to promise to consider my and Alana's vision for what the inn could be."

"Okay," she said. "And if I agree to that, will you listen to me about the nonprofit?"

"Sure." He folded his arms over his chest. "That's my offer. Take it or leave it."

Everleigh pushed the heel of her hand against her sternum. Was her heart racing, or was she imagining things? He was her partner, so she had to respect his conditions and his opinion. And in turn, he was agreeing to respect hers. This could be successful if they worked together.

She smiled and held her hand out to him. "I accept your conditions, partner."

He shook her hand. "It's a deal, partner. Good luck."

As he sauntered out of the kitchen, she leaned back against the counter and massaged her forehead. How was she going to sell the inn on her own? What did she know about real estate?

Her phone vibrated with a text, and when she pulled it from her pocket, she found a message from Quinn:

> Hi! How are things? Let's meet for coffee soon and catch up.

Everleigh smiled. She'd been thinking of her friend and meaning to text her. Then hope surged through her. Quinn had worked in real estate! Maybe her friend could give her some pointers on how to sell the inn. She poised her thumbs over her phone.

Everleigh: How about tomorrow?

Quinn: That was quick! 😊 I'm working, but I can meet you at the Roast Shack on my break. How's ten o'clock?

Everleigh: Perfect! See you then.

Everleigh breathed a sigh of relief. Maybe Quinn would be all the help she needed.

✦ ✦ ✦

Everleigh stepped into the Roast Shack's open-air service area, and the delicious aroma of coffee saturated her senses. She scanned the restaurant, listening to all the customers chatting. One wall featured a gorgeous mural of the beach at sunrise, and the opposite wall had a matching mural of the beach at dusk. She smiled as she recalled Alana sharing how she'd watched the artist working on the sunrise mural while she enjoyed a cup of coffee.

She turned toward the counter and spotted Karis O'Neill. Karis appeared to be in her late sixties by now, and she grinned at a man while taking his order. The brunette with silver roots, bright hazel eyes, and a gap between her two front teeth had owned and operated the coffee shop with her husband, Ted, for as long as Everleigh could remember.

"Everleigh!"

She turned toward the sea of tables, where Quinn waved her over with one hand and held up a cup of coffee with the other.

Everleigh sat across from her, and Quinn pushed a cup her way.

"I took a chance and ordered you an Americano."

"Thanks." Everleigh took a sip and smiled. It hit the spot!

The two friends chatted for a little while, catching up on Quinn's work and family and Everleigh's recent travels. Then Quinn cradled the warm cup in her hands and asked, "So what's going on with the inn?"

"Funny you should ask. I need your help." She shared how she and Cade were at odds, then described the agreement they had made. "So I have two months to sell the inn myself, and I have no clue where to begin."

Quinn was silent for a moment, and Everleigh prepared herself for another lecture about how she was making a grave mistake.

"The first thing you need to do is decide on a price. Then we can purchase signs to post outside the inn and on the major streets leading up to it. If you want, I can come over and help you take photos. Then you can list the inn on a few websites and social media." Quinn named off a few more websites Everleigh might find helpful. "I'm off tomorrow. Would you like me to come over then?"

"Yes!" Excitement mixed with gratitude overtook Everleigh. "Thank you so much, Quinn." She let her shoulders relax and took another sip of her coffee.

"I guess it's not going well with Cade, huh?"

Everleigh rubbed the edge of the table. "He's . . . complicated."

"How so?"

"One minute he's a total grouch and gives me short, one-word answers to questions—if he talks to me at all. But then last night during dinner, he was friendly and funny. It was the first time I've seen him smile. He acted interested when I talked about nursing. Plus, he's a chef and saved the terrible dinner I attempted to make. For a moment, I thought we might be friends." Her smile faltered. "But he completely shut down when I brought up selling the inn."

"And that bothers you."

Everleigh perked up again. "I think he'll come around once we get to know each other. I can tell he cared about Alana, and that means the world to me. At the very least, I hope we can get past our disagreement." She took a sip of her coffee.

"And if you never become friends, then just think of it this way: Soon the inn will be sold, and Cade will be out of your life forever." Quinn tapped her finger on the table. "Now, let's make a plan to sell the place."

CHAPTER 8

"PERFECT!" QUINN TOLD Everleigh the next morning. "Now let's get a shot of the windows overlooking the pond."

Cade leaned against the dining room doorway and glowered while Everleigh and her friend took more photos. Everleigh had spent several hours cleaning the inn from top to bottom—vacuuming, dusting, and wiping down the woodwork—even though he didn't think it necessary. When he'd walked through yesterday, he found her rearranging the furniture in each room before putting it all back where it had been. He felt a twinge of guilt for not offering to help her, but selling the inn had been her idea, not his. He couldn't allow himself to encourage her when he knew Alana would never approve of this.

Cade already regretted agreeing to her advertising the inn, but he held on to Roger's belief that it most likely wouldn't sell without a professional Realtor's help. Everleigh was a nurse, and real estate wasn't anywhere near her wheelhouse.

But had he given her too much time? It was already the middle of

September, and October would be here soon. Maybe he should have told her October 1 was her deadline.

"I think that's it for the inside," Everleigh announced. "We need to get photos of the grounds now." She spun toward Cade, and her smile became hesitant. "I left a draft of the listing on the counter for you. Did you look at it?"

He nodded.

"Are you okay with the price?" She appeared anxious for his approval, which baffled him. Why did she care about what he thought, when she was determined to sell the inn despite his objections?

He shrugged. "Sure." But then he stood up straight. "Ask for more, if you want," he suggested. If she inflated the price, then for sure no one would buy it.

"The comps I ran all pointed to this price," Quinn chimed in.

Thanks, Quinn. He nodded his head and backed out of the doorway.

But Everleigh trailed after him. "Do you have any questions or concerns, Cade?"

He speared her with a sarcastic smile. "I'm sure you've thought of everything, partner."

Her smile dimmed for a fraction of a second, but it lifted again when she turned her attention back to Quinn. "Let's go get the outside shots. The view of the bay is just stunning. Alana loved it so much."

While Everleigh and Quinn disappeared out the back door, Cade lingered in the kitchen for a few minutes and examined the ad she'd written. He hadn't figured on her friend being a former Realtor, but he tried to convince himself that no one would want to buy a bed-and-breakfast.

But as Quinn and Everleigh strolled the property, the truth settled over Cade that Roger's idea might backfire. Who was he kidding? Who *wouldn't* jump at the chance to own six acres with an incredible view? This place would sell for sure, and then what would he do?

He walked out into the humid morning air. Everleigh and Quinn were standing near the bay, where Quinn held up a digital camera. He shook his head and continued to the garage, as Bryant appeared and trotted beside him, meowing.

"Hey, buddy. I promise I'll take you with me no matter where I wind up."

The cat meowed his approval, but Cade winced at the thought of leaving. He had no idea where he would go if the inn was sold. Sure, he'd have the money to go wherever he wanted, but he had no clue where that might be. He could buy himself a house in Coral Cove, so his parents would be close by. But what would he do for a living?

Take a risk and open another restaurant? Probably not. He had no desire to repeat that disaster.

He crossed to his workbench and studied his latest project—a shelf for his shop. He sanded the pieces while he pondered Everleigh. It blew his mind that she was so passionate about her patients—the babies she cared for—and their parents. In fact, he'd been enthralled as she shared how much her job meant to her. He felt her drawing him in when she talked about those newborns, but he was stumped that she couldn't see how selfish she was being about selling the inn out from under him. Had she even considered how it would affect him or what Alana would think about it? She was complicated and confusing, and being unable to understand her was driving him crazy.

His fury sparked. Cade pulled out a hammer and nails and then lined up two pieces of wood. He pulled the hammer back and swung it—and completely missed the nail.

He growled as pain radiated through his thumb and up his arm. He shook his hand and danced around, furious at himself.

The cat hopped up on the workbench and walked back and forth, chirping sympathetically.

"Thanks, buddy." Cade sat on the bench and rested his throbbing hand on the cat.

His annoyance cooled, and he took a deep breath. He couldn't allow Everleigh to get to him. Most likely she'd be out of his life soon, whether the inn sold or not, and the plan was for her to leave. He couldn't wait for the day he would load her one-ton suitcase into the back of her car and say goodbye to her.

After the pain subsided, Cade returned to the shelf in progress. Bryant stayed on the workbench and took a bath.

"Cade?"

He craned his neck over his shoulder and saw Everleigh standing beside his motorcycle. Bryant hopped down from the workbench and ran over to her.

Traitor.

Everleigh bent down and moved her hand over the cat's head. "I'm going to make the listing live today." She rattled off the social media pages and the real estate market websites where she planned to post it.

He swiped the back of his arm over his forehead.

Tension hung in the air between them.

"What are you working on?" she finally asked.

"A new shelf."

"So you build things too? You're a talented guy, Cade."

He remained silent and turned back toward the workbench, hoping she'd take the hint and leave.

"You know," she began, "Alana would be okay with this. She was excited about the nonprofit and how it could help families in need, and I'm sure she wanted me to make this dream come true." She paused for a moment. "There's a reason why she left each of us half of everything. This could be a second chance for you too."

He turned slightly to face her. "A second chance?"

She nodded. "Is there something you shared with Alana that you've always wanted to do?"

"Like what?" he asked.

"You know." She brushed her fingers over his bike's handlebar. "Some dream she knew about that you always wanted to make a reality?"

He stared at her. What on earth was she talking about?

"Alana wants us to live our dreams, Cade. I'm sure of it."

He shook his head and returned to his work. "You keep telling yourself that."

Then he heard her leave, his traitorous cat hurrying along at her side.

✦ ✦ ✦

"I had to pull over Old Man Burns for driving too slowly down Potter Road again yesterday," Landon announced the following evening. "He thinks it's safe when he's going twenty in a thirty-five, even though I've tried to explain to him that it's actually more hazardous to the other drivers."

Dad held up his hand. "I had to do that too." He studied Landon. "Tell me you didn't give him a ticket."

"Nope," Landon said. "But I gave him another warning. Must be his third or fourth."

Everleigh grinned across the table at her brother while the rest of her family members laughed. It was Sunday night, and Mom had insisted that everyone come over for meatball subs. Landon and Amber were there, along with Harlowe and Branson. Everleigh had hoped to get her sister alone later so they could talk.

"What's happening at the inn?" Amber, Landon's girlfriend, asked.

Everleigh swallowed a bite of the sub. "I moved in last week, and I got Alana's suite organized. I took a few bags of clothes to the donation center and brought some of her things to Mom." She met her sister's curious stare. "I brought you a few things too, Harlowe. I didn't know if you'd stopped by Mom's to get it all since you never answered my texts." She had messaged her sister earlier in the week about a couple of bracelets she'd set aside for her, but as usual, Harlowe didn't answer. And that silence hurt Everleigh more than she cared to admit.

"Thanks." Harlowe lifted her glass of Diet Coke. "I meant to text back. Slipped my mind."

"That's okay. I'm sure you're super busy at work." Everleigh smiled at her sister and then turned her attention back to Amber. "How's the fire department?"

"Busy," Amber told her. "I keep telling Landon we're busier than CCPD, but he disagrees."

"There's no way you work harder than we do," Landon said.

Dad shook his head. "I used to hear that when I was at the police department. The age-old rivalry between the police and fire departments never ceases, does it?"

Landon looped his arm around his girlfriend's shoulders. "It keeps things interesting."

Everyone chuckled.

After they finished supper and Mom's scrumptious homemade cheesecake for dessert, Everleigh carried the dishes to the counter, where Amber was loading the dishwasher.

Back in the empty dining room, Everleigh found her sister standing alone by the table. As she approached, she felt the chill of Harlowe's cool gaze.

"Is it true that you convinced Cade to sell the inn?"

"I'm so glad you and Branson came tonight," Everleigh said.

"I've missed you. Maybe we can get together for lunch or coffee this week."

Then Harlowe took hold of Everleigh's arm. "Answer my question, Everleigh. Are you selling the inn?"

Everleigh nodded. "Yeah. It's true."

"Why?" Harlowe searched her eyes. "You loved that place, and so did Alana. Is it greed?"

Everleigh took a small step backward. "No, it's not at all about greed."

"Then what are you going to do with all of that money?" Her sister's eyes demanded an explanation.

"I'm going to start a nonprofit in Alana's memory."

Harlowe scrunched her nose. "Why would you do that?"

"Everleigh? Harlowe?" Mom appeared in the doorway. "We're going to sit out on the patio. Come join us."

Harlowe moved past her, and Everleigh sighed.

✦ ✦ ✦

Later that night, Everleigh hugged her folks good night and then walked out to her blue Chevrolet Trailblazer. She'd been relieved when her father had told her it had been delivered; then he'd offered to pick her up for supper so she could drive it back to the inn.

Harlowe and Branson climbed into their older model Honda Accord and then backed out of the driveway. Everleigh wasn't surprised that her sister hadn't bothered to say goodbye, but the snub still stung.

"I guess you and Harlowe still aren't talking?" Landon sidled up to her and leaned against the hood of her SUV.

"What gives you that idea?"

"The looks she was shooting you during supper and then out on the patio. Yet you never stopped smiling at her, Everleigh.

Why do you put up with her even when she's downright mean to you?"

"She's our sister. I love her no matter what." Everleigh watched as her sister's taillights disappeared into the dark. "Like everyone else, she doesn't like that I'm selling the inn. But I think everyone will understand why when the nonprofit all comes together."

Landon scratched the back of his head and looked toward the porch, where Amber continued to talk to Mom and Dad.

"Let me guess," Everleigh said. "You don't agree with me selling the inn either."

"It's not that."

"Then what is it?" Her worry pricked hard while she awaited his response.

"I get the feeling that Harlowe and Branson are having some sort of issue."

"Oh no," Everleigh said. "In their marriage?"

"More . . . financial."

"What did you hear?"

Her brother hesitated. "I shouldn't repeat this, but I overhead them discussing that they didn't know how they were going to pay for something. I only got the tail end of it. So that could be why she's upset she wasn't in the will."

Everleigh mulled over this troubling news. She'd always admired Branson and how patient, loyal, and sweet he was to her sister. Should she offer to help them somehow? When Harlowe finally opened up to her, Everleigh would do just that.

Landon held his hands up. "Please keep this to yourself."

"I will," she promised. Then she cocked her head to one side. "Do *you* think I'm wrong for selling the inn?"

Landon gave her shoulder a squeeze. "I've known you my entire life, and I've never witnessed you making a hasty decision. I'm sure you have your reasons for selling it, so just stay true to that decision."

"I will."

Amber jogged over to them. "You ready?" she asked Landon.

"Yeah."

Amber pulled Everleigh in for a hug. "See you soon."

Everleigh waved goodbye to her parents, and as she drove back to the inn, she pondered her brother's words. She hoped she could make Alana proud, as well as her family.

CHAPTER 9

CADE STEERED THE lawn tractor toward the pond Wednesday morning, pulling his ball cap lower on his head while the mower bounced and chattered. The leaves of the humongous oak tree shook as a couple of squirrels chased each other up and down the tree's trunk. He peered out toward the birdfeeders near the benches next to the cove and made a mental note to fill them later.

He'd been keeping an eye on the reservation requests on the website, and so far, the inn didn't have any. He hoped some folks would book soon since the inn had been closed for almost a month.

When he drove back toward the inn, he spotted Everleigh sitting on the sunroom porch and talking on her cell phone. He hadn't spoken to her since Saturday, but they'd traded hospitable nods and waves over the past few days. He was grateful he hadn't seen any potential buyers touring the grounds with her, and he hoped it stayed that way.

He made another pass by the benches and swing set, then did a double take when a black Porsche Cayenne motored up the driveway and pulled up by the sunroom. Cade squinted to get a better look, then killed the engine and climbed off the tractor. He made a beeline to the SUV, just as a tall and slender woman with platinum blond hair climbed out of the vehicle. She seemed a little out of place in her bright-red lipstick, expensive-looking sunglasses, designer pantsuit, and high heels.

Everleigh let the sunroom door close behind her, and Cade shared a confused expression with her before the woman spoke.

"Good morning!" she exclaimed. "I'm Valerie Rhodes." She held a manicured hand out to Everleigh. "And you are . . . ?"

"Everleigh Hartnett," she said as the woman squeezed her hand. Cade was almost certain he saw Everleigh wince at the firm shake.

"Such a pleasure," Valerie declared before turning her attention to Cade. "And you?"

"Cade Witherspoon," he said, and she shook his hand.

"Fantastic." Valerie clapped her hands. "Now, let's get down to business. I saw the listing for the inn and was *thrilled*." She pulled two business cards out of her pocket and distributed them.

Cade read it and swallowed a groan. *Of course* she was a Realtor. *And here we go . . .*

Valerie looked at Cade, then Everleigh, then Cade again. "Which of you is the owner?"

"We both are." Everleigh motioned between them. "Equal partners."

"Great. Well, I represent Coral Cove Builders. This property sure is stunning, isn't it?" Her bright-red lips turned up in a smile. "They are *very* interested in purchasing, and they're prepared to make a *very* generous offer."

"Coral Cove Builders?" Everleigh asked.

Valerie nodded. "That's right."

"What do they plan to do with the land?"

Cade slipped the business card into his back pocket and pushed his sunglasses higher on his nose.

"This would be a fantastic place for luxury condos." Valerie motioned toward the bay. "Can you imagine waking up to such a view of Coral Cove Bay? Maybe with a common area and a—"

"No." Everleigh shook her head, and her thick red ponytail bounced off her slight shoulders.

Cade brushed a hand over his mouth to hide a smirk. *Tell her, Everleigh!*

"Excuse me?" Valerie had the nerve to look shocked.

"I said no," Everleigh repeated. "We only want to sell to someone who will keep the spirit of the Sunshine Inn for the sake of my godmother's memory." She turned to Cade. "Right, Cade?"

He nodded. "Yup."

"Oh, Coral Cove Builders will be *very* respectful." Valerie touched her collarbone. "I understand that you want to remember Alana McFadden." She clucked her tongue. "She was a pillar in our community, that's for sure. You have my word that the company will remember her."

Everleigh crossed her arms. "How exactly will they do that?"

"Well . . ." Valerie scanned the area and then pointed toward the water. "They can put a memorial bench by the bay. I'll tell them to add a few plaques there as well. She'll be honored and respected for sure."

Cade turned toward Everleigh and waited for her response. *You got this, partner!*

Sure enough, she was steadfast. "We're not interested in any offers that include knocking down the inn."

"Is that right?" Valerie asked, and Everleigh nodded. "What if they offer cash?"

Everleigh shook her head.

"How about cash *and* twenty-five percent over your asking price?"

"Thanks for your time, but no." Everleigh started to back away from her.

Cade took in the frustration in Valerie's expression.

"Well, it was nice meeting you," Valerie said before strutting back toward her expensive SUV.

Once she was out of earshot, Everleigh threw Cade an annoyed look. "Thanks for helping with that."

He rubbed the stubble on his chin. "You handled it just fine."

Her face lit with a smile. "Really?"

"You didn't need my help at all."

"Thanks, partner."

They shared a look, and for a moment he relished being on the same side as her.

Cade pulled the business card from his back pocket and consulted it. "She'll be back. She doesn't seem like the type who takes no for an answer." He nodded toward the gleaming SUV as it retreated down the driveway. "It takes a lot of yeses to afford a car like that."

"True," Everleigh said. "But we can handle her."

"She might just come back and say she has a different buyer who plans to keep the place as is. Then they'll turn around and build those luxury condos anyway."

"You think so?" she asked, looking surprised.

"You're too gullible, Everleigh."

Her smile wobbled. "I am not."

Cade snorted and then headed back to the lawn tractor. They had fought off one Realtor, but he had a sinking feeling that the game had only begun. Though he doubted it was possible, he just hoped he and Everleigh could somehow stay a united front—at least until she gave up on selling the inn.

✦ ✦ ✦

Later that night Cade checked his email and found a reservation request from one of their regulars. The Newtons, an older couple from Upstate New York, had been coming to Coral Cove since the nineties, Alana had told him. According to their booking, they planned to arrive on Saturday and leave the following Saturday.

"Absolutely," he whispered, approving their reservation. If only more would come through soon.

Bryant hopped up onto the sofa and began kneading the throw blanket beside him.

Cade gave the cat's head a scratch before toggling back to his email. His eyes focused on a message from Declan Hewitt with the subject line: "Important."

"Looks like a scam," he muttered, but when his curiosity overtook him, he clicked on it anyway. He read the first couple of lines of the message:

> Dear Cade,
> I know this sounds crazy, but I think we might be . . .

"No thanks," he muttered, deleting the message. "Hopefully I didn't just invite a virus onto my laptop."

He sank farther into the sofa and yawned as he scrolled through social media, stopping every once in a while to watch a motorcycle video. As he considered the day, he recalled how impressed he'd been with the way Everleigh handled the Realtor. She had stood her ground without being rude, and he admired her tenacity.

But he still didn't trust her. He had stopped giving people the benefit of the doubt when Serena and Clark double-crossed him. When it came to personal relationships, he was better off alone. At least *he* knew his own intentions. Everyone else was a mystery.

He yawned again and stroked Bryant's back. The cat purred and buried his head in the fold of the blanket. "You got the right idea, buddy. It's bedtime."

The phone buzzed with a call, and he saw his mom's number on the screen. "Hey, Mom," he said when he answered.

"Cade!" she exclaimed. "Is it true that you're selling the inn?"

He sighed. "Yeah."

"Why didn't you tell me?"

"It *is* true?" Dad asked in the background.

He winced. "I meant to, but I've been busy."

"Hang on," she said. "Let me put you on speaker." He heard a lot of rustling from the other end as his mom figured out the phone buttons. "Okay. Now—why are you selling it?"

"We thought you loved that place," Dad said.

"I do." He let his head fall against the back of the sofa. "But it's complicated." He explained his initial reluctance and the agreement he'd reached with Everleigh. Then he told them about the Realtor who had stopped by today. "Truth be told, I'm hoping it doesn't sell."

"What will you do if it *does*?" Mom asked.

"Not sure yet."

"Don't say you're going to move away again."

He felt a twinge of guilt. He could still hear the sound of her sobs the day he'd left for boot camp. "I'm . . . considering options."

Dad chuckled. "If you get what the place is worth, I imagine you'll have plenty."

Cade opened the listing on social media and stared at the asking price. Sure, it was a big chunk of change, but he'd give up the money to keep his promise to Alana. "We'll see what happens," he finally said. "Besides, we each have veto power, and I don't want to sell. I'm not planning on agreeing to any offer."

"What a relief!" Mom exclaimed.

"Keep us posted," Dad added.

"And don't be a stranger," Mom instructed. "Stop by sometime."

"I will. Good night." He disconnected from the call and set his phone down. For a moment, he considered what he would do with his half of the sale if he did agree to sell the inn. One idea that had crossed his mind was that he might be able to help his parents. They had struggled financially over the years, so paying off his parents' debts and maybe investing in Mom's store would mean a great deal to his family.

But at the same time, he couldn't imagine discarding Alana's dream. The idea sat like a rock in the pit of his stomach. If only he could convince Everleigh to feel that way too.

✦ ✦ ✦

Everleigh pushed her grocery cart down the aisle on Friday afternoon and stared at her shopping list on her phone. She reviewed the items in her mind—milk, eggs, cereal . . .

Crash!

She looked up to see that she had collided with another cart at the end of the aisle.

The owner of the cart, a man who appeared to be around her age, met her gaze. At the eye contact, heat began climbing up her neck.

She groaned. "I'm so sorry! I was staring at my phone and not paying attention."

To her surprise, he propped his elbows on the cart's handle. He was attractive with a square jaw and shaggy, dark hair that hung over his forehead and dark eyes. He wore a tight-fitting T-shirt featuring the logo for a local gym, and he was stocky, possibly only a few inches taller than she was. "No problem. Are you all right?"

"Yeah." She chuckled and pretended to examine her arms. "No bumps or bruises. You?"

"Fine." His smile was wide, showing off pearly-white, straight teeth.

"Good news." She nodded. "Anyway, sorry again. Have a good day."

She zipped through the aisles, careful not to hit any other carts, then took her place in the checkout line. She read the covers of gossip magazines while she waited for her turn to pay.

"Have you ever been to Tokyo Treasures?"

Everleigh turned around and smiled at the man she'd collided with earlier. He was standing in line right behind her. "No, I haven't," she said. "Is that a restaurant?"

"Sure is. Do you like Japanese hibachi?"

She nodded. "I do."

"I heard it just opened a couple of months ago, and that the name fits." He seemed to study her. "Would you like to check it out with me sometime?"

She paused for a beat. Was this guy actually asking her out? She couldn't remember the last time she'd been on a date. "Uh, well, umm . . ." she stammered.

"Sorry!" He held his hands up. "I didn't mean to be creepy. I just moved here from Florida."

She rested against the handle of her cart. "Well then, welcome to Coral Cove. I'm sure the beaches are much more impressive in Florida."

"More crowded, definitely. But more impressive, not so much."

"Huh." She nodded. "Interesting."

The line advanced, and a woman with a toddler sitting in the seat of her cart began loading her groceries onto the conveyor.

Once the woman's items slid forward, Everleigh began loading her groceries. She dropped a can of peaches, which rolled toward the stranger.

He picked it up and handed it to her. "So, what's there to do around here?"

"Let's see. There's the beach, the boardwalk, plenty of stores, lots of restaurants. And if you don't mind a little drive, we have an amusement park and some museums not too far away."

"If you're ever free," he began, "we could check out some of those places together."

He seemed nice enough, and she was flattered, but she just wasn't interested. "Thank you, but I'm not dating right now." When he appeared disappointed, she added, "I don't plan to be in town long."

"That's a shame. What do you do?"

"I'm a traveling nurse," she said.

"Really?"

"I'm in town to take care of some family business, but I'll be back on the road before the end of the year."

He reached into his back pocket, pulled out a card, and handed it to her.

She read it aloud: "'Trevor Whalen Handyman Services—painting, home improvements, lawn maintenance.'" Then she met his eager expression.

"Give me a call if you change your mind."

"Will do, Trevor."

"And what's your name?"

"Everleigh."

"Nice to meet you, Everleigh." He held out his hand, and she shook it.

She told Trevor goodbye before paying for her groceries and toting them out to her SUV.

✦ ✦ ✦

Cade stopped weeding the front flowerbed when Everleigh's blue Trailblazer rumbled down the driveway. He pulled off his gloves and met her at the back of her SUV.

"Hi." Her smile was bright as she opened the tailgate.

He nodded toward the bags of groceries. "Need some help?"

She thanked him for offering, and they worked together to lug the bags into the kitchen and deposit them on the island. When she saw the vase of red roses, she gave him a shocked expression.

"Who sent those?" she asked.

"Check out the note," he said.

Her happy expression dimmed as she read aloud, "'Hope you'll reconsider. Coral Cove Builders has offered to install benches in memory of your grandmother, along with a garden in her name.'" She scowled. "I said Alana was my *godmother*, not my *grandmother*. Valerie can't even get that right!" She tossed the card into the trash and smelled the flowers before she started unpacking the groceries.

"If you're so worried about Alana's memory, then why do you want to sell?" he asked, setting the milk in the refrigerator.

"Alana is my guardian angel," she said. "She gave me half the inn to make the nonprofit a reality."

He stilled. "Your guardian angel?"

She nodded, and her expression warmed. "I believe she wanted you to have the same opportunity to follow your own dream."

He let her words settle over him while they continued working. What if Everleigh was right about that? What dream would he follow?

Still, it didn't make sense when Alana loved the inn so much. He couldn't imagine her wanting them to let go of it.

A few more moments ticked by while he lined up the new cans of peaches in the pantry. "Heard from any other Realtors?" he finally asked.

"No." She faced him. "What about reservations?"

"The Newtons arrive tomorrow."

"The Newtons?" Her face lit up. "Mrs. Newton always brings her homemade jam. Alana loved the apple jam the best and put it on her toast every morning."

He leaned on the island.

"I haven't seen them in years though." She snapped her fingers. "Have you met the Olsens?"

"The couple with the toy poodles?"

"Yes!" She giggled. "Alana always said no pets until she met them. She loved having those little poodles running around."

"Except when they had accidents in the foyer."

"Oh, yuck. I guess you had to clean it up?"

"Only after stepping in the puddle."

"Ugh. No!"

He nodded, and she giggled again. For some ridiculous reason, he liked the sound.

Her eyes lit up again. "Oh! You know what I was just thinking of? How she'd say the same thing to the guests every morning."

"*It's going to be a great day at the inn. Go out and enjoy some sunshine,*" they recited at the same time, making them both smile.

Her eyes glistened as she sighed and leaned on the island across from him. "I miss her."

"I do too," he whispered, his voice sounding rough.

Their gazes held, and a strange emotion unfurled inside him. For the first time, he felt a connection to Everleigh, something real and palpable.

Even so, they'd been at odds since they met. How could they ever come together?

Everleigh pushed herself up from the island and wiped her eyes. Then her trademark brilliant smile reappeared. "After we finish putting away these groceries, I'll go freshen up the Sunrise Suite. That's the one the Newtons requested, right?"

He cleared his throat. "As always," he told her.

She turned her back to him and slipped a loaf of bread in the breadbox. "Would you mind making breakfast while they're here?" she asked over her shoulder.

"I don't think they'll want burned toast," he teased her. "So, yeah, of course."

She spun to face him. "Had I known guests were coming, I could have picked up something special for you to make. You should have texted me and told me."

"I don't have your number."

"Oh! Let's fix that right now." She pulled her phone from the back pocket of her jean shorts, and Cade rattled off his cell number. She hit a few buttons on her phone before his phone dinged with a text.

"Now you've got my info, and I have yours, partner." She beamed at him. "Let me know if you need me to go back to the store for you."

"Thanks, but I got it," he offered.

They studied each other for a moment, and once again he felt they were on the same side. This emotional tug-of-war when it came to her was frustrating and also . . . bewildering.

"I'll be out front," he told her, and she nodded. Then he slipped outside to the porch, where he pulled his phone from his pocket and read her text: Hi, partner! 😊

Cade saved her number in his contacts, and his mind raced with something he couldn't define. He slipped on his gardening gloves and grabbed a nearby bucket. Then he crouched down and tried to bury his baffling thoughts while he yanked up a handful of weeds.

Why had Everleigh been so excited about the inn's regular guests? She was a puzzle he couldn't solve. On one hand, she wanted to sell the inn, and insisted Alana was their guardian angel. But on the other, she was almost turning cartwheels at the mention of the Newtons.

He leaned forward and pulled another weed, then dropped it into the bucket. As he worked, an idea slowly began to form. Maybe if Everleigh remembered how much she loved the inn, she might not want to sell it anymore. If they hosted more guests and she enjoyed the work, would that compel her to take it off the market?

Hope swelled inside him, and he balanced on his heels. She clearly had some affection for the place, but her idea for the nonprofit was getting in the way. If he could remind Everleigh just how much the inn meant to him, to her, and to the guests who loved to stay there, then maybe, just maybe, they could keep it.

And he could keep his promise to Alana.

CHAPTER 10

"THIS WAS SO fun," Mom said. "I'm glad you finally made time to go shopping with me."

It was Saturday morning, and the warm breeze brought with it the scent of salt water and cocoa butter. While Everleigh and her mother walked along the boardwalk at the Coral Cove oceanfront, the rhythmic cadence of the waves, along with the happy sounds of children playing, hovered over them. Although Everleigh enjoyed the smell of the beach, she could only stand to watch the waves from a distance. Any closer and she was reminded of the time she'd almost drowned when she was ten. She trembled despite the heat as the memory gripped her.

Pushing her sunglasses up higher on her nose, she stepped to the side to allow a few giddy teenage girls to hurry past her. "The new shops are so cute, Mom. The handbag store has some good deals."

"Maybe too good." Mom held up her large shopping bag. "It's a shame Harlowe couldn't join us though."

Everleigh did her best to mask the frown that threatened to overtake her face. She hadn't heard from her sister since their family dinner, and she tried not to let it bother her.

They came to the end of the boardwalk, and Mom's face flickered with concern. "How are things going at the inn?"

"Fine." Everleigh sang her answer just as a line of riders on colorful bicycles sped past as if in a parade.

"Have you gotten any offers?"

She filled her mother in on Valerie's visit. "Cade and I aren't going to budge though. We won't accept an offer from anyone who wants to demolish the inn." They sat down on a bench beside each other. "But we have officially reopened the inn, and some of Alana's favorite visitors are checking in later today. They always bring the best homemade jam."

"How nice!" Mom said.

A couple who looked to be in their mid-twenties strolled by while holding hands.

"I'm hoping Landon finally proposes to Amber this year." Mom shook her head. "I don't know what your brother is waiting for. He's almost thirty, and they've been together almost five years." Then she focused on Everleigh. "And what about you? You're not too far behind him. Are you going to spend the rest of your life single and traveling?"

Here we go again. Everleigh could count on her mother bringing up this conversation at least once a year. And each time, she gave the same answer. "I love my job, Mom."

"I know," Mom agreed. "You love those babies. But don't you want one of your own?"

Everleigh's smile never faltered. "Sure. Someday."

Mom slipped her arm around Everleigh's shoulders. "You'll be a great mom."

"That's because I have the best example to follow." She rested her head on her mother's shoulder.

After a few moments, Mom checked her watch. "Oh, dear. We'd better get going."

They walked to Mom's Subaru, and Mom hugged her. "Will I see you soon?"

"You will." Everleigh waited until her mother backed out of the parking space before she waved and crossed the street. She headed down Main Street, and when she came to Crafty Creations, she peered in the window. Customers milled around Cade's mother's store, moving through the aisles carrying baskets overflowing with everything from markers and stickers to frames and pipe cleaners. Behind the long customer service counter was a whiteboard advertising a list of available classes—jewelry making, painting, drawing, wreath making, and a variety of classes for kids.

Everleigh recalled the shelf she'd caught Cade building. It was obvious he inherited his creativity and talent from his mother. Perhaps she'd even encouraged his interest in cooking.

As she continued down the block toward the parking lot where she'd left her SUV, she recalled their conversation in the kitchen yesterday. She'd been surprised by how quickly they'd both enjoyed discussing the visitors. And oh, his smile! It had taken her by surprise and sent a thrill through her. But when they discussed Alana, the vibe quickly changed. And the way he studied her reminded her of when she was telling him about being a nurse—his intense expression had awoken something deep within her. She felt something powerful and new stirring, and she had no idea what to make of it.

The Coral Cove Library came into view, and Everleigh picked up her pace, hoping Quinn was at work. She entered the front door and moved through the large foyer until she reached the reference desk, where Quinn sat talking on the phone.

When Quinn spotted her, she held up her hand, indicating she'd be a moment or two. Everleigh meandered over to the periodicals area and flipped through an entertainment magazine.

"Everleigh!"

Quinn walked over and stood on her tiptoes to pull Everleigh in for a tight hug. "What brings you out here today?"

"I was just nearby and thought I'd stop in."

"I got your text about the Realtor and her flowers." Quinn clucked her tongue. "Talk about nerve."

"I know." Everleigh shook her head.

"Hopefully you'll get some more offers soon." Her friend suddenly snapped her fingers. "Hey, what are you doing later?"

"Just chores around the inn. Why?"

"Want to go to the beach?"

"I don't know . . ."

"How long have you been back home now?"

Everleigh eyed her friend. "This seems like a trick question."

"Just answer it, please!"

"Three weeks."

"And have you been to the beach yet?"

"I walked the boardwalk today. Does that count?"

"Have you actually *sat* on the beach with your toes in the sand?"

Everleigh sighed. "No."

"Why not?"

"You know I'm not a beach person."

"But you were raised at the beach, Everleigh," Quinn said. "I know you don't like the waves after what happened to you." She frowned. "But you can still enjoy the view, right?"

"What are you getting at, Quinn?"

"Tiffany Davis from high school texted me earlier, and I was going to send you a message anyway to let you know a group of us are getting together. We're going to grill out, swim, and play volleyball."

"Really, I . . ."

Quinn folded her hands as if saying a prayer. "Please come. It will be *so* fun. And I bet you haven't had a chance to relax since you got home, have you?"

Everleigh hesitated. "No, not really."

"Then come. If you aren't having fun, I'll give you permission to go home, okay?"

Everleigh chuckled. "Fine, fine," she said, finally giving in. "I'll come, but I won't swim."

"Completely understand. I'll text you all the details."

✦ ✦ ✦

"Cade?" Everleigh hollered from somewhere out in the hallway. "You up here?"

"In here!" he called. He consulted the instructions on his phone one last time, then climbed up a stepladder. He pulled out the filter from the mini-split heating and air unit in the Sunrise Suite.

"Where?" she called, sounding closer this time.

"In the Sunrise Suite," he announced.

"Oh!" He heard her footfalls before she appeared in the doorway.

He angled his body to face the door and tried not to stare. She wore a short, lemon-yellow sundress that flaunted her slim thighs and long legs. Her red hair was pulled into a messy bun on top of her head, and ties from a pink swimsuit peeked out from under the dress at the nape of her elegant neck. A large bright-purple beach bag was draped over her arm, and a floppy green sun hat dangled from her hand. She was the perfect mix of stunning and cute.

He winced slightly as he took her in. Why did she have to be so pretty?

"Heading to the beach?" he managed to ask.

Her smile was radiant. "Yes." She jammed her thumb toward the end of the hallway. "I thought Alana kept a couple of collapsible beach chairs in the utility room, but I can't find them. Do you know where they might be?"

"In the shed." He hopped down from the stepladder.

She appeared befuddled. "We have a shed?"

"Alana put it up a couple of years ago during her decluttering phase."

"Huh." She spun the hat in her hands. "So, uh, where's the shed?"

"I'll show you."

"No, it's okay." She pointed to the mini-split. "I don't mean to interrupt your work. I'll find it."

"It's not a problem." He met her in the hallway and made a sweeping gesture toward the stairwell for her to go first.

They traipsed downstairs, and he retrieved the shed key from the utility room before they continued outside. The afternoon sky was clear, and the air was heavy with humidity. Bryant met them on the path and trotted alongside them.

"What sparked your beach day?" Cade asked.

"I met my mom at the boardwalk earlier and then stopped by the library to see Quinn. She convinced me to join her and some of our old friends." Her smile dimmed slightly. "The Newtons won't be here before eight, right?"

"Right."

"I'll only be gone a few hours. I can help finish any last-minute chores when I get back."

"I've got it handled." He led her behind the garage to the large white shed with a gray roof.

She clucked her tongue. "I had no idea this was back here."

He unlocked it and pushed up the door. "One or two chairs?" he asked, climbing in and using his phone as a flashlight.

"One." She paused. "Unless you want to join me."

He turned to face Everleigh, and her smile seemed almost coy. How . . . confusing.

"You want me to go?" he asked.

"When was the last time you did something fun, Cade Witherspoon?" Her brown eyes glittered.

"Uh . . ." He rubbed the stubble along his jawline. "Well." He was stumped.

She pointed at him. "I thought so."

"Hold on. Don't nurses work twelve-hour shifts?"

She nodded.

"Maybe I should ask you the same question," he said. "Am I right to assume you don't always make time for fun either?"

Her brow furrowed. "You are. I can't remember the last time I went out with friends." She paused. "Or on a date."

He found that little tidbit surprising. He imagined she was not short on offers. Not that it was any of his concern. He climbed past a few rakes, shovels, and bikes before he located the two beach chairs folded up in the back corner and brought one to her.

"Thanks." Then she gave him an exaggerated frown. "I guess that means you're not coming with me."

"I'll think about it."

"I knew you wouldn't go for it."

He propped his shoulder against the doorframe. "Is this a challenge?"

"Maybe." She shrugged, but the eagerness in her expression was unmistakable.

"I need to finish cleaning the filters, but then maybe I'll head that way."

She grinned. "Sure, you will," she teased.

"See you there, partner."

"We'll be around Fourth Street. Look for the volleyball net. Not that I actually expect to see you." And with that, she turned and strutted toward her waiting SUV.

Cade shook his head. He wanted to accept her challenge, but he also didn't want to feel like the odd man out among her friends. Plus, he hated crowds.

He texted Roger: Meet me at the beach?

Roger: Now?

In about a half hour.

Okay. Finished a job early today.

"Can't believe I'm doing this," he muttered on his way back to the inn. But for some insane reason, he couldn't resist Everleigh's little game.

✦ ✦ ✦

"Everleigh!" Penny Robinson nearly knocked Everleigh over with a hug. "It's been, like, forever since I've seen you!"

"It has, but you look exactly the same," Everleigh told her high school friend. And she meant it. Penny had unblemished dark skin and bright hazel eyes. "You're still a knockout."

"Speak for yourself. So, where've you been since graduation?"

"Oh, here and there," Everleigh said with a laugh. She shared a bit about her work with Penny, and soon a group of their friends from high school were gathered around to listen. As she spoke, she found herself searching the crowd for Cade. Their playful banter before she'd left the inn had surprised her, and now she couldn't stop thinking about him and hoping he would show.

"Time for volleyball!" Penny announced.

While the group began dividing up into teams, Quinn sidled up to Everleigh. "You look distracted. What's up?"

"I'm just thrilled to see everyone," Everleigh exclaimed. "Are you going to play?"

Quinn pushed her sunglasses up on her head. "It's not really a short person's sport." Then she brightened. "But I'll play if you're on my team."

"Deal."

They plodded in the direction of the net, and the hot afternoon sand squished between Everleigh's toes. She adjusted her sun hat, scanned the beach, and froze when she saw Cade standing on the boardwalk with the guy who had accompanied him to the memorial service.

"I can't believe it," she whispered. "He actually came."

"Who?" Quinn's petite nose wrinkled.

"Cade." She tried in vain to pull her stare away from him. Dark sunglasses shielded his eyes, and he wore a gray tank top that emphasized his athletic arms. Black swim trunks did wonders for his muscular legs. A towel was slung over his shoulder.

"And his friend too." Quinn made a noise of approval. "That Roger is handsome."

Everleigh's eyebrows shot up. "Quinn! Do you like him?"

"I didn't say I *liked* him. I just like to *look* at him." Her grin made Everleigh laugh. "Should we ask them to join us for volleyball?"

"That's a great—"

"Everleigh?"

She turned at the sound of her name and saw Trevor Whalen approaching her. "I thought that was you," he said. "How's it going?"

Quinn's face registered confusion.

"Hi, Trevor." Everleigh motioned between them. "This is my friend Quinn. Quinn, I met Trevor yesterday at the grocery store."

Quinn offered him a little wave.

He nodded and then turned his attention back to Everleigh. "What are the chances I'd see you here again today? Seems like it's meant to be. What are you all up to?"

"Oh, uh . . ." She needed to politely get rid of this guy so she could go see Cade. "Just a little volleyball."

"Do you come to the beach often?"

"I'm not really a beach person." She turned toward where Cade and Roger stood, and when her gaze collided with Cade's, she tried to read his expression. But those dark sunglasses didn't make it easy.

"No kidding! You grew up here, right?" Trevor asked.

"Uh-huh." She folded her arm over her sundress.

"But you don't like the beach?"

"It's not that . . ." She hesitated. She didn't know Trevor well enough to share a personal story about nearly drowning. "I'd just rather sunbathe than swim. Not a big fan of the waves."

"I wouldn't have guessed that. I love the ocean. In fact, I'm a surfer. I guess you don't surf then."

"Nope. I sure don't." Out of the corner of her eye, she spotted Cade and Roger moving toward her. She just *had* to find a way to end this conversation. Could the guy not take a hint?

"Everleigh," Quinn interjected. "Should we go?"

Thank you, Quinn!

"Go ahead. She'll meet you at the net," Trevor told Quinn. "Are you staying with family while you're in town?" he asked Everleigh.

Everleigh gave Quinn an apologetic look, and Quinn rolled her eyes in Trevor's direction before heading over to the net. Everleigh curled her lips into a polite smile for Trevor. "I'm over at the Sunshine Inn."

"Like a hotel?" he asked.

"It's a bed-and-breakfast. My godmother owned it, and I inherited it recently."

"So sorry for your loss. How big is it?"

Everleigh shared some sparse details, but what she really needed was an escape route. Where was Cade? Why wasn't he walking over? And why couldn't this Trevor guy get a clue?

CHAPTER 11

"WELL, NOW WHAT?" Roger said. "Volleyball? Swimming?"

Cade glanced around, taking in the groups of people and families enjoying the sun and the waves. *This was a bad idea,* he told himself. "I'm not sure. I hate crowds. And sand in my clothes."

"You're always such a grouch."

Cade snorted. Maybe, but he wasn't one to back down from a challenge—especially from his redheaded partner. There was something about the glimmer in those dark-brown eyes . . .

And there she was—still wearing that dress. The floppy hat was perched on her head with her knot of red hair peeking out the top.

She was standing with her arms crossed, nodding and smiling while a stocky guy with shaggy dark hair talked her ear off. Everleigh's wide eyes suddenly locked on Cade's as the guy continued to yap. A strange feeling threaded through him.

The guy said something, and she turned back toward him. Who was he? And why did it bother Cade so much that he had stolen her attention?

"Who's that guy talking to Everleigh?"

"Don't know. Don't care. Let's swim," Cade grumbled.

They chose an empty spot to drop their towels, sunglasses, phones, and keys, then Cade pulled off his tank top and jogged into the water. He dove through a wave and enjoyed the feel of cool, salty water on his skin. When he came up for air, he shoveled his hands through his hair and focused on the shoreline, where the guy remained with Everleigh. She continued to give him a winning smile, probably because she was enjoying the conversation too. Why did the sight of them jerk a knot in Cade's gut?

"Her friend Quinn is here too," Roger said.

Cade had been so focused on Everleigh that he had forgotten about Roger for a moment.

"We should invite them to join us in the water."

"Good idea." Cade made his way to the shore and walked up the beach past a group of kids building an elaborate castle. He continued through the hot sand to where Everleigh stood with the guy.

"Eight bedrooms," she was saying.

"And it's on the bay?" The guy appeared impressed. "How many acres did you say?"

But Everleigh had turned her attention to Cade. "Hi, partner. You actually came!"

"Told you I would. I know how to have fun." He folded his arms over his chest. "Do you?"

"I do," she said with a wink.

The guy held his hand out to Everleigh. "Let's play some volleyball."

A strange expression traveled over her face, but instead of taking the guy's hand, she locked eyes with Cade. "Want to join us?" she asked.

Cade shook his head. "I'll sit this one out." He pointed toward the water. "I'll be out there."

He wasn't certain, but she seemed a little disappointed. "All right," she said. Then she turned her attention back to the other guy. "I'm a little rusty. Haven't played since high school."

"Don't worry," the guy said. "I'll help you."

Cade held back an eye roll. It was probably best for him to back off anyway, since he didn't want to give her the wrong idea. Even more, he didn't want to be the third wheel with Everleigh and this other guy.

Still, watching her walking over to the net with him irritated Cade.

Quinn and Roger joined Everleigh and the guy, and soon they were playing on the same team. Cade watched the guy miss a shot, and then he shook his head before loping back into the waves.

✦ ✦ ✦

Everleigh jumped up and spiked the ball over the net. When the opposing team missed it, Roger, Trevor, and Quinn cheered.

"We won!" Quinn hollered. "Even with me on the team, we won!"

Everleigh laughed as Quinn hugged her.

"Great job." Roger pulled Quinn in for a hug, and she beamed even brighter.

Trevor held his hand up to Everleigh. "You aren't rusty at all."

"Neither are you." She gave him a high five, then stepped away in hopes of avoiding a hug.

He puffed out his chest. "Well, I did play a bit in college. I like to stay in shape, you know."

Trevor seemed like a nice enough guy, but he sure enjoyed talking about himself. She'd found out way more than necessary about his surfing skills, although, to be fair, he had asked her several questions about the inn.

While Trevor detailed his workout regimen at the gym, Everleigh scanned the beach for Cade. She located him trudging out of the water and onto the shore, and she felt a tingle in her chest. Water dripped from his short, wavy, light-brown hair and glistened on his tan skin; he had just the right amount of hair in the center of his impressive chest. She tried to pull her eyes away from him but found it impossible. He stopped over by a towel and flopped down onto it.

"Another game?" Trevor asked.

"Huh?" Her gaze pinged back to his confused expression. "I need a break, but thanks." Before he could respond, she trudged past the cluster of chairs, blankets, and kids digging in the sand until she came to Cade's towel. "How's the water?"

Tenting his hand over his eyes, he lifted his gaze to meet hers. "Perfect. You should get in."

"No thanks."

He patted a spot beside him on the towel. "Want to tell me about your boyfriend?"

"He's not my boyfriend." She remained standing. "I met him at the grocery store yesterday."

"Yesterday?" Cade's brow furrowed.

"Yeah, yesterday. I ran my shopping cart into his, and he struck up a conversation with me when I was in line to pay. Now he's here on the beach for some reason."

"He's definitely interested." When he looked behind her, his eyes narrowed. "And here he comes. See? He can't stand to be away from you."

She gave Cade a look, and he appeared amused.

"Thirsty?" Trevor held a bottle of water out to her.

"Thanks." She took the cold bottle from him and then pointed between them. "Trevor, this is Cade."

"Trevor Whalen." He held his hand out for a shake.

Cade stood up to his full height, which had to be at least four inches taller than Trevor, and grasped his proffered hand. "I'm her partner."

"Partner?" Trevor asked.

"We own the Sunshine Inn together," she explained. "My godmother left it to us equally."

Trevor's eyebrows sailed upward. "Is that right? And you both decided to sell it?"

Cade crossed his arms over his chest and remained silent.

"We've worked out an agreement," Everleigh said.

"What do you do for a living, Trevor?" Cade asked.

"I'm a handyman right now," Trevor said. "Just moved up here from Florida, so I'm getting settled in."

Cade seemed to study him. "What brought you here?"

"I've visited the area in the past on vacation, and I liked it. So, you know, I decided it was time for a change and all that."

Cade's expression remained blank. "What kind of work are you looking for?"

"I'm not really picky. I have some money saved up, so I'm kind of going with the flow right now."

"Going with the flow, huh?" Cade lifted an eyebrow.

"You know how it is," Trevor said. "I'm doing work here and there. I'd like to get back into construction, but I'm just doing my own thing first. Enjoying life and all that."

Cade's lips formed a thin line. He clearly was not impressed with Trevor.

"Do you need any work done at the inn?" Trevor asked. "I can paint, replace flooring, repair heating and air systems, rebuild decks . . . If there's work to be done, I'm your guy."

"Thanks, but I've got it handled." Cade's tone was borderline sarcastic now.

"How about painting sunrooms?" Everleigh asked.

Trevor's expression brightened. "Sure, I can do that."

Cade groaned. "Everleigh, we've been through this."

"You said, and I quote, 'Whatever knocks your socks off, partner.'" She made air quotes with her fingers. He shook his head, but she spotted a playful glint in his eyes.

"I can paint it, or I can help you," Trevor offered.

"I just might take you up on that."

"Cade!" Roger called as he and Quinn joined them. "Let's get back in the water." He took Quinn's hand, and they jogged together toward the waves.

Trevor rubbed his hands together. "Great idea." He set his bottle of water down, pulled off his shirt, and grinned at Everleigh. "Race ya!" Then he took off running and splashing into the waves.

But Everleigh didn't move. The memory of being dragged under, blacking out, and waking up on the shoreline with lifeguards standing over her took her mind hostage. She pulled on the hem of her dress and tried to keep smiling.

Cade watched her. "You okay?"

"Yeah." She feigned offhandedness that she didn't feel. "I just don't do waves."

His expression rippled with surprise. "Then I'll stay here."

"No. I insisted you come to the beach, so go have fun." She pointed toward the water. "I can watch."

This time, Cade was the one who stayed put. "Are you sure?"

The care in his voice touched her deep inside. "Go enjoy the waves. I promise I'll have fun watching everyone from right here."

"Whatever you say, darlin'." He headed toward the water—and she really did enjoy the view.

She also hoped he'd call her *darlin'* again soon.

✦ ✦ ✦

"I love the ocean this time of year," Roger told Cade later after they'd spent some time swimming.

They were back on the shore and drying off with their towels. Cade found Everleigh perched on the beach chair. She had removed her sundress, and she was lounging in a modest two-piece pink suit that made the most of her svelte figure. Her floppy hat blocked her face while she studied her phone. Quinn walked over to her, and Everleigh smiled as her friend spoke and pulled a towel over her shoulders.

He'd been disappointed when she didn't join them in the water. In fact, she'd seemed almost twitchy when he asked her why she didn't want to swim.

"I'm gonna ask Quinn for her number," Roger confessed.

Cade nodded at his friend. "Good for you."

"It's time for me to get back out there." He patted Cade's shoulder. "And you should do the same."

Cade shook his head. Dating was the least of his worries right now, especially with his career on the line. "Go for it, man."

"Maybe I haven't found 'the one,' but I'm not giving up. You and I both ought to be grabbing life by the horns and enjoying the ride."

Cade frowned. Roger made it sound so easy.

"Listen, man," Roger began, "Serena did you wrong, but not every woman is Serena."

Cade's eyes slid back over to Everleigh. For the first time since she'd arrived, he wondered if they might become real friends.

But was she trustworthy? He had pledged his future to Serena, but she had stabbed him in the back. What proof did he have that Everleigh might not do the same thing? After all, she was still bent on selling the inn—a motive so at odds with his own that he could imagine himself getting really, really hurt again.

✦ ✦ ✦

"Hey, Everleigh," Trevor called, rushing over to her. "I need to head out, but I'm so glad I ran into you today." He held up his phone. "Would it be okay if I called you?"

She couldn't stop her eyes from wandering over to where Cade spoke to Roger. "Trevor, you're a nice guy, but I hope you're just asking as a friend. I already told you I'm not planning to stay in town."

Trevor grinned. "I understand. But friends can see each other and go out every once in a while, right?"

"I suppose so."

"Great." He pointed to her phone. "What's your number?"

This guy really wasn't going to give up, was he? Everleigh smiled despite her annoyance. "I have your card. I'll call you."

"If you decide to paint that sunroom, give me a call."

He reached out to hug her, and she awkwardly patted his back. "See ya," he said before sauntering up to the boardwalk.

Quinn stood beside her. "If you only met Trevor yesterday, how did he know you were going to be here today?"

"I have no idea," Everleigh said. "I'm just as surprised as you are. He asked me out yesterday, but I told him I only wanted to be friends."

"Interesting." Quinn twirled her sunglasses in her hand. "He seemed really eager."

"And what about you and Roger?" Everleigh inclined her head closer. "It's pretty obvious he likes you."

"Right?" she exclaimed. "I'm hoping he'll ask for my number. But if he doesn't, then I'll ask for his."

Everleigh beamed. "Good plan!"

Everleigh glanced toward Cade and Roger again and admired Cade's handsome profile. She was proud she'd gotten him out of the house. Then she gave Quinn a hug. "Thanks for inviting me today." They said their goodbyes, and she started toward the boardwalk.

"Hey, partner!" Cade called out, and she spun toward him. "I'll see you at home."

She smiled and gave him a thumbs-up.

✦ ✦ ✦

Cade nosed his pickup truck into the garage, and Everleigh parked behind him. He climbed out of the truck and walked over to her SUV as she got out. "*You* lost the bet."

Her expression was playful. "Who said we were betting?"

"You said you didn't believe I'd show up, which means I won." He pointed to himself.

Her grin was coy and adorable. "Actually, *I* won because I convinced you to go. It was more of a dare than a bet."

He had to admit she had a point. "Fine. You won."

Seemingly satisfied with that, she hefted her giant tote bag onto her shoulder. "I'll get changed and then give the Sunrise Suite a once-over before the Newtons get here." She started toward the inn. "I'll leave the beach chair in my trunk in case I need it again," she called over her shoulder.

"Hold up." He started after her. "Why didn't you swim?"

She stopped in her tracks but turned toward him. "I don't swim in the ocean." Her fingers moved over the stitching on her tote bag strap, and her expression was suddenly solemn. This wasn't an emotion he was used to seeing on her face.

"Did something happen?" he asked gently.

"I . . ." She swallowed. "I don't like to talk about it."

He held his hands up. "Didn't mean to overstep."

She nodded, started toward the house again, and then stopped. She seemed to be working through something in her mind. Then she pulled in a deep breath, her shoulders rising and falling before she faced him.

He took in the pain in her eyes and braced himself for her words.

"When I was ten," she began, "I almost drowned."

His eyes widened, and he closed the distance between them. Her scent wafted over him—cocoa butter combined with something sweet—and he basked in it.

Her dark eyes glistened. "I normally don't talk about it, but since you asked . . . I feel safe sharing it with you."

He was so honored that she trusted him with something so personal. A lock of her hair cascaded down from her messy bun and floated over her cheek. Without thinking, he pushed it behind her ear. "What happened?"

"I . . . I was almost swept out to sea in a riptide."

"Everleigh," he breathed. "How scary that must have been."

She looked past him as if gathering her words. "I was swimming with my brother and a couple of his friends, but I remember going under." She sniffed. "I panicked all of a sudden and couldn't breathe."

Her gorgeous eyes met his again, and tears leaked down her cheeks. His chest constricted as he took in her fear and anxiety. He brushed the tears away with the tip of his finger, and he was almost certain that she shivered at his touch. Surely she was only reacting to the horrible memory.

"Everything went black." She gripped the strap on her bag. "When I woke up, my mom was screaming and crying. If I close my eyes, I can still hear the terror in her voice. The memory is so vivid, like it just happened yesterday."

Unable to stop himself, he took her hand in his, and she held on.

"A couple of lifeguards were standing over me." Her voice trembled. "I remember choking and coughing up water. It was in my lungs, and they had to do CPR."

He couldn't imagine the depth of her fear. She had been so young. And her family must have thought they'd lost her. He ached for her and for them. "You must have been terrified."

"Yeah," she whispered, her voice reedy. "I spent a few days in the hospital, and my mom stayed with me every second. But ever since then, I've stayed away from the water." She sniffed and then laughed. "I guess you think I'm a big chicken, huh? It happened so long ago, but I still can't bring myself to even put a toe in."

He shook his head, and he was silent for a moment. But an idea gripped him. "Would you want to go in with me?"

She blinked. "What do you mean?"

"We could go back in the water together," he suggested. "Maybe I could help you overcome your fear—if you want to, I mean."

She released his hand and shook her head. "I don't think . . ." Her words trailed off, and she wiped her eyes.

"I promise I won't let anything happen to you."

She gave him a watery smile. "That's really sweet of you, Cade, but I don't think I could do it."

"I understand," he said, storing the idea in the back of his mind.

In a flash, her face seemed to transform. "But enough about that. I'd better make sure the suite is ready for Mr. and Mrs. Newton. Thanks for coming along today, Cade." Then she turned on her heel toward the inn.

"You're welcome," he called after her. "And by the way . . ."

She spun toward him. "Yes?"

"I don't like your boyfriend."

"Cade, I already told you he's *not* my boyfriend."

Cade's mouth quirked up in a grin. "He sure *wants* to be."

"I know." She sighed. "He asked me out, but I told him no."

Though he didn't admit it aloud, relief tumbled through him. "There's something about that guy, Everleigh. Seriously, I don't trust him."

"Why do you say that?"

He leaned on her bumper. "I can't put my finger on it, but I felt like he wasn't telling me the truth about why he moved here and what he does for a living. It almost sounded like he was making up answers as he went along."

She studied him for a moment, then fixed him with a look. "Tell me something, Cade. Do you trust anyone?" When he didn't respond, she nodded as if she already knew the answer. "If you need me, I'll be inside."

As he watched her walk away, he felt himself starting to trust her—but he knew the risks of letting her in. He'd been burned by Serena, and no matter what, he couldn't allow anyone to get that close to him again.

CHAPTER 12

MRS. NEWTON AMBLED up the front steps of the inn later that evening and threw her arms around Everleigh. "Sweetheart!" she gushed. "It's been too long."

Everleigh held on to her. "It's so good to see you, Mrs. Newton. I'm surprised you remember me!"

The sky above them was dark and sprinkled with bright stars. A few moths circled the porch lights while a chorus of cicadas and frogs serenaded them.

The older woman clucked her tongue. "You're a grown woman now. Call me Maggie." Her dark curly hair shimmered with gray, and her bright amber eyes were still full of life. Her smile fell. "Sweetheart, I was so sorry to hear about Alana."

"Thank you."

"I brought you a gift." She turned toward their Dodge Caravan, where Mr. Newton spoke to Cade. "Henry, will you get that basket out for me?"

When Cade's eyes met Everleigh's, her heart gave a happy flutter. She recalled how sympathetic and concerned he'd been this afternoon.

She could still feel his strong hand holding hers, and the pad of his thumb tracing her cheek as he'd brushed her hair behind her ear.

She pushed away the thought. Cade was her business partner, and she would soon be back on the road for work. She turned her attention to Mr. Newton as he waved to Everleigh and passed a basket to Mrs. Newton.

"This is for you." Mrs. Newton handed her a basket full of jars of jam.

Everleigh grinned. "Cade and I were just talking about your jam. Alana loved the apple the best."

"I know, dear. I named it Alana's Apple Jam for a reason." She held up a jar, and Everleigh's eyes stung as she read the name.

"That's so sweet of you. Thank you so much."

"Let's take this inside while the men handle the bags," she said.

The two of them headed into the kitchen, and Everleigh set the basket on the counter.

"Mrs. New—" Everleigh began. "I mean, Maggie, let me pay you for all of this."

Maggie shook her head. "Not a chance." She gestured around the kitchen. "This inn has brought Henry and me so much joy over the years. Giving you and Cade a basket of jam is the least I can do." Her eyes glistened. "Alana was so special, and she loved you dearly."

Everleigh nodded as sadness rolled in like a heavy fog.

"She bragged about you all the time and talked about your adventures as a nurse. She was so proud of you."

Everleigh sniffed. "Thank you," she managed to say.

"Henry and I love coming here to Coral Cove," she continued. "We've often talked about moving here. How wonderful would it be to live on the coast year-round? And it's much closer to our grandchildren than where we are now in Upstate New York."

Everleigh found her smile again.

Mrs. Newton waved off her own idea. "But we talk about a lot of things and never do them. I suppose coming to visit is less of a hassle than packing up and moving." She pointed toward the window. "I saw the sign out front though. You're selling the inn?"

"We are."

Mrs. Newton's face lit up. "We?" She inclined forward as if sharing a juicy secret. "Did you get married?" She took Everleigh's left hand in hers. "I don't see a ring."

"No, no, no. Alana left the inn to Cade and me. We've put it on the market."

Mrs. Newton frowned. "That's a shame. It's such a lovely place to visit. I'd hate to see it sold."

The front door opened, and Cade trudged past the kitchen with two suitcases.

"Let me carry one up the stairs, son," Mr. Newton told him.

"No, sir, I got it," Cade insisted.

The two men disappeared, and soon footfalls sounded on the steep staircase.

"That Cade is such a nice young man. I always look forward to his breakfast." Mrs. Newton grinned. "Please tell me he's cooking for us tomorrow morning."

"I'm sure he has something delicious planned for you."

"Oh, good." Mrs. Newton clapped her hands. "He's so talented. Alana said she knew he was special when she first met him. She said he's just a sweet soul who's had a tough time. She always believed he just needed some time to shine and find his courage again. Then he would make some young lady a wonderful husband."

Everleigh nodded, glad to take in these details about Cade.

"And what about you? Do you have a special fella in your life?"

"No, ma'am."

"I'm sure you'll meet someone soon." She cupped her hand to her mouth to shield a yawn and then pointed toward the doorway. "But enough about that tonight. We've had a long ride, so I'll see you in the morning, sweetheart."

"Good night," Everleigh told her. "Let me know if you need anything for your stay."

Mrs. Newton disappeared through the doorway, and Everleigh began examining the jars of jam—apple, grape, strawberry, apricot, cherry, peach, and blueberry. She picked up a jar of apple jam and read the label: Alana's Apple Jam. Memories of sharing breakfast with Alana swirled through her mind, and her eyes felt wet again.

Footsteps sounded behind her, and Everleigh set the jar down and wiped her eyes.

"What's in the basket?" Cade's deep voice was close to her ear, sending a chill up her spine.

"Mrs. Newton's jam." Everleigh stepped aside. "She named the apple jam after Alana."

Cade examined it. "What a generous gift."

"I know." Everleigh pushed against the anguish threading through her and perked up. "Do you need any help with breakfast tomorrow?"

He shook his head. "I got it."

"Have you decided what you're going to make?"

He rested his forearms on the island, and an impish look overtook his handsome face. It nearly knocked the wind out of her for a moment. "It's a surprise."

"You can tell me."

"But can I trust you?" His expression was playful, and she was captivated once again. "Fine." He lowered his voice. "Bananas Foster Belgian waffles."

Her mouth began to water. "Please tell me you're going to make enough for you and me too."

He chuckled. "Of course I will."

"And you don't need any help?" When he shook his head, she lifted her chin and said, "I'll have you know that I'm an expert at setting the table."

He laughed again, and she savored the sound. "Okay, then that would be helpful."

They both were silent for a moment, and then he pushed off the island. "Right. Then I'll see you bright and early."

"Good night," she told him.

While he sauntered toward the back door, Mrs. Newton's comments about Cade replayed in her mind:

"She said he's just a sweet soul who's had a tough time . . ."

Once again, Everleigh wondered why Alana never told her about Cade. And now she also wondered what his story was and what had led him to the Sunshine Inn.

✦ ✦ ✦

"This is outstanding." Everleigh pointed her fork toward her plate of bananas Foster Belgian waffles. "I have never had anything as delicious as this."

Cade and Everleigh sat across from each other the following morning. She'd arrived in the kitchen at seven, singing a pop song to herself. She bopped around, smiling and humming, while she put the fruit cups together, made coffee, filled juice glasses, and then set the table before asking what else she could do.

Although he thought Everleigh had way too much energy for someone who had just woken up, he had to admit she was a tremendous help. All he had to worry about was cooking, and thanks to

Everleigh, breakfast was on the table when Mr. and Mrs. Newton arrived exactly at eight.

The older couple had enjoyed the meal and then left for the beach, leaving Cade and Everleigh to eat together while sitting on stools at the island.

"Did you serve this at your restaurant?" she asked. "Because if you didn't, you sure should have."

Cade took a long draw from his mug of coffee. He wished he'd never admitted to her that he'd owned a restaurant. It wasn't something he wanted to share with anyone. Those memories were best left in the past, just like his memories of his time with Serena.

"Occasionally I featured it as a special on Sundays." As soon as he'd spoken, he regretted this admission too. Her dark eyes lit up with excitement.

"What else was on your menu?"

He pressed his lips together, wanting to change the subject. "Mostly American fare, but we had specials highlighting certain countries on certain days."

"Like what?" She rested her chin on her palm and studied him as if he were the most interesting person she'd ever met.

"We'd have a German day with bratwurst or sauerbraten."

"Yum! I love German food. What else?"

"Lasagna or eggplant parmesan on Italian day."

"Also yum. What other international meals did you make?"

"Burritos and things like that." He ate another forkful of waffle.

"What was your favorite meal?"

He shrugged. "I like to cook, so anything is fine."

"What was the name of your restaurant?"

He took a long drink of coffee. "Sully's."

"Sully's?" she asked. "Who's Sully?"

Cade ate more of the waffle and considered his answer. He didn't want to tell her about his business partner who had double-crossed him and run the business into the ground. That level of detail was too much to share with her, even though her eyes seemed to pull him in.

Still, he knew better than to trust her.

"I didn't pick the name," he finally said.

"Who did?"

"My business partner."

"Oh." She looked curious. "Who was Sully?"

He moved his fingers over his warm mug. "It was his grandfather's nickname."

"Super cute," she declared.

They ate for a few moments, and he felt himself start to relax.

"Mr. and Mrs. Newton were very impressed with your breakfast," Everleigh said. "What are you going to make tomorrow?"

"Eggs Benedict."

"Oh, I can't wait!" Her smile was brilliant as she pulled out her phone. "We need to take a selfie."

"What?" he asked. "Why?"

"Because this is the first breakfast we've prepared together for our guests." She hurried around the table and held up her phone.

"Whoa," he protested. "I don't do selfies."

She scrunched her nose. "What do you mean? Everyone takes selfies."

"Not me."

"Just try it, Cade." She stood up on her tiptoes, angled the phone toward him, and leaned in close. "Now smile," she exclaimed before her face lit up. She snapped the photo, then turned and showed him the shot. "See? That wasn't so bad."

He snorted as she returned to her stool. "So you liked helping with breakfast?" he asked.

She nodded and ate another bite.

He hoped she was finally remembering why she loved the inn so much, which would mean his plan was working. "I want to add suppers too."

"When we sell the inn, you should take your half of the money and open another restaurant." She made a sweeping gesture. "It would be the talk of Coral Cove. You can have your international food days and make bananas Foster Belgian waffles for breakfast. It will be a hit, Cade. I'm sure of it."

He stilled, and his lips turned down in a frown. So they were back to this. Just when he felt like they were making strides together, she had to bring up selling the inn.

Her smile faded. "Cade? What did I say wrong?"

"I'm done running restaurants."

She leaned forward. "Why? Just because it didn't go well the first time doesn't mean it won't when you try again."

He glowered at her. Couldn't she see how selfish she was being? What business did she have telling him what to do with his half of the money he didn't even want? He was done with this conversation. He dropped his fork on the plate and hopped off his stool before carrying his plate, utensils, and mug to the counter.

"Hold on, Cade," she said, and the earnestness in her voice made him face her again. "You said your first restaurant didn't work out, but I believe in you. You should believe in yourself."

"Thanks for the pep talk, but it's not that easy."

"Why not?"

He rested his hip against the counter. "Running a business is tough work, but a restaurant is a lot tougher than this place."

"But if we get what we want for the inn, you can hire a great staff. You won't have to do it on your own." She gestured all around the kitchen. "Maybe Alana wanted you to give it another try with your half of the money. She obviously knew you were an amazing chef with talent to share with others."

He shook his head. She had no idea what she was talking about. He supposed that in her happy-go-lucky mind everything was simple and straightforward. It must be nice to live with permanent rose-colored glasses covering your eyes.

He rinsed off his dishes and set them in the dishwasher.

"I'll clean up." She appeared at his side. "You cooked."

"No, I got it." He stayed rooted to the spot as he continued to fill the dishwasher, but he was aware of her standing behind him.

After a few moments, she said, "I didn't mean to upset you, Cade."

He sighed and looked over his shoulder at her. "I'm fine. Go do whatever it is you have to do today."

She retreated to the dining room and reappeared with an armload of the Newtons' dishes. They finished tidying up the kitchen together, and the silence between them clawed at him. Once the dishwasher was full, he added the dish detergent and started the machine, which hummed in response.

Everleigh gave him a hesitant smile. "Thanks for breakfast. I can't wait to try your eggs Benedict."

He nodded, and she hurried off in the direction of her suite.

Cade leaned against the counter and crossed his arms. Maybe Everleigh's intentions were good, but he couldn't just ignore her obliviousness. Everything inside him screamed that trusting her would only lead to heartache and disappointment—another devastation he would do anything to avoid.

He closed his eyes and released a long, weary breath. He was already exhausted, and it wasn't even noon yet.

"Why, Alana?" he whispered into the stillness. "What on earth were you thinking?"

CHAPTER 13

THREE WEEKS LATER, Everleigh hummed along to a pop song streaming from a portable speaker while she mopped the kitchen on a Saturday morning. She and Cade had hosted two more couples after the Newtons left, and she was enjoying getting reacquainted with the regular guests while also spending time with her family and Quinn. She hadn't spoken to Harlowe, except for brief encounters at her parents' house. But that wasn't for her lack of trying.

Although she and Cade hadn't had any personal conversations, he'd been friendly enough. They hadn't received any other offers on the inn, and she was beginning to wonder if it would ever sell. But giving up hope would be going against her nature, so instead she spent her days working at the inn. Thankfully, another couple planned to check in tomorrow.

Ding-dong!

She leaned the mop against the counter and moved to the front door. The warm mid-October air rushed in, and she found a man who appeared to be a few inches shorter than Cade standing on the porch. His light-brown hair was cut short, and his facial structure and blue eyes seemed familiar. She guessed he was in his mid- to late thirties.

"Can I help you?" she asked.

"I hope so," he said. "I'm looking for Cade Witherspoon."

"Sorry, you just missed him."

Disappointment fell over his features. "Do you expect him back soon?"

"He ran out to the grocery store but should be back within the hour."

"Are you his wife?"

A bubble of laughter escaped from her. "No, no, we're business partners. For now, anyway."

"Oh." The man's forehead rumpled. "I've been trying to connect with him for a while now."

Curiosity gnawed at her. "I can take a message and have him call you."

"Fantastic." The man's face relaxed sightly. He reached into his pocket and pulled out a card. "I'm staying over at the Rosewood Inn. It's really important that I speak to him." He handed her the card, and she read the name "Declan Hewitt, Financial Advisor."

"I'll make sure he gets this as soon as he gets back."

"I appreciate it." He started down the stairs, then stopped and turned back around. "By the way, what's your name?"

"Everleigh."

"Nice to meet you, Everleigh," he said before climbing into a dark-colored sedan and driving toward the main road.

She leaned against the railing and studied the card. Why would a financial advisor want to find Cade? And what was so urgent?

"Strange," she whispered as she closed the door behind her. Back in the kitchen, she finished mopping and then moved to wiping the baseboards. She'd reached the end of the hallway when the inn's phone began to ring.

She jogged to the office to answer. "Thank you for calling the Sunshine Inn. How can I help you?"

"Alana?" a woman asked.

"Oh no." Her hands began to tremble, and she dropped onto a chair. "This is Everleigh."

"Everleigh! You must be all grown-up now. I don't think I've seen you since you were a child," the woman said. "Oh, and I've forgotten my manners. This is Loretta Walker. Maybe you remember my husband and me?"

"Hi, Mrs. Walker." She tried to sound as if she recalled her, but Everleigh couldn't place the name.

"Is Alana there?"

Everleigh closed her eyes and pressed her hand against her forehead. "I'm sorry to tell you this, Mrs. Walker, but she passed away this summer." She pulled in a gulp of air, preparing herself for the woman's response.

Mrs. Walker gasped. "What? No! What happened?"

Tears pressed against Everleigh's eyes. "She had cancer."

"Oh, honey. I'm so sorry to hear that. What kind?"

Everleigh stared up at the ceiling as her tears threatened to pour from her eyes. Didn't Mrs. Walker know how difficult this was for her?

"Liver, but it spread to her lungs." *Please don't ask for more details. Please let it go!*

Mrs. Walker clucked her tongue. "Oh no. That had to be so painful. Poor thing."

Everleigh gnawed her lower lip and slammed her eyes shut.

"Did you take care of her?"

"Um . . ." Everleigh swallowed as her tears began to fall. She grabbed a tissue from the box on the desk and dabbed at her eyes. "No, ma'am." Her voice sounded small.

"I'm surprised to hear that. You were so close, and I believe she mentioned you were a nurse."

Everleigh took a deep breath, trying in vain to collect herself, but the tears continued to pour down her hot cheeks.

"Alana talked about you all the time," Mrs. Walker continued. "You were the daughter she never had. She adored you."

Everleigh opened her mouth, ready to change the subject. Then she sat up straight, wiped her face, and cleared her throat. "So, Mrs. Walker, how can I help you?"

"Bernie and I wanted to come down before it got too late in the year. Do you have any openings?"

"We sure do." Everleigh pulled up the reservation page on the website. She booked the Walkers for the first week in November, then quickly ushered her off the phone.

When she hung up, she cupped her hands to her face. The guilt she'd kept bottled up inside her boiled over, and tears poured from her eyes again. Why hadn't Alana told Cade to call her and ask her to come home? Everleigh could have been helpful during her treatments, could have comforted her and wiped her tears when she cried, could have told her she loved her one last time . . .

Mrs. Walker's words echoed in her mind. Surely the cancer had been painful. Had Cade done all he could to keep her comfortable? Somehow, she was certain he had. She already sensed Cade had a good heart, but that didn't stop the anguish from blooming inside her.

"Everleigh?" Cade called from somewhere inside the inn. "You here?"

"In the office." Her voice was tight.

As soon as he appeared in the doorway, worry raced across his chiseled features. "Are you okay?"

"Yeah." She tried to curl her lips into a smile, but it felt more like a grimace. "I'm fine."

"No, you're not." He pulled a chair over to her. "What happened?"

She waved off his worry. "Mrs. Walker called to make a reservation, and she didn't know Alana had passed away. She asked me questions about her death, and it was . . . I just found it difficult to respond."

"I remember Mrs. Walker." He frowned, and she was certain it was his concerned frown. "She never knows when to be quiet."

"It's okay. Really. I'm sure she meant well." She wiped her eyes with the tips of her fingers. "How was the grocery store?"

He rested his arms on the desk. "Uneventful."

"You had a visitor while you were out."

His eyes briefly narrowed. "Who?"

"Some guy named Declan." She handed him the business card. "He's anxious for you to call him."

Cade studied the card, and his brow furrowed. "Declan Hewitt. Declan Hewitt . . ." He whispered the name as if trying to place it. "Where have I seen that name?" He tapped the business card against his palm and then snapped his fingers. "I think this guy has emailed me about something. Seemed odd." He dropped the business card into his pocket.

"He seemed pretty serious about talking to you." Everleigh finally conjured up a genuine smile. "Ooh, what if you won a sweepstakes?"

"That would be a miracle since I can't remember entering one."

"You need to try positivity, Cade. The guy could have good news."

He scoffed. "The last time I did that, things turned disastrous. Why waste the energy on getting my hopes up?"

"Take a chance sometime. You might be glad you did." She reached out and touched his arm.

"This is about more than just dreaming, partner."

"You're allowed to dream, Cade," she told him. "You deserve it."

Shaking his head, he started toward the doorway. "Thanks for taking the message. I'll go finish putting the groceries away."

✦ ✦ ✦

Later that night, Cade flopped down on the sofa beside Bryant and opened a can of Coke. "What a day, huh, buddy?"

The cat stretched his large paws out in front of him and yawned before snuggling deeper into his blanket.

Cade took a long draw from his can before setting it on the end table beside him. He found the remote and flipped on the television. While the evening news anchor talked about how the weather would continue to be warm during the next few days, Cade's thoughts wandered back to earlier in the day when Everleigh had handed him the business card.

He pulled the card from his pocket and studied the stranger's name. He couldn't for the life of him imagine what Declan Hewitt wanted. When he recalled Everleigh saying he could have won a sweepstakes, Cade shook his head and chuckled to himself. If only he could muster an ounce of her positivity. At the same time, he'd done too much living to believe people only had good intentions. Many people were only out for themselves, and Cade had encountered the worst of that.

He set the business card down on the end table and focused on the television. While the anchors began reading the latest news, his eyes defied him and kept returning to the card. He picked it up and studied it once again.

Huffing out a frustrated breath, Cade weighed the idea of calling the man. Curiosity finally overcame him. The guy had been so determined to find him that he'd tried emailing him *and* visiting his place of work. Maybe he truly did have important information to share with him.

Cade pulled his cell phone from his pocket. What was the worst that could happen? If the guy had bad intentions, he could hang up on him and block him. And if the guy was genuine, Cade might be glad he called.

He turned to the cat, who had buried his snout in the blanket. "Should I call this guy?"

Bryant blinked up at him, yawned, then readjusted himself on the blanket.

"Fine. I'll call him." He muted the television and shook a finger at the cat. "But if he's up to no good, I'm going to blame this on you and Everleigh."

Cade dialed the number and then held the phone up to his ear. He settled back on the sofa and drummed his fingers on his lap while the phone rang.

"Hello?" a man asked.

"Is this Declan?"

"Yes." He paused. "Cade?"

"Yeah. Everleigh said you stopped by earlier to see me."

"I'm glad you called. I tried emailing you, but I don't know if you received the message."

"I did." Cade rested his elbow on the arm of the sofa. "What's this about?"

Declan hesitated. "There's something I need to discuss with you."

"I'm listening."

"I'd rather talk in person."

What was it with this guy? Cade let his head fall backward and land on the sofa cushion. "Why? I don't even know you."

"It's . . . awkward."

Like this conversation? "All right," Cade said, relenting. "When?"

"My schedule is open, and I'm in town for a while. I'm staying at the Rosewood Inn."

Cade hesitated, but he had a feeling that if he didn't agree to meet this guy, he wouldn't give up. It was in his best interests to see what he wanted and then get rid of him. "How about lunch tomorrow?"

"Perfect." Declan sounded relieved. "Where?"

"Do you like pizza?"

"Who doesn't?"

Cade felt himself relax, but only slightly. "Meet me at Slice of Heaven at noon."

"Perfect," Declan said. "Thanks, Cade."

"Sure thing." He disconnected the call and tossed his phone onto the cushion beside him. He groaned. He'd probably just made a colossal mistake. He couldn't believe he'd let Everleigh talk him into reaching out to this guy. What if he was only out for money or something to do with the inn? Or what if this was just the next step in some elaborate scam?

Possibly worse yet—what if his reason for tracking down Cade was legitimate? *What on earth,* he wondered, *could it be?*

Cade tried to concentrate on the news anchor babbling about NASCAR while photos of a race team flashed on the screen. His apartment suddenly felt too small. He needed to burn off this nervous energy.

He crossed to the window facing the bay. The sun had begun to set, sending a brilliant rainbow of colors across the sky. Movement drew his attention to the swing set, where Everleigh was slowly gliding back and forth.

Curiosity propelled him down the stairs and out the door. As he approached Everleigh, he found her eyes were trained on the water. She seemed deep in thought, as if the weight of the world was balanced on her slight shoulders. He couldn't take his eyes off her. She was beautiful with the fading light illuminating her ivory skin, the same light also stoking her red hair like a blaze.

He stopped moving forward and jammed his hands into the pockets of his shorts. For a moment he felt ridiculous for longing to talk to her about the mysterious Declan Hewitt. Why would Everleigh care about his life? She seemed to be burdened with her own thoughts, and he didn't want to bother her with his nervousness about meeting the stranger tomorrow.

He started back toward his apartment. He was better off just finding something to watch on television and putting his confusion and concerns about Declan out of his head.

"Are you spying on me?"

Cade paused and faced her again. Everleigh was looking over her shoulder at him from the swing, the sunset still lighting up her features. "Not exactly," he said, kicking a pebble with the toe of his shoe. "But you look stressed. Wanna talk about it?"

Everleigh pushed her swing back into gentle motion. "I was just thinking about Alana and how she meant so much to so many people." Her lip wobbled, but she tried to smile anyway. "What's on *your* mind?"

He walked over to stand next to her. "I called that Declan guy."

Her expression brightened. "And?" As her swing moved and a warm evening breeze drifted over him, her scent—something flowery mixed with vanilla—wafted over him as well. His pulse blipped and stumbled, and the corners of her mouth quirked upward. "Did you win a sweepstakes?"

He tried to shake off his confusing feelings for her. "No, but I agreed to meet him for lunch tomorrow."

"What does he want?"

"Don't know."

She scrunched her nose. "Hmm . . . Maybe he *is* sketchy. Do you want me to go with you?"

He shook his head. "Thanks, but I can handle it."

"Humph. Suit yourself then." She patted the swing next to her. "Want to join me?"

He was tempted. Enjoying the warm evening beside her sounded like heaven, but he was afraid to get too close. He already was growing more attached to her than he cared to admit, which was only putting his heart in danger. "No, but thanks for the offer."

Her face seemed to fall slightly, but then her smile returned. "Well then, good night, partner."

"Night." He stood still for a moment, then started back toward his apartment. As he approached the garage, he pondered how sad Everleigh had seemed when he first spotted her by the pond. He longed to know what she was *really* thinking, but he couldn't allow himself to open up.

Then a thought hit him. He could design a memorial gift—something special that would remind Everleigh of Alana. Instead of going up to his apartment, he unlocked the garage and crossed to his workbench. Before long, all sorts of creative ideas had engulfed his mind.

CHAPTER 14

CADE STROLLED TO Slice of Heaven and pulled open the front door. The savory aromas that hit him normally would have caused his stomach to gurgle, but anxiety had tied his insides into knots. He's spent a sleepless night puzzling over who Declan Hewitt was and what he wanted.

He'd managed to keep the conversation to a minimum with Everleigh while they made breakfast for the inn guests, and he'd agreed to let her tidy up the kitchen when breakfast was over. He'd spent the remainder of the morning in his shop, tinkering with a project he'd started for Everleigh until it was time to drive into town.

Cade scanned the walls of the pizzeria, which were lined with photos of mouthwatering pizzas, breadsticks, and calzones as well as beach landscapes. The black-and-white tile floor was worn, evidence of the family-owned restaurant's longevity—here since Cade was a child. His folks had always bought pizzas from this place, and it was still his favorite.

He searched the dining room as he made his way to the line, finding several families gathered around tables and sitting in booths.

Pulling his phone from the back pocket of his jeans, he scrolled through his text messages, looking for one from Declan. He wished he'd asked Declan how to identify him. Meeting a stranger was so awkward. He had a flashback of the blind date he'd been set up on when he met Serena, and he bit back a groan. The two of them had had instant chemistry, and before the end of the night, he'd been certain he'd found "the one." He almost laughed at himself out loud at the naïveté of it all. He'd been such a hopeless romantic back then, but he'd learned his lesson—the hard way.

"Cade?"

His head popped up just as a man approached him with his hand outstretched. "I'm Declan."

"Hey." Cade shook his hand.

Declan pointed to a corner booth in the back. "I took the liberty of getting you a gigantic piece of pepperoni and a Coke. Sound okay?"

"Yeah." Cade followed him to the booth and sat across from him. Although the pizza smelled delicious, his appetite was nonexistent. He took a sip of Coke and then waited for the stranger to speak.

"You're probably wondering why I've been determined to track you down."

"You could say that."

Declan hesitated and then set his phone on the table. "The truth is," he began. "Well, the truth is . . . you're my brother."

Cade blinked and then blinked again before he laughed. "Is this a joke?" He looked around the restaurant. "Did someone put you up to this? Am I being recorded on a hidden camera?" He waited for Declan to laugh, but the man just pressed his lips together and shook his head.

"We're brothers, Cade."

"I hate to burst your bubble, but I'm an only child. You've got the wrong guy."

Declan steepled his hands, his expression stoic. "I was adopted as an infant."

Cade rubbed his elbow. "I don't see what that has to do with me."

"I've spent my entire adult life searching for my family. I joined every DNA website I could find, including Family Tree."

The muscles in Cade's shoulders stiffened.

"I submitted a saliva test, and I finally got a hit." Declan paused. "And I found a relative, and that relative was you."

"Th-that can't be true." Cade's leg began to bounce.

"It's true. We're brothers." Declan hit a few buttons on his phone and swiped a few times before holding the screen up for Cade to read. "We have the same mother."

Cade's mouth opened and then closed, and the world around him tilted. "That has to be a mistake. I'm an only child."

Declan set the phone on the table and pushed it over to Cade. "That's why I've been trying to reach you. When you didn't answer my email, I came here and asked around until I found out where you worked."

Cade's gut tightened as he stared at the DNA results—he and Declan had the same mother, which meant Mom had given up a baby for adoption before Cade was born. How could that be true if his parents had never told him he had a brother?

Confusion overwhelmed him, and he fought the urge to flee the restaurant. But a mixture of curiosity and suspicion kept him cemented in place.

He finally met Declan's eyes. "What do you want from me?"

"I've wanted to know my biological family ever since my parents told me I was adopted."

Cade sagged on the booth seat and pushed the phone back over to Declan.

"I went to see your mother." Declan moved his finger along the edge of the table. "*Our* mother." His lips turned down in a deep frown. "I found her store, but she refused to talk to me. Turned her back on me and hid in the back room until I left." He rested his forearms on the table. "That was right before I came to see you."

Cade just stared at him while questions swirled in his mind. If his mother had another child, why hadn't she ever told him? Would she have kept this secret from him? Did his father know? None of this made any sense!

"How old are you?" he asked.

"Thirty-nine," Declan said. "I'll be forty in January." He tilted his head. "You?"

"Thirty-three." His voice sounded thick.

Declan shifted in his seat. "Look, I know this is a shock, but I didn't know how else to tell you. It didn't seem right to share this over the phone. To answer your question, I don't want anything from you. I just . . ." He paused. "I just would like to have you in my life. I've always wondered about my family, and now that my wife and I are starting our own, it's become even more important to us both."

Cade stared at him as his words soaked through him. Not only did he possibly have a brother, but he also had a sister-in-law. And soon, he'd have a niece or nephew.

His head was spinning. It was too much.

"I'll be in town until next Sunday," Declan continued. "It would be great if you could help me arrange a meeting with our mother. Maybe if you were involved, she'd consider talking to me." There was desperation in Declan's eyes, and Cade could feel him pleading with him for help.

Cade scratched his shoulder. "I'll see what I can do."

"Thank you." Declan picked up his piece of pizza and took a bite.

Cade just stared at the slice in front of him, not sure when he'd be able to eat again. His world had just been turned upside down.

✦ ✦ ✦

Later that evening Cade nosed his pickup truck into the garage. He killed the engine and stared at the dark dashboard. After meeting Declan for lunch, he'd driven around for hours, parked by the beach, and sat on a bench while watching the waves, trying to make sense of the bomb Declan had just dropped. He'd spent his entire life believing he was an only child, but now he had a half brother whom his mother had kept a secret for all of his thirty-three years. It didn't make any sense, and he had no idea how to process this information.

Wrenching the door open, Cade dragged himself out of the truck. He exited the garage and hit the code on the door to close it before unlocking the door that led to his apartment. Footsteps crunched on the gravel driveway, and he turned just as Everleigh caught up to him.

"I've been waiting for you for hours. How'd it go?" Her pretty face beamed.

"Not great."

Her smile dissolved. "What happened?"

"I'd rather not talk about it tonight." He pushed the door open.

"Wait!" She grabbed the door before he could close it. "Cade, talk to me."

He closed his eyes and held the bridge of his nose. He was too emotionally and physically exhausted to deal with her constant bright outlook. "Everleigh—"

"It's not healthy to keep things locked inside. You can trust me."

Could he? At that moment, he did trust her—*completely*—though the admission unnerved him. At the same time, he longed to unpack some of his confusing feelings with someone.

He took a deep breath, and something in her bottomless brown eyes compelled him to confess it all. "He says he's my brother."

Her eyes narrowed, and her brow pinched.

"He insists that DNA on a website proves it, but it has to be some sort of mistake, right?" he asked, hoping she'd agree with him.

"Why would it be a mistake?"

"He showed me the results, but don't those websites make mistakes sometimes?"

"I don't know, Cade." She looked unconvinced. "Haven't law enforcement officials used those websites to solve crimes?"

His posture wilted. "Yeah, I've heard that."

"Maybe he's telling the truth?"

"But that's just not possible," he replied. "He's six years older than me. There's no way my mom had another baby and didn't tell me."

Everleigh considered this. "How long have your parents been married?"

"Thirty-four years."

"And you're thirty-three, right?"

He nodded.

She paused for a beat. "Maybe she did keep it from you. How old would she have been when she had him?"

Cade swallowed and calculated it. "Barely seventeen."

"She was young. Maybe she was scared or had no choice but to give him up for adoption." Everleigh's expression warmed. "Cade, I'm a NICU nurse. I've met plenty of terrified new moms. I've seen teen moms in all kinds of situations, and many weren't good at all. Sometimes adoption is the best option, but it's never easy."

"But why wouldn't she have told me?" He could hear the strain in his voice. "I've spent my entire life thinking I was an only child, Everleigh. I'm just so—"

"Confused and hurt?" As she finished his thought, she took his hand in hers. The warmth of her skin gave him comfort. "Your mom must have her reasons, and you need to forgive her, okay? I know you're hurting, but she deserves the benefit of the doubt. Go talk to her and ask her to be honest with you, then listen without judgment."

He stared at her as he tried to make heads or tails of his swarming emotions.

"If you want, I can go with you to talk to her." Her expression glowed, reminding him of the midday sunshine. "I'm happy to be your emotional support friend."

"Thanks, but I can handle it." He pulled his hand away, and the disappointment in her face sent guilt flooding through him. But he ignored it. He'd already shared too much with her. "It's late. I'm heading to bed."

Her smile seemed forced. "Good night, Cade."

"Night," he called as she walked away. Once she was gone, he closed and locked the door before ascending the stairs to his apartment, dropping onto the sofa, and wishing he could stop the doubt and confusion buzzing in his head.

✦ ✦ ✦

The following afternoon, Everleigh knelt on the sunroom floor and covered the woodwork with painter's tape. She'd woken up that morning and decided it was the day to finally brighten up that room. She'd planned to ask Cade to help her in hopes of taking his mind off the situation with Declan, but he'd been so quiet at breakfast that she decided to back off. It was against her nature to let him be, especially when she could feel the anxiety pouring out of him. It pained her to see him so upset.

He'd hardly said two words to her while he cooked chocolate chip pancakes for the guests. Then he'd agreed to allow her to do the dishes and disappeared again. She'd heard his truck drive away earlier, and she considered calling him to check on him. But she forced herself to give him the space he needed. She just hoped he would come to her when he needed her. *If* he needed her.

Since Cade was gone and their visitors had left for the day, Everleigh had ventured out to the hardware store for paint and supplies. Back at the inn she changed into an old, bright-blue tank top and shorts and then started on her project. It had only been an hour since she began, and she already regretted it. But she wasn't one to waste money. She'd purchased the supplies and now had to follow through with it—unfortunately. Besides, the outcome would be a nice, bright, and happy room, which was always the best kind!

With a sigh, she continued taping the woodwork. When she heard a noise, she stopped and listened again.

Ding-dong!

The doorbell! She jumped to her feet and jogged to the front of the house. She yanked the door open and found Trevor on the porch.

"Trevor. Hi." She pushed her hand through her hair and examined her old clothes. "I wasn't expecting company."

He gave her a sheepish smile. "Sorry for just showing up. I was in the neighborhood, and I hadn't heard from you so . . ." He grimaced. "That sounded creepier than I wanted it to."

She chuckled and rested her arm against the doorframe. "It's fine. How are you?"

"Great." He jammed his thumb toward the driveway. "I saw the For Sale sign. Have you had any offers?"

"None we're taking."

"It's lovely out here on the bay. In my opinion, this is the most scenic part of Coral Cove. I'm surprised no one has snatched it up."

"It's a really special place. My godmother cherished it, and I loved working here with her."

"You said she passed away?"

She nodded. "Cancer."

He pointed to the wicker love seat on the porch. "Can you sit for a minute?"

"Sure."

They sat down beside each other, and she breathed in the warm mid-October afternoon air.

"So, your godmother," he began, "she meant a lot to you."

"She was like my aunt, but sometimes she was like my second mom." While she spoke about Alana, Trevor smiled and seemed completely engaged and interested. She wondered why Cade had said he didn't like or trust Trevor when he seemed like a decent guy—not anyone she was interested in romantically, but certainly not a dangerous person either. What had happened to Cade to make him so leery of everyone he met?

"I'm sorry," she finally said. "I didn't mean to go on and on about Alana. When I start talking about her, I just can't seem to stop."

Trevor took her hand in his. "It's okay. I understand. I feel the same way about my grandpa. I miss him every day."

She tried to subtly pull her hand back. "So, what are you up to today?"

"I'm actually between jobs, which is why I stopped by. Do you need any help with anything around here?"

"Well, I did buy yellow paint this morning."

"For the sunroom?"

She nodded, and he laughed.

"What kind of yellow?"

"Lemonade." She raised her index finger. "But I don't expect you to paint the room for me."

"It'll go faster with two people, right?"

She hesitated. "How much can I pay you?"

He shrugged. "Dinner?"

"Just dinner? That's it?"

"Yup." He stood. "But we're wasting time. Let's go paint that room."

"Follow me!" she said, laughing. They headed into the house, and soon Trevor was helping her tape the woodwork before they set to painting.

While they worked, Trevor shared stories about his life in Florida. Everleigh tried to concentrate on what Trevor shared, but her mind kept meandering back to Cade. She couldn't stop worrying about him. She longed to call him and ask how he was, but she didn't want to pry. She hoped he wouldn't be upset that Trevor was helping her since the work at the inn had been Cade's job for so long. But Everleigh was doing him a favor by handling the task herself, and maybe Cade could appreciate that.

Regardless, she couldn't wait for him to get home—and she would keep worrying about him until he did.

CHAPTER 15

CADE SAT ON a stool in the break room at his mom's store, Crafty Creations. He tried to interpret his mother's expression while he shared the story of meeting Declan, but her face was an unreadable mask. "So this guy Declan says he's my half brother, Mom. He submitted a saliva sample, and according to the Family Tree website, we're related. Isn't that ridiculous?"

Mom remained silent, and he took her reticence as a declaration that he was right.

Relief fluttered through him, and he stood. "I *knew* it wasn't true. I'm sorry to have wasted your time, Mom. I know Monday is always a super busy day." He hugged her and then started for the door. "Just forget about all this. I'll talk to you later. Tell Dad I said hi."

"Cade, wait," she called after him.

Something in her tone made him freeze. He spun and found tears rolling down her cheeks. "Mom?" His eyes widened, and his pulse picked up. "Wh-what is it?"

She took a deep breath and wiped her eyes. "I had a baby boy when I was sixteen."

Mom's words felt like a blow to Cade's chest.

"I gave him up for adoption." Her voice was small.

He stared at her as shock rolled through him. He gripped a nearby counter to steady himself.

"It was a closed adoption, and I didn't think he'd ever find me." She wiped her eyes with the back of her hand. "I never even told your father about him."

"What?" he whispered, trying to make sense of her words. "Dad doesn't even know?"

She shook her head, and the news rocked him to his core.

Mom ripped a paper towel off a nearby roll and mopped up her face. "I always assumed no one would find out about him. Back then, no one had DNA tests like the ones they have now."

Cade stared at her, unable to move and unable to speak. This all felt like a bad dream—a nightmare, even.

"He came to see me." More tears trailed down her cheeks. "And I asked him to leave." Her voice grew thinner and thinner with each word. "He looked so hurt," she said, almost inaudibly.

"Declan?" he asked, and she nodded.

She swiped the paper towel over her face. "I should have known this could happen."

Cade waited for her to continue.

"He looks so much like you." She took a shuddering breath. "He has your eyes and your chin. But I never imagined how much he would look like you." She examined her shoes. "I guess I tried to block all memories of him and avoid thinking about the man he might become."

Cade nodded. He had no idea what to say to his mother.

She cupped her hand to her forehead. "I don't know what he wants from me." She studied Cade. "Do you know what he wants from us?"

Cade stood up straight. "I can't say for sure, but I think he just wants to know his family. He asked me to arrange a meeting with the three of us—you, me, and him. That's why I'm here."

Mom's expression darkened. "No. Absolutely not. I left him in the past, and that's where he belongs."

Cade stared at her, and for a moment, he didn't recognize her. She was talking about her son, her firstborn child. How could she be so cold, so callous? Declan was family, her flesh and blood. Who was this woman, and what had she done with Cade's mother?

His confusion transformed into irritation, and he suddenly felt the need to defend Declan—this man who was his *brother*. "He's a person, not some doll you left behind." Anger simmered under his skin. "You can't just pretend he doesn't exist, Mom."

"Oh yes, I can! I opted for a closed adoption for a reason."

He was so disgusted that his nostrils flared. He pulled Declan's card out of his wallet and slapped it on the table in front of her. "Here's his number in case you change your mind."

Without saying goodbye, he stalked out the back door and to his truck. He unlocked the door and began to climb in, but when he heard children calling to each other in the distance, he stopped.

He faced a park across the street, where a group of children played tag on the grass. Instead of driving away, he closed the truck door, traipsed over to the park, and took a seat on a bench. Cade had a *brother*, an older brother. While he watched the kids play, he wondered what it would have been like to grow up with an older brother. If his parents had chosen to raise Declan and him together, he could've had a playmate, a best friend, a confidant. His life could've been so different.

Hugging his arms tight against him, Cade let his thoughts whirl. He tried to imagine an alternate timeline with Declan in his life—someone to spend time with, to laugh with, to share things with. Someone to give him advice and share milestones with. Maybe Declan would have taught him how to ride a bike, how to swim, how to drive, how to ask a girl out. Grief for something he'd never known overtook him, and his eyes began to sting.

He pondered his confusing conversation with his mother, and he tried to make sense of her words. While he could understand why his mother had to give up Declan for adoption, he couldn't wrap his mind around why she would deny him now. After nearly forty years, why would she push him away? Didn't she want to know the son she hadn't seen for forty years? Didn't she feel something for him—a bond that only a mother and child had?

And if she pushed him away, did she expect Cade to do that same thing?

So many things didn't make sense, but Cade knew one thing for sure: Life as he'd known it would never, ever be the same, and neither would he.

Today had changed him forever.

✦ ✦ ✦

Cade steered the truck into the inn's driveway later that evening and breathed a sigh of relief when he spotted a cozy yellow light glowing in the kitchen. He was desperate for someone to talk to, and Everleigh was the warm, supportive friend he needed at that moment.

After parking in the garage, he ambled up the path and through the back door, where he was greeted by the delicious scent of Asian food and the melodious lilt of Everleigh's laugh. A whiff of wet paint also floated over him. What had she been up to while he was gone all afternoon?

The sound of a man's voice drifted through the air, and Cade's entire body stiffened. She wasn't alone, but he hadn't recalled seeing a vehicle parked in the driveway. He must've been so caught up in his thoughts that he missed it.

He stepped into the kitchen doorway and stopped short when he found Everleigh and Trevor sitting at *their* kitchen island—the place where Cade and Everleigh shared breakfast together every morning. A muscle jumped along Cade's jaw as Everleigh laughed at something Trevor said.

Cade tunneled his hand through his hair. The guy he suspected was up to no good was sharing a meal with Everleigh, and she was enjoying every minute of it. Trevor didn't belong there. An unpleasant emotion overwhelmed Cade, something ugly and almost painful that squeezed the air from his lungs.

Could this day get any worse?

Everleigh turned toward the doorway, and her expression lit up. "Cade!" She beckoned him. "Come eat with us. I promise I didn't cook it." She grinned and pointed to the food. "It's takeout from that new Japanese place, Tokyo Treasures. I have hibachi shrimp, and Trevor has steak. There's plenty left. You can have half of mine."

"Cade, how's it going?" Trevor waved, but Cade focused on Everleigh.

"Sorry," Cade said, his tone flat. "Didn't mean to interrupt."

"Don't be silly, man," Trevor insisted, his smile a little too bright. "Join us. It'll be fun."

Cade's stomach turned sour. This guy was so fake it was almost funny.

Everleigh's face flashed with worry. "Everything okay?"

"Yup. Enjoy your meal," he told her. Then he headed toward the back door.

Footsteps sounded behind him, and a headache began to throb behind his eyes. He kept moving, wishing he could sprint to his apartment. *Just leave me alone, Everleigh.*

"Cade!" she called after him. "Wait!" She caught up to him, grabbed his arm, and tried to turn him toward her. "Hey. Hold on. Did you talk to your mom?"

He nodded.

"What happened?"

He frowned. "Don't trouble yourself."

"Cade." Her eyes pleaded with him, and when she touched his shoulder, he edged away from her. The hurt in her eyes nearly tore him in two, but he couldn't help himself from rebuffing her. He'd already allowed her to become too important to him. "You look terrible." She reached for his face but then stopped.

"I'm fine." He ground out the words. "Please, just go back to the kitchen."

She hesitated. "Talk tomorrow?"

He nodded.

She lifted a suspicious eyebrow. "Promise?"

"Yeah. Now go back to your . . . your . . . Trevor." The words tasted bitter in his mouth.

Her pink lips formed a thin line. "I've already told you he's *not* my boyfriend."

"Could've fooled me," he muttered as he walked away from her.

He continued to the door leading up to his apartment, grateful Everleigh didn't follow him this time.

He heard a meow.

Bryant blinked up at him, and Cade felt the tension in his shoulders start to ease. "Hey, boy."

As soon as he unlocked the door, the cat scurried up the stairs. Cade dragged himself behind him, feeling as if he'd been hit by a bus. The emotions of the day had knocked the wind out of him.

When he reached the kitchen, Bryant circled Cade's feet like a shark stalking his prey. The cat sang his usual chorus of meows while Cade spooned a stinky seafood meal into the cat's bowl and set it on the linoleum. Bryant began inhaling it while Cade propped his hip against the counter and rubbed the heels of his hands in his eye sockets. He tried to erase the image of Everleigh laughing with Trevor, but it was permanently burned into his brain now, along with his disturbing conversation with his mother. He felt like he was trapped in an upside-down world where nothing made sense.

"What should I have for supper, Bryant?"

The cat continued guzzling down his meal.

He opened his refrigerator and stared at his containers of leftovers. He considered cooking something since throwing together impromptu recipes had always calmed him. It had been his best therapy after Serena left him and since he'd lost his restaurant.

But choosing ingredients sounded like too much work when he was emotionally and physically spent. He grabbed a container of leftover chicken Alfredo and pasta and stuck it in the microwave. Once it was warmed through, he flopped down on the sofa, turned on the television, and found an old action movie to stream. He tried to lose himself in the cliché story while he ate, but his mind kept replaying his mom's callous words about Declan and the scene of Everleigh laughing with Trevor. Both made his stomach roil.

Cade had no idea how he would ever recover from this terrible day.

✦ ✦ ✦

Everleigh watched Cade disappear into the doorway leading to his apartment. The pain in his eyes had stolen her breath, and she wished she could've held him captive and insisted he talk to her. She couldn't stand it when he shut down, and she knew to the depth of her soul that he was hurting. His conversation with his mother must have gone badly, and she longed to offer him some solace.

She stood in the driveway while the lights in his apartment

illuminated, and a warm golden glow escaped through the slats in the blinds. She was grateful Bryant had gone inside with him. At least Cade wasn't alone.

Her flip-flops crunched along the rock path leading back toward the inn. She climbed the back steps and returned to the kitchen, where Trevor remained eating his supper.

"Everything okay?" he asked.

"Yeah." She curled her lips up into a smile. "Sorry about that."

Trevor watched her. "Is Cade all right?"

"Uh-huh." She took a sip of Diet Coke. "He has a family situation he's working through, but he's going to be just fine." She sat up taller on the stool. "You were telling me about the time you tried water-skiing and wound up drinking more water than you meant to."

He chuckled. "Right. I was surprised to find out I'm not a very good water-skier."

Everleigh tried to focus on Trevor's story, but her thoughts were stuck on Cade. She longed to ask Trevor to leave so she could pound on Cade's apartment door until he invited her in and poured out his feelings.

But she knew she'd be wasting her time and her breath. Cade Witherspoon was the most stubborn man she'd ever known. He kept his feelings locked up tight, and she would have to figure out how to locate the key.

"So," Trevor began after they'd finished eating and cleaned up the kitchen, "should we put another coat of paint on the sunroom before I head out?"

"I'm down if you are."

He rubbed his hands together. "Then let's do it."

They spent the next couple of hours repainting the sunroom, and Everleigh continued to struggle with her worries over Cade.

"So you've gotten some offers on this place but haven't accepted them?" Trevor asked while he stood on a ladder and painted the top part of the far wall.

Everleigh worked on the trim around the door leading to the outside. "Only one from a developer."

"What did they offer?"

She swiped the back of her hand over her forehead. Even with the row of ceiling fans humming above them, the room was stifling. "A generous price—more than we're asking—but they want to knock down the inn and build luxury condos."

Trevor was silent for a few moments while he painted. "So that's why you turned them down."

"Exactly. Cade and I agree we don't want the inn demolished." She gave a little laugh. "It may be the *only* thing we agree on."

"Interesting."

She spun to face him. "What do you mean by that?"

"Oh, nothing. It just seems like you and Cade are close." He finished where he was painting, climbed down the ladder, and moved farther down the wall.

She shook her head. "We're acquaintances. Maybe we're friends?" She shrugged. "I don't know what we are, but we're definitely business partners—at least for now."

She glimpsed out the window toward the detached garage, where the lights still glowed in Cade's apartment. Once again she felt an invisible force pulling her to him.

"So you and Cade are just looking for a buyer who'll keep the inn going?" Trevor asked, swishing his paint roller back and forth.

"That's right."

"Well, I hope you find them."

She smiled. "I'm sure the right buyer is out there. We just have to be patient."

They finished the second coat, then Trevor helped her clean up the painting supplies. When it was getting dark, she walked him out to his black late-model Toyota pickup truck.

"Thanks for your help tonight," she told him.

He grinned. "It was fun."

"You and I have different ideas about what's fun," she said, laughing. "Painting is more work than fun."

"Nah. Just spending time with you is fun." He reached out and brushed his finger over her shoulder. "You have some paint there."

She found both white and yellow paint splotches dotting her blue tank top. She laughed again and then met his hopeful gaze. "I'm a mess."

"You're not a mess. You're pretty perfect," he said, and the compliment took her by surprise. He pulled his phone from his pocket. "Since I spent the afternoon and evening helping you paint, have I finally earned your phone number?"

"Oh." She paused for a moment. "I-I guess so." She rattled off the number, and he programmed it into his phone before winking at her.

Then he waved his phone in the air. "I'll call you, okay?"

"Sure. Thanks again."

"Anytime." He jogged over to his truck, which beeped as he unlocked it.

"Good night." She watched him drive away and then returned to the kitchen, where she consulted the window. Cade's apartment was dark now, and she imagined him tossing and turning in his bed.

Pushing away from the counter, she padded down the hallway toward her suite. As she stepped into the shower, she tried to oust all thoughts of Cade. She couldn't wait to see him in the morning, and when she did, she planned to force that stubborn man to open up—whether he wanted to or not.

CHAPTER 16

"GOOD MORNING," EVERLEIGH sang. She swept into the kitchen around seven o'clock, and the delicious scent of bacon washed over her. She had set her alarm for six forty-five and was planning to help him cook, but it seemed he'd gotten an early start. "What smells so incredible?"

Cade kept his back to her as he worked. "Quiche," he mumbled.

"Yum." She came to stand beside him at the counter, where he was assembling yogurt parfaits in tall glasses. "You're up early." Her heart pinched when she took in his chiseled profile and found dark circles under his dull eyes. "That looks delicious *and* beautiful."

He kept working as if he didn't hear her, and renewed worry twined through her.

"Need some help?" She pushed a lock of her hair behind her ear.

"You can set the table," he muttered. "Make coffee."

"All righty!" She tried to keep her tone light despite the anxiety nibbling at her. After starting the coffee maker, she began pulling Alana's fine china out of the buffet in the dining room. Cade continued to work at the counter, his spine and shoulders rigid and his expression empty, almost unreadable.

She set the dishes on the table but couldn't take it anymore. "Are you mad at me, Cade?" she suddenly blurted out. The silence was tearing her apart.

Cade stilled but never turned to face her. "No."

"I can't stand it when you're quiet," she whined, almost embarrassed by the desperation in her voice. "Please tell me what's wrong."

"It has nothing to do with you."

She carefully placed the silverware and racked her brain for a way to convince the man to speak. After the table was ready for their four guests, she walked back into the kitchen. "Cade, last night you promised to talk to me." She folded her hands as if saying a prayer. "Please, I wish you would," she pleaded. "I'm worried about you, and I want to help."

He finished the last parfait before scrubbing his hands.

Everleigh held her breath. The only sound in the kitchen came from the running water and muted footsteps of the guests milling about above them.

When she'd almost given up hope, Cade leaned back against the sink and wiped his hands on a paper towel. The sadness in his eyes sent a pang through her. Whatever was bothering him was serious. "I'm not angry with you, Everleigh."

"Then what is it?"

He tossed the used paper towel in the trash can. "Yesterday was a disaster."

"With your mom?"

He nodded. She waited for him to elaborate, but he remained silent, his jaw set in stone.

"What happened?"

"I'd rather not talk about it." He examined the timer on the stove.

"Cade . . ."

He held his hand up. "Not now, Everleigh. I need to finish getting breakfast ready."

The man's silence nearly drove her bonkers. The urge to take his arm and force him to sit and talk to her made her feel almost mad. But she had to respect his boundaries, no matter how they irked her. Besides, it was probably a bad idea to have a discussion like that within earshot of the guests.

"Okay," she finally conceded before busying herself with the juice glasses and mugs.

Soon the appetizing scent of the quiche was drifting into the dining room, and the two middle-aged couples who were staying at the inn were ready for their breakfast. Everleigh and Cade served them and made small talk while they ate.

Cade plastered a manufactured smile on his face while he listened to Mr. Becker's story about the fish he caught during his trip to Maine a few weeks earlier. He also nodded along with Mr. Hill's tale about the classic car show he and his wife had attended on Main Street the night before.

Soon their quiche, coffee, and parfaits were gone, and Everleigh was stacking up their dishes and carrying them to the counter. Meanwhile the guests were making their way outside to spend the day in Coral Cove.

She hoped Cade would start talking soon, but he stripped off his black apron and hung it in the pantry.

"Mr. Hill said their commode won't stop running. I bought the supplies to fix it before Alana got sick and then forgot about it. If you don't mind cleaning up the kitchen, I'll take care of it."

"Sure." She nodded, trying hard not to look flustered.

"Thanks." He hesitated and then headed for the doorway.

Everleigh sighed and shook her head. Cade was a complicated

man, but she was determined to crack him open somehow. Maybe he had good reasons for his reticence, but she *knew* she could be the friend he needed.

Everleigh hummed as she filled the dishwasher, and soon the dining table was cleared, the floor was swept, and the dishwasher was humming. She stowed the dustpan and broom and then headed to the sunroom to uncover and rearrange the furniture.

A knock on the door stopped her in the hallway, and she made a beeline to the front of the house. She opened the door, and an attractive, middle-aged woman with bright-blue eyes and graying light-brown hair stood on the porch. She looked familiar, but Everleigh couldn't place the woman as she fidgeted with her shoulder bag.

"Can I help you?" Everleigh asked.

"I'm Trisha Witherspoon, Cade's mother."

Everleigh hesitated and then smiled. "Oh, hi." She remembered her from the memorial service. "I'm Everleigh." She opened the door wide and waved her in. "Please, come inside." A lump formed in her stomach when she considered the rough conversation Mrs. Witherspoon had had with her son. She sincerely hoped she was here to clear the air.

"Thank you." Mrs. Witherspoon toyed with the hem of her shirt and gave Everleigh an uncertain expression. "I was hoping to talk to Cade."

"He's working in the Sand Fiddler Suite. Follow me." She escorted Mrs. Witherspoon up the open staircase to the first suite on the right, which included a double bed, a sitting area with a television and love seat, and a row of windows overlooking the bay.

"This is lovely." Mrs. Witherspoon moved her hand over the arm of the love seat and the cherry coffee table. "I love the antique furniture and the lace curtains."

"This was one of Alana's favorite rooms. She inherited the furniture from her grandparents' house, and she wanted to share it with her visitors." Everleigh crossed to the bathroom and rapped on the door, which was ajar. "Cade?" she called. "You have a visitor."

Movement sounded before he pushed open the door and wiped his forehead on the sleeve of his gray T-shirt. His eyes homed in on his mother, and they narrowed. "What are you doing here, Mom?"

The strain between them was unmistakable. Mrs. Witherspoon shifted her weight on her feet. "We need to talk."

Everleigh tried to make a graceful exit, but Mrs. Witherspoon and her son already seemed to have forgotten she existed. So she sneaked out of the room, softly closing the door behind her before retreating down the stairs.

While she rearranged the sunroom, she worried and worried over Cade. Were he and his mother upstairs working things out? Surely this was something the two of them could fix.

✦ ✦ ✦

"She's pretty." Mom pointed toward the doorway.

Cade ignored Mom's comment about Everleigh. "What do you want, Mom?"

"I told you—I just want to talk." She pointed to the sitting area and sat on the love seat. "Join me?"

He did as he was told and dropped onto a wing chair across from her. "What else is there to say? You made it crystal clear yesterday that you want nothing to do with your firstborn."

"I'm late for work, but I didn't want to talk to you over the phone." She blew out a deep breath, and he noticed that she somehow looked older. The gray streaks in her short, light-brown hair were more prominent, and the wrinkles around her mouth and her eyes seemed deeper. Had this unexpected news aged her overnight?

Cade settled into the chair and tried to prepare himself for whatever bomb she was going to drop today.

"Last night I told your father about . . . about Declan." Her fingers moved over the arm of the love seat.

Cade rested his elbows on his knees. "And?"

"He was shocked to say the very least."

"Rightfully so." Cade considered his father—a kind, generous, and patient man who rarely raised his voice, even when Cade was a bratty teenager. "Why didn't you tell him sooner—like thirty-four years ago?"

"It was too painful to talk about." Her voice hitched.

"But Dad would've supported you, Mom. You should know that." He brushed his hands over his shorts. "I would have too." He paused. "We both love you."

She pulled a tissue from her pocket and dabbed her eyes. "I know that. But that was a difficult part of my life that I'd tried to put behind me."

Cade was speechless, still trying to make sense of what his mother had just shared. How could anyone just forget about a child they'd brought into the world? He wasn't a father, but he hoped to become one someday—at least, he'd wanted to before Serena destroyed his belief in love. He couldn't imagine forgetting his own child. His mother's words made no sense to him at all.

If his mother could forget her older son so easily, did that mean she could forget him too?

"I can tell you're disappointed in me, Cade," she began, "but I hope you'll understand that I am just not able to let Declan into my life. And I need you to accept that."

"Why?"

"Because I need you to respect my feelings," she said, standing from the love seat.

"Mom, I'm really trying to respect your feelings, but I can't." He stood and held his palms up. "Please help me understand how you can deny your own child."

She wiped her eyes and then stashed the tissue into her pocket. "I'm not ready to see him. Please tell him I can't meet with him right now."

"But he's leaving Sunday," Cade said. "It's Tuesday, Mom. He's your family." He pointed to his chest. "He's *my* family too. Why can't you get past whatever is holding you back and go see him?"

"I can't *get past it*." She nearly spat the words at him. "You make it sound so easy, but you have no idea what I've been through," she said, her voice shaking.

He took a step toward her. "No, I don't know what you've been through. So, tell me. I'm here, and I'm listening, Mom." He paused and waited for her response, but she remained silent as she stared at him. "Please, Mom. Tell me so I can understand why you feel the need to reject your own son."

Her fingers moved over the strap of her purse as her expression paled. After a moment, she shook her head. "I can't." She glanced at her watch. "And I need to go," she muttered, hurrying across the room. She stopped in the doorway and faced him again. "If I change my mind before Sunday, I'll let you know."

Cade nodded his head.

"If you want to get to know him, that's fine. But I-I just can't." She pulled a business card out of her pocket and set it on a shelf by the door. "Bye," she said before disappearing from the suite. Seconds later, her footfalls sounded on the stairs.

He picked up the card from the shelf and wasn't surprised to see it was Declan's. Cade studied Declan's name and phone number and sighed. Sadness, hurt, confusion, and frustration roared through him. He once again pocketed the card and trudged back to the bathroom.

He tried to concentrate on his work, but his hands felt like lumps of clay. What on earth had happened to his mother? What else was she trying to forget?

✦ ✦ ✦

Cade was lost in thought later that afternoon when he spotted movement in the doorway behind him. He turned to see Everleigh standing there, leaning against the doorframe. She was effortlessly pretty, clad in a bright-pink tank top and blue jean shorts. Her face was makeup-free, and her hair was styled in a messy bun on the top of her head. Her dark eyes were focused on him, and her brow was crumpled.

"Hey," he said.

"Hey yourself." Her smile somehow eased the coiled muscles in his back. "You missed lunch."

"What time is it?"

"After two." She stepped into the bathroom and sat on the edge of the tub. "I saw you leave and then come back earlier."

"I got some supplies at the hardware store and decided to repair the toilets in all of the bathrooms while I was at it." Staying buried in mindless jobs was the best way for him to cope with stress. It was either that or cooking.

She studied him, and an expectant expression crossed her face. He could feel the curiosity and worry radiating from her, and guilt nagged at the edges of his conscience for how he'd dodged her questions earlier in the day. He'd been aware of how anxious she was to find out about what had happened with his mother, but he didn't want to risk the guests hearing their conversation. Plus, he just wasn't ready to talk about it. Doing so would feel like baring his soul.

But now he was feeling calmer, and a little more ready to share.

He stood and pointed to the sitting area in the Sand Piper Suite. "Want to talk?"

Her eyes lit up. "Yes! Please!"

He almost chuckled at the eagerness on her face. "Come on." He held his hand out to her, and when she linked her fingers with his, his pulse picked up speed. He towed her to the sofa, where she sat. Then he took the armchair across from her.

She folded her long legs under her and stared at him, looking as if she might burst with anticipation.

"Has your life ever been completely blown up?"

Her face pinched. "I'm not sure what you mean."

"I found out yesterday it's all true. I have a half brother I never knew existed."

"Really?" she squeaked.

He nodded and brushed his hands down his face. "My ex had convinced me to register with one of those DNA websites, and she picked Family Tree." He glowered. "She wanted to find out about our heritage before we had kids someday."

"Your ex?" she asked, intrigue glimmering in her eyes.

Uh-oh. He was not prepared to tell her about Serena, so he chose to avoid the question. "I sent in my swab sample, but I was never really interested in learning about any mystery relatives. Well, not until Declan found me. Sometimes Family Tree emails me updated info, but I usually just delete their messages."

"Wow," she said, drawing the word out.

"Everleigh, what would you do if you found out your mother had lied to you for your entire life? Or if you discovered a long-lost sibling?"

"I-I don't know." She paused. "How do you feel about having a brother?"

He leaned back in the chair and tried to sort through the emotions churning inside him. "I can't really explain it. It's a mixture of elation and shock." He rested his right ankle on his left knee. "My childhood was lonely. I was jealous of my buddy who was the oldest of four." He thought back to those days. "Ryan always had companions around when he went on vacations. He had someone to share things with." He scoffed. "Someone to fight with too."

"I can relate to that."

"You can?" he asked, and when she nodded, his intrigue sparked. He paused for a moment, but when she didn't elaborate, he continued. "Sure, we had a dog and even a couple of cats, but it's not the same. You can't ride your bike to the beach with your cat or play on the swing set with your dog. You know?"

She nodded.

"But it's also so shocking that I can't put it into words. I mean..." His voice trailed off while his thoughts raced.

She reached out and blanketed her hand over his, and a wave of heat careened from his hand up his arm. "I'm sorry you had a lonely childhood. That must have been difficult."

He took in the warmth in her eyes, and something inside him shifted. He licked his lips and tried to keep his thoughts on track. "I think I want Declan in my life, but I don't know how to make that happen."

"What do you mean?"

"My mom doesn't want to see him. She flat-out refused when I brought it up." He explained how Mom had rebuffed Declan and then wouldn't even consider sitting down with the two of them. "She won't tell me what happened that made her choose to reject her own child. And I can't understand why she's acting this way now."

Everleigh gave his hand a squeeze, and he took comfort in her touch. "It must have been something terrible."

"Yeah." His voice was shaky, and he cleared his throat. "Declan said he'll be in town until Sunday, so maybe my mom will change her mind before then."

She nodded, and her lips turned up in a faint smile. "I'm glad you finally told me. I was so worried about you last night and this morning." She was silent for a moment. "Cade, I'm always here for you if you need someone to talk to. Don't forget that, okay?"

Her words touched him deep in his heart. At that moment, he felt closer to her than he'd ever felt to anyone in his life. The thought scared him, and he pulled his hand back and leaned away from her in the chair. Once again, he was falling into the trap of trusting someone—a trap he recognized all too well. "Let's talk about something else."

She blinked in surprise.

"What did you mean when you said you could relate to fighting with a sibling?"

She sighed. "Harlowe and I have never gotten along."

"Never?"

She shook her head. "She's always seen me as a pain or an inconvenience. I suppose it's because when I was born, she suddenly had to share her bedroom while Landon had his own. She'd yell at me for getting into her things or interfering when she had friends over. Usual kid stuff. Sisters fighting sisters."

She shrugged, but he could tell from the wrinkle in her forehead that the situation hurt her deeply. "When we got older, I thought maybe we'd work it out and become friends. I've known other women over the years who always called their sisters their *best* friends. I always dreamed of reaching that level with her. Well, I'm twenty-seven now, and she's thirty-one, and she still can't stand me. She acts like I'm a nuisance."

The sadness flickering over her expression touched him. "That's gotta hurt," he told her.

"It does, but . . . who knows? Maybe it will get better eventually," she said, her hallmark sunniness taking over the moment. "Someday, she'll change her mind about me. I won't let her forget how much she means to me."

"And what about your brother?"

"Landon's great." Her smile widened. "We check in with each other when I'm away working, and we like to share memes or updates. He's always excited to see me when I come home. The two of us have always gotten along."

"Well, you are pretty easy to get along with." Then he held a hand up. "Most of the time, anyway."

She laughed, and his pulse bumped. "That's sweet. I'm hoping to get Harlowe to agree." Her smile dimmed slightly. "We had an argument at Alana's memorial, and she's still upset with me from that, I think."

He grimaced. "I hate to admit this, but I saw your heated discussion."

She groaned and covered her face with her hands. "I was afraid of that. So embarrassing."

"I bet it wasn't your fault. What did you fight about?"

"Well, on *that* occasion, she was mad that I had missed our dad's birthday party because of work. But I also think she's upset about Alana's will, and the fact that we're selling the inn." She sank back onto the sofa. "I've tried calling her and texting her, but she won't respond. When I see her at my parents' house, she barely says two words to me."

"I'm sorry."

"Thanks, but she's my only sister. I'll find a way to convince her I'm not her enemy."

As their gazes held, Cade's thoughts turned to Trevor and how cozy he and Everleigh had seemed last night. He had to know if she cared for him, and he prayed she didn't.

"Why was Trevor here yesterday?" he asked, already dreading the answer.

"He said he was in the area and just came by to say hi." She rested her hands in her lap. "He helped me paint the sunroom and then we ordered food." She lifted her hands as if to stave off his anger. "I only let him help me paint the room because I knew you weren't interested in doing it."

Cade studied her as frustration built inside him. "You painted the sunroom?"

She nodded.

"What color?"

"Lemonade."

He blew out a sigh.

"You told me to do it if I wanted to, and I wanted to." A proud expression overtook her face. "And it does look nice, if I do say so myself. Even Trevor agreed."

Cade pursed his lips. He didn't trust that guy, and he didn't like that she was spending time with him. Trevor seemed so comfortable with her last night, but Cade didn't want him anywhere near her *or* the inn.

"Did Trevor the handyman charge you for his time and labor?"

"No, but I paid for his dinner. And—"

"Everleigh! This guy, he's—"

She groaned. "Don't say it, Cade. He's not my boyfriend."

"I wasn't going to say that."

"Right." She chuckled and then reached over to pat his hand. "Trevor is no one to worry about. You, on the other hand?" She let out a long sigh. "I hope you won't give up on your mom, Cade. You can change her heart."

"There you go again, making it all sound so easy. You really wear rose-colored glasses."

"Maybe it's time you tried on a pair." She smiled and stood. "Can I make you a late lunch? I promise I won't set off the smoke detectors."

"No thanks. There's some leftover quiche I can eat—unless you ate it all."

"There's still some left, but I *did* eat the last yogurt parfait." She headed toward the door and then stopped. "You really are a talented chef, you know."

He sighed as he watched her leave. His life was a mess, no matter what she said. But after talking to her, he sure felt a lot better.

CHAPTER 17

ON THURSDAY, EVERLEIGH walked down the path leading to the garage. It was midmorning and she found Cade crouching next to his motorcycle and running a rag over it, shining the engine and the wheels. She rested her hands on her hips. He'd hardly said more than four words to her since their conversation, only making small talk with the guests while they served breakfast. Their friendship seemed to have taken ten steps backward, and once again, she had absolutely no clue as to why.

Cade had become important to her, and she couldn't stand to see him hurting. She had searched her mind for a way to cheer him up, and after cleaning up the breakfast dishes, an idea had finally come to her.

"All right, Cade Witherspoon," she began. "You've moped around here long enough. Today, you're coming with me."

He stood up to his full height. "I know you're not attempting to order me around." His eyes sparkled.

"I sure am. Now, come on." She waved him toward her. "Let's go, partner."

"Where are we going?"

"I need to get another coloring book, and you're going to drive me to Beach Reads."

"Coloring book?" His eyebrows drew together. "You like to *color*?"

"It relaxes me after a long shift in the NICU." She rested her hands on her hips. "What's wrong with that?"

"You really want me to answer that honestly?" His lips quirked, and for a moment, she couldn't take her eyes off them.

Then she shook herself. "Come on, Cade! Time's a wastin'! Let's go."

"Just hold on there a minute, red." He held up two fingers. "I have two conditions before I agree to this trip to town."

"Really, Cade? More conditions?" she whined.

"Yup." He propped his back against the bed of his pickup truck. "First, we take my bike." He pointed to the motorcycle. "And second, you put on your bathing suit."

A chill cascaded over her despite the warm October morning, and she stilled, her lips pressing into a flat line.

"What do you have against my bike?" he demanded, but his tone held a note of teasing.

"Nothing." She paused. "But I'm not going to swim." She pointed to the sky. "Besides, who swims in October?" She tried to laugh, but it came out as a squeak.

"You're a local. Surely you've been to the beach this time of year. The water temperature is probably in the mid-seventies."

She knew he was right, but she didn't respond.

His eyes seemed to assess her, and another chill gripped her, a different kind. "Do you trust me?" he asked, his voice low and warm.

She hesitated but then nodded. "For some silly reason, yes. I do."

He grinned, and her heart came alive. "Then put on your suit, partner. I'll grab mine and meet you back here."

She hurried to her room and donned her two-piece bathing suit before pulling on her favorite jean shorts and a bright-green tank top, along with her green high-top sneakers. Fear gripped her as she thought about stepping into the ocean water, but she dismissed it. Right now, she was focused on brightening Cade's world, and she'd worry about her own issues later. She crammed two towels into a backpack and then slipped it onto her shoulders before rushing out the back door.

Back at the garage, Cade stood by his motorcycle and held out a black helmet. He wore dark-gray swim trunks and a pale-blue T-shirt that complemented his glorious eyes.

He nodded toward the bike, and she noticed that he'd added a seat that was positioned on the fender. "You ready?"

"I think so." She gnawed her lower lip.

"I promise I won't let anything happen to you." He held up the helmet. "Would it be all right . . . ?"

"Yeah."

He slipped the helmet onto her head and then closed the straps under her chin. His nearness made her insides burn. "Okay?" he asked.

She nodded.

He donned a matching helmet, and for a moment she wondered if the helmet she wore once belonged to his ex. Had she ridden on the back of this same motorcycle?

More questions about this woman invaded her mind. What was her name? What did she look like? Were they engaged? Had she broken his heart, or had he broken hers? How long had they dated?

Does he still love her?

"Everleigh?"

Her eyes snapped to his, and she realized she'd been staring into space. "Yeah?"

"Everything all right?"

"Uh-huh." It was a good thing he couldn't see her face since she was certain it was crimson.

He climbed onto the bike and held his hand out to her. She took it, and he guided her onto the back, where she perched on the seat. "Hold on to me as tight as you want to. You won't hurt me."

She wrapped her arms around his middle and silently marveled at the taut muscles in his back and chest. She breathed in the scent of him—laundry soap mixed with sandalwood and something uniquely Cade—and rested her head against his back.

Cade started the motorcycle, and the engine roared before he steered out of the garage. He paused to close the door before they set off down the driveway, passing the beautiful view of the bay with its rolling water glimmering in the sun.

Everleigh closed her eyes and held on tight, enjoying the feel of his body next to hers. All too soon he was steering into a space in front of Beach Reads. He killed the engine and pulled off his helmet. "What do you think?"

"It was okay." She tried in vain not to grin while removing her helmet.

"Just okay, huh?"

She shrugged, and he gave her a look of disbelief. He took her hand and helped her off the bike.

"I'll wait here," he said, retrieving his phone from his back pocket and staring at the screen.

"Oh no, you won't." She tugged his hand, but he didn't budge. "If you come with me, I'll buy you ice cream."

"Can I get a lollipop and a sticker too?" he deadpanned.

She rested her hands on her hips. "Cade, you are the most stubborn man I've ever known."

"Funny." He touched his chin. "I think you've told me that before."

"Please come with me," she begged.

"Nope."

She stared at him as determination rolled through her.

After an awkward moment, he crammed his phone into his pocket. "Fine. I'll come, but I refuse to have fun."

"We'll see about that."

They walked through the store's double doors, and she breathed in the welcoming smell of books mixed with coffee. Everleigh turned toward the front counter and spotted Callie Lewis, the owner and manager of Beach Reads. With short-cropped brown hair, large red glasses, and a distinctive voice, she always reminded Everleigh of Annie Potts's character in the original *Ghostbusters* movie—one of Alana's favorite childhood films.

A familiar pop song sang through the speakers, and Everleigh bopped along with the music while they wandered through the stacks. She spotted a sign for adult coloring books, found the book she wanted, and did a little dance as she picked it up. When she turned, she found Cade smiling at her, and her pulse stuttered.

"What?" she asked.

"You're cute when you dance."

Heat infused her cheeks. She set the book down, took his hands and started swaying back and forth. "Like this, you mean?"

His smile flattened. "I don't dance."

"Come on, Cade," she sang. "Don't be such a sourpuss. Loosen up." When he still refused to dance, she pulled her phone out. "Let's take a selfie instead."

"Why? We're in a bookstore."

"Exactly! Bookstores are some of the happiest places on earth." She held her phone up in front of them. "Lean down by me since you're so tall," she instructed, and he did as he was told. "Say cheese, Cade," she said, then snapped the photo and dropped the phone into her backpack.

"You and your selfies," he muttered, shaking his head. But the ghost of his smile remained on his lips, and his compliment echoed in her mind. *"You're cute when you dance."* Happiness bubbled through her, but she tried not to let it boil over. Soon she would be back on the road, and Cade had made it clear he was a loner. Still, she found herself wondering: *What if our circumstances were different?*

Shaking off her ridiculous thoughts, she paid for the book, and together they walked out to his motorcycle. "Ice cream?"

"I'm good," he said.

She pointed to the pizzeria. "Pizza?"

"Everleigh, it's eleven o'clock, and I'm still full from breakfast," he said. "We had a deal, remember?" He pointed to the strap peeking out from behind her shirt. "You wore your suit for a reason, right?"

She nodded.

"I'll take good care of you. I promise." He held his hand out to her.

She allowed him to guide her to the beach, where they walked out onto the warm sand. While it wasn't as crowded as it had been during the height of tourist season, about a dozen kids hooted and shrieked as they bobbed in the waves. A few families were scattered around the area, sitting on chairs and under umbrellas, and a group of teenagers laughed and jumped in the air during a rowdy game of volleyball. The aroma of cocoa butter hovered over Everleigh, and seagulls soared above them through the cloudless blue sky.

Cade reached over his head and whipped off his shirt, and she tried not to stare at his tanned chest and arms. "Ready?"

No. She gulped air. As she stared out at the waves, her legs began to shake. Fear gripped her as memories of the rip current, the lifeguards, the darkness, the choking, all rolled through her mind.

Cade's expression became warm, and his hand caressed her shoulder. "Trust me, darlin'."

Oh, that nickname really turned her to jelly.

"Okay." The word was barely audible over the cacophony around them. Shaking even more now, she pulled off her shirt, shorts, and shoes.

Cade's gaze roamed over her, and the approval in his eyes made her heart flutter. He held his hand out to her, and she hesitated before linking her fingers with his. They proceeded to the edge of the water together, and then she released his hands and stopped, frozen in place while the waves rolled toward her. The water kissed her toes and she jumped back, nearly falling backward onto the sand.

"Everleigh." Cade's voice was close to her ear and reminded her of velvet. "It's okay." He rested his hand on the small of her back. "I've got you. I'll be beside you the entire time."

She gripped his hard bicep and took one step onto the wet sand.

"Good job," he said.

She took another step just as a wave crashed, and the water rushed around her feet and up to her ankles. Her body trembled like a leaf in a windstorm.

"Let's take another step together," he said.

The encouragement in his eyes propelled her forward. She took two steps and then froze.

"You're doing great," he told her.

Another wave crashed, and the water reached her shins.

Cade leaned down. "Ready to go out a little bit farther?"

She studied the waves, and a memory swelled in her mind. She was back in the water with her brother and his friends, and the ocean was dragging her under. Her throat began to close, and she shook her head. "I-I can't. I can't do this anymore. I need to get out of the water."

"It's okay, darlin'." Cade took her hands in his. "I got you."

"I-I . . ."

A wave crashed, and she gripped his biceps and flung herself against him. She nestled her head against his chest and held on as the water moved around them. Her breath came in short bursts as she stared up at him.

Cade smiled. "You got this."

She nodded and held on to him.

"Want to try to go a little farther?"

She turned back toward the water and felt a surge of confidence. "Maybe."

"That's the spirit."

They slowly plodded out until the water was up to her thighs. Then she stopped and held on to Cade's arms as the waves broke around them.

She took a deep breath. "I . . . I think I want to go in up to my waist."

"What a daredevil." He grinned, and she basked in his joy.

They moved out farther, and when the water was up to her waist, she stopped. They rode a wave up together, and when they came back down, she grabbed Cade as tightly as she could. He held her close against him, and the chill of air above the water raced across every inch of her bare skin. She wrapped her arms around his neck, and he wound his around her waist. She rested her head on his shoulder while they rode out a few more waves. She felt her fear beginning to dissolve, as she silently enjoyed the warm, salty water and the sound of the ocean.

Everleigh relished the feeling of being in his arms. For a moment, she let herself wonder what it would be like to be more than Cade's friend, to have him be someone special in her life. But it was a fleeting thought.

When the waters calmed, she released his neck and pulled slightly away from him. Her embarrassment crept in the moment she realized she'd been clinging to him for dear life. "I'm sorry."

"Don't be." He raked his hand through his wet hair and then reached for her, his brow pinching. "Are you okay?"

"Yeah." She started toward the shore. "But I'm ready to go." The moment she said it, a wave pulled her backward, crashing over her and knocking her off-balance. She teetered, and a scream tore from her throat.

Cade grabbed her waist and pulled her upright. "Hey! It's okay." He held her close again. "I got you."

She nodded and allowed him to steady her through another wave.

"Relax." He inclined his face next to hers. "Just trust me, okay?" His voice was husky next to her ear, sending a tremor through her. "Close your eyes."

She did as she was told.

"Take a deep breath and clear your mind," he said. "Just breathe and let the water move over you. Try not to think about the past. Instead, try to feel the water in the moment."

She breathed in deeply and cleared her mind. She concentrated on the feel of Cade's body holding hers in place, and his hands resting on her hips. She allowed the waves to flow, gently lifting and surrounding her, and her body relaxed. Her fear seemed to dissolve, and the peacefulness of the water and the security of Cade's strong presence combined to enfold her in a warm hug. For a moment, Everleigh was in control. She was confident.

A few more waves crashed around her, and she craned her neck over her shoulder and smiled up at Cade. "Oh my goodness."

He lifted his eyebrows. "You good?"

"I'm perfect."

He grinned, and her heart kicked hard. "Ready to go?" he asked.

"Yeah."

"Hold on to me," he ordered.

She gripped his magnificent bicep, and he guided her back out to shore. When they reached the dry sand, she smiled up at him and rested her hand on the muscled plane of his chest. "Thank you."

"You're welcome."

Then she threw herself into his arms and hugged him with all of her might. She closed her eyes and listened to the steady cadence of his heartbeat for a few moments.

Suddenly, a bark of laughter burst from her mouth. "I actually went into the water. I waded up past my waist. I can't believe I did it." She pulled him closer, and he rested his hands on her lower back.

"I guess that means you're glad you did it." His voice rumbled in his hard chest.

She reluctantly released him. "I am. I beat my fear, Cade. All because of you."

"Pretty sure I just helped." He touched her nose before turning to find her backpack and pull out the towels. They dried off and pulled on their clothes, the autumn beach air whistling across their skin.

"We need to take a selfie."

"Another one?" he asked.

"Yes! This is a momentous day."

"That's two today, Everleigh. You're approaching my lifetime selfie limit," he said.

She fished her phone out of her backpack, and when he leaned down into frame, he rested his hands on her shoulders. A pleasant shiver traveled through her body. His smile was bright when she snapped the photo, and she was *certain* she hadn't reached his selfie limit. In fact, he seemed to like taking photos with her more than he wanted to admit.

"How'd we look in that one?" he whispered in her ear, sending more chills dancing through her.

"Perfect," she managed to say. While they headed back up the beach toward the boardwalk, she wondered if it was the right moment to ask about Declan. "Have you heard from your mom?"

His happy expression darkened. "Afraid not."

"How about Declan?"

"Nope."

She could feel the sadness radiating off him, and her chest ached. They continued across the boardwalk and down the street to his waiting motorcycle. He put on his helmet and attached the strap while she pulled on hers and climbed on the bike.

Before they pulled away, she spotted a large poster she hadn't noticed on the front window of the bookstore. It advertised the Coral Cove Fall Festival on Saturday, and an idea overtook her. Cade had helped her today, and now she was going to help him.

She smiled as the plan took shape in her mind.

CHAPTER 18

CADE PARKED THE motorcycle in the garage, and as soon as Everleigh disentangled herself from him, his body felt cold without her touch. He had relished every second she'd held on to him while they drove to and from the shops on Main Street. And holding her while they were in the water was almost too much for his heart.

Once again, he could feel himself getting too attached to her, but he couldn't help it. He couldn't resist her—her laugh, her kind and caring heart, her sense of humor, her fun-loving demeanor, her adorable antics, even dancing in the bookstore—not to mention how drop-dead gorgeous she was.

He had to evict those ridiculous thoughts from his head. Not only was he not interested in a relationship, but she was also planning to leave. Any feelings he developed for her would just send him spiraling with another broken heart, and he couldn't survive that again.

Cade climbed off the bike and then held his hand out to her. She took it and allowed him to lift her off the seat. He enjoyed the feel of her soft skin. In fact, he would never get used to how it made his own skin heat up.

"That was so fun!" She struggled with the straps on the helmet. "Um, Cade? A little help, please?"

He chuckled. "Allow me." He unclipped the strap and then lifted the helmet off her head.

"Thank you." She adjusted her backpack on her shoulders. "I'm going to get changed and run to the grocery store. Need anything?"

He considered the question. "We're getting low on eggs."

"Anything else?" she asked, and he shook his head. "Okay then. See you later." She gave him a little wave before heading toward the house with a spring in her step.

Cade placed the helmets on a shelf in the garage.

Bryant meowed and rubbed against his shin.

"I guess it's time to feed you." Cade and Bryant climbed the steps to the apartment, and just as Cade set the bowl full of cat food on the floor, his phone rang.

Roger's name lit up the screen. "What's up, Rog?" he asked.

"I could've sworn I saw you riding through town with a redhead on the back of your bike."

Cade plucked a can of Coke from the refrigerator. "You following me?" He flopped down on the sofa and opened the can, which fizzed in response.

"You and Everleigh looked good on the bike together."

Instead of responding, Cade took a long draw from the can. He wasn't going to admit out loud just how much he had enjoyed having Everleigh on the back of his bike, feeling her pressed against him.

"I haven't talked to you in a while. What's new?"

"Not much. How about you?" He wasn't sure it was time to share about Declan and the drama with his mother yet.

"Well, I've been out with Quinn a few times."

"How's that going?"

"Great." He could hear Roger's smile in his voice. "Have you had any bites on the place?"

Cade set the can on the end table. "A couple more developers came by, but Everleigh turned them down. That's been it so far. I'm still hoping she gives up and tells me to run it while she goes back on the road." Even as he said the words, he dreaded the idea of Everleigh leaving. That said, there was no way he and Everleigh could ever be more than friends. Any other notion seemed ridiculous.

"Did anything happen with that guy that was at the beach?"

"Which guy?"

"The one who was hanging around Everleigh?"

Cade frowned. "He was here the other night and helped her paint the sunroom."

"Is she seeing him?"

The cat jumped up on the back of the sofa and rubbed his head against Cade's shoulder. "She says she isn't seeing him, but *he's* definitely interested."

"What about you?"

"What about me?"

"Are *you* interested in her?"

"No." Cade angled his body toward the cat and began massaging his fuzzy ear. Bryant relaxed over the back of the sofa and purred with his eyes closed. "Regardless of what happens with the inn, she's not staying in town anyway."

"You sound disappointed."

"Just stating a fact. If the right buyer comes along, maybe we'll sell the B&B. And if not, she'll go back to working as a traveling nurse, and I'll run the place myself. End of story."

An engine rumbled, and he looked out the window to see Everleigh driving her Trailblazer toward the road. She seemed awfully excited to go to the grocery store. What was she up to?

"Well, I'll let you go. Give me a call soon, and we'll get together."

"I will. Bye." Cade disconnected the call and continued to pet the cat while trying to banish the memory of Everleigh in her two-piece bathing suit. The feel of her holding on to him, the sound of the gentle rolling waves at the beach . . . He had to get his feelings for her under wraps. Anything more would only mean disaster for Cade Witherspoon.

✦ ✦ ✦

Everleigh's heart began to race as she parked her SUV in front of Cade's mother's store, Crafty Creations. Now that Cade had helped her overcome her fear of the ocean, she yearned to do something nice for him in return. The flyer for the fall festival had sparked an idea in her mind—something she could do to help bring his family together.

She could tell the situation with Declan and their mother was breaking Cade's heart. And she cared about Cade, even though they'd never be more than . . . What even *were* they? Acquaintances? Friends? Business partners?

Everleigh hefted her purse onto her shoulder and yanked open the door at Crafty Creations. A bell chimed to announce her entrance, and a buzz of conversations swirled around her as customers lingered in the aisles, filling up their shopping baskets with art supplies. She weaved past a group of teenagers discussing a beaded bracelet making kit and trading friendship bracelets for an upcoming concert.

Her plan came together in her mind as she approached the register, where a young woman with a nose ring and pink highlights in her blond hair stood.

Everleigh waved to her. "Hi. I saw the poster in the window advertising the fall festival on Saturday, and I heard that many of the Coral Cove retailers were going to have booths there. Will you have one too?"

The young woman shrugged. "We always do."

"Great." Everleigh searched the store for Cade's mom but didn't see her. "Will Mrs. Witherspoon be there?"

"In the booth?"

"Yeah." Everleigh paused, hoping the answer would be yes.

The young woman nodded. "She's holding a wreath-making class to try to drum up more business."

"Fantastic!" Everleigh clapped her hands.

The young woman studied Everleigh as if she were nuts, then pulled a clipboard out from under the counter. "We're already taking reservations. Did you want to sign up for the class?"

"Nope, but thank you." Everleigh started backing away. "I'll see you Saturday."

"Um. Okay . . ."

Everleigh moved through the aisles and out to her SUV. She drove through Coral Cove toward the bay and followed the winding road to the Rosewood Inn, a sprawling gray colonial with a wraparound porch decorated with swings and planters containing colorful flowers. She steered into the parking lot and smiled when she spotted a dark-colored sedan with a North Carolina tag. She hoped it was Declan's car.

She hurried up to the sidewalk, and as she reached the porch steps, the front door opened. As if by fate, Declan stepped outside. She waved to him. "Declan, hi."

"Everleigh, right?"

"That's right. I was hoping you'd be here."

His brow puckered. "You were?"

"Yeah." She folded her hands. "I wanted to invite you to the Coral Cove Fall Festival on Saturday so you can get a real feel for the town before you go home."

His expression flashed with suspicion.

"Cade will be there."

He studied her for a moment, and her skin felt itchy under his scrutiny. "Did Cade ask you to invite me?"

"Uh-huh. Yup. He sure did." She squirmed at the half-truth, but she considered this a harmless little white lie—something she didn't ordinarily do. Surely Declan and Cade would understand she was fibbing for the sake of bringing their family together. "Will you meet us there around eleven on Saturday?"

"Meet you where?"

"In front of the bookstore, Beach Reads."

Declan paused, and she held her breath.

Finally, he nodded. "Yeah. I'll be there."

"Great!" She resisted the urge to jump up and down like an excited child. "We'll see you then."

They said goodbyes, and Everleigh started toward her car. When Declan called her name again, she spun to face him. His eyes seemed to sparkle with hope, and at that moment, they reminded her of Cade's.

"Thank you," Declan said.

"You're welcome," she told him. As she climbed into her SUV, she compared how much Cade wanted Declan in his life to her rocky relationship with her sister. Renewed hope plunged through her as she fished her phone out of her backpack purse and dialed Harlowe's number.

When it went to voicemail, she tried to disregard the ache deep inside her.

After the beep, she said, "Harlowe, I miss you." She took a deep breath. "I'll be at the fall festival on Saturday, and I hope you'll be there too." She pressed her hand to her forehead. "Let's work this out," she said, her voice sounding thin. "You're my only sister, and I love you. Call me back. Bye." Surely this message would touch Harlowe's heart and encourage her to reach out.

✦ ✦ ✦

Everleigh hummed to herself while she carried a cup of coffee down the rock path toward Cade's apartment. It was Saturday morning, and the sun was hidden behind a cluster of dark clouds. The mid-October air was warm, and the marigolds danced in the breeze. It was almost ten, and she was surprised she hadn't seen Cade yet. But since their guests had left earlier that morning and insisted they would get breakfast on the road, Cade had most likely taken the opportunity to sleep in.

She checked around for Bryant, but when he didn't appear on the porch, she assumed he had spent the night in Cade's apartment. She hurried over to his door and knocked. After a few beats, she knocked again.

"Cade? Cade!" she called. "You up?" She rapped on the door again, and after a few moments, muted footsteps sounded on the stairs.

The door swung open, and Cade, yawning, dragged a hand through his messy, light-brown hair. He wore a black tank top and athletic shorts, and Everleigh yearned to run her finger along the scruff lining his angular jaw. "Where's the fire?" he asked before yawning again.

"Good morning." She held the coffee out to him. "This is for you." She lifted her chin. "Just how you like it. A little bit of creamer and two sugars."

He took a sip. "Thanks. It's perfect." He took another drink and studied her. "Why are you up so early?"

"It's almost ten, and you need to get dressed." She pointed to his shorts and tried not to stare at his legs.

"Why?" His eyes questioned her.

"You're taking me to the fall festival."

He shook his head. "Sorry, darlin', but I'm not a fan of crowds. I don't do festivals."

"But I haven't been to one in years, and you're going to take me." She clapped her hands. "So, chop-chop. Let's go."

He drank more coffee, his eyes watching her over the top of the mug. "Why don't you ask Trevor to take you?" His tone held a hint of snark or possibly something else.

She rolled her eyes. "Because I want *you* to take me, Cade."

Surprise traveled across his face, and he tapped the doorframe with his free hand. "Give me ten minutes. We'll take my truck."

"Wonderful!" she said with excitement. Then she peeked past him. "I haven't seen Bryant today. Is he with you?"

Cade grinned, and her pulse spiked. "He's still in bed. He didn't want to get up either."

She laughed. "I'll meet you at your truck." She did a little dance as she took off toward the inn. Today was going to be perfect.

✦ ✦ ✦

Cade glanced at Everleigh beside him on the bench seat of his truck. She kept shifting—crossing and uncrossing her long, slender legs before folding her arms over her pink T-shirt. "Too much caffeine?" he asked.

"Huh?" Her dark eyes met his, and an attractive flush tinged her cheeks. "Sorry. What'd you say?"

He swept his hand over his mouth. "You seem preoccupied."

"Oh." She faced the window again. "It's been years since I've gone to this festival."

"Oookay." He had a feeling it was more than that, but he'd gotten used to how excited Everleigh got about mundane things and even found it endearing. He parked in one of the last free spots a couple of blocks away from Main Street, and together they started down the sidewalk.

Everleigh consulted her phone and then stuck it in the back pocket of her jean shorts. Then she picked up speed.

"What's the rush?" he asked.

"No reason." She continued to walk briskly.

She was up to something, but he couldn't imagine what.

They reached Main Street, and the enticing scents of popcorn, funnel cakes, nachos, and fresh-baked pastries greeted him. Booths lined the middle of the road, selling everything from food to jewelry to collectibles, and groups of people moved around them. Pop music floated out of nearby speakers. A gigantic inflatable slide sat at the end of the street, and children took turns hurling themselves down it while shrieking at the top of their lungs.

Everleigh placed her hand on his bicep and nudged him along. "Follow me."

"Where are we going?"

"To have fun."

"Can you be a little more specific?"

"Just hurry up!" she exclaimed.

He sighed. "Yes, ma'am." She steered him past nearly a thousand families with strollers until they reached the sidewalk in front of Beach Reads. Then she searched the crowd as if looking for someone.

"Care to clue me in on who we're looking for?" he asked.

"No one," she sang.

"Everleigh," he began, "I can tell you're up to something."

She beamed and grabbed his arm. "Look! There's Declan! What a coincidence."

He followed her gaze and spotted Declan milling about near a group of kids eating cotton candy.

So *that* was what she'd been up to. He couldn't stop his smile. It was the perfect day, and he was with his gorgeous friend. And now, his brother too.

His brother.

His heart felt light.

"Declan!" She cupped her hands around her mouth and hollered, "Declan! Over here!"

His brother turned and waved before sidestepping the kids and joining them on the sidewalk. His expression was sheepish. "Hi there. This festival is crowded."

Everleigh's smile bounced between Cade and Declan. "Let's enjoy it."

CHAPTER 19

THE SKY ABOVE them was dotted with dark clouds as they began walking around the festival together. Everleigh continued to grin, appearing as if she might burst with happiness that her plan to bring Cade and Declan together had succeeded. Silence extended between them though, and Cade tried to think of something to say to his brother.

"Where are you from, Declan?" Everleigh finally asked.

"Elizabeth City," he said. "It's about four hours from here, depending upon traffic."

"That's near the coast by the Outer Banks, right?" she asked.

Declan nodded.

"It's pretty there."

"It is."

A group of teenagers, each of them licking an ice cream cone, came toward them, and Cade moved to the edge of the sidewalk to let them pass.

He scratched his neck. "You mentioned that you and your wife are starting a family, right?"

Declan nodded.

Everleigh's face lit up even more. "When's she due?"

"January."

"Congratulations," Everleigh told Declan before smacking Cade's arm. "You're going to be an uncle."

Cade's heart expanded. In the blink of an eye, he'd gone from being an only child to having a brother *and* a sister-in-law and soon a niece or nephew. He was so overwhelmed that he couldn't speak for a moment.

"How long have you been married?" Everleigh asked.

Cade silently marveled at how she effortlessly kept the conversation going. He considered himself socially awkward, always racking his brain to think of something to say. But social graces came naturally to Everleigh. He imagined she was always the life of the party.

"Almost eight years. It took us longer than we expected to start a family."

Everleigh nodded. "I'm sure that was very frustrating."

Declan rubbed his jaw. "Yes, it was."

They continued walking for a few moments, and then Everleigh suddenly held up her phone. "This is a special day. Let's take a selfie!"

Cade couldn't stop his smile as a pleasant feeling moved through him. Leave it to Everleigh to want to commemorate this.

She pushed her phone into Cade's hand. "You're the tallest, so you need to take it." Then she held on to his arm and rested against him. "Come on, Declan," she instructed. "Lean in close."

Cade's brother complied, and Cade's grin was wide as he snapped a few photos before giving her phone back to her.

"Perfect!" she exclaimed, examining the shots. Then she pointed toward an empty bench. "You two sit, and I'll get us some drinks," she said before taking off toward a food truck.

Cade shared an awkward smile with Declan.

"I get the feeling you weren't expecting to see me today," his brother said.

"No, I wasn't." Cade shook his head. "Everleigh woke me up less than an hour ago, banging on my apartment door and insisting she wanted me to bring her to the festival."

Declan sat on the bench. "She arranged this."

Cade sat beside him. "Looks like it."

Everleigh took her spot in a long line at the food truck several yards away from them, and examined her phone while she waited.

Cade nodded toward her. "I guess she wanted us to have a chance to get to know each other."

"Yeah." Declan chuckled. "Seems that way." He looked out toward Everleigh and then back at him. "Are you two . . . ?" He waved a finger between them.

"No, no." Cade shook his head. "We're just running the inn together."

"She told me that when I stopped by, but it seems like you're more than just business partners. You two have chemistry."

Cade considered that while he rested his arm on the bench. "She's . . ." *Pretty special.* "A really good friend."

"A really good friend, huh?" Declan nodded, looking unconvinced.

"What's your wife's name?" Cade asked.

"Stephanie." Declan settled back on the seat. "We met through mutual friends. We dated for a few years before I finally found the courage to propose. Ever been married?"

Cade moved his fingers over a loose piece of wood on the arm of the worn bench. "Almost. At the last minute, my fiancée decided she had other plans. Better plans, I suppose."

"Ouch."

"That's an understatement." Cade gave him a wry smile. "I was living in Alabama. After the breakup I decided to move home to Coral Cove, and that's when I got the job at the inn." He explained how Alana had passed away and left the inn to him and Everleigh.

"I noticed it's for sale."

Cade nodded. "Everleigh wants to sell. She's convinced Alana left it to us so we could use the money to make our dreams come true. But I still don't want to sell it." Eager to change the subject, he asked, "Did you grow up in Elizabeth City, Declan?"

"Nearby in Moyock. I went to Elizabeth City State and then just settled there. I was never very adventurous. How about you?"

"I joined the army after high school. I didn't have the grades or interest in college." He shrugged. "Then I wound up in Alabama, almost got married, and came home."

Everleigh turned toward them and waved.

Cade couldn't help but wave back at her. She was just so cute. Actually, she was radiant with her thick red hair swinging in a ponytail and a pair of pink sunglasses shielding her eyes.

He turned his attention back to his brother. "Did you have a good childhood?"

Declan rested his right ankle on his left knee. "Thankfully, yes. My folks are great. My mom taught second grade but retired a few years ago. Dad works in finance, and that's how I got my start. I work for his firm, and he wants me to take it over when he retires—or *if* he retires. But we spent a lot of time at the beach swimming, sailing, fishing, and all that. I was an only child, but my folks have always made it clear that I was a blessing to them. They spent years trying to conceive and then went to an adoption agency. We're grateful to have each other."

Declan turned his attention toward the crowd, but he seemed lost in thought. "They told me I was adopted when I was about ten." He was silent for a few moments, and a family moved past them. Three identical toddlers rode in a long stroller, pushed by two haggard-looking parents. "I've always wanted to know where I came from. And with the baby coming and all, it seemed like the right time to start my search for answers."

"How'd you find me?" Cade asked.

"It wasn't that difficult." Declan's expression seemed sheepish. "I started out with that Family Tree website and tried contacting you through there, but you didn't answer."

Cade grimaced. "Sorry. My ex signed me up for it, so when we broke up, I sort of forgot it existed."

"Makes sense. When I didn't hear back that way, I searched social media. I sent you a friend request."

Cade held his hands up. "Sorry again. I don't spend much time on social media anymore."

Declan laughed. "Well, I get it. But your email address is set to public on your page." He winced. "I sound like a stalker, don't I?"

"Not a stalker, just a determined sleuth."

Declan pointed at him. "Exactly. That sounds less creepy. Anyway, after you didn't answer my email, I searched the internet and found your name on the inn website." He tapped his chin. "Also, thanks to social media, I found the connection to your mother and quickly figured out she owned a store here in Coral Cove." He tapped his fingers on his thigh. "I just kept digging until I found you both."

"I'm glad you did," Cade said softly. He was once again overwhelmed with emotion for this new person in his life.

Declan smiled. "I appreciate that."

"I'm sorry I haven't reached out to you since we first met. I just wasn't sure . . ."

"I get it." Declan nodded. "Really, I do. This is uncharted territory for me too."

"I hope you like Coke, Declan." Everleigh appeared in front of them balancing a drink tray with three large cups, along with three baked pretzels. "And pretzels."

Cade popped up. "Let me help you." He took the tray from her, and when their fingers brushed, a zip of heat raced through his body.

"Thanks." She smiled at him.

"Please, sit." Cade nodded toward the bench. "I'll stand."

They dug into their pretzels and watched the crowd while Everleigh peppered Declan with questions about his life in Elizabeth City.

After their pretzels were gone, she popped up to her feet. "Come on. There's so much to see at this festival." She led them around, pointing out different booths. Cade relaxed and sipped his soda while relishing the time spent with both his brother and Everleigh.

"Let's go this way." She took Cade's arm and guided him past a booth selling beach-themed shirts and accessories. Then she stopped when they reached the booth beside it. "Oh, look. It's Crafty Creations!"

Cade scanned his mother's booth. She had various art supplies for sale, along with sign-up sheets for classes and a newsletter. In the back he spotted his mother teaching a wreath-making class.

"Oh, wow!" Everleigh sang. "I've always wanted to make a fall wreath." She held on to Cade's arm and yanked him toward the booth.

But this time he pulled back. "Hold on a sec, Everleigh." He turned to Declan and found anxiety flickering over his features. "My— I mean, *our* mom is here."

"I see that." Declan swallowed, and his Adam's apple bobbed.

Everleigh bounced on the balls of her feet. "Should we go say hello to her?"

The muscles in Cade's shoulders compressed as he turned to Declan and waited for his reaction. "Do you want to?"

"Yeah," Declan said, determination replacing his worry. "Yeah, I do."

"Then let's go." Cade waved Declan over, and they moved to the back of the booth. Mom was instructing her students how to attach bows to their wreaths. Everleigh stood near the front of the booth, perusing a display of adult coloring books. It seemed her plan today was not only to bring Cade and Declan together but also to bring them together with their mom. He wondered how long she'd been cooking up this scheme, but he'd ask her about that later.

Mom glanced over at Cade and Declan, then did a double take. Her eyes widened and her face went slack, and she whispered something to the young blond woman beside her. She wore a pastel tie-dye shirt and what looked like dozens of beaded bracelets. Lorna, her assistant manager, he realized.

"Okay, folks. Now you can decide which fall flowers you'd like to include on your wreaths," Lorna announced.

Mom scurried over to Cade and Declan and divided a look between them. Fear and confusion seemed to overtake her face. "What's going on here?"

"Can you step away from your class for a few minutes?" Cade asked.

She hesitated. "Why?"

"So we can talk," Cade said, working to keep his voice even despite the irritation curling through him.

Mom shook her head. "No, no, I can't." She took a few steps backward, away from them.

Cade took in the pain in Declan's eyes. He was determined to help Declan get through to their mother. He had to. He wanted Declan in his life, and he yearned for Mom to accept him too.

"Mom, please." Cade could hear the desperation in his tone. "Just give us a few minutes. Then you can get back to your class."

Her lip trembled. "No."

This couldn't be happening. Declan was standing right in front of her! How could she reject him as if he were nothing? "Mom," Cade began, his voice rising, "Declan is your *son*."

She sniffed and wiped her eyes, and then her spine straightened. "I'm sorry," she said, her tone wavering. "I-I-I just can't."

Cade's lip curled. "His wife is expecting their first child. You're going to be a grandmother."

Her eyes glistened. "This isn't a good time." Her words sounded scratchy.

"When will be?" Cade's voice boomed loudly—louder than he'd anticipated. Out of the corner of his eye, he spotted a couple of older women staring at him from behind the yarn display.

Declan rested his hand on Cade's shoulder. "It's okay, Cade. Really."

How could Declan be so calm?

"I-I don't know," she blurted out before making a beeline back to her class. "I'm sorry about that interruption." She gave her class a stiff smile. "How are we doing with those flowers?" she asked, and when she held up her hands, they were visibly trembling.

Cade shook his head while disappointment and fury warred inside him. "Declan, I'm so sorry. I thought maybe if she saw us together, she would be willing to talk to you."

Declan stared at their mother while hurt and longing glistened in his eyes. "I did too, but for some reason, she can't stand to even look at me."

Even Everleigh looked deflated. "What if I ask her to meet us somewhere later? Do you think she'd consider it?"

Declan's posture wilted. "It's no use. I've tried." He held out his hand, and Cade shook it. "I'm glad I finally got to meet you, but I think it's time to head home. If your mother changes her mind about me, let me know." Then he turned and headed down the sidewalk.

Anger and grief churned in Cade's gut as he watched his brother walk away.

"Declan, wait!" Everleigh called after him. "Wait!" She started after him, but Cade pulled her back to his side.

"Everleigh," he said as she called out for Declan again. *"Everleigh!"*

She quieted and spun to face him. "What?"

He shook a finger at her as fury plunged through him. "You set this up."

"I was only trying to help." She took Cade's arm and attempted to yank him forward, but he stood in place as if cemented to the sidewalk. "You can't let him go, Cade. He's your brother."

"You're right. He's *my* brother." He pointed to his chest. "Do me a favor and stay out of *my* family business. You've done enough damage." Then he stomped away from her and headed toward his truck.

He couldn't get out of there fast enough. The entire day had been a disaster. He'd found his brother, and just as he was getting to know him, he'd lost him again. And he had Everleigh to thank for it. This was exactly why he couldn't get close to people. As soon as he let someone in, they blew up his life.

He was better off alone. Always had been and always would be.

✦ ✦ ✦

Everleigh's insides were tangled up as Cade disappeared into the crowd.

Grief poured over her, and she sniffed, hoping to hold back the tears stinging her eyes. She couldn't lose it here in the middle of a festival. She'd look like a complete weirdo if she did. She observed Mrs. Witherspoon conducting her class, and Everleigh tried to comprehend how that woman could deny her child in public. At the same time, how could Everleigh judge her? She didn't know the circumstances around her choice to give Declan up for adoption—but it still didn't make sense that she wouldn't want to know him now.

She'd hoped that by arranging this impromptu family meeting, Cade, Declan, and their mother would be able to connect and bond. But it had all blown up in her face. Now she'd lost Cade's precious friendship and messed up his relationship with his mother and brother. She was only trying to help, but she'd made a mess of things instead.

Everleigh's heart sank while Cade's harsh words echoed in her mind:

"Do me a favor and stay out of my *family business. You've done enough damage."*

Another sob brewed in her chest, and Everleigh took off toward the park. She found a secluded bench and dropped onto it just as her tears broke free. She covered her face with her hands and tried to get her emotions under control.

She wiped her eyes with a tissue and then looked out toward Main Street. It would be a long walk back to the inn—around four miles—but at least the cloudy sky offered some relief from the sun. If she started walking now, she could be home before supper. Not that she was hungry. Food was the furthest thing from her mind.

More tears fell, and she covered her face with her hands again. She had to get it together. Crying wasn't going to solve anything.

"Everleigh?"

She looked up and found Trevor standing over her, holding out a napkin. Unable to speak, she accepted the napkin and wiped her eyes and nose. "Thanks," she finally eked out, nodding to the empty seat beside her. Trevor lowered himself down.

Concern clouded his features. "Want to talk about it?"

She slouched over the bench. "I made a mess of everything."

"I find that hard to believe." He took her hand, but she felt nothing special about his touch.

She recalled the heat coursing through her skin when she'd dragged Cade by his arm through the crowd in search of Declan. Of course, her pulse always sped up whenever that man smiled at her—and when he'd whispered against her ear as they stood together in the waves, she thought her heart might explode. But she shoved the thought away. Cade wasn't even her friend anymore. Any silly attraction she felt for him was in vain.

A middle-aged couple walked by holding hands and laughing together, and more sadness tugged at her. Would she ever experience a relationship with someone who truly loved her?

That dramatic thought almost made her laugh. Why was she thinking about relationships at all? She didn't have room in her life for anyone. She was always working, always moving. Love didn't exactly fit into her schedule.

But what if she stayed in Coral Cove and built a life here? Then she'd be close to her family, the inn, *and* Cade . . .

She slammed her eyes shut. What was her problem? Cade had made it clear he didn't want her around. She had wrecked their relationship. He was done.

"Everleigh," Trevor began, "please talk to me."

She rubbed her eyes. Cade's family issues weren't her business to share. "I tried to help a friend, and instead, I made a mess. Now he's angry with me, and I feel terrible." Then she lifted her head and tried to smile. "But we'll work it out somehow. I'm sorry for being such a blubbering mess."

"Is your friend Cade?"

Was it that obvious? She met his knowing look and nodded.

He stretched his arm over the back of the bench behind her. "Are you and Cade a couple?"

"No, no, no." She tried to laugh, but it sounded like a croak. "We're . . . partners. Business partners. I've already explained how we own the inn together."

He looked out toward the road and then turned toward her. "Have you gotten any offers on the inn?"

She frowned. Why was he asking about the inn? "Yeah, a few, but all of them are investors who don't want to run the inn. They want to put up luxury condos or cram a few dozen townhouses on the property to take advantage of the beautiful view of the bay. But that's not what my godmother would've wanted. Cade and I can't in good conscience sell to them."

He seemed to consider her words as he tapped his fingers on the edge of the bench. "Don't you think your godmother's legacy can live on without the inn? I mean, you could find another way to memorialize her. I'm sure you have some ideas."

Everleigh studied his earnest expression. She wondered why he would say something almost identical to what Valerie Rhodes, the Realtor, had said about Alana. What were the odds they would have the same suggestion?

But his face seemed full of concern for her—*genuine* concern. Then Cade's warning about him echoed in her mind:

"I can't put my finger on it, but I felt like he wasn't telling me the truth about why he moved here and what he does for a living. It almost sounded like he was making up answers as he went along."

She almost laughed out loud at herself. Why would she worry about Cade's hunches after the way he'd treated her earlier? He was the most stubborn, moody, hurtful man she'd ever met. After the way he yelled at her, why would she trust his view on anything?

Because despite everything, I'm starting to care for him . . . deeply.

"I'm sorry, Everleigh." Trevor shifted toward her. "I didn't mean to upset you." He pointed toward the Roast Shack. "Why don't I buy you a cup of coffee and a snack, and we can talk?"

Everleigh felt her stomach start to settle ever so slightly. "Thank you," she said, wiping her eyes. "I think that'd be really nice, Trevor."

CHAPTER 20

CADE PACED IN the kitchen at the inn later that evening. A steady cadence of rain drummed the kitchen windows and the roof. He cupped his hand to the back of his neck as anger whirled through him.

After snapping at Everleigh, he had sat in his truck for a while and contemplated how terribly the day had turned out. He had enjoyed his talk with his brother, getting to know more about him and his family, but he was hurt and disappointed that his mother had given up on Declan the way she did. He'd almost called his dad and asked for his advice on how to get through to Mom, but even that seemed like a lost cause.

Next, he considered going back to his apartment to cool off—but despite how furious he was with Everleigh, he felt like a real jerk for leaving her without a ride. So instead of driving himself home, he had wandered around the festival for more than an hour looking for her.

When she was nowhere to be found, he decided it would be better to just go home and cool off after all. Considering the stress-filled events of the day, he didn't want to risk losing his temper with her again. So he drove home and sulked in his apartment. He tried working in his shop and then streaming a movie, but he couldn't concentrate on either thing.

After a while, he went to the inn and sat on the porch and waited for her to get home. When it got dark, he headed inside and sat in the kitchen. He pulled his phone from his pocket and stared down at the screen. It had been several hours since he'd fussed at her, and he was starting to get worried. He pulled up her contact information and considered calling her, but he couldn't bring himself to do it. He was still too irritated with her for butting into his life. He believed she truly cared about him and his family, but this time she and her antics had taken a step too far for anyone's good.

He growled out his annoyance and locked his phone before dropping it into his pocket. Headlights swept across the front of the inn as a pickup truck steered down the driveway. Cade reached the porch just as Everleigh climbed down from the passenger seat.

"Thanks," she told the driver. "Good night."

Cade recognized that black Toyota Tacoma. It belonged to Trevor. His hands balled into tight fists.

Everleigh started toward the porch. When her eyes locked with Cade's, her gait slowed, and her pleasant expression dissolved.

"Hey," he said, his tone hesitant.

She stopped at the bottom of the steps and remained silent, her face a mask of uncertainty.

"Look," he began, "I know you were trying to help, but—"

She lifted her hand. "Just stop right there, Cade. You were right. I have gotten too involved in your life and your family, and I was wrong." Her chest lifted and fell with a deep breath. "I've realized we're not friends and never will be," she said, her voice breaking. "I-I can accept that. In fact, it's better that I do accept that."

Her words pierced his heart. "Everleigh, wait. I didn't mean—"

"From now on, let's just go back to being business partners, okay?" Her dark eyes glittered in the porch lights. "You stay out of my life, and I'll stay out of yours. Deal?"

He nodded despite his disappointment. "Deal."

"Good night," she whispered as she hurried past him into the house.

He stood on the porch alone and wiped his hands down his face. He couldn't imagine not having her in his life, but she was right. They were better off on their own—and the sooner he got used to not having her in his life, the better.

And that truth left him gutted.

✦ ✦ ✦

"So, Everleigh, you and I haven't spoken in a while," Quinn said Thursday morning, sitting across from Everleigh at the Roast Shack. "What's new with you?"

Everleigh took a sip of her vanilla latte and debated how much to share. It wasn't her place to tell Cade's business about his long-lost brother, but she didn't know how else to explain why she and Cade weren't talking.

Quinn set her forearms on the table. "I can tell when you're holding back, and I have to be back in the library in thirty minutes. Just go ahead and tell me what's on your mind."

"Fine." Everleigh dropped back against her seat. "Cade's been busy all week. We haven't spoken since Saturday."

Quinn nodded. "Roger told me Cade's been helping him fix his little sister's car. Melanie doesn't have the money to take it to a shop, and since Roger's sunroom company is slow right now, Cade's been over there every day helping them rebuild whatever broke in the engine. It's really nice of him."

"Yeah. It is." Everleigh began folding a napkin. "Our last guests left Saturday morning, and since we don't have anyone booked for a couple of weeks, I haven't seen Cade." She tried to act as if not talking to him for five days wasn't slowly breaking her apart. Then she smiled. "But that's how it is with friendships and partnerships sometimes. Right?"

Quinn leaned forward again. "Everleigh, what's going on?"

"It's . . . complicated." She continued folding the napkin over and over until it was a tiny square. Then she unfolded it and started over. "We sort of had an argument on Saturday, and we haven't spoken since."

"You and Cade?"

Everleigh nodded.

"What happened?"

Everleigh's lips turned down. "I can't tell you the details, except to say it was totally my fault."

"Your fault?" Quinn asked. "I doubt that."

"I interfered in a family issue he's been dealing with. I was trying to help fix it, but I only made it worse." She shook her head. "He got upset, and I told him it's obvious we can't be friends. And now that we don't have anything going on with the inn, we have no reason to talk. But I *have* been staying busy focusing on trying to sell the place," she chirped. "I renewed our ads on all of the websites and even updated the text a bit."

Quinn seemed impressed. "That's exciting. Have you gotten any bites?"

"Only developers. Even that first Realtor with the Porsche SUV called me again yesterday." Everleigh rolled her eyes. "And she sent us a fruit basket! As if that would convince us to sell."

"A fruit basket?"

"Yeah. You know, the ones that come with the chocolate-covered bananas?"

"Mmm." Quinn grinned. "Those are delicious."

"They are, but they aren't going to do the trick. We're not selling to someone who plans to knock down the inn." She rested her elbow on the table and her chin on her palm. "And recruiters keep calling me too. I considered taking down the ads yesterday, going back to Texas to work, and letting Cade take over running the inn without me. But I still believe Alana was invested in our nonprofit, and I can't give up that dream just yet. Not before Thanksgiving, and that's a month away."

Quinn was silent but took a loud sip of her Americano.

Everleigh could tell her friend had an opinion. "Go ahead and say it."

Quinn shrugged. "It just seems like you're very conflicted when it comes to Cade."

That was an understatement. She felt something deep for him, something she hadn't felt for anyone before, but he was the last man on earth she'd ever want to get involved with—especially when she didn't plan to stay in Coral Cove.

Though in certain quiet moments, she felt Coral Cove and something deeper beckoning her to stay.

"We don't mesh very well," she said. "It's best if we steer clear of each other. And that's okay."

Quinn nodded toward the window. "I heard there's going to be a bad storm tonight. The wind gusts are supposed to be strong, and there's a flood watch too. I need to get home early tonight and bring in all of my patio furniture and garden decorations."

"I saw that on the news this morning." Everleigh stopped folding the napkin. "I'd better walk around the inn and store all our little decorations too."

Quinn consulted her watch and sighed. "Looks like I need to get back to the library." She stood. "I'll walk you to your car."

Everleigh headed out into the warm air and took in the dark clouds above them. The scent of impending rain was unmistakable. She gave her friend a long hug. "It was so good to see you."

"Don't stay away too long." Quinn patted her arm. "And don't give up on Cade. I have a feeling you two are going to work out your differences."

Everleigh smiled. "By the time I get back on the road, it'll all be worked out." But those words stabbed at her heart more than she cared to acknowledge.

Quinn stuck out her lip. "But I'll miss you."

"And I'll miss you too." Everleigh waved goodbye as Quinn started down the street. She climbed into her car and tried to put thoughts of Cade out of her mind.

Was it even remotely possible that Cade—the grumpiest, moodiest man she'd ever met—missed Everleigh as much as she missed him?

✦ ✦ ✦

Everleigh stared through the darkness at her bedroom ceiling later that night. The heavy rain pounding on the roof reminded her of when she and her family had gone to see a drum corps competition when she was little. And the howling wind sounded like it might be tearing the shingles right off.

She hugged her long pillow against her body and rolled onto her side, trying to tune out the sound of the storm. The rain had started shortly after supper, and she'd been relieved upon hearing Cade's truck motoring down the driveway about an hour later. The meteorologist on the news had reported that a line of storms was going to rage throughout the night, and the rain and wind would worsen with each hour. She was grateful Cade had gotten home safely before the storms picked up.

Why am I still thinking about Cade?

She groaned and snuggled deeper into her pillow. She had to shove that man out of her head and her heart, but she had no idea how to do it. They had no future, and the facts confirmed it. So why was she holding on so tight?

A gust of wind howled, and the rain pounded even harder. Everleigh squeezed her eyes shut. Maybe if she fell asleep, the storm would be gone by the time she woke up.

Crack!

Boom!

The house shook as if hit by a bomb, and Everleigh leapt out of bed. Her heart pounded against her rib cage as she groped for her phone on the nightstand and stumbled across the room toward the light switch. She flipped it up and down several times, but the room remained cloaked in darkness.

Uh-oh. The power was out. She found the flashlight app on her phone and rushed out to the hallway. She ran to the windows facing the back of the house and gasped at the sight illuminated by lightning: Branches from the ancient oak tree had crashed through the sunroom on the other side of the wall, just feet away from her suite.

"No. No, no, no!" Not thinking straight, she dropped her phone into the pocket of her shorts and raced outside. The cool late-October rain bit into her skin, and she quivered as her bare feet squished through the cold mud. The wind whipped her wet hair around her face, and her vision blurred as she took in the gigantic branches crushing her godmother's beloved sunroom.

A flash of a memory came to her of the day Alana had invited Everleigh's family over to see the sunroom for the first time. Alana's proud, gracious smile flickered in her mind's eye.

And now . . .

"No, no, no," Everleigh cried. A torrent of wind crashed into her, and she dropped to her knees in the soaked grass.

Grief built up in her chest, and she hugged her arms over her middle. Alana was gone. And now her beloved sunroom had been crushed by a tree.

Cade was no longer her friend. She'd lost him too.

Everleigh's life was falling apart. And her heart was torn to shreds just like the wreckage before her.

Soon her tears mixed with the pouring rain, drenching every part of her.

✦ ✦ ✦

Cade sat up with a start. "That sounded close," he mumbled. Through the dark he could see the silhouette of his cat sitting like a statue at the foot of his bed, ears raised on high alert.

He crossed to the window, pushed back the shade, and spotted nearly half the oak tree lying in the sunroom.

Wait. What?

He blinked and rubbed his eyes, but the scene in front of him didn't change. Panic clawed at his chest, and adrenaline raced through his veins.

The sunroom was on the other side of the wall from Everleigh's suite! What if she was hurt . . . or worse? He couldn't bear the thought.

"Everleigh!" he hollered.

He dashed through his apartment, down the stairs, out the door, and down the path toward the back of the inn. He disregarded the rocks biting into his bare feet as the wind gusted around him and rain soaked through his hair, T-shirt, and shorts.

He spotted the outline of a person hunched on the ground, and when he recognized Everleigh's red hair, he picked up speed. What on earth was she doing outside in the storm?

"Everleigh!" He screamed her name over and over, but his voice was lost in the sound of the howling wind.

When he reached her, he took hold of her and tried to pull her to her feet. "Everleigh! Come on!"

She remained on her knees, pushing him away.

"Come on!" he yelled before wrapping his arms around her waist and lifting her to her feet. "We need to go! You're not safe here!"

When she seemed unwilling to take a step, he had no choice but to hoist her up in his arms. As he strode toward safety, another crack rang out. Cade held her tight against himself and continued to run.

Boom!

Two more large branches crashed through the sunroom, flattening the structure as if it had been built with Popsicle sticks. Another branch landed just feet from where they stood.

If they hadn't moved . . .

Dismissing the terrifying thought, Cade raced toward his apartment. Everleigh clung to him until they reached the door, which he managed to wrench open. Once inside, he gently released her and set her on her feet. "Go," he said, nudging her toward the stairs.

She wiped her feet on the doormat and then trudged up the steps while he closed and locked the door behind them. He hit the light switch at the bottom of the stairs, but the stairwell remained dark. "Great," he grumbled.

Adrenaline continued to plunge through him as he jogged up the stairs and into the tiny laundry room. With the help of the flashlight app on his cell phone, he found two old Coleman lanterns he had used for camping years ago.

Please work! He flipped the switches, and they lit up the room with a soft yellow glow.

He carried them to the den, where Everleigh stood in the middle of the room, hugging her arms against her drenched gray T-shirt. In the dim glow of the lamplight, he could see that the shirt read "Sleep All Day. Nurse All Night."

Cute.

He set a lantern on the counter, grabbed a beach towel from the hall closet, and wrapped it around her shoulders. She held it against her body and shivered.

"Want some dry clothes?" he offered.

Her teeth chattered as she nodded.

What on earth did he own that might fit her narrow frame?

"Come on," he said.

She followed him into his bedroom, where he set the second lantern on the dresser and searched through the drawers. He found a pair of drawstring shorts and an old, faded concert T-shirt and held them out to her. "These should work."

"Thanks," she whispered. She kept her attention focused on the clothes, and he was certain she was averting her eyes.

"Bathroom's there." He pointed to the doorway beside his closet. "Help yourself to anything—towels, face cloth, whatever you need."

She nodded. Then she carried the lantern into the bathroom and closed the door.

He chose a pair of sweatpants and a dry shirt for himself and then slipped out of the room, closing the door behind him. He changed in the laundry room and then paced around the apartment. He couldn't wipe the sight of the demolished sunroom from his mind.

What if the branches had fallen a few feet away? What if they had landed on Everleigh's room, trapping her—or worse? If they had, their last conversation would have been an argument. And . . .

Stop it! Get ahold of yourself!

Everleigh was fine. She was in his apartment, and she was safe. In fact, she was in his bathroom *putting on his clothes.*

Despite that assurance, his heart still tried to pound itself out of his chest. He needed something to occupy him, to take his mind off what could have happened to Everleigh.

He spun toward the kitchen, and his eyes landed on an old kettle his mother had given him. He kept it on the counter since he had no room for it in the cabinet.

Tea.

He would make some tea. Yes, that would keep him busy for a minute or two.

After using a long wand lighter to ignite a burner, he filled a kettle with water and set it on the stove. Then he collapsed against the counter and took a few cleansing breaths to soothe his frayed nerves. The rain continued to pound the roof while the wind howled around them.

He waited for his bedroom door to open and Everleigh to appear in his clothes, but he didn't hear any movement coming from his room.

What was taking her so long?

Had she curled up in his bed with the cat and fallen asleep?

He rubbed his chin and debated what to do. He didn't want to intrude upon her, but he was worried. She'd seemed to be in one piece when he brought her to his apartment, but maybe she'd gotten hurt. She could've fallen in the mud and injured herself and was looking for bandages.

Or maybe she didn't want to see him? She'd told him days ago that they needed to stay out of each other's lives.

He gritted his teeth. He couldn't stand the idea of her avoiding him, especially now that the inn was in jeopardy.

But she'd clearly been upset when he found her kneeling in the mud, and she hadn't looked him in the eye since he'd brought her into his apartment.

Stop stalling, Witherspoon. Go check on her!

He crossed to the door and knocked softly. "Everleigh?"

He waited a moment while rain continued to beat a loud cadence on the roof.

He knocked again. "Everleigh?" He rested his forehead against the cool door. "Everleigh, please answer me. Are you okay?"

Then he held his breath.

CHAPTER 21

"YEAH." EVERLEIGH'S VOICE sounded soft, unsure, and hesitant.

Cade couldn't recall a time when Everleigh had been timid since he'd met her. Maybe she was injured and too stubborn to ask for help. Worry spun in his gut. He needed to get in there and see her for himself.

"Can I come in?" he asked.

"Sure."

He opened the door and found her perched on the corner of his bed, stroking Bryant's chin. The cat lounged on his back with his eyes closed, eating up the attention.

And Everleigh was gorgeous in his clothes. The shorts showed off her long legs, and the shirt hung perfectly over her. For a moment he got lost in the yearning swirling inside him while he drank in the scene.

Focus, Cade!

"Are you hurt?" he asked.

Keeping her attention glued to the cat, she shook her head.

"Want to come out to the den?"

She hesitated for a moment. When she finally nodded, his worry morphed into irritation. *Talk to me!*

The past five days had been pure torture without their daily conversations. Though Cade was a much better chef than mechanic, he'd agreed to help Roger work on his sister's car, if only to get away from the inn. Handing Roger tools and watching car repair videos sounded better than hanging around after Everleigh told him they couldn't even be friends. Aside from that, he hadn't heard from his mother or his brother. The combined stress was slowly eating away at him.

At the same time, being away from the inn wasn't any fun either. The only thing Cade had figured out during the past five days was that he missed Everleigh, and he regretted yelling at her. And now that she sat on his bed petting his cat, he wanted nothing more than to talk to her, reconnect with her, bring her back into his life.

Although holding her against him like he had out in the rain was another enticing option.

Stop it, Cade. Concentrate on getting her to talk to you.

When she didn't move, he took that as his clue to leave her and Bryant alone. He returned to the kitchen and stared at the kettle. Why did boiling water always take forever? One of his grandmother's favorite sayings echoed in his mind: *A watched pot never boils.*

"You were right, Grandma," he whispered to himself.

He located two mugs and two tea bags. When a powerful gust of wind shook the windows, Cade braced himself for another loud *crack* followed by a *boom*.

Instead, he heard soft footsteps, and he turned just as Everleigh climbed onto the corner of the sofa, folding her long legs under herself. She grabbed a blanket from behind her and wrapped it around her body. Bryant hopped up next to her before resting his chin on her lap. She murmured softly to him, and Cade smiled.

Cade joined her, sitting down on the opposite end of the sofa from Everleigh, who continued to pet the cat. He was sure she was avoiding his eyes, and he racked his brain for something to say. Coming up empty, he settled back on the arm of the sofa and waited for her to speak as the storm continued to roar outside.

A sniff sounded, and Everleigh covered her face while she cried.

His lungs constricted, and he shifted toward her. "It's okay," he whispered. "You're safe. We'll get the damage to the inn fixed."

"It-it's not that," she managed to say between sobs.

"Okay . . ." He inched closer to her. "What is it?"

She wiped her eyes with the backs of her hands. "It's everything." Another sob burst from her, and she collapsed forward, bending at her waist and shielding her face with her hands.

"Everleigh," he said softly. "Come here."

She leaned toward him, and he took her into his arms. She rested her cheek on his shoulder and wrapped her arms around his neck. He rubbed her back and breathed in her scent: something flowery—possibly shampoo?—mixed with vanilla and something sweet. He closed his eyes as every one of his nerve endings was set aflame. Holding her close felt like heaven.

He rested his cheek on her head. "When I looked out the window and saw the tree had crashed through the roof, I was terrified something had happened to you." He heard the catch in his voice.

She snuggled closer against him.

A wave of relief flitted through him. If she was comfortable enough to let him hold her, then maybe she hadn't given up on him. If only she'd talk to him! After several moments, he couldn't take it any longer.

"Please say something," he pleaded with her. "I can't stand the distance between us."

Bryant hopped down from the sofa and sauntered into Cade's bedroom, clearly bored with the conversation.

Everleigh cleared her throat. "I miss Alana so much." Her voice was raspy. "And I'm so hurt she didn't tell me she was sick."

He could hear and feel her anguish, and grief swamped him. Unable to speak, he nodded.

She shifted out of his arms and leaned back against the sofa with her side pressed against him. He was grateful she hadn't broken the connection. He stretched his arm out behind her, and she rested her head against his shoulder before looking up at him. "Why didn't Alana want us to know—my mom and me?"

He moved his fingers through her damp hair, and it was just as soft as he'd imagined. "I asked her more than once if she wanted to call your mom, and she said no. I knew how close they were, but Alana didn't want to be a burden to anyone."

"A burden?" Everleigh asked, looking shocked or possibly more hurt. "I wouldn't have ever considered her a burden. I would've broken my contract with the hospital and come right home. I could've taken her to her appointments, held her hand during her treatments, held her hair while she was sick, made her meals, and even fed her if she was too tired to pick up her utensils. I could've kept her comfortable, Cade. Washed her clothes. I could've been her nurse, but she never gave me a chance. After all those years of supporting me, she didn't give me the opportunity to do the same for her. And I—I—" Her voice cracked, and more sobs broke through her trembling body.

When she covered her face with her hands again, he pulled her against him and massaged her back. He longed to take away her pain, but the only way he knew how was to hold her close. Her body shuddered, and he closed his eyes.

"It's okay, Everleigh," he murmured. "I know you would've taken good care of her. It's obvious how much she meant to you."

She rested her head on his shoulder and seemed to be working to calm herself.

When she pulled away from him, she hugged her arms against her middle. "I'm sorry," she whispered. "I don't know why I'm such a basket case tonight. Seeing the tree crash through the sunroom just unlocked all of this grief I've been carrying around with me since . . ."

"You don't need to apologize." He handed her a box of tissues from the end table beside him.

She mopped up her face with a tissue and then inclined her head against his shoulder once again. "Did she go for treatments?"

He shook his head. "She was diagnosed and had an appointment at UNC–Chapel Hill. She planned to tell your mom everything after the appointment for her treatment plan, but she never made it there."

"I'm so angry with her for not telling me." Her chin wobbled. "And I'm angry at myself for being angry with her."

He pushed her hair back from her face. "I can relate. I was angry when she finally admitted to me that she hadn't felt well for a while but wouldn't go to the doctor. If she'd gone sooner, they might've been able to help her."

They were both silent, and he enjoyed the feeling of her head resting against his shoulder. He could get used to sitting with her like this. Snuggling with her. Touching her. Sharing his most private thoughts with her.

Stop it! She's your friend and only your friend.

"Thank you for taking care of her," she finally said.

"I didn't do much." His voice was rough. "But I did everything I could. She became like family to me. In some ways I felt closer to her than to my mom. She was easier to talk to."

"I know what you mean. I could tell Alana things that I couldn't tell my mom too. I guess I knew I could be completely honest with her and not worry about disappointing her." A tear trailed down her cheek, and he wiped it away with the tip of his finger. "I miss our talks. There's so much I wish I could tell her, and I'd love to hear her opinion on things, especially about the nonprofit and the inn."

"She was a wonderful person."

Everleigh touched his cheek. "You're such a good man, Cade. Thank you for taking such good care of her when I couldn't. I know she was in good hands with you." She ran the tip of her finger along his jawline, her touch leaving a sizzle of desire in its wake.

His eyes locked on her lips, and for a moment he couldn't stop himself from wondering how soft they were and how they tasted. His blood heated, and when he dipped his chin, he thought he heard her breath hitch.

Then warning bells screamed in his head, and he froze. What was he doing? Everleigh was planning to leave soon. Getting involved with her was the last thing he should—

"Cade?" she asked. "Is that the kettle?"

"What?"

She pointed toward the galley kitchen. "The kettle?"

His brain suddenly engaged. The kettle was whistling—not warning bells wailing in his head.

"Oh!" He popped up from the sofa and rushed to the kitchen, where he brewed the tea and brought the two mugs over to the coffee table.

"It sounds like the storm finally calmed down," she said, pointing to the ceiling.

The wind gusts weren't as fierce, and rain tapped softly on the roof above them.

"You're not setting foot in the inn until we know it's safe," he said.

She nodded and sipped from her mug.

"I'm glad we don't have any visitors right now. What a disaster that could've been. You're staying here tonight." He pointed toward his bedroom. "You take my bed, and I'll sleep out here."

"If you say so." She set the mug down and rested against the sofa, her leg still pressing against his. "Can I ask you something?"

He angled his body toward her. "Sure."

She picked up the blanket and hugged it against her body. "You mentioned that your ex insisted you sign up for the Family Tree website. How long were you together before you broke up?"

Oh boy. He should have known this question would eventually come up. He studied the earnestness in Everleigh's face, and for some reason, he didn't mind telling her the truth—the *whole* truth—about Serena. "Almost five years." Her eyes looked like they might bug out of her head, and he couldn't stop his laugh. "Are you shocked I could maintain a relationship that long, darlin'?"

"Um, yeah. Kinda." She laughed, and he enjoyed the sweet sound. But her smile faded. "It had to have been painful when you broke up after such a long time. What happened?"

"You really want to hear the sad and sordid tale?"

She folded up her legs, then rested her elbows on her knees and her chin on her palms. "I'm ready."

He laughed and rolled his eyes. "Fine. I met her on a blind date when I moved to Alabama. I fell head over heels quickly because I was an idiot. She encouraged me to follow my dream of opening my own restaurant, and I encouraged her to follow her dream of going to law school. She convinced me to partner with her cousin at the restaurant, and I helped her pay her tuition. Next thing I knew, I was in hog heaven. I had everything I ever wanted." He counted them off on his fingers. "I had her, I had my restaurant, and we had a bright future—or so I thought. I took out a loan, bought a ring I couldn't afford, and proposed. And that's when it all fell apart."

Everleigh's mouth dropped open. "You were engaged?"

"Wait. You haven't heard the best part yet." He gave her a sardonic smile. "Now remember I told you I was paying her tuition, right?"

Everleigh nodded.

"I was running a business, paying her tuition, *and* helping with her rent. I was spread way too thin. And then three weeks before the wedding . . ." He held up three fingers. "Three weeks! She decided she wasn't ready to get married. She came to me all crying and upset with some nonsense excuse. We argued, and she threw the ring at me. Then her stupid cousin, who I never wanted to partner with, sent my restaurant into a tailspin. He knew nothing about running a business. Ruined our relationships with all of our vendors. Didn't pay our bills. We didn't have enough to cover payroll, and it all went up in smoke."

He threw his hands up in the air. "Poof! I was grateful I was able to return the ring and get some of my money back. But that was when I came home to Coral Cove with my tail between my legs. I had no money, no future, nothing to my name except for my motorcycle. I had to move back in with my parents at the age of thirty-one. Do you have any idea how humiliating that was?"

Everleigh's beautiful face was full of sympathy.

"Alana was generous enough to give me a chance to start over, and I'm so grateful for it. I love the inn and what I do here." He paused and took a breath. "And now you know everything." To his surprise, sharing the story with her had been cathartic. He felt as if a weight had been lifted from his chest.

"I'm sorry that happened to you." She reached over and took his hands in hers. "Your ex has no idea what she lost."

Her words warmed him from the inside out. "Thanks, but it also taught me a valuable lesson."

"What's that?"

"Not to trust people."

"Not everyone is like her."

"But many people are. That's why I'm done with romance, love, and all that. It only leads to heartache. Why set yourself up for disappointment when you're better off on your own?"

She clucked her tongue. "Why would you cut yourself off like that, Cade Witherspoon?" She squinted slightly as she studied him. "You don't ever plan to settle down and have a family?"

"Probably not." He shook his head. "I let that dream die when I left Alabama."

"That's a shame."

Questions about Everleigh and her past spun in his mind. "How much have you dated?" he asked.

"Not much since college. It's not easy maintaining relationships when you move every thirteen weeks."

He recalled Trevor dropping her off last Saturday, and his spine went rigid. "What about Trevor?"

"Cade . . ." She sighed.

"Do you like him?" He held his breath, dreading her response.

"As a friend?" she asked. "Yes." Her tone was laced with impatience.

He tried to hide his relief. "That's all?"

"Ugh." She rolled her eyes. "How many times do I have to tell you we're just friends?"

Cade couldn't shake the feeling that the guy wanted more—*a lot* more. He tried to swallow back his jealousy. What was wrong with him?

I'm really losing it . . .

She cupped her hand to her mouth to cover a yawn. "I think I need to head to bed." She started into the room but stopped in the doorway. "Thank you."

"For . . . ?"

"Saving me." She pointed toward the window. "If I had stayed where I was when the second branch fell . . ."

He shuddered. She didn't need to finish that sentence. He couldn't even think about what could have happened.

"I need to grab a pillow and blanket." He followed her into the bedroom and plucked an extra pillow from his bed and a blanket from the top of his closet.

She stood at the foot of the bed and rubbed Bryant's ear. The cat rolled onto his back, and his purrs rumbled as loudly as the rain pelting the roof above them. "Who named him Bryant?" she asked.

"Alana. I wanted to call him Bear."

"He's definitely a Bryant." She smiled down at the cat and then lifted her eyes to Cade's again. "I don't feel right taking your bed. Let me sleep on the sofa."

He shook his head. "My mama would tan my hide if she found out I put you on the sofa."

"But you're taller than I am." She pointed to the doorway. "I'll be more comfortable out there. You should stay here."

"Nope." He patted the cat's round belly and then nodded at Everleigh. "Night."

She gave him a sweet smile that went straight to his heart. "Good night, Cade."

He closed his bedroom door behind him and then tried to get settled on the sofa. Everleigh was right—he was much too tall for it—but after resting his feet on the arm, he found a semi-comfortable position. He stared up at the ceiling and listened to the steady drumming of the rain on the roof.

The night had been unexpected—from the tree crashing through the sunroom to holding Everleigh in his arms while she sobbed. And when he'd almost kissed her . . .

A shiver moved through him at the memory.

Thank goodness the kettle whistled when it did! He'd almost made a huge mistake. Getting involved with Everleigh would make things even more complicated than they already were.

At the same time, it was a relief to unload what had happened between him and Serena. Everleigh was easy to talk to and always empathetic. But that didn't mean he should fall for her.

He blinked up at the ceiling. If he was being honest with himself, he had to admit he already *had* fallen for her.

Oh no . . .

He had to find a way to bury those feelings. He couldn't make it through another rough breakup.

Cade tried to adjust himself and his pillow—but he knew that between the uncomfortable sofa and his confusing feelings for Everleigh, it was going to be a *very* long night.

CHAPTER 22

EVERLEIGH ROLLED ONTO her back and yawned. Opening her eyes, she spotted sunlight sneaking in between the slats in the blinds. For a moment, she didn't know where she was. Then the previous night came rushing back—the storm, the tree crashing through the sunroom, collapsing in the mud under the cold rain, Cade rescuing her, sobbing in Cade's arms, Cade holding her close . . .

Cade.

She moved onto her side and breathed in his scent imprinted on his pillowcase—the fragrance of laundry detergent mixed with sandalwood. His smell had surrounded her and reminded her of his warm hug as she had snuggled under his gray sheets and blanket last night. A thrill slipped through her as she recalled how safe and secure she'd felt in his strong arms, releasing all the grief she'd been carrying around since her mother told her Alana was gone.

For some stupid reason, she couldn't stop herself from confessing everything that was weighing on her heart when she was with Cade. It didn't make sense at all—especially since it had been six days since she'd told him they shouldn't be friends, and he had agreed.

Had all of that flown out the window when the trees flattened the sunroom?

When she was around Cade, she just naturally opened herself up to him. And she'd been almost certain he had done the same last night. She'd been stunned to discover that he'd been engaged, and that his fiancée had broken up with him three weeks before the wedding. She'd never expected him to share so much. The pain she saw in his eyes when he spoke about his ex tore at her heart. The woman had obviously hurt him deeply—so deeply that he'd completely given up on love.

It was all so overwhelming. But even more than that, she'd been almost sure that Cade was going to kiss her. She touched her lips, and goose bumps ran down her arms as she imagined what it would have felt like for his mouth to claim hers. If only the kettle hadn't chosen that exact moment to whistle!

She rubbed her forehead as confusion and disappointment warred inside her. It was probably for the best that he hadn't kissed her. Why was she imagining kissing Cade when she was planning to get back on the road after the inn sold? Thinking about having a relationship with him was insane, especially when he made it clear he had no interest in love or romance. They would never make sense as a couple. They were too different—and they had opposite ideas about the inn too. He was distrustful of nearly everyone, but she always saw the bright side of things. If they were together, they'd probably do more bickering than kissing.

But she was certain those kisses would be worth the hassle . . .

Stop it, Everleigh!

She had to ignore these ridiculous feelings. Cade would never be more than a friend to her, and that was that.

Something stirred near her legs, and then Bryant appeared at her side and meowed.

"Good morning to you too." She stroked his head, and he purred.

The delicious scent of bacon filtered in from the kitchen, and her stomach growled. She pushed herself up from the bed and grabbed her phone from the nightstand. The cat grunted as he jumped off the bed and raced to the bedroom door. She surveyed the room, finding a triple dresser, a tall dresser, and a chair.

The tops of the dressers were neat and tidy. The triple dresser held a tray with a handful of coins and a wallet, along with a couple of framed photos. Curiosity launched her across the room, where she picked up one of the frames.

The first photo featured a young Cade posing with an older couple on a dock with a small boat in the background. She surmised by their ages they were his grandparents. She guessed he was around ten or twelve, and his hair was sunshine blond. He beamed at the camera, and she smiled as she imagined him as a young man fishing and laughing with his grandparents.

The second included Cade standing with a couple on the beach. He appeared sixteen or seventeen, and she recognized the woman as his mother. He definitely had his mother's bright-blue eyes, but she saw glimpses of his father's smile in his. What had teenage Cade been like? Did he enjoy school like she had? Or had he yearned to be anywhere else?

"Meow!"

Everleigh turned to where the cat paced by the bedroom door. "Sorry! I'm coming."

She set the photo back on the dresser and then let the cat out before slipping into the bathroom. She flipped the bathroom switch, but the light didn't come on. After retrieving the lantern from the nightstand, she washed her face and rinsed with mouthwash before frowning at her reflection. Her hair was a frizzy disaster. She picked up Cade's brush and stared at it, taking in the golden-brown strands tucked between the bristles. He'd said she could use anything she wanted, but would he mind her using his brush? Shaking her head, she placed the brush on the counter and then finger-combed her hair into a more presentable mess.

"It is what it is," she declared before traipsing toward the door. As she stepped out into the den, she breathed in the delicious smells of breakfast.

Cade worked at the stove with his back to her, and she couldn't help herself from staring at his broad shoulders and sculpted legs while he cooked. He craned his neck over his shoulder at her and grinned, sending her pulse into hyper speed. "Good morning, sleepyhead."

"What time is it?"

He consulted his phone on the counter. "Ten."

"I don't usually sleep this late." She yawned and stretched. "How'd you sleep?"

He shrugged. "Well enough."

"You're not a very good liar, Cade. I knew you should've taken your bed, and I could've slept out here." She sidled up to him and breathed in the delicious smell of western omelets cooking in a large pan while bacon sizzled in another. "Need any help?"

When the kettle began to whistle, he grinned. "Pour the tea?"

"Sure." She fixed two mugs of tea while he carried two full plates to the small table. Then they sat down across from each other. "Oh my goodness." She picked up her fork and admired the western omelets. "This is amazing, Cade."

"If we had power, I would've made toast and coffee to go with it. But this is all I can manage on my little stove."

"I'm still impressed." She took a bite of the omelet and rested back on the wooden chair, her taste buds dancing with delight. It was the most flavorful omelet she'd ever had. "This is outstanding."

"Glad you like it."

She pointed her fork toward the plate. "You need to make omelets for the guests."

"I have." He sipped the tea. "When we have more guests, I will."

"Did you ever make omelets at Sully's?"

He nodded and swallowed a bite of bacon. "We had breakfast on weekends, and it was pretty popular."

"What else did you offer for breakfast?"

He considered the question for a moment. "The basics mostly—waffles, eggs, different kinds of toast, pancakes, bacon, and sausage."

She took in the excitement dancing in his eyes while he talked about his restaurant, the happiness reverberating in his deep voice as he shared more about the menu and his favorite dishes.

"Tell me about the menu you were working on before Alana passed away," she said.

He stilled, something like dismay flashing over his handsome features.

"You said you and Alana were talking about taking the B&B to the next level," she explained. "And you mentioned a menu. Remember?"

"I know what you're talking about, Everleigh. I'm just surprised you want to hear about it."

She smiled. "I want to know everything."

"Okay." He crossed to the den, opened a drawer in the entertainment center, and returned with a stack of papers and pushed them toward her.

She perused the potential menu, finding pages for appetizers, main courses, and desserts, with everything from salads to burgers to cakes. "This sounds phenomenal."

"We discussed hosting dinners for our guests but then opening it up to the public, if only just for special occasions like Mother's Day or Valentine's Day." His eyes sparkled.

"I'm sure it would be popular. Where would you seat everyone?"

He pointed toward the windows. "We talked about erecting some sort of structure that would take advantage of the bay view. Something like a permanent tent or gazebo." He made a face. "A gazebo would be too small, but you know what I mean. Maybe a pavilion. We'd make use of the good weather."

Everleigh studied the mouthwatering menu. Why hadn't Alana told her about this? She met his eager eyes again. "You and Alana couldn't have handled the cooking and serving alone."

"Right." He nodded. "I would've definitely needed help in the kitchen, and help with service too."

She flipped through the pages of the menu and tried to imagine bringing this to life with Cade. They might cook together, or she could help serve. A smile took over her lips as she considered how fun that would be.

But how could she stay in Coral Cove and run the inn with Cade while also making her nonprofit a reality? At the end of the day, she just couldn't do both. And was she willing to give up nursing too? She could work at a local hospital part-time, but she'd only make a fraction of what she earned as a traveler. And how would she . . . ?

"Everleigh?"

She looked up at Cade, and his intense stare made her throat dry.

"Sorry." She smiled. "Lost in thought." She pushed the menu back over to him. "This is really something, Cade. I'm surprised Alana never told me about it."

"She didn't?"

She shook her head. "I had no idea she wanted to expand the B&B."

"Well, now you know." His expression warmed. "Your turn now. Tell me more about the nonprofit." The sincerity in his face caught her off guard.

She took a deep breath. "About three years ago, I was working in Iowa, and there was this young couple." She drew invisible circles on the tabletop while the memories played through her mind like a movie. "They were in town visiting family, and the pregnant wife wasn't due for another two months. But she went into labor, and their twins were born at thirty-one weeks. They had a survival chance of maybe sixty to seventy percent." She kept her eyes focused on the table.

"They were so young and so scared. The parents, I mean. And their medical insurance wasn't the best. The husband had to go home for work, and the wife just sat in the NICU and cried with her babies. She worried about everything—when she'd see her husband again, how she'd afford their care, the future . . . The babies were going to need help beyond the NICU, and there was a possibility that they would need care for the rest of their lives."

She sniffed, and her gaze collided with Cade's. He was completely still, his focus on her. "One night I couldn't sleep. I texted Alana, and she told me to call her. I told her about this couple and how I couldn't get them out of my mind. I wanted to help them. I wished the husband could take a leave of absence and stay in Iowa with his wife and newborns, but then who would cover their bills? The extended-stay hotel was not inexpensive, and in a perfect world, a nanny could assist when they went home, help provide all of the resources they needed for their babies and give them some peace of mind. But all of that had a price tag."

"What did Alana say?"

Everleigh smiled despite the tears filling her eyes. "She said, 'Then find a way to do it, Everleigh. You can do anything you set your mind to.' And I said, 'What if we started a charity together and helped these little angels?' She loved the idea. For the next three years I researched how to start a nonprofit, and . . . well, you know the rest of the story. I tried and tried, but I couldn't find a financial backer willing to subsidize our dream."

Silence stretched between them, and then a thought took hold of her: *What if we made both of Alana's dreams come true? What if we took the B&B to the next level and started the nonprofit? Would Cade be willing to do that with me?*

Cade tilted his head. "What's going through your mind right now?"

She twirled her fork in her hand and debated telling him the truth—that she wasn't sure she wanted to leave Coral Cove or even sell the inn, but she didn't know how to bring the nonprofit to life without a sale.

Alana is our guardian angel. What would she want us to do?

Everleigh knew for sure that she didn't want to argue with Cade again. She wanted to keep talking to him like this.

Her thoughts wandered to their argument last Saturday, and the urge to clear the air between them surged inside her. They had discussed so much since he'd brought her to his apartment last night, but that subject hadn't come up once. It was the elephant standing in the room with them, and she needed to find the courage to address it.

"All right." He set his fork down and rested his elbows on the table. "Your mood suddenly changed when I asked you about the nonprofit. I really think it's a great idea, Everleigh. I understand why it was important to you and Alana."

"Thanks, but that's not what's troubling me."

His lips formed a thin line. "Troubling you?"

She moved her hand over her warm mug. "I'm sorry for interfering with your family last Saturday. I never should have arranged for you to see Declan or to ambush your mom that way. I was totally out of line."

Cade scratched his cheek. "And I'm sorry for being such a jerk about it. I never should have yelled at you or left you stranded." He pushed his knife around on his plate. "I looked for you at the festival after I stormed off, but you'd found a ride."

Surprise doused her. "You looked for me?"

He nodded. "I should have called or texted you to say so, but I was too angry." He turned sheepish. "Sometimes my temper prevents me from doing the right thing." He scoffed. "Okay, let's be real. It *always* does."

They were both silent for a moment, and her mind clicked through so many questions. Should she have gone looking for him instead of running to the park and going to the coffee shop with Trevor? If she had, then maybe they could have worked things out Saturday night instead of spending five painful days apart.

"Have you talked to your brother since the festival?" she asked.

"We've texted here and there, but we haven't discussed my mom. I don't even know what to say about her."

"Have you reached out to her?"

He shook his head. "I'm too bitter." He settled back on his chair. "Have you talked to Harlowe?"

Everleigh shook her head.

He held up his mug toward her. "A toast to our dysfunctional families."

She snickered and tapped her mug to his.

"There's that smile," he said.

They continued to eat their breakfast, but Everleigh's thoughts turned toward the mess at the inn. She hadn't looked out the window yet—she almost didn't want to—but she assumed the damage was extensive.

"What should our plan be for the sunroom?"

Cade took a long, deep breath. "Well, I haven't been outside to look yet, but through the window, the sunroom looks completely flattened."

"Ouch."

"First and foremost, we need to cancel all of our reservations until the inn is back to normal."

"Once we have power and the internet is back online, I'll take care of that," she offered.

"Great," he said. "Roger builds sunrooms for a living, so I'll get him over here to take a look. Also, I'm going to call my dad. He's a plumber, and he knows plenty about construction. They can help me determine if it's safe for you to go inside or not."

She considered her shirt and shorts. "Can I at least run in for something more presentable to wear before we have company?"

"I think you look perfect, darlin'." The hint of a smile played over his lips.

The sound of that nickname made her insides melt. For a moment she allowed herself to imagine what it would have felt like if he *had* kissed her last night.

Down, girl!

"Let me see how the roof and the walls look first," he said. "I can't risk you getting hurt."

"Okay." His concern for her sent a warm glow through her.

"I'll call the insurance company too."

"We should take the inn off the market while we're working on repairs, right?"

He nodded. "Probably."

She hesitated for a moment. "But then we'll relist it when construction is done?"

He opened his mouth to say something just as her phone chimed with a text. She pulled it from her pocket.

Trevor: That storm was bad last night. You okay?

Everleigh studied the text and then lifted her eyes to Cade's. His lips had turned down, and his eyes focused on her phone. She could feel his irritation from across the table.

"Trevor?" he asked.

"Yeah."

He nodded toward her phone. "What does he want?"

"He asked if I was okay after the storm." She locked the screen and took a bite of bacon.

"You going to answer him?"

"Later." She nodded. "Maybe he can help with the cleanup."

His eyes narrowed. "We don't need his help."

"From what I could see through the dark last night, that entire tree broke in half and flattened the sunroom. I think we need all the help we can get."

"We have insurance."

"And how many other people sustained damage last night?" she asked. "We'll have to wait our turn in line to file a claim and then have a crew come out to clean up the mess. The more people who come out to help us in the beginning, the better."

Cade pushed his chair back, his blue eyes suddenly frosty. "We still don't need *his* help."

"I don't understand why you hate him so much. He's been nothing but nice to me."

"Because he wants something, Everleigh. You can't possibly be that naïve."

"Stop calling me naïve," she insisted. "Just because I'm younger than you doesn't make me naïve." She stood and stacked their plates. "I'll do the dishes. You can get dressed."

Cade hesitated for a moment, his jaw set in a stubborn line, but then he stalked toward the bedroom and closed the door behind him.

Everleigh plopped down onto the chair and rubbed her forehead as frustration rushed over her. This was exactly why she and Cade could barely be friends. It seemed like every one of their conversations ended in an argument. Why couldn't they just stay civil?

She pulled up Trevor's text and poised her thumbs over the phone. Then she drooped back on the chair and let out a frustrated huff. She could answer him later, she supposed. But she was still unsure of why her friendship with Trevor made Cade so angry.

Shoving away her annoyance, she headed to the sink and began washing the dishes. They needed to focus on getting the sunroom repaired no matter how much they bickered.

She scrubbed one dish and set it on the drainboard. Then she pulled the phone out again. It wasn't Cade's business if she wanted to be friends with Trevor, especially since Trevor had been so kind and supportive to her in a time of need.

She began typing: Hi. I'm okay, but we had some damage last night. A tree fell through the sunroom.

Immediately, conversation bubbles began to dance on her phone.

Trevor: Oh no! Do you need help?

Everleigh turned toward Cade's bedroom door. He'd be furious if she invited Trevor over, but they did need help if they were going to get the area cleaned up and the inn back on the market. And if Cade was angry, so be it.

Everleigh: Thanks, but I'm sure you're busy.

Trevor: Not busy. I'll come by later and see what I can do to help.

Everleigh: You sure?

Trevor: That's what friends are for, right? 😊

Everleigh smiled. That was *exactly* what friends were for, and it was a shame Cade couldn't see that.

Everleigh dropped her phone into her pocket. Maybe Cade just needed to see for himself that Trevor didn't have any ulterior motives. And even if he couldn't be convinced, he'd just have to accept that Trevor and Everleigh were friends.

CHAPTER 23

THE WHIRR OF chainsaws buzzed through the air later that afternoon as Cade and his father cut up the branches from the old oak tree. They'd been working for more than an hour, and they'd barely made a dent in the debris scattered around the yard. The sky was bright blue and cloudless, showing no sign of the line of storms that had wreaked so much havoc on Coral Cove overnight. The late October air was comfortable, and the last remnants of summer were gone.

Cade's arms already ached, and his head throbbed too. He was overwhelmed by the destruction but grateful that only the sunroom had been destroyed, aside from minor damage to the roof at the back of the inn. He turned off the chainsaw and began gathering up the branches into a neat pile.

Dad's chainsaw stopped too, and the murmur of conversations around the yard floated over to Cade. A group of volunteers had come to assist with the cleanup, and he was so grateful Everleigh had called her family and asked them for help. Everleigh's brother,

Landon, and his girlfriend, Amber, along with a few of Amber's coworkers from the fire department, were up on the roof covering the damage with a tarp. Roger was already busy working on plans for the sunroom rebuild, consulting with a few of his employees on the other side of the yard. And Bryant sat on a nearby fence post supervising everyone's work.

"We're getting there, Cade."

He tented his hand over his eyes and turned toward his father. "I'm not so sure about that." He took in the monstrous branches that had crushed the sunroom. "We've only just begun."

Dad chuckled. "At least you've got some help." He nodded toward the roof, where Landon, Amber, and the other four firefighters were climbing down the ladder. "And it could've been much worse."

Cade didn't want to think about what could've happened. He turned toward where Everleigh and her parents picked up debris and tossed it into large trash cans her father had brought. She had changed into jeans, boots, and a bright-green hoodie. A chill rippled over him as he recalled how attractive she'd been dressed in his shorts and T-shirt last night. He'd never get that image out of his mind.

Cade tried in vain to stop a yawn from overtaking him. He'd spent a restless night contemplating Everleigh and how it felt to hold her in his arms. Thanks to her, the wall he'd built around his heart was slowly breaking down, and it both thrilled and terrified him. Allowing himself to fall for Everleigh was a dead-end street.

Still, he couldn't control his feelings anymore. And from the way she reacted when he'd almost kissed her, he knew she felt something for him too. But if he told her how much he cared for her, he risked giving her the power to destroy his heart. He'd sworn he'd never make that same mistake, yet here he was—head over heels, all over again.

And then there was the issue of the inn. He'd been shocked when she took an interest in what he and Alana had envisioned for its future. He'd also been touched by her passion about her nonprofit. For a brief moment, he wondered if they could somehow take the inn to the next level *and* start the nonprofit at the same time. But that plan was impossible without the liquid funds they needed.

But could he convince his heart to give up on her?

Stop making yourself crazy!

He turned his attention back to his father and their task at hand.

"Thanks for coming to help," Cade told Dad. "I called the insurance company, but they can't get out here before next week."

Dad patted his shoulder. "You know I'm always willing to help." He paused for a moment. "Your mom had to work, but she wanted to be here too."

Cade glowered and picked up the chainsaw. He didn't want to talk about her.

"Hold on there, son." Dad held his hand up, sadness flashing over his face. "Your mom misses you. I've tried to encourage her to reach out, but she's not sure what to say. Maybe you should call her."

Cade frowned as that familiar grief saturated him. "I know. I'm just so confused."

He peered over to where Landon, Amber, and the other firefighters had started picking up debris. Landon said something to Everleigh, and she smacked his arm while he laughed. He took in their comradery, and his heart twisted. He'd missed out on so much with Declan. If they had grown up together, they could've been buddies. And his mother was standing in the way of them coming together as a family now. It didn't make any sense.

His eyes darted to his father's again. "I don't understand why Mom doesn't want Declan in her life."

Dad nodded. "It's complicated."

"That's an understatement."

"But one thing isn't complicated, Cade. Your mom loves you."

Anger shot through him. "What about Declan? She *abandoned* him, Dad, and now she refuses to even acknowledge him. Think about how that makes him feel."

"It's not that simple." Dad's tone remained even.

"Don't you feel betrayed, Dad?" he demanded. "That she never told us about him?"

Dad considered that for a moment. "I feel bad that she didn't trust me with the truth, but I don't feel betrayed. It was her burden, her secret. Not mine."

Cade's posture stiffened. How could Dad always remain so calm, no matter the circumstance? He couldn't remember one time when his father had lost his cool, not even when Cade wrecked their sedan when he was sixteen, a week after he'd gotten his driver's license.

And at this moment, he yearned for his father to lose his temper—to feel for himself all the confusing emotions that Cade had swirling around in his chest.

"Yeah, but that was a long time ago," Cade said, his voice trembling. "Don't you think it's time she accepted him into her life? He's a part of her, which means he's *our* family." He pointed to himself. "He's *my* brother and *her* son."

Dad's expression remained serene. "I know. I've been working on getting through to her."

"You have?" Hope lit in his chest.

Dad nodded. "We just need to give her time."

Cade watched while Landon looped his arm around Everleigh's shoulders. "I've always wanted a brother. I've been texting Declan, but I want him to be a part of our family. I want to invite him to join us for the holidays, but I feel like I can't do that without Mom's blessing." He kicked a small branch with the toe of his work boot.

"I don't know how to handle this. So I haven't mentioned Mom to him since the disaster at the festival."

Dad stood beside him. "Give yourself time too."

Cade shook himself. He had work to do, and standing around talking about the unsolvable problems with his mother and brother weren't going to accomplish anything. "I guess we'd better get back to work."

Dad smiled. "Yes, we should, son."

✦ ✦ ✦

"I'm just so glad you're okay," Quinn told Everleigh while they gathered bottles of water from the pantry at the inn. She'd hastened over as soon as her shift ended at the library that afternoon. "If that tree had fallen a few feet in the other direction . . ."

Cade's voice from last night echoed in her mind:

When I looked out the window and saw the tree had crashed through the roof, I was terrified something had happened to you.

She could hear the hitch in his breath, and it sent a swell of heat rushing through her. She picked up the pack of water. She and Cade hadn't spoken except in passing since they'd had words about Trevor this morning. Trevor had responded that he was tied up with a project but would check in soon. She was grateful he hadn't shown up today since he tended to cause so much friction between her and Cade, and especially since they didn't even really need his help. After all, her family had come through, along with Amber, a few of Amber's coworkers, Quinn, and Roger. They had plenty of assistance, and they had already made a dent in the cleanup, although it would take at least another day or two to clear out the tree debris. The demolished sunroom, however, would take even longer.

"I'm glad only the sunroom was damaged," Quinn continued. "You must have been so scared when the tree fell."

Everleigh smiled. "Cade took good care of me last night." She explained how he had carried her in from the storm and how she'd slept in his room. "We're grateful to everyone who came to help today."

"I got off work as soon as I could. I heard that a few other places in Coral Cove got hit hard, too, but power should be restored soon."

Everleigh tried the light switch, but the kitchen remained dark. "Hopefully tomorrow. At least the weather isn't too hot or too cold. I'll be all right without heating or air."

"And Roger's company can rebuild the sunroom after you get the check from the insurance company."

Everleigh pointed to the stools at the island. "Sit for a minute?"

Quinn complied. "What's up?"

"You tell me." Everleigh rested her elbow on the island and her chin on her palm. "I want the 'tea' on you and Roger."

Quinn beamed. "We're good. Really good."

"Details, please!"

Quinn blew out a happy sigh. "He's sweet and thoughtful. When he's working near the library, he'll stop by and bring me a cup of coffee or a snack if he has a lunch break." She shifted on the stool. "We have fun together. We like the same movies, and we never run out of things to talk about."

"That's amazing," Everleigh gushed. "I'm so happy for you."

"Now how about you and Cade?"

"What?"

Quinn rolled her eyes. "There's definitely some tension between you two. Even Roger has commented on it."

"Tension, huh?" Everleigh asked, and Quinn nodded. "I mean, I'm definitely attracted to him." That was for sure. Her cheeks heated as she recalled how it felt to be tucked safely in his arms. "But I don't think anything can come of it."

"Why not?"

"Because I'm planning to go back on the road." She motioned toward the back of the house. "We need to get this place back on the market, and hopefully someone will buy it. Then I'll start my nonprofit, and maybe Cade will open another restaurant since working as a chef is his passion," she explained. "And that will be that. I probably won't see Cade unless I come home to visit my family and he's still living somewhere around here." And why did that thought send sadness coursing through her?

Disappointment covered Quinn's features. "That's a shame, Everleigh. I think you two would be a great couple."

"If we could stop arguing, maybe."

"Arguing about what?"

"Different things." She shrugged. "Right now, he really dislikes Trevor and is convinced he's up to no good."

Quinn gave a knowing look. "He's jealous, I bet."

"Jealous?" Everleigh scrunched her nose. "No, he just has serious trust issues."

Quinn shook her head. "I think it's more than that. Cade cares about you."

"That might be true, but nothing is going to come of it." Everleigh hopped down from the stool. "Anyway, we should get back out there. I think everyone is waiting for some water."

She lugged the case of water outside and handed out bottles. When she approached Cade and his father, she contemplated what Quinn said about Cade. He did seem to care about her, but did he care about her as more than a friend? Was he as attracted to her as she was to him? That possibility sent a shudder through her.

"Thanks." Cade took the bottle, opened it, and drained almost half of it. "What should we do about supper? Should I make something for everyone? I don't even know what we have in the fridge or freezer that's still good since the power's been out."

She took in the exhaustion in his eyes and shook her head. Cade was completely worn out, but he was worried about feeding everyone who had helped. He was such a good man. "You're too tired to cook, Cade. You've been doing manual labor all day."

Landon appeared beside her and swiped a bottle of water from the pack. "Mom was talking about getting pizza at their house." He pointed toward the sky. "It'll get dark soon, so we need to wrap it up for the day." He focused behind her. "Dad! Are we heading to your place for pizza?"

"Yup." He pulled his phone from his pocket. "I'll order a bunch of pies, and we can all eat at our place since we have power."

Everleigh's eyes met Cade's. "Sound okay?"

"Sure." He examined his clothes. "I just need to get cleaned up first."

An hour later, Cade nosed his truck into the driveway at her parents' house and parked behind Landon's and Roger's pickups. He killed the engine and angled his body toward Everleigh. "This is where you grew up? At Endless Summer?"

"Didn't your parents name your childhood home?"

"Nope. It's just a plain ol' nameless house." He gave her a dramatic frown. "My folks are not nearly as cool as yours."

She laughed as she unfastened her seat belt and pushed the door open. "Come on in."

The delicious aroma of pizza coupled with the murmur of conversations greeted them when they walked inside the house. Everleigh guided Cade through the den to the kitchen, where her parents, Landon, Amber, Roger, and Quinn had packed around the table.

"You finally got here," Landon announced.

Cade picked up a can of Coke. "I had to shower."

"Yes, he did," Everleigh agreed, and everyone chuckled.

Mom pointed to the line of pizzas on the counter. "We have every flavor imaginable."

"Even Hawaiian." Landon made a face. "Putting pineapple on pizza is just plain wrong."

Cade tapped Everleigh's shoulder and leaned in close. "I learned early in the restaurant business that people get very emotional about their pizza toppings." His voice against her ear sent an electrical current cascading down her spine. "What kind would you like, partner?"

"Pepperoni works for me," she told him.

He picked up two plates. "Coming right up." He filled a plate with pepperoni pizza and one with meat lover's before they squeezed in at the table, their legs resting against each other.

Everleigh smiled while Landon shared his police patrol stories, and Cade laughed along with the rest of the group. Amber joined in and told a few of her rescue tales from the fire department.

Later Dad pulled out ice cream and all the fixings, and Everleigh felt herself relaxing as they built ice cream sundaes and ate them.

"What's your current plan for the inn?" Dad asked before shoveling a spoonful of vanilla smothered in chocolate syrup into his mouth.

Cade swallowed a bite of his sundae. "After we get the check from the insurance company, I was going to talk to Everleigh about having Roger's company rebuild the sunroom."

"Why would I disagree with you about that?" she asked.

Landon snickered. "At least not in front of Roger."

Roger shrugged, and everyone laughed.

"We'll need to find a tree service first to cut back the oak tree," Everleigh said.

Cade nodded. "I thought about that too."

"I can get you a list of recommended companies," Amber said.

"Fantastic," Cade said.

Mom squirted whipped cream onto her sundae. "Alana often told me how much she loved working with you, Cade. I'm sure you have plenty of great stories about being at the inn with her."

"I do." Cade nodded.

"Well, what are you waiting for?" Landon asked. "Share!"

Cade leaned back on his seat, and his arm brushed Everleigh's, sending a rush of warmth through her. "One time we had some guests coming from Europe, and she insisted we have a more sophisticated breakfast than I usually serve."

"What?" Everleigh squeaked. "Your breakfasts are delicious."

He held his hand up. "Hold on. So I made some pastries and had fruit and bagels."

"I can feel the punch line coming . . ." Landon said.

"Yeah." Cade rubbed a spot on his chest. "They asked me to make scrambled eggs, bacon, and home fries for the rest of their stay."

Everyone laughed.

Mom wiped her eyes while she continued to giggle.

"You've got to tell us some more stories," Dad said.

"Let me think." Cade tapped his chin.

Everleigh felt someone watching her, and she looked over to where Quinn grinned. Her heart felt light. Cade fit in with her family, and she was relishing every minute with them.

Once again she wondered if she should forget the idea of going back on the road. What would it be like to stay in Coral Cove and run the inn with Cade? She studied his handsome profile while he shared another tale about Alana, and her heart tightened.

But if she remained in Coral Cove, she hated the thought of abandoning Helping Angels. She felt led to help those parents who couldn't provide the care their children needed. She'd witnessed their suffering firsthand, and a nonprofit seemed like the perfect way to make a difference in the world.

Yet the Sunshine Inn was Alana's legacy, and now she understood how Cade and Alana had plans for it to grow and change. Even more than that, the inn had become Cade's home. Selling it would change his life forever. And after getting to know Cade, she would never be the same either.

Lately the idea of leaving her family and Cade felt like a knife to her soul. How would she recover after leaving them behind? Coral Cove was her home, and for the first time in her adult life, she missed it deeply. Was it time for her to settle down? And if so, did it make sense to settle down here?

Everleigh hugged her arms to her middle as confusion swamped her. All she knew for sure was that she felt the pull of Cade and Coral Cove—and she had no idea what that feeling meant or what she should do about it.

✦ ✦ ✦

"Your family is great," Cade said as he slipped his truck in park by his garage later that evening. He had not only enjoyed the delicious food, but he'd also appreciated sharing stories with people who cared about Alana. He'd been completely at ease with Everleigh and her family. He hit the button on his sun visor to open the garage, then rested his hand on his forehead. "I keep forgetting we don't have power."

She chuckled through a yawn. "I am completely worn out, but tonight was fun."

He turned toward her. She was gorgeous in the light from the dashboard. Her skin was flawless, and she didn't need any makeup. She inclined her head to the side.

"Why are you staring at me?" she asked.

"No reason." He considered the inn, cloaked in darkness, and imagined her padding around with only the light from her phone guiding her. "Are you okay staying alone at the inn?"

Her brows crouched. "Why wouldn't I be?"

"It's completely dark."

She grinned. "I'm an adult. I promise I'll be okay." She was silent for a moment. "When do you think we can get started on the sunroom?"

"Hopefully in the next couple of weeks. Roger will give us a good deal on the rebuild, and I can help him with the work—as long as he gives good instructions."

"My dad can help too," she offered. "He says he's bored in his retirement. I think he drives my mom crazy, which is why she told him he needs to come over and help us." She seemed to study him for a moment. "I saw you and your dad talking earlier. Is everything okay?"

"Yeah." He rested his back against the door. "He says I should give my mom some time to process Declan coming into our lives." He frowned. "I still don't understand why she's having such a tough time, but I can't force her—as much as I'd like to."

Reaching over, she took his hand in hers, and his pulse trotted. "I think it's all going to work out."

His throat dried as he took in the determination in her eyes. Her hope gave him strength. He recalled their discussion at breakfast about his plans for the inn and her nonprofit, and he wondered where her head was when it came to her plans for the future. Could they possibly involve him at all?

"So, you still want to put the inn back on the market after it's fixed up, right?" he asked, hoping she'd tell him no.

Her expression flashed with surprise before her smile returned. "Yeah. Of course." She nodded, but did he see uncertainty in those beautiful brown eyes?

"The deadline is coming up fast."

"Thanksgiving is coming up soon," she hedged. "Do you want to give me until Christmas?"

His body felt heavy with disappointment. It was obvious she wanted to sell the inn and leave. "Is that what you want?"

"Is it what *you* want?" she asked, her words seeming to challenge him.

A heavy silence expanded between them as they stared at each other, neither of them responding. Finally, he turned off the engine, and darkness covered the cab of the truck. His eyes adjusted, and he could see the outline of her.

"Do you want me to walk you to the door?" he offered.

She flipped on her camera's flashlight and shook her head. "I charged my phone at my parents' place, so I'll be fine."

They climbed out of the truck and met at the tailgate. Everleigh gasped and pointed her flashlight down toward the ground, where Bryant now rubbed against her shins. She giggled. "He nearly scared the life out of me."

"Bad boy. You need to stop sneaking up on us." Cade rubbed the cat's back. "Now, you go with Everleigh and keep her company tonight."

Everleigh hesitated, then threw her arms around Cade's neck. "Thank you for taking care of me."

"Anything for you, partner." He held her close and breathed in the sweet scent of her shampoo.

She stepped out of the embrace. "I guess I'll see you tomorrow," she said softly.

"Good night." He stood in the driveway and waited until she and Bryant were safely tucked inside the inn. As he climbed the stairs to the apartment, he tried to accept that soon she'd be gone from his life, though he didn't know how he'd move on without her.

CHAPTER 24

"THE LUMBER WILL be delivered this afternoon, and then we'll get your sunroom framed and rebuilt." Roger pulled his keys from his jacket pocket, and they jingled. "My crew will be there in a couple of hours."

"Great." Cade breathed in the cool November air as they crossed the parking lot at the home improvement store. It had been two weeks since the storm, and Cade had managed to work everything out with the insurance company. A tree service had disposed of the remaining branches as well as cut back the rest of the tree. The roof had been fixed, and Cade and Everleigh had hired Roger and his company to build the replacement sunroom.

He smiled when he thought of the events of the past two weeks. They had actually been . . . nice. He and Everleigh had cooked together, and they'd even played cards a few nights, spending most of the evening laughing. Their interactions had been good for his soul. He was grateful they were back on track as friends, and he tried not to think about how she planned to leave soon. He longed for her to give up the dream of selling the inn, hoping instead that she'd agree to let him run it. In that case, she'd only need to visit a few times a year. Or more, if he were lucky.

With a frown, he shoved away those thoughts. He was kidding himself. Everleigh had made it clear that her heart was not in Coral Cove. Instead, her heart belonged to nursing, and he admired her for that.

Actually, he admired her for many things.

Stop it, Cade!

"Did you hear what I said?"

"Sorry." Cade turned to his best friend. "What was that?" he asked as they approached Roger's twenty-year-old Chevrolet pickup.

Roger unlocked the doors. "I said we'll have the sunroom framed by Monday afternoon, and then the electrician will do his thing. We may have it closed in by the end of next week. It's a good thing you've already picked out flooring and paint."

"Lemonade," Cade muttered. Everleigh was so proud of that paint that he couldn't help himself from picking it again.

He bit back a growl at the thought of Trevor helping her paint that room. He couldn't stand that guy.

He'd noticed Trevor's name popping up on her phone a few times when they were together. She insisted he was only checking in to see how the sunroom rebuild was going. He hadn't stopped by to help, and they didn't need or want it as far as Cade was concerned.

Cade hopped into the passenger seat, and Roger cranked the diesel engine, which rumbled to life.

"You need to give me a lesson in framing this afternoon," Cade told his friend. "I can learn."

Roger grinned. "We'll see about that, chef." He steered through the parking lot.

"I did some plumbing work with my dad when I was a teenager. And I learned I was not cut out for it," Cade said, snickering. His eyes scanned the parking lot as they drove. "I mean, I can hold a wrench, but I—" He stopped speaking when his eyes locked on a black Toyota Tacoma. "Stop." He held his arm out toward his friend. "Please, stop here."

Roger hit the brakes. "Why?"

"You've got to be kidding me," Cade muttered. Fury boiled inside him as Trevor climbed out of the pickup truck and strolled over to a black Porsche Cayenne.

"What am I missing?" Roger asked.

The driver's side window lowered on the Porsche, and Trevor leaned into the SUV. Cade shifted in his seat, and when he spotted Valerie Rhodes, he felt as if a match had been lit in his veins. Now he had the proof he needed that Trevor was up to no good. He was working with Valerie Rhodes, who was representing the builders. He should have known it all along!

"That rat," Cade growled. "I knew it!"

"Cade?" Roger asked. "What's going on?"

"That's Trevor over there talking to Valerie Rhodes, the Realtor representing the developer that wanted to build luxury condos on our land. I knew that guy couldn't be trusted. He always told us he was just a handyman, but he's actually working with her." He glowered. "Everleigh says she and this guy are only friends, but I had this feeling he wanted more. Now I know for sure he's just using her—angling for an opportunity to buy the Sunshine Inn. And she's too sweet and trusting to realize his attention isn't genuine."

Trevor reached in the SUV and touched Valerie's cheek, and Cade grumbled. "I can't let him hurt her, but that's exactly what he's going to do."

"But she likes him, right?" Roger asked.

"Unfortunately," Cade groused.

"That means she might not believe you."

Cade massaged his forehead, where a headache brewed. "She already thinks I'm too suspicious of everyone, but look"—he pointed to Trevor as he laughed at something Valerie said—"they're clearly in cahoots. I can't let him get away with this."

"Just tread lightly," Roger warned him. "If she considers him a friend, she'll take his side."

Cade sat up straighter. "I'll handle it." He'd make Everleigh see he was right before it was too late.

✦ ✦ ✦

Everleigh turned toward the driveway just as Roger's truck steered in. She smiled at her father and brother, grateful they had come to help with the framing. "Wait here. I'll be right back."

She scooted down the driveway just as Trevor's black Toyota Tacoma pulled in. He had texted to check on her yesterday and mentioned that he'd try to come by and help, but she hadn't heard from him again. He'd been promising to offer a hand ever since the storm two weeks ago, but today was the first time he'd actually shown up.

Curious.

She picked up speed just as Cade climbed out of Roger's truck. Trevor approached him and said something before holding out his hand. Cade gave him a black look, scrutinized his hand, and then walked away.

Everleigh's stomach twisted. Why was Cade always so rude to Trevor? He didn't deserve it. He'd come over to help them.

Then Quinn's words from the day of the storm echoed in her mind: *"He's jealous, I bet."*

But how could that be true? Everleigh hadn't seen Trevor since well before the storm, but she'd spent every day since the storm with Cade. Didn't Cade know he was special to her—much more special than Trevor could ever be?

"Hi, Everleigh," Trevor said. "Sorry it took me so long to come by." He opened his arms to hug her, but she gave him an awkward pat and backed away from him.

"We appreciate the help."

Trevor turned toward the empty concrete pad where the sunroom had once stood and gave a low whistle. "All of that painting was for nothing, huh?" He touched her arm. "I guess we'll have to paint the new sunroom Lemonade."

"Right."

"You know, you don't have to go through all this," Trevor began. "You could just let the place go to a developer and not have to worry about rebuilding the sunroom."

Everleigh blinked and then blinked again. Had she heard him right?

Trevor lifted his hand, and his expression was mildly sympathetic. "Just think about it. A developer won't care if there's a sunroom or not. You won't have to deal with the hassle." He gestured around the property and then flashed a winning smile.

She looked over to where Cade was speaking to Roger, and when Cade started toward her, her insides turned and dropped.

Oh no. He's going to make a scene.

"I know your godmother meant a lot to you, Everleigh, and I'm not trying to make light of that." Trevor touched her hand. "But think about it. You want to get back on the road, and you mentioned you had to take the inn off the market while you deal with this headache. If you just sold it to a developer, all your worries would be solved."

The dark expression on Cade's face sent a cold chill through her as he approached. *This is going to be bad.*

"Trevor, why are you so invested in convincing Everleigh to sell the inn to a developer?" Cade demanded.

"I'm just looking out for her," Trevor said. "I'm sure this has been so stressful, and as her friend—"

"Her *friend*?" Cade gave him a derisive snort. "Please. You're not worried about Everleigh." He pointed at Trevor. "You're out for yourself."

Trevor's lips worked, but no words came out.

Everleigh folded her arms over her middle as anxiety hurtled through her. She had to do something to break this up. But what?

Cade took another step toward him, and he stood almost a head taller than Trevor. "Why don't you just do us all a favor and leave?"

She grabbed Cade's arm. "Please stop."

"No." Cade pulled his arm away. "This guy is up to no good, and it's time to face it, Everleigh. Stop being so naïve."

She gasped at the barb. Hadn't their friendship moved beyond that? "I'm not naïve. I'm just not rude like you." She pointed to his chest.

"Cade . . ." Roger appeared behind him. "This isn't what I'd call treading lightly."

Everleigh stared at him. What on earth was he talking about?

Trevor held his hands up. "If you really want me to go, then I will."

"No." Cade shook his head. "I want you to tell Everleigh the truth. Why are you *really* here, Trevor?"

"I'm here because Everleigh is my friend."

"Yeah, right!" Cade bellowed. "The truth, Trevor. I saw you before you came here."

Trevor looked confused. "What does that mean?"

"I saw you over at Beach Home Improvement. I know who you were talking to."

Something unreadable traveled over Trevor's face, and a sick feeling drifted over Everleigh.

"What's he talking about, Trevor?" she asked.

Trevor's countenance turned haughty. "I have no idea."

"Come on," Cade demanded. "Are you going to tell her, or should I?"

Trevor took a step toward Cade. "You know what your problem is?" he asked. "You think you know everything, but you don't."

"Is that right?" Cade's hands balled into tight fists. "Do you want to know what *your* problem is?"

"I thought you'd never tell me." Trevor's dark eyes glittered. Was he enjoying this?

Cade jammed his finger into Trevor's chest. "You're a liar, a user, and a phony. And it's time that Everleigh knew the truth about you."

Trevor's hand formed a fist, and he pulled his arm back.

Oh no! Worry shot through Everleigh. She had to do something!

The two men stood nose to nose, and panic grabbed Everleigh by the throat.

"That's enough!" She wedged herself between them, then pushed them away from each other. "Just calm down." Her focus pinged from one to the other, and she shook her finger in both their faces. "The two of you need to grow up."

Cade's lips twisted.

"If you're not going to help with the framing, then leave," she told them, her pulse galloping.

Cade glared at Trevor before sauntering toward the garage, muttering to himself.

Everleigh swiped her hands over her face, hoping her cheeks would cool down.

"Hey." Trevor touched her shoulder. "I'm sorry. I didn't mean to—"

"What was Cade talking about?" she demanded, interrupting him.

"Wh-what do you mean?"

"He saw you at the home improvement store. What were you doing?"

Trevor shrugged and focused on something behind her. "I honestly have no idea."

"Were you at the home improvement store before you came here?"

He rubbed the dark stubble on his jaw. "Uh, yeah." He pointed toward his truck. "I had to run by there to pick up a new hammer. The handle on mine broke last week. I traded it in under the warranty and got a new one."

"And who did he see you talking to?"

He shook his head. "I have no idea who he's talking about. I talked to the guy working over in the tool section."

She searched his face for any sign of a lie, but she wasn't sure if she saw one or not. She turned toward the garage, where Cade and Roger stood just inside the bay door. She couldn't see Cade's face, but he was gesturing wildly as if telling a story—or complaining about Trevor.

What had Cade seen? Had he misinterpreted it?

Cade was no dummy. Still, he was suspicious of people because he'd been hurt.

"Everleigh," Trevor said, "I just want to help you. You know that, right?"

She took in the sincerity in his eyes. She wanted to believe him, but Cade had made it clear that he wanted to help her too. He'd proved that more than once. In fact, he'd helped the first time she met him when he ran through the rain to bring her an umbrella and handle her suitcase. And since then, he'd gone out of his way to take care of her while Trevor had only shown up here and there.

"I'm sorry," Trevor said. "I really am just trying to help." His phone began to ring, and he pulled it from the pocket of his jeans and studied the screen. "Sorry, but I've got to take this." He walked away from her. "Bob. What's up?"

"Whoa. That was intense!"

Everleigh swiveled just as Quinn sidled up to her. She frowned. "How much did you see?"

"Uh, Cade and Trevor almost punching each other. I didn't want to interfere."

Everleigh blew out a deep sigh. "I really thought Cade was going to start World War III." She peered over to where Trevor walked near the pond with his phone up to his ear. "But Cade said something that has me concerned. He said he witnessed Trevor doing something shady at the home improvement store, but Trevor is denying it all." She turned to her friend. "Do you think Trevor is genuine?"

Quinn shrugged. "I can't really give you any advice since I don't know him. You need to go with your gut on this one." She patted Everleigh's arm. "Ask Cade what he saw. Something tells me he wouldn't lie to you."

Everleigh sighed. "Why is this so complicated?"

"I know one thing for sure: You guys can use all the help you can get, and if Trevor works in construction, then let him help with the framing. Many hands make light work, right?"

"Right." Everleigh nodded, but unease still gripped her stomach.

✦ ✦ ✦

Cade sat on the top of the picnic table later that evening and studied the framing. Thanks to Roger's crew and their volunteers—Landon, Everleigh's father, and even Trevor—they'd finished the framing in one day. Dave, Everleigh's father, had left a while ago, and Roger and his team were packing up their tools and getting ready to head out for the night.

Trevor and Everleigh were engrossed in a conversation near the back door, and Cade narrowed his eyes. He wished that guy would just disappear. He'd managed to avoid another run-in with Trevor, but the two of them had traded glares throughout the day while working on opposite sides of the site. It irked Cade that Trevor had stuck around, but it didn't surprise him. Of course he would want all of Everleigh's attention, and he was showering her with compliments on her work. He couldn't be any more obvious, but sweet Everleigh seemed oblivious. That, too, was irritating.

Landon climbed up on the picnic table, sat next to Cade, and handed him a bottle of water. "You look like you could use this."

"Thanks." Cade opened the bottle and took a long drink. *Ahhh.* The cold liquid was just what his parched mouth craved. Although the evening air was cool, the job had worn him out. He had a new appreciation for construction. He didn't know how the workers did this every day. He couldn't wait to take a long, hot shower and relax for the rest of the evening.

Landon drank from his bottle too. "We got it done." He held his bottle out to Cade, which he tapped as an informal toast.

"We sure did, man," Cade said. "Thanks for your help."

Landon shrugged. "No problem. I was off today, and my dad told me I should lend a hand. I'm just grateful my baby sister is in town for a while. I'm happy to spend some time with her." He grinned. "Even if it does involve manual labor."

Cade chuckled and took another drink of water. "Is it better than driving around in a patrol car and giving out tickets to people who drive too slow?"

"I guess Evie told you about my run-ins with Old Man Burns?"

Cade nodded. "I see him around town occasionally."

Landon took another long drink and peered out toward the back of the house, where Trevor spoke animatedly to Everleigh, who was listening with an indecipherable expression. "What's with that Trevor guy?"

Cade's eyebrows shot up. "What do you mean?"

"I don't know." Landon set his water bottle down on the tabletop and rested his elbows on his thighs. "There's something about him. He's just . . . sketchy." He squinted as he looked in their direction, then nodded as if to confirm his judgment. "Yeah. Definitely sketchy."

"That's an understatement."

Landon turned toward him. "How so?"

"Where should I start?" Cade moved his hand over the stubble on his neck. "He's working with the Realtor who's been hounding us to sell to a developer. I saw them together at the home improvement store, and it just solidified what I've suspected all along. That guy is bad news. He's pretending to be someone he's not."

Landon's eyes slid toward Trevor and Everleigh again and then back to Cade. "And let me guess. My sister doesn't believe he has any bad intentions."

"Bingo!" Cade pointed his water bottle toward Landon. "I've tried to convince her, but she thinks I'm just suspicious of everyone."

Landon let out a long-suffering sigh. "My sister has always believed the best in people—no matter what. You should've seen the guys she brought home in high school and college." He rolled his eyes. "She was always convinced she could 'save' them." He made air quotes with his fingers.

"Really?" Cade was fascinated.

Landon frowned. "The guys treated her badly. They'd never be there for her when she needed them. They'd cheat on her and break up with her and leave her devastated. But then she'd move on to another guy who wasn't any better. She'd bend over backward helping them with homework, paying for their dates, things like that. My folks would try to tell her she deserved someone who treated her as well as she treated him, but she'd never listen."

Cade considered Everleigh, and everything Landon said made sense. She'd always been a giving, caring, and trusting person—to a fault. None of that disappointment broke her belief in people, which might have been why she'd become a nurse. Her loving nature had guided her toward helping people and to the idea of a nonprofit to help parents of critically ill children. Cade admired how she always put everyone else before herself. But it was also her downfall when it came to men like Trevor.

"She can't see the writing on the wall." Landon leaned back on his hands. "Or she chooses not to."

Cade took another drink. "I suppose there's no getting through to her."

"I hope she's learned something over the years." A deep frown contorted his face. "Tell me she's not dating him."

"No, she's not, but she refuses to see the truth about him. I'm not going to give up until she acknowledges it. I don't want to see her hurt again."

Landon finished his bottle of water. "I have a feeling you'll get through to her."

"I'll do my best to get through to Trevor, too, since he hasn't gotten my point yet." He set his jaw.

Landon pushed himself off the picnic table. "I'm meeting Amber for supper, so I need to head out soon. But I'll go check on my dad and see if he wants help cleaning up."

"Thanks, Landon. I'll be there in a few minutes." Cade shook his hand before Landon started down the driveway toward his car.

When Trevor headed down the drive carrying a tool bag, Cade took off after him. He was going to handle the situation right now.

CHAPTER 25

"TREVOR," CADE CALLED him. "Trevor! We need to talk."

Spinning to face him, Trevor fixed his face with an apologetic expression. "Look, man, I feel like we started off on the wrong foot," he said. "I'm sorry if I've given you the wrong impression. I'm not trying to take advantage of Everleigh. I just want to help. That's it."

"Is that right?" Cade shook his head. Did this guy think he was an idiot? "You can save the song and dance. I know you're working with Valerie Rhodes."

Trevor tapped his chin. "Valerie Rhodes? I don't know who that is. I'm not working with anyone. I'm new in town, and I just wanted to—"

"Give it up," Cade insisted, his voice rising. "You think I'm an imbecile, but I'm not. It's obvious what you're doing here."

"Cade, I'm telling you the truth. I'm not trying to do anything underhanded." Then he paused and took a step toward him. "Wait a minute. Are you worried that I'm moving in on your girl? I never meant to do that either. You like Everleigh, right? But you haven't found the courage to tell her. If that's the case, then I'll back off."

"Please do back off," Cade snapped. "You can try to pull one over on her, but it's not going to work with me. You're trying to convince Everleigh to sell to the developer Valerie represents. I haven't figured out your connection to the developer, but I will. And you're taking advantage of Everleigh to do it. You can rest assured I won't let you double-cross her. I'll be sure she knows the truth. Besides that, we own this place equally, and she can't sell without my consent."

"You've got it all wrong, Cade." Trevor's expression and tone was so sleazy, Cade's skin began to crawl. "I'm not trying to convince Everleigh to do anything. I'm just trying to be a good friend."

This guy was a professional snake, and Cade's fingers itched as he balled them into fists.

Keep it together! Deep breaths, Cade.

He was determined to somehow rein in his temper. He had to, or he'd look like the bad guy to Everleigh. "Come on, man. I saw you at the home improvement store. You were leaning in the window of Valerie's Porsche. And you two looked very comfortable with each other."

"I don't know anyone named Valerie. You must have seen someone else with her. I was in the tool section."

Cade's body vibrated. He wasn't getting anywhere with this guy. It was clear he was wasting his time. But Cade wasn't a quitter.

Trevor glanced past Cade, and a sugary-sweet smile formed on his lips. Cade looked over his shoulder as Everleigh headed toward them, a serious expression overtaking her face.

Cade glared at Trevor. "When I tell her the truth, your charade will be over."

"I think there's been a misunderstanding here, Cade. There's no charade, and I'm sorry if I did something to offend you."

Cade glared at him before marching toward the back of the inn. If he was going to tell Everleigh the truth, he needed to tamp down his fury first. He knew for sure Trevor wasn't who he said he was. Problem was, Cade didn't know exactly why Trevor was playing this game at all.

✦ ✦ ✦

Everleigh dashed over to Trevor. "Sorry about that. I had to run inside for a minute." Her glance rotated from Trevor to where Cade talked to Landon and her dad. His dark expression sent worry through her. "Did you and Cade have words again?"

"It's fine." He waved it off. "Just a misunderstanding."

Not again! "I'm sorry about that. Without your help, we wouldn't have finished the framing so quickly today."

"It's no problem." Trevor shrugged. "He's just protective of you, which I understand." He took her hands in his. "I would be too. I'm just here to help you. That's all."

Everleigh studied his dark eyes as Cade's warnings filtered through her mind. Why was Trevor so eager to help her? And why was he always asking so many questions about the inn?

Trevor cocked his head to the side. "Everything all right?"

"Yeah." She pulled her hands out of his grasp and then glanced toward where Cade spoke to her brother and father. It was time to put an end to this stress. She was tired of the constant arguing. "I think it might be best if you stayed away for a while. The inn is half his, so I need to take his feelings into account."

Trevor nodded slowly. "That makes sense."

"But I appreciate your help today."

He pushed himself off his truck. "Sure thing." He pointed toward the skeleton of the sunroom. "If you decide you want an extra set of hands when it's time to hang the Sheetrock, let me know."

"I will. Thanks."

He opened his arms to hug her, but she held out her hand. He shook it before he climbed into his truck and drove away.

Everleigh made her way over to where Cade, Landon, and Dad were cleaning up the worksite. She pushed her hands into the pockets of her jeans and smiled. "Thanks for your help today, Dad. And Landon too."

"You know I'm always game to help my baby sis." Landon looped his arm around her neck and rubbed his knuckles on her head.

"Hey!" she squealed as she pushed him away. "I'm not ten anymore."

Dad chuckled, and Cade's eyes glittered as a ghost of a smile played over his mouth.

Landon's face lit up with his signature goofy grin. "Evie, you'll always be ten to me." He checked his phone. "Uh-oh. I'm going to be late meeting Amber, and she'll yell at me." He tapped Dad's shoulder. "Tell Mom hello for me." He and Cade shook hands. "Call me when you need help." Then he reached for Everleigh again.

"Don't you dare . . ."

Landon hooted and then waved. "See ya later," he called on his way to the driveway.

"I should get home too," Dad said.

"Would you like to stay for supper, Mr. Hartnett?" Cade asked.

"I told you to call me Dave, and no thank you." He patted Cade's shoulder. "You look exhausted. Get some rest." He hugged Everleigh. "You too."

Everleigh held on to him for a moment. "Thanks again, Dad."

"Anytime, honey. Let me know what else I can do to help, Cade."

"I will, sir." Cade grimaced. "I mean, Dave."

Dad smiled and then walked toward his car.

Everleigh scanned the backyard. "Did Roger and his crew already leave?"

"Yeah." Cade dropped a small piece of wood into a nearby trash can. "Your dad has a point. I'm worn out. How about we order something for supper?"

She folded her arms over her middle. "Let's talk first."

"Okay." He dropped a few more pieces of wood into the can. "Let me guess. Trevor?"

"Yeah." A cool breeze blew over her, and she moved her hands down her arms. "I want to know why you lost it with him earlier. What happened at the home improvement store?"

"He didn't tell you?"

She shook her head.

"Why am I not surprised," he mumbled. "Everleigh, I saw him with Valerie Rhodes."

"You saw him with Valerie Rhodes?" she asked, and when he gave her a solemn nod, her stomach pitched. "What exactly did you see?"

He explained that he and Roger were driving out of the parking lot, and he spotted Trevor's truck. Then he witnessed Trevor leaning into a Porsche Cayenne and talking to Valerie. "They seemed very . . . comfortable with each other. He was touching her face."

"Are you sure?"

"Yes, I'm positive." He dropped down onto the sunroom's temporary staircase. "I've suspected he was up to something from the beginning, but now I have proof that he's working with her."

Everleigh stilled while Trevor's comments about selling to a developer clicked into place in her mind. It was all starting to make sense—the way his friendship seemed forced, the way he was always overly affectionate, the way he constantly steered their conversation back to the inn.

"Everleigh, I know you want to trust him, but he's not who he says he is."

She opened her mouth and then closed it as embarrassment set in.

Trevor was using her, and she'd been a fool. Heat covered her cheeks. Cade had been right all along.

"Come on, Everleigh," Cade exclaimed. "He's not one of the loser boyfriends you brought home in high school or college."

She blanched at the sting of his words.

Oh, no he didn't!

"Excuse me?" she squeaked. "Who told you I brought home loser boyfriends in high school and college?" Then she recalled seeing him sitting with her brother earlier in the evening. "Was it Landon?"

"This is a prime piece of real estate, and some people will do anything for a deal," he continued, ignoring her question. "They'll take advantage of you to get what they want."

Her hands began to quiver while hurt thrummed through her. "Now I know what you really think of me." She gestured widely. "You believe I attract losers who use me. And you think I can't make good business decisions." Her voice was thick. "You also think I'm naïve, which you've made clear more than once. I bet you're pretty upset Alana didn't leave the inn to only you." She sniffed. "Oh, that's right. You already admitted that to me the night of the storm. You think I'll run this place into the ground just like your partner did when you lost your restaurant."

His lips thinned. "I didn't say that."

"But you're thinking it." She shook her finger at him. "How about this, Cade? Let's go back to our original plan the day I interfered in your family drama." She pointed to the garage. "You stay out of my way, and I'll stay out of yours. Sound good to you? It sure sounds fantastic to me."

He looked stricken. "Everleigh, I didn't—"

"No." She shook her head. "I know how you feel about me." She rubbed her stinging eyes. "I'm nothing but a pain to you. An annoying little sister, right? Just like how Harlowe feels about me."

"No, Everleigh," he began, his expression grave. "I never—"

"It's okay. Really." Her words vibrated with her grief. "Once the sunroom is rebuilt, I'll get the inn back up on the web. Maybe it will sell before Thanksgiving, but no matter what, I'll be out of your life by December because it's obviously time for me to leave. Deal?" Her voice broke.

He studied her. "Is that what you want?"

No! She paused for a beat. But then she nodded. She couldn't tell him the truth—admit that she cared about him—and let him hurt her more than he already had.

"You sure?"

"Positive," she whispered, the word sounding strained.

He hesitated for a moment, and her heart pounded in her ears.

"Fine," he muttered before he started for the garage, Bryant trotting at his heels.

As Everleigh watched him go, her tears broke free and raced down her face. Not only had she been kidding herself thinking she and Cade could be friends, but she'd also been stupid enough to think he respected her—maybe even loved her and wanted her to stay. But it turned out she'd been wrong about everything.

Everything.

And now it was time to wrap things up in Coral Cove. She needed to sell the inn, get back on the road, and put Cade Witherspoon behind her.

✦ ✦ ✦

Dad gave a low whistle as he stepped into the sunroom. "This is better than the first sunroom." He scanned the light-yellow walls, recessed lighting, ceiling fans, and slate flooring. "You've been busy."

"You could say that," Cade quipped. It was Wednesday afternoon, and "busy" didn't seem to do the work justice. Cade felt as if he,

Roger, and Roger's crew had been working nonstop for days on end to finish it.

"Looks like you're done," Dad said.

Cade plowed his hand through his hair. "We just have to hang the blinds." He pointed toward the large windows. "Roger went to pick them up. He got a great deal with one of the vendors he always uses."

"Where's Everleigh?" Dad asked.

"At the store with Quinn looking for furniture." Cade rubbed his knuckles over his sternum and looked out toward the bay just as Bryant trotted by as if on his way to take care of something important. His stomach sank as he considered how strained things had been between him and Everleigh since their argument a week and a half ago.

"Everything all right?"

Cade turned toward his father's concerned expression. "Why?"

"You seem anxious." Dad gave him a knowing look. "I can read your moods, son."

Cade nodded. "Yeah, I know." He cleared his throat. "Things have been tense around here."

"I can understand that. You've had a lot of stress with the aftermath of the storm." Embarrassment flashed over his face. "I'm sorry I haven't been around much to help. That job over in Wilmington turned out to be more than we anticipated."

Cade rubbed his elbow. While he longed to tell his father everything, he wasn't quite sure how to put it into words. But the stress had been eating him alive. He couldn't stand the distance between him and Everleigh.

Dad's face lit with concern, and he beckoned Cade toward the doorway. "Why don't we sit and talk while we wait for Roger? When he gets back, I can help y'all hang the blinds."

Cade led his father to the kitchen, where he handed him a bottle of Coke. As they sat at the island, he recalled all the times he'd sat there with Everleigh, talking and laughing. Now she barely spoke to him.

"You look like you're about to explode," Dad said. "What's going on, son?"

Cade took a deep breath and then unloaded all of his burdens. He shared how he had suspected Trevor was bad news and caught him interacting with Valerie Rhodes. Then he shared how he and Everleigh argued, and how she'd told him her plans to leave. "I've tried everything to get her to open up to me. I've apologized. I've tried cooking for her, but she said she wasn't hungry. I've begged her to talk, even telling her she could yell at me, but she says she's too tired. No matter what I say or do, she just walks away or doesn't answer me."

He spun his bottle cap, sending it spiraling around the island. "I feel like I'm coming apart at the seams. I never meant to hurt her, Dad. I never intended for her to think I considered her an annoying younger sibling. That's not even in the ballpark of how I feel about her. But she's so stubborn—more stubborn than I ever imagined." He found Dad watching him. "I can't just let her leave thinking I don't respect her, but I don't know how to get through to her." He scoffed. "I guess she's just as stubborn as I am, huh?"

Dad remained silent, and Cade sighed. He craved his father's advice. "Say something, Dad. Anything."

"You care about her." Dad rested his forearms on the island.

"Of course I do. We're partners and friends." He twirled the bottle cap again. "At least, I thought we were friends." His posture drooped as the truth settled over him. "I guess the best option is for us to go our separate ways. We can't get along. We drive each other crazy."

Dad grinned.

"You find this funny?" Cade grumbled.

"Yeah, I do." Dad continued to smile. "Because I've said those very words about your mother more than once."

Cade stared at his father. "You're comparing Everleigh and me to you and Mom?" he asked, and Dad nodded. Shock and confusion rocketed through him. Had Dad lost his mind? "That makes no sense. We're not dating. We've never dated. So why would you even think that?"

"You and Everleigh seem to . . . click."

"Click?" Cade guffawed. "All we do is argue," he exclaimed. "We're total opposites. We can't agree on anything."

Dad nodded slowly. "I've been there with your mom. I don't have to tell you that she and I are opposites too. She's much more . . . reserved. And getting her to open up sometimes requires a can opener." He pointed to himself. "But I'm an open book."

"That's true."

Dad pointed to him. "And you're like your mom."

Cade couldn't deny it. And Everleigh was an open book like his father—warm, giving, kind, always willing to help someone. She was a ray of sunshine while he tended to be a gloomy day. They *were* opposites. Yet there was that old saying that opposites attract. And he was definitely attracted to her.

That familiar stitch radiated in his chest.

He scrubbed his hand down his face. Why was he driving himself insane? Soon she'd leave, and life could go back to—normal? What was normal now? Now that Alana had died, nothing would ever be normal again. And now Everleigh had walked into his life and turned it upside down.

"You okay, Cade?" Dad asked.

"None of this matters." He tossed the bottle cap toward the trash can, and it bounced off the counter before rolling under the refrigerator. "She's made it clear she'll be gone by the beginning of December."

"How do you feel about her leaving?"

Broken. Devastated. Distraught. "It's what she wants."

"Is it what *you* want?"

No. Cade ousted the thought from his mind. He needed to change the subject. "Has Mom spoken to Declan?"

Dad frowned. "I've tried to get her to open up about him, but as always, she refuses. She shuts down whenever I mention him."

Cade began pulling the label off the bottle of Coke. "What happened that made her want to forget her child?"

"I wish I knew." Dad took another drink. "It had to be really bad."

"Yeah," Cade whispered. He didn't want to think about someone hurting his mother. "If she told us, we could help her cope with it, and then maybe Declan could be a part of our lives." He ripped the label completely off the bottle and then dropped it onto the island. "I've texted Declan a few times since he was here. We've made small talk, but he hasn't mentioned Mom, and I haven't either. I'd love to find a way to help her deal with whatever is holding her back."

"There's one thing I've learned about your mother, Cade. You can't force her into anything." Dad pointed his bottle toward Cade. "And, like I said earlier, you're just like her."

Cade sighed. "I know."

"Let me give you a little piece of advice, son."

"Go ahead."

"Don't let your stubbornness stand between you and your happiness."

The front door opened with a squeak, and Roger came into the kitchen. "Ready to hang some blinds?"

"Let's do it." Cade gave his dad's shoulder a squeeze and tossed the two empty bottles into the recycle bin under the sink. Then he followed Roger out to the truck, his father's advice echoing in his mind.

CHAPTER 26

QUINN POINTED TO a white wicker patio set, including a love seat, two matching chairs, and a coffee table. "How about this?"

Everleigh examined the price tag. "It's within our budget." She ran her hand over the cushion. "I like the bright blue." She shrugged. "Honestly, anything is okay with me."

Her phone buzzed with a phone call, and she found the number for one of her recruiters on the screen. She clicked the button to silence the call and returned the phone to the back pocket of her jeans.

Quinn lifted her eyebrows. "Who was that?"

"Recruiter." She sighed.

Quinn touched her shoulder. "Is everything all right?"

She managed a smile. "Of course." She dropped onto the wicker love seat. "I reposted the inn on the websites last night since all we have left to do is hang the blinds and put new furniture in the sunroom." She moved her fingers over the wicker arm. "Cade and Roger really did a great job with it. And they even painted it Lemonade, the color I had painted the walls just before the storm. Alana would love how it turned out." A bubble of sadness expanded inside her, and she tried to wish it away.

"Hey." Quinn sat beside her. "I can tell when you're trying to convince everyone else that you're happy, but something is really bothering you. You can talk to me, Everleigh." Her expression held concern. "What's going on?"

"I'm fine." She pinned a smile on her face. "I told Cade I'd be gone after Thanksgiving, and Thanksgiving is next Thursday—only eight days away."

Quinn was quiet for a moment. "You're really not going to stay?"

Everleigh could feel her heart breaking as she shook her head. "I need to go."

"Why?"

"Because it's always been my plan." She studied her hand as if her short fingernails were the most fascinating things on the planet. "It's best if Cade and I part ways, whether the inn sells or not."

Quinn remained silent, but Everleigh could almost feel her friend analyzing her words. She turned toward her. "Go on and say it, Quinn."

"What?" Quinn gave her a feigned shocked expression. "I didn't say anything."

"But you're thinking it."

Quinn angled her body toward Everleigh and rested her back against the arm of the love seat. "I take it that you and Cade still aren't speaking."

"That's true." Everleigh folded her legs under her. "He's been trying to get me to talk, but he really hurt me, and there's nothing left to say."

Quinn's smile was glum. "Roger and I have noticed that there's something between you and Cade, and I was hoping maybe you'd stay because of it."

Everleigh's heart skipped a beat. *I was hoping so too . . .*

"You two seem to really care about each other."

Everleigh remained quiet. She did care for him—*deeply*—and she couldn't deny it even to herself. But that didn't mean they could have a future.

"Don't you care for him?" Quinn asked.

Everleigh nodded. "I do, and at one point I thought maybe we could be more than friends." She played with the zipper on her jacket while her mind replayed the night of the storm. "I was convinced he cared about me the night the tree fell through the sunroom. He actually said he couldn't imagine something happening to me. And the way he carried me out of the rain, then held me close while I cried . . ." A quiver rushed over her, but she renounced it. "But we argue *all the time*. If Cade cared so much, he wouldn't have treated me like an annoyance or a fool." An ache radiated in her chest. She couldn't lose it here in the middle of the busy home improvement store. She'd melt from embarrassment if she allowed herself to give in to grief so publicly.

"I need to get back on the road. It's where I belong." That's what she needed to focus on instead of her broken heart.

Quinn rested her hand on Everleigh's shoulder. "I don't want you to go." She sniffed. "I'll miss you."

"I'll miss you too." She squeezed her friend's hand. "But I promise I'll stay in touch and visit when I can."

"I'm going to hold you to that."

Everleigh smiled and then pushed up from the love seat. "I'm going to find a salesperson and see when I can get this set delivered." She zigzagged through the store, trying to shove away the sadness that burrowed deep in her soul.

✦ ✦ ✦

Everleigh loaded her groceries into the back of her Trailblazer Monday morning. She hugged her jacket closer against her body as a chilly late November breeze brought with it the aroma of salt water and moist sand. She climbed into the driver's seat and rubbed her cool hands together for warmth. She started her SUV, and a pop song serenaded her through her speakers.

She'd spent the last couple of days considering offers for hospitals all around the United States. Her top choices were Houston and Atlanta, but she hadn't narrowed them down further yet. She'd almost signed a contract to go back to Texas but then convinced herself to wait until after Thanksgiving. Not that anything crucial was going to change.

Steering out of the parking lot, she turned onto Main Street and stopped at the red light. The small Coral Cove government center came into view, and she gripped the steering wheel tighter. Her sister's office was located on the second floor. She hadn't heard from Harlowe in weeks, but a pit still expanded in her stomach every time she thought of her.

Everleigh sat up taller in the seat, and she slapped on her blinker. She was going to find her sister and insist they work out whatever issue Harlowe had with her. She couldn't leave Coral Cove without resolving it once and for all. Maybe today would be the day their relationship changed. Perhaps they could forge a renewed sisterhood. Everleigh smiled as she imagined how the talk would go.

After parking in the municipal lot, Everleigh hastened through the cold and into the government center before taking the elevator up to the human resources office. She was grateful for the warm air pumping through the heating vents as she pulled open the door to Suite 201.

"Everleigh!" Betty Jean Gorman exclaimed. She rushed around

the desk and pulled Everleigh in for a tight hug. The older woman barely came up to Everleigh's chest. "You're a sight for sore eyes. It's been so long, honey!"

Everleigh smiled down at her. "It has been." She jammed her thumb toward her sister's closed office door and the nameplate that read Harlowe Kessler. "Is she in?"

"Oh, no." Betty Jean shook her head. "She's in a meeting downstairs."

"For how long?"

Betty Jean's little nose crinkled. "At least another hour."

"Oh." Everleigh's spirit deflated like a balloon. So much for working things out with her sister before Thanksgiving.

Betty Jean pushed a notepad and pen toward her. "You can leave her a note." Then she waved her off. "Silly me! I'm so old-fashioned. You'd probably rather text her, right?"

But texting hadn't worked. Maybe an old-fashioned method was a better course of action. "Actually, I'd love to write her a note." She took the pen and began to write:

> Harlowe,
>
> I was in the area and thought I'd stop by and see how you are. Sorry I missed you.
>
> Looking forward to seeing you and Branson Thursday.
>
> Love,
>
> Everleigh

She handed the notepad back to Betty Jean. "Have a nice Thanksgiving with your family."

"You too, honey." Betty Jean's eyes twinkled behind her glasses.

Everleigh's phone chimed with a text just as she climbed back into her SUV, and she found Trevor's name on her screen. She hadn't heard from him since she'd told him to keep his distance more than two weeks ago. What could he possibly want now?

She opened the text message:

> Trevor: Hey. Just checking in. How's the sunroom?

Everleigh had reposted the ad for the inn five days ago. Valerie had texted twice and left two voicemails saying she wanted to discuss an offer over asking price, but Everleigh hadn't responded. Cade's warning rang through her mind. Surely Trevor's true purpose in texting her was to find out why she hadn't answered Valerie's calls.

Everleigh tapped her fingers on her steering wheel as a surge of confidence overtook her.

> Everleigh: Sunroom is done and the inn's back up for sale. Is that why you're really texting me? Are you looking for inside info on any offers we've received?

She held her breath as the moments ticked by. Suddenly the dancing dots appeared on her screen.

> Trevor: Why would you think that?

She snorted before dropping her phone onto the passenger seat and starting her SUV. She flipped on the radio, and a pop song sang through the speakers. Her phone chimed again, and she turned the radio up louder. She wouldn't allow Cade or anyone else to call her naïve ever again. And as far as she was concerned, she was done with Trevor.

✦ ✦ ✦

Cade wrenched open the exit door at the bank and stalked out onto Main Street. The cold breeze rushed over him, and he jammed his hands into the pockets of his coat. It was Tuesday afternoon, two days before Thanksgiving, and disappointment weighed heavily on his shoulders.

He'd spent the past week trying to find a way to buy out Everleigh's half of the inn. He'd applied for a couple of loans online, getting turned down for each of them, then applied in person at his bank. He'd tried putting his truck and motorcycle up as collateral, but that didn't help. No matter what he attempted, his bad credit—all thanks to Serena and his failed restaurant—haunted him and squashed his opportunities.

He continued down Main Street, taking in the passing traffic both on the sidewalk and the road. Since the roof was fixed, the sunroom was completed, and the online ads for the inn were active again, he and Everleigh hadn't spoken in a few days. He'd waved to her when he saw her outside with Bryant earlier in the day, but other than that, their friendship seemed to have gone the way of his credit. He tried in vain to ignore the grief that nagged him.

Why should he even be surprised? Everleigh had turned out to be just like Serena. Her actions reminded him why he'd worked to guard his heart and push away people who had tried to get close to him. It was better in the end to just remain alone.

His mother's store came into view, and he quickened his steps. He needed to discuss plans for Thanksgiving with her, and he also wondered if she had spoken to Declan. Last he'd heard from his brother, their mother hadn't made any efforts to contact him. Cade was determined to resolve that issue as soon as possible.

He pushed open the door, and the bell above it rang. He scooted past customers perusing a display of miniature car models and made a beeline for the counter, where a cute blond with a nose ring and streaks of pink in her hair stood looking bored. Her green eyes locked on his, and a bright smile lit up her face as she propped herself against the counter. "Can I help you?" she asked.

Cade looked down at her name tag. "Hi, Missy. Is Trisha here?" he asked.

Her brow wrinkled. "She's in the back, but I can help you." She stood up taller.

"I'm her son."

"Oh." Understanding overtook her face, and she gave him a once-over before twisting a lock of her pink and blond hair around her finger. "So you're the famous Cade."

He nodded before slipping through the door marked with an Employees Only sign. He found Mom sitting at her desk, staring at her computer screen.

"Cade!" She pushed her reading glasses up on her head and waved him over. "Give me a hug."

What's up with Mom? He couldn't remember the last time she'd demanded a hug from him, but he complied before sitting on a chair in front of her desk.

"What's going on, sweetie?"

He rested his right ankle on his left knee and drummed his fingers on his thigh. "I wanted to talk to you about Thanksgiving. I'd like to cook. I'll pick up the turkey and all the fixings after I leave here. We can eat in the kitchen at the inn."

"Great. What can I bring?"

He shrugged. "Dessert?"

"I'll get a pie."

"Perfect." He hesitated, searching his mind for the best way to start a dialogue about his brother.

"Your dad said the sunroom was coming together."

"It's done," he said. "The new furniture is supposed to be delivered tomorrow."

She nodded, and an awkward silence stretched between them.

Then he took a deep breath. *Here goes nothing.*

"I'd like to invite Declan and Stephanie to join us for supper Thursday. I'm going to tell them they can stay at the inn for a few days, so we can get to know them."

She shook her head with emphasis. "No, Cade."

"Mom—"

"No," she said, more forcefully this time. "I'm-I'm still not ready."

He worked to hold back his anger. "When will you be ready?"

"I don't know." She picked up a pen and rolled it between her fingers. "Maybe Christmas, but not now. Not yet."

He studied her. Frustration and confusion rained down on him.

She threw her hands up. "It's too soon, Cade." Her words faltered. "I can't do it."

He leaned forward. "Mom, can you explain to me why you've chosen to cut your firstborn out of your life like this? Because I just can't understand it."

Her desk phone rang, and she jumped with a start. "I need to get this." She picked up the phone. "Crafty Creations, this is Trisha." As she listened, she covered the receiver with her hand and addressed Cade. "I'll see you Thursday at the inn. Text your dad the details."

Cade watched her, but she focused on the edge of her desk, avoiding his eyes. After a few moments of listening to her discuss providing arts and crafts kits for a day care, he gave up and retreated to his truck.

He sat in the driver's seat and stared down at his phone. His plan of inviting his brother and sister-in-law to join him for Thanksgiving had gone up in smoke, just like his plan to buy out the inn. But he couldn't give up the dream of having his brother, sister-in-law, and future niece or nephew in his life.

After unlocking his phone, he dialed Declan's number and hoped his brother would answer.

"Cade," Declan said. "Hi."

Cade moved his free hand over the cool dashboard. "Hey, Declan. I was going to invite you and Stephanie to come for Thanksgiving, but when I mentioned it to Mom . . ."

"Let me guess," Declan began. "She said no."

Cade slumped back on the worn bench seat. "I'm sorry, man."

"It's not your fault, Cade. She's just not ready to talk to me."

"I'll keep working on her." Cade rubbed his forehead as an idea gripped his mind. "Give me a couple of days, and I'll get back to you. Just promise me you won't give up hope yet."

Declan chuckled. "Hope is all I have at this point."

After he hung up, Cade started his truck. He had an idea that might finally bring his family together, and he couldn't wait to put his plan into action.

CHAPTER 27

EVERLEIGH STOOD IN front of the full-length mirror in her suite and examined her reflection. She almost didn't recognize herself. Since Mom always insisted they dress up for holidays, she'd pulled on her little black dress and heels. Her hair fell in curls past her shoulders, and minimal makeup highlighted her eyes. She was much more comfortable in jeans, a hoodie, and a pair of Converse sneakers, but she couldn't let her mother down.

After swiping gloss over her lips, she shouldered her purse and headed out into the hallway. As her shoes clicked along the hardwoods, the delicious aroma of roasting turkey permeated her senses and made her stomach gurgle. When she reached the kitchen she stopped in the doorway, and her eyes roved over Cade standing at the counter with his back to her.

Hello, snug-fitting jeans. And oh, how that black T-shirt stretches over that muscular back and those arms . . .

He turned toward her, and heat crawled up her neck to her cheeks. *Did I say any of that out loud?*

His eyes widened, then returned to their normal size. "Hi," he said.

"Happy Thanksgiving," she managed to say.

"Happy Thanksgiving." He inclined back against the counter, and his eyes moved over her. She was almost certain he was checking her out and liked what he saw.

Huh. Interesting. Does that mean he might still care about me?

"You look . . . nice," he said, rubbing his hands over that fantastic five o'clock shadow. "Really nice."

She studied her dress for a moment. "Thanks. It's been a while since you've seen me in a dress and heels. Not since Alana's memorial service."

He swallowed, and his Adam's apple bobbed. "Heading to your folks' place?"

She nodded and propped herself against the doorjamb. "It smells amazing in here. I assume your parents are coming over?"

He nodded.

She pointed to the freezer. "I need to grab that chocolate pie. They put me in charge of buying dessert since I can't mess it up."

"Don't blame them." He grinned, and her heart did a little dance. He retrieved the pie from the freezer, and she met him at the island. He held it out to her and then pulled it back. "You're more than welcome to join us." His expression became sheepish. "But I'm sure your family would miss you." He handed her the pie. "Maybe you can have dessert later with me and my folks."

"Yeah. Maybe."

They stared at each other, and a longing started deep inside her. She took a step away from him and then two more before she turned and started toward the door. She had to get out of there before she said something stupid. He had hurt her, and she couldn't give him the power to do it again. But she also missed him more than she could express.

"Everleigh," he called, and his voice sounded strange.

Keep walking!

But she couldn't. Her feet refused to move forward.

She froze in the kitchen doorway with her back to him and closed her eyes, her breaths coming in short bursts.

"Everleigh," he repeated, his voice suddenly hoarse. "I-I never meant to hurt you."

She fixed her lips in a sweet smile and then pivoted toward him. "I know."

His expression flashed with suspicion. "So we're okay?"

"Uh-huh. Of course." She pointed toward the door. "I'd better go." Her heels clacked toward the front door, where she sat the pie and her purse on the bench. She retrieved her coat from the closet and quickly pulled it on.

"Wait."

When she spun to face him, his handsome countenance flashed with contrition, and her lungs constricted.

"Have we gotten any offers on the inn since you reposted the ads?" he asked.

She swallowed against her dry throat. "Only from a few developers, and I told them no." She paused for a beat. "I know today's the deadline. I'll take the ads down tomorrow."

"You will?" His eyebrows shot up.

She nodded. "I'm considering a couple of hospital contracts. I haven't decided between Houston or Atlanta."

"Oh." He shoved his hands into the pockets of his jeans and leaned his shoulder against the doorframe. He appeared . . . sad? Disappointed? A little of both? They were both silent, and then he stood up straight. "Enjoy the holiday with your family. Tell them I said hello."

"You too." She picked up the pie and headed out the door, and once she reached the stairs, she released the breath she didn't know she'd been holding.

❖ ❖ ❖

Cade ran his hand over the back of his head after Everleigh was gone. She'd been stunning in that dress and those high heels that showed off her long and lithe legs. Just the right amount of makeup accentuated her dark, gorgeous eyes and pink lips. And, as usual, her shiny, thick hair bounced off her slight shoulders. He yearned to thread his fingers through those red curls. He'd had to force himself to stop staring at her.

And all at once he found himself almost begging for her forgiveness. What was his problem? He was wasting his breath thinking she felt something for him. The woman was already considering hospital contracts out of state. There was nothing between them except for the inn, and that was how it should be. After today, he'd go back to running it, and she'd be the silent partner he'd hoped for from the beginning.

You're better off without her here.

But for some irritating reason, a twinge of disappointment mocked him.

He read the clock. Mom and Dad would be here soon, and he still had to make the gravy, green bean casserole, and mashed potatoes.

Cade buried his confusion in cooking and then set the dining room table with Alana's china. He tried to forget the last time he'd eaten there—with Everleigh.

Stop thinking about her!

He did his best to concentrate on the meal. By the time his father's sedan parked in the driveway, he had the turkey and all the fixings ready.

"The inn smells heavenly," Mom said as Cade took her coat.

Cade hung his parents' coats in the closet by the front door. "I hope you brought your appetites with you."

"We did." Dad balanced two pies in his hands. "And plenty of dessert."

"Everything's ready." Cade led them into the kitchen and then pointed to the dining room. He set the pies on the counter while his parents took their seats. Then he stood in the doorway and waited for his mother to react to the two extra place settings. It was time to put his plan into motion.

"Are you expecting someone else?" Dad asked.

Mom seemed hopeful. "Is Everleigh joining us?"

"Nope." Cade sat down across from them and beside the two extra seats. He steepled his hands and took in their confused expressions.

Mom's eyes bounced between Cade and Dad. "What am I missing?"

Dad held his hands up. "Don't look at me. I have no idea."

"You insisted I not invite Declan and Stephanie for Thanksgiving, but I set two places for them. This way, we can be reminded of who's missing from our family today," Cade explained.

Shock flittered over his mother's face as it contorted with a frown. Dad brushed his hands over his mouth before shooting Cade a pointed look. The room was mortuary quiet, and Cade waited for his mother to speak.

"Cade," she finally said. "This isn't going to change my mind."

He sat forward in his chair. "Then what will, Mom? I understand that you need time, but I've already lost an entire lifetime with my brother. I want to get to know him and his family, and I want to do it now." He pointed to the table.

"Why does this mean so much to you, Cade?" Mom asked.

He took a deep breath. "I appreciate everything you did for me when I was a kid and everything you gave me. I had a happy childhood full of love and opportunities." He paused. "But it was lonely growing up an only child. I was always envious of my friends who had siblings to play with, to argue with, to learn from. I had no one to play with when we went on vacation. I had no one to share secrets with or get advice from. I always felt I'd missed out on something important."

Mom sniffed and wiped her eyes with a napkin, and his heart wrenched.

"I'm not saying this to hurt you, Mom," he explained. "But I want Declan, Stephanie, and their child in my life, and I don't want to do it behind your back. I want you and Dad to be a part of this. You kept this secret from me for thirty-three years, but now that I know the truth, I'm not going to act like my brother doesn't exist. He *does* exist. He's *my* flesh and blood. And he did nothing to deserve to be treated this way."

Mom pushed her chair back and stood. "I'm not going to sit here and listen to this." She started for the door. "I'm going home."

Cade took off after her. "Mom!" he called. "You can't keep running from the truth."

The front door opened and then slammed shut.

Cade whirled around toward his father. "Why is she making this so difficult?"

Dad shook his head and started after her.

Cade followed him. "Dad. Don't tell me you agree with her."

His father retrieved their coats from the closet. "When you're married, you have to be a team, a united front no matter what." He opened the front door. "I'll call you later," he said before fleeing out the door.

Cade stood in the foyer alone.

And the silence was deafening.

✦ ✦ ✦

Everleigh plastered a smile on her face while Landon shared a story about chasing a guy on foot who'd stolen a sandwich and soda from a gas station. She scanned the table and tried to focus. But her thoughts were tied up with Harlowe and Cade.

Her sister hadn't shown up for supper. Instead, she and Branson had decided to join his family, and the sting of her absence was raw. Not only had Harlowe not contacted her since she'd left her a message at her office, but she'd decided not to come to supper on Thanksgiving.

To make matters worse, Everleigh was struggling to forget how Cade's intense eyes had sent heat skipping over her skin when he'd stared at her in the kitchen.

I'm losing it. Officially off my rocker.

She studied her untouched turkey, gravy, green bean casserole, cranberry sauce, and sweet potatoes. Was Cade enjoying supper with his parents right now? Was he thinking of her?

Stop it!

"Everleigh?"

Her head snapped up, and she found all the eyes around the table locked on her. She set her fork down and smiled. "What did I miss?"

"Is everything okay?" Dad asked.

"Yeah." She moved her finger over the red tablecloth. "Is Harlowe coming for dessert?"

"We hope so." Mom's smile seemed unsure.

Everleigh did too. Surely Harlowe wouldn't skip seeing her family on a holiday. She turned toward Amber. "How are your folks doing?"

"Fine," Amber said. "My mom is talking about finally retiring from the bank. I hope she does. My dad keeps saying he wants to travel, and he's been retired for a couple of years now. Says he's ready to enjoy his golden years."

Everleigh relaxed while Amber continued to talk about her parents. She nibbled her supper even though her stomach was tied up in a knot.

Once everyone had finished eating, she carried a stack of plates into the kitchen and began filling the dishwasher.

Amber set the silverware in the sink while Landon put the glasses on the counter.

"We need to get going to Amber's parents' place." Landon touched Everleigh's shoulder. "We promised we'd be there for dessert."

Everleigh recalled how Cade had called her exes "losers," and irritation nipped at her. But she didn't want to make a scene. She peeked toward the doorway, where Amber was engrossed in a conversation with Mom. "Landon, can I ask you something?"

"Sure."

"Did you tell Cade that all of my ex-boyfriends were losers?"

Landon stared at her for a moment before recognition glimmered in his eyes. "Oh. Um, maybe?" He cupped his hand to the back of his neck.

"Why would you betray me like that?"

"Whoa." He lifted his hand. "I didn't betray you, Evie. I didn't say anything I wouldn't have said to your face. In fact, I probably *have* said that to your face."

"Then what did you say?" she asked. "Why were you even talking about me?"

"Hold on there, little sis," Landon began, his words gentle. "We were discussing Trevor. I told Cade I didn't trust him, and we talked about how you always look for the best in people. I mentioned that you used to bring home guys who . . . weren't the best choice for you. I said they treated you badly, but you acted like you could save them."

"I wish you'd kept that to yourself."

"Cade knows how you are, Evie. He agreed that you always give people the benefit of the doubt, even if they don't deserve it." He grinned. "And that's what makes you so lovable."

She rolled her eyes. "Just don't talk about me anymore, okay? It makes me uncomfortable."

"Fine." His expression held contrition. "I didn't mean to upset you."

"I know." She smiled, and his face relaxed.

"Landon," Amber called, "we've got to go. You know how my mom gets if someone's late."

"Be right there, babe." He gave Everleigh's shoulder a gentle punch. "See you later."

Everleigh waved to Amber before she and Landon disappeared from the kitchen. She turned her attention to the dishwasher, making quick work of adding the dishes, utensils, and glasses before squeezing in the serving platters. Then she added the soap powder and started the machine.

The coffee maker spluttered, and the delicious scent of coffee wafted over her. Mom opened the cabinet and pulled out three mugs. "Ready for dessert, or is it too soon?"

"It's never too soon for chocolate pie," Dad said.

Everleigh grinned. "I'll get the plates and forks."

When they returned to the dining room, Everleigh's phone began to sing, announcing an incoming call. She found her purse on the sofa and pulled out her phone, which registered an out-of-state call. She poised her thumb on the button to silence it, but something compelled her to answer.

"Hello?"

"Is this Everleigh?" a familiar female voice asked.

"Yes."

"Hi, sweetie. This is Maggie Newton. I'm sorry to bother you on a holiday, but Henry and I needed to speak with you right away," the older woman said. "We've been dreaming of retiring in Coral Cove, and running the inn together would be a dream come true. We didn't want to risk losing the opportunity to someone else, so . . . how would you and Cade feel about a full-price offer for the Sunshine Inn?"

CHAPTER 28

CADE PACED IN his apartment. He had cleaned up the leftovers—well, the entire meal since he had lost his appetite after his mother stormed out—and then locked up the rest of the inn. He'd called for Bryant and retired to his place to try to cool off, but anger and disappointment still churned in his gut.

After taking a shower, he considered just going to bed. But it was too early for that, and he knew he would only wind up staring at the ceiling and stewing over his frustration toward his mother.

He had finally settled on an old Western movie when his phone began ringing. He was surprised to see his brother's name and number on the screen. After pausing the movie, he picked up the phone. "Declan. Hi," he said.

"Happy Thanksgiving," Declan sang while voices sounded in the background.

"Same to you," Cade said. "Sounds like you have a full house." A painful longing gripped his heart—the urge to be included in that house full of people, along with his parents and Everleigh, instead of being alone on this holiday. He slammed his eyes shut and worked to dismiss those thoughts. Thanks to his mother, Declan would never be included in their family—and Cade didn't know if he'd ever find a way to accept that.

The background noise faded away. "We're at Stephanie's parents' house, and she has a huge family. I'll try to find a quiet corner." A door squeaked open and then clicked shut. "I wanted to check in with you. How's your holiday going?"

"It was fine."

"Was?" Declan asked. "It's not even eight yet. Did you eat early?"

"Uh, yeah. I'm relaxing now, just me and the cat. We're watching an old movie. How's everyone there?"

Cade listened while his brother talked about Stephanie's family and the delicious meal they had eaten. More sadness expanded in his chest as thoughts of what could have been overtook him. Had Mom agreed to include Declan and Stephanie today, they all could have been talking and laughing and eating too much food together right now.

"You still there, Cade?" Declan asked.

He cleared his throat. "Yeah."

"Something wrong?"

Cade hesitated. He hated lying, but how could he explain what had gone haywire today without hurting his brother? Neither lying nor telling the truth seemed all that great an option.

"I may not know you well enough to say this, but something seems to be bothering you, Cade. Did something happen with your mom today?" Declan's voice held a thread of worry or hesitation—maybe both.

Cade rubbed Bryant's back, and the cat's purr provided a much-needed boost of courage. "Yeah, I guess you could say that."

"What was it?"

"Really, it's not . . ." Cade hesitated. "Why don't you call me in a few days?"

"Just tell me," Declan insisted. "I can handle it."

Cade took a deep breath. "I tried to talk some sense into my mom, and it fell flat." He shared what happened when Mom and Dad came over and he had the two empty place settings at the table. "She still refuses to acknowledge you and Stephanie, but I'm not giving up." He hesitated. "I mean it. You're my brother, Declan, and I want you and Stephanie to be an active part of our family. I'm going to do whatever's in my power to make that happen."

Silence hummed across the line.

"Declan?" Cade asked. When his brother didn't respond, he studied his phone to see if the call had dropped. "Declan? You there?"

"Yeah." Declan's voice was somber.

"I'm sorry." Cade closed his eyes as disappointment and grief overtook him. "The last thing I wanted to do was ruin your holiday."

"You didn't. You just drove home what I've already been thinking."

Cade's stomach plummeted. "What do you mean?"

"That it's time for me to move on." His voice trembled with anger and possibly anguish. "I've had enough heartache to last me a lifetime."

Cade shook his head as if his brother could see him over the phone. "No. You can't give up."

"I appreciate all you've tried to do, but I can't keep allowing her to hurt me." He paused for a moment. "Stephanie told me to give up after the fall festival. I was still grasping onto the hope that my child would know my biological family, but it's been too hard."

Cade nodded. "I can't even imagine."

"If I keep going through this, it will start taking a toll on her too. I don't want to put her in jeopardy, you know? It took us a long time to get pregnant, and if something happened . . ."

Cade returned to petting the cat to try to lower his spiking blood pressure. "I understand."

"I'm sorry, Cade. This stress isn't good for me or Stephanie."

Cade held his hand up. "Let's give Mom more time. She told me earlier in the week that maybe she could see you at Christmas and—"

"No, Cade. I'm done."

"Declan, listen." He could hear the desperation in his voice. "What if I came to see you and Stephanie at Christmas? We can celebrate as a family, and maybe that will inspire Mom to finally come around."

A voice sounded in the background, and then a rustling came over the phone, like Declan was holding his hand over the speaker. Then Cade heard more muffled voices.

"Cade," Declan finally said into the phone. "I'm sorry, but I have to go."

"Of course," Cade said. "Can you call me later or tomorrow?"

Declan was silent for a beat, and muscles tensed in Cade's shoulders. "I think it would be best if we didn't communicate anymore."

Cade's gut knotted. "Wh-what do you mean?"

"Look, Cade. I'm glad I met you," Declan began. "I've wondered nearly all my life if I had siblings, and I'm so grateful to have a brother." He paused. "But I've got to be honest. If I can't have our mother in my life, then it'll be too painful to maintain a relationship with you."

"I'll work on her," Cade promised, searching for anything to convince Declan not to give up. "Just give me a little more time. I can get her to come around."

"I've tried calling her, writing her, and visiting her, and nothing has worked. She's made it clear that when she gave me up for adoption, she was done with me." Declan's voice was raspy. "Just back off, okay? It is what it is."

"Declan—"

"Have a good life, man. Take care," Declan said before disconnecting the call.

Cade stared at the phone as anger, bereavement, and regret crashed through him. He'd gained and lost a brother in less than two months, and his head was spinning.

But he knew one thing for sure: His mother was to blame. They'd had a chance to add Declan to their family, but she'd prevented it.

His finger shook as he dialed his mother's number.

"Hello?" Mom said.

"Well, you've finally done it," Cade snapped. "I just talked to Declan, and he's cutting both me and you off."

He waited for her to speak, but when she didn't, his anger morphed into white-hot fury. How could she get away with this? His pain went all the way to the bone.

"And guess what, Mom? Now you've lost *both* of your sons."

"Wh-what do you mean?" she stammered.

"Declan's done with us, and I'm done with you." Then he disconnected the call, collapsed back on the sofa, and let the emotion pour out of him.

✦ ✦ ✦

"Everleigh, are you okay?" Dad asked. "You're white as a ghost. Who was on the phone?"

Her entire body trembled as she stood in the doorway of the kitchen. "That was Mrs. Newton. She and her husband come to the Sunshine Inn every year, and she always brings homemade jam." She sat down at the table where her parents were already sipping coffee and eating pieces of pie.

"I remember you and Alana talking about her," Mom said. "What did she want?"

"Well." Everleigh took a shaky breath. "She and her husband want to buy the inn. They offered full price, and they want to close as soon as possible. She said they're going to meet with their lawyer and put together an offer and then email it to me."

Mom and Dad shared a shocked look.

"Today was the deadline Cade gave me." She fiddled with her fork. "But I actually made the sale happen." Now she could get back on the road, and more importantly, finally start the nonprofit in memory of Alana. A swarm of emotions crowded her chest—shock, confusion, and . . . regret?

What was wrong with her? This was what she'd hoped for, right? This way, the dream she shared with Alana would come to life—an organization that, if successful, might live on well after both Alana *and* Everleigh.

"*An angel always finds its way to you, even in your darkest moments.*"

The words Alana had written echoed in her mind, and she tried to convince herself that selling the inn was the right path for her and Cade.

But if it was what Alana, her guardian angel, had wanted for her, then why did the thought of leaving Coral Cove make her want to sob instead of celebrate?

Her parents continued to watch her.

"Does that mean you're going back on the road again?" Dad asked, and the disappointment in his expression tweaked her heart.

She rested her elbow on the table and her chin on her palm. "I've been considering hospital contracts in Houston and Atlanta."

"Please choose Atlanta," Mom said. "Then you'll only be six hours away."

Dad touched Mom's hand as if to comfort her. "I agree. You'll be less than a day's drive from us."

"Okay," Everleigh said, the word sounding thin.

Mom wagged a finger at her. "And that means you'll need to visit us more often. No more staying away for more than a year."

"I promise I won't do that again," she said, and she meant it.

"Good." Mom's dark eyes glistened with tears. "I know you've always wanted to travel, but I was hoping you'd stay home for good this time." She sniffed. "I really thought maybe you'd decide to run the inn with Cade and work part-time for a local hospital."

The walls of Everleigh's chest closed in, and her eyes felt wet. Leaving her family this time was going to be so much more difficult than it had ever been.

"You know, your dad and I will support whatever you choose to do. But we'll also always miss you because we love you."

Everleigh reached across the table and covered her parents' hands with hers. "I'll miss you too, but I promise I'll visit. I'll also call at least once a week."

Dad gave her hand a gentle squeeze. "Honey, we're proud of you."

After finishing dessert and helping clean up, Everleigh took the long way home. She parked her SUV by the boardwalk and sat on a bench while looking out over the ocean. She hugged her coat against her body, pushed her hair behind her ears, and glimpsed the stars twinkling in the sky. The crisp, salty air filled her lungs while the waves' cadence serenaded her. She tried to commit the sights, sounds, and scents of her hometown to memory. More than ever, she was going to miss Coral Cove.

When the cold air seemed to seep into her skin, she returned to her car and made the short drive to the inn. She sat in the driveway and stared up at the dark colonial. She had expected Cade's parents to still be visiting.

Everleigh drove around back and parked outside of the detached garage, where lights glowed in Cade's apartment. She knocked on his door and shifted her weight while trembling in the cold. After a few moments, his footfalls sounded from inside.

He pushed the door open, and his normally bright eyes were dull. "Hi."

Bryant sat on the stairs behind him and yawned.

"Hi." She smiled despite the worrying look on his face. He seemed exhausted and so sad. "You okay?"

He rested his forearm on the open door. "Great as always."

Something was off, but she couldn't put her finger on what. "How was dinner?"

He examined his shoes for a moment. "Perfect." Then he moved his hand over his chest. "Yours?"

She tried to detect signs of a lie, but she couldn't tell if he was being sarcastic or not. His handsome face was a mask of indifference, reminding her of when she'd first met him. What had caused him to change? "Same."

An awkward silence grew between them, and a pang of grief radiated through her.

Talk to me, Cade!

"What's up?" he asked.

"I have news." She took a deep breath. "We sold the inn for full price."

His eyes flashed with something unreadable, and he stood up straight.

"You'll be shocked at who made the offer," she said.

"You got me," he replied.

"The Newtons." She hid her quaking hands in her pockets and

stopped speaking for a moment, waiting for him to respond. But he continued to watch her with a blank expression.

"Mrs. Newton called me while I was at my parents' house," she explained. "They want to retire here and run the inn. They're anxious to make this happen, so they plan to email me an offer soon."

He folded his arms over his chest. She tried to decipher the emotion on his face, but she couldn't. And his silence was tearing her apart inside.

"That means we got an offer we can both agree on just within the deadline." She paused and waited for him to speak. When he didn't, she added, "What do you think, Cade?"

More silence. Had it been summertime, they would have heard crickets. Instead, a car passed in the distance, and a dog barked. Everleigh held her breath, waiting for his reaction, but he only stared at her in silence.

"Cade, please talk to me." Desperation echoed in her words.

"That's great," he finally said, but his face and his voice were void of emotion.

"You think so?"

"Sure." He shrugged.

"Do you want to accept their offer?" she asked.

"It's what you wanted, Everleigh." His eyes assessed her, and her heartbeat pounded in her head. "What was it you said . . . ?" He rubbed his chin. "You said you believed Alana was our guardian angel, and we were supposed to sell the inn so we each could follow our dreams. Isn't that right?"

Her throat felt as if it were full of sand. "Yes," she managed to whisper.

"So, you got what you wanted, Everleigh. You can go on your merry way and start your nonprofit, and I'll try to figure out how to restart my life—again." He cocked his head to the side and studied her for a moment. "Why do you look so sad about it? All of your hopes are coming true." His words held a note of sarcasm that cut her like a knife.

She was silent for a moment as grief and regret plunged through her. "What if we refused their offer?" she asked.

A few moments ticked by.

"Why would we do that?" he asked.

"You had plans for the inn. What about adding the pavilion and opening a little restaurant here?" She paused. "Besides, this place is your home." Her voice sounded strained. "I'm sorry, Cade. I'm so, so sorry. I never meant to railroad you with this sale. I never meant to push so hard and hurt you." She took a deep breath. "We can reject their offer. Just say the word, and I'll call her back tonight and tell her we changed our minds."

He shook his head, and his eyes remained almost lifeless. "I'll be fine. I've moved plenty of times. No big deal."

She blinked. Had she heard him right? "So, this *is* what you want, Cade?" she asked. "You want to accept their offer?" *And you want me to leave?*

"When do they want to close?" he asked, his expression still unreadable.

"Soon," she said. "Around Christmas."

"Great. I guess that means you'll come back for the closing."

She worked to find her voice. "My parents asked me to accept the hospital's offer in Atlanta, so I won't be too far away. Only about six hours."

A guarded look shadowed his face. "I'm sure they're happy about that."

Are you?

She nodded, but an ache started in her belly and worked its way up to her chest. *Tell me to stay and run the inn with you. Tell me you love me, and you want to build a life with me.*

"Everything worked out the way you wanted it to, Everleigh." His face was blank—almost cold. "Congratulations." The word sliced through her.

Her voice was stuck in her throat.

"Let me know when you get the offer, and I'll sign it," he told her before closing the door in her face.

Everleigh felt tears building up in her eyes. She raced to her car before Cade would have the opportunity to look outside and see her cry. She slammed the car door, drove around to the front of the inn, and put the car in park. A powerful wave of anguish overcame her, and she couldn't stop her sobs. At that moment, she realized that Cade was right: It *was* better not to get attached to people. Their friendship had meant much more to her than to him—and that reality crushed her heart.

✦ ✦ ✦

Cade slumped back against his closed door and covered his face with his hands. Just when he thought this day couldn't get any worse, it had. The inn was sold, and the rug had been ripped out from under his feet. Not only had he lost his brother and his mother, but now he'd lost his home, his job, and . . . *Everleigh.*

His life was in complete shambles now. He had nothing left. Sure, he'd get a nice check after the closing, but everything he loved was right here at the inn, and now it was gone.

He was completely and utterly alone—*again.* A block of ice invaded his chest where his heart had once been.

Cade slid down to the floor and sat with his back against the door, his body limp and his head falling forward. He'd never expected

Everleigh to show up tonight. In fact, he'd been studying his phone waiting for his brother, mother, or father to call. But the phone had remained silent, proof that he'd lost everyone he'd ever cared about.

And why should that surprise him? Everyone in his life had wronged him. Serena and his former business partner were the first. Then he found out that his mother had lied to him his entire life. Then his brother gave up on him, and his father had chosen his mother's side.

And now the final nail had been pounded into his coffin: Everleigh was moving on with her life and leaving him behind.

There was no reason for him to stay in Coral Cove. Once he got his half of the inn profits, he'd figure out where he wanted to go. So long as it was somewhere far, far away, he'd be satisfied.

Bryant appeared at the top of the stairs and meowed.

"Hey, buddy." Cade wiped his eyes and ignored the anguish quavering in his voice. "Where should we move to?"

Meow! the cat yelled.

Cade picked himself up and started up the stairs toward the cat. "We'll find somewhere nice to live, buddy. You're all I need."

If only he could believe that.

✦ ✦ ✦

"It's only Wednesday," Quinn whined. "Can't you at least stay for the rest of the week?"

"I wish I could, but I start work on Friday." Everleigh felt a pang as she took in her friend's sad expression. She folded another pair of jeans and put them in her suitcase.

She'd been surprised when the Newtons sent their offer Monday afternoon. The older couple hadn't been kidding when they said they wanted to take care of things quickly. They had added in some extra money to purchase the inn's contents—including the furniture, which made life easier for Cade and Everleigh. Cade had agreed to the offer, and they both signed before Everleigh sent it back to the Newtons' lawyer. The closing was scheduled for the week after Christmas, and she had negotiated with the recruiter to take off the day before and after the closing so that she could travel home.

She was grateful she'd managed to sign the Atlanta contract, and she'd already found a new place to live. Last night she'd had supper with her parents, Landon, and Amber, and they all said they would miss her but were happy for her new post. She shared a tearful goodbye with them, and she tried to overlook her disappointment that her sister hadn't bothered to come even though Mom had invited her.

Everything seemed to be falling into place so easily—so why did she feel like she was constantly on the verge of tears?

Everleigh had texted Harlowe last night to tell her she was leaving and would miss her, but once again, her sister had remained silent. Her indifference was another stab to Everleigh's heart, but she would try again. Maybe she could call Harlowe during her six-hour drive to Georgia, and they could talk for part of the way. She smiled at that thought. Alana had always helped make her long drives seem shorter, and perhaps Harlowe could fill that role.

Cade had been reticent too, which was more painful than she could express. When she asked him what he planned to do after the closing, he had shrugged and mumbled, "Not sure yet," before walking away from her. He was back to the grumpy version of Cade she'd met when she first came to Coral Cove. The special friendship she thought they'd shared seemed to have evaporated like raindrops on a summer sidewalk.

Maybe she had longed for more from him, but she'd been kidding herself. Apparently their heart-to-heart the night of the storm had meant nothing to him. She'd imagined he might care about her—

possibly even love her—but she had been completely wrong. Had all of the good she'd seen in him been a facade? Then again, maybe she just wasn't Cade's type.

All she knew for sure was that he'd broken her heart, and she'd have to give herself time to heal—if healing was even possible.

Quinn set a few books into a box and then turned to her. "Do you want all of these too?"

Everleigh nodded at the stack of Alana's photo albums. "Yes. Thanks."

Ding-dong!

"Are you expecting anyone?" Quinn asked.

"No. I'll be right back." Everleigh headed toward the hallway and out to the foyer. When she yanked the door open, she did a double take. Her sister was standing on the porch. "Harlowe!"

Her sister fiddled with the zipper on her coat. "Can we talk?"

"Of course! Come in." She led her sister into the kitchen. "Want something to drink?"

"No thanks." Harlowe twisted her hands. "I got your message."

She scoffed. "I've gotten *all* of your messages."

Everleigh hopped up on a stool at the island and took in her sister's apprehensive expression. Why was she acting like they didn't know each other? "Why are you here now?"

"I need to say something to you." Her dark eyes glittered, and her upper lip trembled. "I'm sorry."

Everleigh was so shocked that she stilled for a moment. Had she heard her right? After all this time, had Harlowe apologized? Then she shook herself back to the present.

Stay focused! This is what you've waited for your entire life.

"What exactly are you apologizing for?"

"For being a terrible sister." Harlowe frowned and hopped up on the stool beside her. "The truth is . . ." She rubbed her cheeks. "How do I even say this?" Then her eyes met Everleigh's. "I've always been jealous of you."

Everleigh guffawed. "Jealous of me?" She pointed to herself, and Harlowe nodded. "Why on earth would you be jealous of *me*?"

"Oh, please!" Harlowe exclaimed. "You were always the beautiful one. The smart one. The talented one. You got straight As. When you walk in a room, all of the guys gravitate toward you." She frowned. "I remember I took you with me to a party when you were in high school and I was in college. Everyone wanted to talk to you. Even my own boyfriend ignored me. I was just invisible."

The memory of that party flashed through Everleigh's mind. "Harlowe, they talked to me because I was new." She pressed her lips together and waved her off. "And your boyfriend at the time was a creep. He wound up cheating on you, and you were better off without him. Besides, you have no reason to be jealous of me. You're pretty and talented, and *you're* the one with the husband."

"You don't realize just how magnetic you are. Everyone loves you. You're sweet, funny, kind . . . You're a ray of sunshine, and I always wished I could be like you." She rested her chin on her palm. "And don't even get me started on your hair, Everleigh. What I would do to be a real redhead."

"What?" Everleigh touched her hair. "I'd do anything to have hair like yours! I've always wished I looked more like you and Mom. I was teased mercilessly in school for having hair the color of orange crayons."

"Why would you want to look like me?" Harlowe asked. "You're stunning, Evie. Exotic, even." Then she laughed. "I never told you I tried to dye my hair red in college. It was a disaster. Thankfully, I convinced one of my sorority sisters to fix it for me."

"I need to see photos of that!"

"Hopefully none exist," Harlowe said.

Everleigh laughed, and Harlowe joined her. Something inside Everleigh warmed. It felt so good to laugh with her sister. For a moment, she was certain she was dreaming.

Harlowe wiped her eyes. "When I found out that you got the inn, I thought I was going to lose my mind." She chose a napkin from the holder on the island and began shredding it. "Branson and I have been struggling financially for a while, and that news . . . Well, it was the straw that broke the camel's back."

Everleigh took Harlowe's hand in hers. "I've been saving money for a long time, and I can help you. How much do you need?"

"I can't take your money, Evie." Harlowe rubbed her eyes. "We've just spent a lot of money trying to get pregnant. We've been doing fertility treatments, and we haven't had any success yet."

"Oh, Harlowe," Everleigh whispered. "I'm so sorry. Why didn't you tell me?"

"I was too embarrassed."

"But I'm your sister, Harlowe. You should trust me."

"You're right, and I'm sorry for that." Harlowe gave her a tremulous smile.

Everleigh's heart twisted. "Please let me help you."

"I can't do that." Harlowe sat up straighter. "But thank you. Branson's folks are helping, and we'll be okay." She gave Everleigh's hand a squeeze. "I'm really sorry, Evie. You're my sister, and I shouldn't have let my petty jealousy come between us."

"It's okay. You've been going through a lot." Everleigh wiped her wet eyes. "I just wish you'd told me. I could've been a sounding board for you. A support."

"Can we start over?"

"Of course we can."

Harlowe gestured around the kitchen. "You're the one who was always here with Alana, and you deserved the inn. I knew that in my heart, but admitting it to myself was hard." Tears spilled down her cheeks, and she brushed them away. "Can you forgive me?"

"Always." Everleigh hopped off her stool and pulled her sister in for a hug, and it felt so good. She'd dreamed of this day, and it had finally arrived!

Harlowe held on tight. "Thank you," she whispered.

"Do you have to get back to work?" Everleigh asked.

"No. I took the day off. I wanted to see you before you left." Harlowe climbed off the stool. "Do you need any help?"

"Sure." Everleigh led her back to the bedroom, where Quinn was loading books into boxes.

For the next hour they continued to pack. Once everything was loaded into her car, Everleigh hugged Quinn and Harlowe and said goodbye, promising to keep in touch. The three of them were still wiping their eyes as Quinn and Harlowe drove away from the inn.

Everleigh was climbing the steps just as a black Toyota pickup truck pulled into the driveway and parked. She wasn't exactly surprised to see Trevor and Valerie climbing out together.

She set her jaw and jammed her hands on her hips as Trevor and Valerie reached the bottom of the steps. "What do you want?"

"We heard you got an offer on the inn," Trevor said.

Valerie nodded. "We're here to counteroffer. Whatever they're giving you, we'll give you another $100,000." Her smile was smug. "What do you say?"

"You've got a lot of nerve coming here after you both tried to trick me." She pointed toward the road. "Get off my property, or I'm going to call my brother. He's a police officer, and he'll escort you off!"

"Come on, Everleigh." Trevor held his hands out to her. "I thought we were friends."

She marched down the steps and glared at him. "Were we friends, Trevor?"

"Sure." He shrugged.

She glared at him. "You even tried to get me to date you. Did I mean anything to you?"

Trevor turned to Valerie, and love twinkled in his eyes. Then he focused on Everleigh. "No. Not more than a friend, anyway."

Disgust roiled through her. "I was *so* naïve," she muttered. "Cade was right all along." She divided a look between them. "What was the connection then? What are you getting out of this, Trevor?"

"My stepdad owns Coral Cove Builders."

"And Valerie is your girlfriend," Everleigh finished.

"No. Fiancée, as of last week." Valerie's expression was arrogant as she held up her left hand, showing off a large twinkling diamond.

"Well, good for you," Everleigh snapped.

"Let's get down to business," Valerie said. "What's it going to take to get you to sell to us? What if we doubled the price?"

Trevor shook his head. "You need to ask my stepdad before you make an offer like that."

"Get out of here," Everleigh demanded. "If you're not out of here by the time I get to the front door, I'm calling my brother." She held up her phone. "Go!"

She waved the phone in the air while Trevor and Valerie scrambled into his truck. As she watched them speed away, a sick feeling overcame her. She'd been such a fool to trust Trevor.

Cade was right about everything, it seemed. She *was* too trusting. But she wouldn't make that mistake again.

CHAPTER 29

EVERLEIGH STOOD IN the center of the bedroom that had become her own during the past couple of months. "Goodbye, room," she whispered. "I'll miss you."

Memories of her time spent in Coral Cove rolled over her. She recalled first meeting Cade, and how he'd dragged her heavy suitcase into the lawyer's office.

"Brought your rock collection?"

Her eyes stung. She was going to miss his dry sense of humor. She'd considered going over to say goodbye to him, but he'd made it clear he was done with her.

Everleigh's chest felt heavy while she walked around the suite one last time. She retraced her steps in the bedroom, making sure she hadn't forgotten anything, then rested her finger on the light switch. As she turned to go, she spotted something behind the dresser.

She peeked behind it and found an envelope there. She took hold of the end of the dresser and tugged, trying to move it. She grunted and groaned until she was able to shift it back a few inches, then dropped to her knees and stretched her arm out as far as she could. Grabbing the very tip of the envelope, she pulled it to her.

She examined the envelope and familiar penmanship spelling out her name. Her heart lurched. It was Alana's handwriting. She opened the envelope and then read the letter.

> Dearest Everleigh,
>
> If you're reading this, it means I've passed on. I'm sure you're upset with me for not telling you that I was sick. I know you would've dropped everything to take care of me, but I didn't want to be a burden. I wanted you to enjoy your life.
>
> I can't begin to tell you how proud I am of you. You've grown into a lovely young woman. Not only are you beautiful and brilliant, but your loving heart is your most special quality. I'm so very proud of how you've followed your dream of caring for others. You're courageous too. I'm in awe of how you've traveled around the country sharing your gifts with your patients.
>
> When I found out I had terminal cancer, I met with my lawyer, and he told me I had to make plans. I had to draw up a will, and I had to decide what to do with my assets. Of course, I immediately thought of you. You're the daughter I never had. You're my goddaughter, my niece, my special friend. I never doubted my decision to leave everything to you. But then I realized this was an opportunity to make an introduction.
>
> I'm sure you're wondering why I only left you half of my assets. I hope you're not angry with me. I'm writing this letter to explain.
>
> Everleigh, I've already told you what you mean to me

and what I admire most about you. But I'm also selfish. I've missed you ever since you took off for college and never looked back. That's not fair for me to say, right? Who am I to tell you where you belong? I've always dreamt of seeing you settle down here in Coral Cove. The inn was your home away from home, and we have so many memories of our time spent here together. I cherish every single one. But honestly, I've also felt you belonged here.

When Cade Witherspoon came into my life, I wasn't looking for a handyman. I've known his mother, Trisha, for years, and we're good friends. She told me she was happy her son had finally come home, and she asked me if I needed a groundskeeper. I told her yes. I met Cade, and I immediately took a liking to him. He doesn't beat around the bush. He says what he's thinking, and his dry sense of humor keeps me in stitches.

I soon discovered there's so much more to Cade than meets the eye. When you first meet him, you'll think he's sarcastic and a bit prickly. Yet underneath that hard exterior is a kind, loyal, and thoughtful man who's been hurt. He's been used and betrayed. He has a lot of love to give, and he proved that to me when I got sick. He insisted on driving me to appointments and taking care of me. He's held my hand and consoled me. He's sat up with me all night long just to make sure I'm okay.

And, oh my goodness, can that man cook! Not only have I benefited from his talent, but so have our guests!

Cade is special to me just like you are, Everleigh. That's why I wanted you to meet him. I believe deep in my heart that you and Cade are meant to be together. Now, before you convince yourself that I'm completely losing it, I assure you that I am of sound mind—body, not so much—but I know what I'm saying. I acknowledge that you and Cade are complete opposites. I'm sure if you say the glass is half full, Cade will insist it's half empty. But you're the same where it counts. You and Cade have warm and generous hearts. You're both loving, giving, loyal people. And I believe Cade is your match, Everleigh. I feel it in my soul.

Well, I have rambled on for pages, and I'm tired. I need to finish this letter and get some sleep, but I need to tell you this, Everleigh—I'm leaving you my inn, but I'm also leaving you an offer for your future. Please consider making the Sunshine Inn your home, your second chance. And please consider making Cade a part of your life too.

If it's meant to be, I'd love for you and Cade to plan a future here together. Build a home here. Start a family. And most importantly, please fill the Sunshine Inn with love.

Don't forget me, and don't forget that I love you, sweetheart.

Forever and always.

Sincerely,

Alana

Sobs broke free, and Everleigh dropped onto the floor. She read the letter over and over until she had nearly committed it to memory.

The letter rested on the floor while she yanked her phone from her pocket and swiped through the selfies she'd taken of her and Cade—in the kitchen the first time they prepared breakfast for guests, at the bookstore, at the beach after he'd helped her conquer her fear of the ocean, and the day they'd met Declan at the festival. She zoomed in on Cade's brilliant smile while he posed with Everleigh and Declan. He'd looked so happy that day, and she studied his handsome face.

Grief expanded inside her, and she knew it to the depth of her heart: She *loved* Cade Witherspoon. She cherished his smile, his laugh, his dry sense of humor, and his loving heart. She adored how he'd taken care of her the night of the storm and the way he insisted on helping her overcome her fears. She appreciated how he listened to her and how easy it was to talk to him. Most of all, she loved how he'd taken care of Alana when she needed him most.

She was desperately in love with Cade, but he didn't love her back. When she told him about the offer on the inn, she had fervently hoped he would want to reject it. She did her best to hint to him that she wanted him to ask her to stay. But he hadn't.

And when they received the offer in writing, she gave him another chance to turn it down. But once again, he had accepted the terms. Then he had muttered a goodbye and left.

Alana had been right when she predicted Everleigh would fall for Cade, but he hadn't fallen for her. There was no future for her here. Her only option now was to leave him and the Sunshine Inn behind.

As she stared around the suite that had been her home, she wondered if Cade had been the love of her life. Perhaps he had been, and she would never, ever get over him.

Everleigh pulled herself up from the floor and stared at the letter. "I'm sorry I let you down, Alana," she whispered. "But I'll never forget you. I'll always love you and carry you in my heart."

Then she dashed out to her car. As she drove away, she glanced in her rearview at the Sunshine Inn. Tears blurred her vision as she motored down the road.

She was leaving a piece of her heart there.

✦ ✦ ✦

Cade sat at his workbench and sanded another piece of wood. He'd spent most of the day searching the internet for business opportunities, but he'd come up empty. He couldn't concentrate enough to even consider what he wanted to do next with his life. All he could think about was that he'd lost everything—his family, his job, his home, and Everleigh.

In fact, Everleigh was packing up to leave, and no matter how hard he tried, he couldn't ignore it. She was going to drive out of his life, taking his heart with her. And he would never be the same.

But she'd made her choice, and he had to live with it.

Somehow.

"Cade?"

He turned and found his mother standing by his truck. Her expression was humble and hesitant. He spun on the stool and stared at her, unsure of what to say. He hadn't heard from her, Dad, or Declan since Thanksgiving, and he'd all but given up on them. He assumed they'd given up on him, too, which hurt him the most.

"Can we talk?" she asked.

He nodded.

She walked over to him and pointed to the planter he'd finished over the weekend when he couldn't sleep. "That's really nice."

"Thanks." He nodded at the second stool. "Have a seat."

They sat in awkward silence for several moments, and he waited for her to share the reason for her visit.

She finally took a deep breath and said, "I'm sorry for keeping your brother's existence a secret." Her eyes glistened with tears. "The truth is, that time of my life was too painful for me to revisit."

The anguish in his mother's face sent grief spiraling through Cade.

"When I met Declan's father, I was young. Very young. I thought I was in love, and when I found out I was pregnant, I believed he'd marry me. A happily ever after." She sniffed. "As soon as I told him the news, he took off, and I never heard from him again. I tried to find him, but I couldn't."

Cade reached over and touched her hand, hoping to offer her comfort.

"My parents were very disappointed in me." She paused and then shook her head. "Actually, that's an incredible understatement. They were more than disappointed. They were furious, and so . . . they disowned me."

"What?" He stared at her. "I thought they died when you were young. Is that why your grandmother raised you? Because your parents gave you up?"

"That was another lie. My parents didn't die until you were about two years old."

His thoughts spun. "I-I don't understand, Mom."

She paused and licked her lips. "They threw me out, and I had no choice but to move in with my grandmother. She lived on a fixed income and had very little money, which meant the only choice I had was to give my baby—Declan—up for adoption."

Cade tried to comprehend this. "So your folks threw you out, you gave him up for adoption, and you stayed with your grandmother?"

She nodded.

"And what did your parents do?"

"I told you, Cade. They disowned me. We never spoke again." She moved her hands down the thighs of her jeans. "I lost everything when I got pregnant. My parents, my boyfriend, and my friends since I had to move from Charlotte to Wilmington to be with my grandmother. I'm so grateful that she took me in. She was all I had. Then she passed away shortly after I married your father."

Cade once again felt as if his world had tilted. "I am so sorry you went through that." He hesitated and tried to take it all in.

Then guilt raised its ugly head and tangled up his insides. He'd assumed the worst about her when she had endured something too painful to comprehend. "Mom, I . . . I completely misjudged you."

She gave him a sad smile. "It's not your fault, honey. You only knew what I'd told you. I'm sorry I never shared the truth with you."

She dipped her chin and moved her thumb through a small pile of sawdust on his workbench. "I was so devastated that I promised myself that I would just pretend my past didn't happen. That was how I dealt with it—I stuffed it down deep inside myself. When I met your father, I was cautious. I was scared, really, that he'd leave me too." Regret seemed to crease her face. "Your poor dad had to prove himself over and over before I finally agreed to marry him." She patted Cade's arm. "He's one patient man."

Cade sniffed.

"I never told your father about my ex or my baby or the truth about my parents either. That wasn't fair to him or you, but I didn't have the tools to deal with it. I still don't think I do, actually. I closed myself off, thinking that would protect me from more hurt, but I know now that was a mistake."

Cade nodded. "That had to be so difficult for you, Mom." He touched her hand again. "And I'm sorry for everything I've said. I can't imagine going through life without you and Dad."

The grief etched on her face squeezed his heart. "Seeing Declan brought back all the pain and grief I thought I'd buried." She wiped the back of her hand over her eyes. "I was too much of a coward to face it all, so I pushed him away."

He swallowed as his throat began to close up.

"That was the wrong response." She frowned. "Cade, I see that now. But it took losing you before I could see how wrong I was." She pulled in a shuddering breath.

Cade dabbed at his own tears with the hem of his T-shirt.

"You've opened my eyes, son." Her words sounded thick. "You've forced me to come to terms with my past, and you've helped me see the truth. By rejecting Declan, I was being just as cruel, heartless, and callous as my own parents, and I never, *ever* want to be like them. I don't want to inflict that pain on my sons." Her expression became fierce despite the tears streaming down her cheeks. "They wounded me so badly, and I could never forgive myself if I did that to you or your brother."

Cade wiped his face with a clean shop rag and handed one to his mom.

"I reached out to Declan," she continued. "He's agreed to give me a second chance, and I couldn't be more thankful. I want to know him and his wife." Her lip trembled. "And I want to know my first grandchild."

"You mean that?" Cade whispered as hope ignited deep inside him.

"Yes, I do, with all my heart." She took his hands in hers. "This is a new start for our family. It's time for us to grow. You were right about everything, Cade. We need to embrace each other."

He sniffed.

"Will you forgive me?"

He reached over and hugged her, holding on tight. "Of course I forgive you. I hope you forgive me for pushing you so hard. I'm sorry we ambushed you at the fall festival. I never meant to hurt you. I love you, Mom."

"I love you, too, and I understand why you were so anxious to welcome your brother into our family." She gave him a squeeze and then released him. "When I called Declan this morning, we talked for three hours."

Cade brightened. "You did?"

She nodded. "He was so gracious." She paused and sniffed. "I invited Declan and Stephanie to come for supper Saturday night, and they said yes." She smiled. "You and Everleigh must come."

Hearing Everleigh's name was like a dagger to his heart. "It'll be just me." He paused. "She's gone."

"What do you mean?"

"We sold the inn, and she left for Atlanta." He tried to sound causal even though the words cut deep.

Mom gasped, her expression horrified. "She left?"

"It was her choice." He fiddled with a piece of wood in order to avoid her stare.

Mom was quiet for a moment. "How do you feel about Everleigh?"

He kept his eyes trained on the workbench as the truth drenched him. *I love her.* "I care about her—a lot."

"Benjamin Cade Witherspoon III, look at me," she ordered, and he complied. "You're just as stubborn as I am."

"Funny. I believe I've heard that before," he deadpanned.

"Then take my advice. Don't make the same mistakes I did. I'm grateful Declan is giving me another shot."

He shook his head. "It's pointless, Mom. This is just like Serena all over again. She left me. She's gone, and that's it."

"If you love her, Cade, don't let her slip through your fingers."

He rubbed his chin.

"Go after Everleigh. You'll be glad you did."

They talked for a while longer before he walked her to her car. Once Mom was gone, Cade dropped onto the porch steps. A memory of the first time Everleigh had come to the inn flashed in his mind. He hadn't been sure what to make of her that day, but as the weeks progressed, she became more and more important to him. And it had also become easier to open up to her. In fact, sharing his deepest secrets with her was something he'd never experienced with another woman in his life.

Then he recalled the night of Thanksgiving when Everleigh had told him about the Newtons' offer. She'd seemed different—

not at all her happy-go-lucky self, and maybe even a little sad. But why *wouldn't* she have been happy? She'd finally gotten what she'd wanted all along—the money from her "guardian angel" to start her nonprofit and her new life.

As his mind replayed their conversation, something suddenly occurred to him. He'd been so hurt and angry that he hadn't been truly listening to her. Instead of gloating about it, she was trying to talk him out of it.

Her gravelly words echoed in his mind:

"Just say the word, and I'll call her back tonight and tell her we changed our minds."

Cade gasped. Why hadn't he read between the lines? He'd been so caught up in his own emotions, so worried she was going to hurt him, that he hadn't realized what she'd been trying to say to him.

Everleigh had *wanted* to stay.

"Oh no." He covered his face with his hands and groaned. "How could I have been so stupid?"

Once again, his stubbornness had been his undoing—and he had pushed away the woman he cherished more than anyone else in this world.

His heart thumped as he bolted through the back door. "Everleigh?" he called. "Everleigh? Are you here?"

He checked the den, study, and kitchen before rushing into Alana's suite. "Everleigh!" he called. "Everleigh?"

He slipped through the door, and his hope took a nosedive when he found the den area bare—no framed photos on the windowsills, no books on the shelves, no shoes strewn about. The bedroom was empty too.

I'm too late.

He dropped down onto the edge of the bed, which groaned under his weight. Melancholy, regret, and frustration swamped him. His eyes scanned the room and found a few pieces of paper sitting on the floor beside the dresser. He grabbed them and started to read.

When he realized it was a letter addressed to Everleigh from Alana, he stopped. This was personal, and he felt like a snoop, but then another thought hit him: Maybe Everleigh had dropped it there on purpose. It was the only item she'd left in the room. Maybe she'd *wanted* him to find it.

Curiosity forced him to read on.

When he came to the end of the letter, his eyes were brimming with tears.

Suddenly, the last conversation he'd had with Alana echoed in his mind:

"Promise me you'll find your sunshine. Don't keep your heart closed forever."

He stilled, and understanding flowed through him. Alana was trying to tell him that Everleigh *was* his sunshine.

Wise, wonderful Alana had hoped to set him up with Everleigh. She'd wanted them to meet and fall in love. That was her grand plan all along.

And he had. He had fallen head over heels in love with sweet and beautiful Everleigh. Memories of their times together played through his mind like a movie—laughing at her cooking, disagreeing over painting the sunroom, watching her dance in the bookstore, helping her wade back into the ocean, sharing his deepest secrets with her, holding her the night of the storm.

Alana was right—they *did* belong together. He closed his eyes and smiled. "Thank you, Alana," he whispered.

Pulling his phone from the pocket of his jeans, he dialed Everleigh's number.

CHAPTER 30

CADE PACED AROUND the bedroom while the phone line rang. "Answer!" he grumbled. "Answer!"

After what seemed like an eternity, Everleigh picked up, and road noise sounded over the line. "Cade?"

Finally! He stared up at the ceiling, and relief twined through him. "Hey."

"Did you butt-dial me?" she asked.

He let the jab go. "Where are you?" He folded the letter and slipped it into his pocket before he hustled out of the inn toward his garage.

"Uh, I'm *driving*. I'm headed to Atlanta."

"No kidding," he quipped as he half trotted, half speed-walked down the driveway. "*Where* are you exactly?"

The hum of her car filled the line. Had the call dropped? But he wouldn't have heard the road noise if the call had disconnected, and the screen still displayed her name.

Had something happened to her?

Renewed adrenaline barreled through his veins.

"Everleigh?" he asked, panic filling him. "You still there?"

"Yeah, I'm here," she finally said. Then more silence. "Why do you care where I am, Cade?" Her words were measured.

He ground his teeth together as he punched in the garage code. The door hummed on its way up, and Bryant appeared at his feet. "Because I'm coming after you."

More silence.

"Why?" she asked.

He blew out a frustrated breath. Oh, this woman drove him crazy! "Let me know where you are, and I'll meet you." He crossed to his truck and leaned on the hood.

"Tell me why, Cade," she insisted.

"I need to talk to you."

"Go ahead and say what you need to say," she said. "I can listen and drive."

He moved his fingers over the cool metal hood. "I need to talk to you in person."

More silence was punctuated with the buzzing road noise. He closed his eyes and held back a groan. Why did she have to make everything so difficult?

"Everleigh," he began, his voice vibrating, "*please* tell me where you are. I will come to wherever you are." After a beat, he added, "Stop being so stubborn."

"I'm not being stubborn. I'm just being honest, Cade," she said, her words sounding throaty. "We said everything we needed to say when we signed the offer on the inn. Our partnership is over." She paused for a moment. "It's time to move on."

Oh, he wasn't giving up that easily. There was a reason his parents called him stubborn. "No, it's *not* time to move on," he said, retrieving his keys from the workbench.

"What are you talking about?"

"I found Alana's letter." He touched his back pocket, where he'd stowed the handwritten pages.

Another beat of silence. "That was private."

"Really?" he snapped. "Then why did you leave it in your bedroom for me to find?"

"I didn't—I mean, I shouldn't have," she stammered. "You had no right to read that."

"You think so?" he asked, challenging her. "Then let's talk about this *in person*." He rested his free hand on his forehead. "Now tell me, Everleigh, *where* are you?"

She remained silent.

It was time to try another approach. "Everleigh, I'm begging you to tell me where you are. We need to talk." He took a deep breath. "Please."

"Fine." She sounded tenuous. "I'm on I-95 South." She told him which exit she was near, and he recalled the area in his mind.

A smile overtook his lips. He'd taken that interstate so many times he could almost draw a map from memory. "I know exactly where that is. There's a rest area coming up in a mile or two. If you'll pull over there and wait for me, I'll be there as soon as I can."

"Okay." Then she disconnected the call.

With his pulse galloping, he spooned food into Bryant's garage bowl and gave him a quick pet. "I'm going to get Everleigh and bring her home, buddy. Wish me luck."

He picked up the project he'd been working on and loaded it onto the passenger seat. Then he hopped into the driver's seat and started the engine. His hands quavered as he steered out of the garage.

He was going after the love of his life and didn't have a moment to lose.

✦ ✦ ✦

I'm standing by your Blazer.

Everleigh stared down at the text message from Cade, and her pulse picked up speed. For the past hour and a half, she'd tried to stay busy. She'd walked around the grassy picnic area at least twenty times.

She'd paced by the vending machines until she was certain the security guard considered her suspicious—or at least a bit off her rocker. She purchased snacks and ate them and then bought more snacks and ate those too. She drank three diet sodas and was so hyped up on caffeine that she'd bitten her already short nails down to the quicks. But she couldn't blame her nutty behavior on the caffeine. No, it was her anticipation and confusion about why Cade was coming after her.

What did he want from her? And why had he found and read her letter from Alana? She groaned. She should have secured the letter in her pocket after reading it, but she'd been so distraught that she must have dropped it.

And Cade had found it. And read it!

He hadn't taken the time to see her before she left. So why was it so important to talk to her now? Had something in Alana's letter caused him to change his mind?

Her phone chimed with another text.

Cade: Where are you?

She took a deep, shuddering breath and then responded with: On my way.

Pushing herself up from the uncomfortable, wobbly plastic chair in the vending machine room, she moved through the crowd and stood by the doors leading out to the parking lot. Her eyes locked on

Cade, leaning against the front end of her SUV, while his eyes sorted through the people walking past.

He didn't seem to notice when three young women sauntered by him and eyed him with appreciation, but Everleigh agreed with their obvious assessment. She held on to the cold door handle and studied him—his tall stature, chiseled jaw, full lips, muscular arms and shoulders, trim waist, that messy, light-brown hair, and oh, that spectacular five o'clock shadow. A buzz of warmth spread through her as she recalled how she'd enjoyed the feel of his stubble and angular jaw the night of the terrible storm.

A sigh escaped her lips, and she tried to memorize his every detail in case this was the last time she saw him. She would never forget Cade. Sadness and regret spread through her.

"Uh, excuse me, miss," a voice said. "Are you going to stand here all afternoon or are you going outside?"

"Huh?" Everleigh spun to face a middle-aged man whose face was inked with irritation. "Oh. Yeah, sorry." A flush rose to her cheeks. "I was just—um—distracted." She held the door open for him.

His wide forehead wrinkled. "Thanks," he grumbled before muttering something about how strange young folks are these days.

Everleigh plunged her hands in the pockets of her jacket and slowly made her way toward Cade.

When his eyes found hers, relief seemed to fall across his handsome features.

"Hi," she said as she approached him.

"Hi." His voice was deep and rich, and she tried to commit that sound she loved so much to memory.

They were silent for a moment before they both started to talk at once.

He stopped himself, then made a sweeping gesture. "You first."

"Okay." She cleared her throat. "What's so important that you have to tell me in person?"

He pulled a folded stack of papers from his pocket, and she recognized it immediately.

"That was personal. Why'd you read it?" she asked.

He held it out to her, and she took it. "Why'd you leave it for me to find?"

"I didn't mean to." She stuffed it into the pocket of her jacket.

"What did you think of what she said about you and me?"

Her hands trembled as she shrugged.

"Do you think she's right about us?"

Everleigh longed to read his expression, but he was a master at hiding his feelings. If she told him she cared for him, would he let her down easy and then turn around and leave?

Then again, why had he driven ninety minutes and met her at a highway rest area to talk to her in person?

Nothing made sense, but she was determined to guard her already broken heart. "What are you getting at, Cade?"

"I asked you a question."

She tried to keep her expression blank. "I don't know."

"Fine. I'll go first." Cade licked his lips and then stood up to his full height. "Everleigh, when I met you, I had given up on everyone. Serena had broken our engagement, and my business partner had run our restaurant into the ground."

She nodded. "You told me the night of the storm."

"I was bitter that Alana had left the inn to you and me, and I had to negotiate plans with you. I was also angry when I found out that my mother had been lying to me all of my life when she told me I was an only child." The tremor in his voice made her throat thicken. "But somehow, you managed to break down the wall I've spent years building around my heart."

She sniffed and rubbed her eyes.

"When I had given up on everyone and thought I was completely alone, you showed up. You've taught me how fun, exciting, and amazing life can be. And as much as I thought I could let you walk out of my life, once you left, my heart was ripped to shreds. I'm tired of being alone. I'm tired of being bitter and resentful all the time."

Her eyes started to sting, and she wiped them. His words were music to her ears.

He threaded his hand with hers, and she enjoyed the feel of his warm skin. "I have something for you."

He steered her through the parking lot to his truck. He opened the passenger door and pulled out a lovely wooden planter bearing a handwritten plaque that said "In Loving Memory of Alana McFadden," along with the year she was born and the year she passed away.

"Cade!" she gasped. "You made this?"

He nodded. "For you."

"Oh, Cade. I-I don't know what to say." She rested her hand on his hard chest. "Thank you."

"You were so upset the day you had to tell that guest that Alana had died. You were crying on the swings, and I wanted to make you something to always keep in memory of her. You can plant her favorite flowers in it."

"Gerbera daisies," they said in unison.

Then Cade took the planter from her and set it back in the truck before taking her hands in his. "Everleigh," he began, "there's so much I want to say to you, but my mind is a jumbled mess right now." He shook his head. "Thank you for helping me learn how to trust again and how to love again. You've always believed in me even when I didn't believe in myself."

He paused, and she sniffed as tears rolled down her hot cheeks. "I came here to stop you from leaving, but if you really want to go to Atlanta, I'll understand. M-maybe I can survive without you, Everleigh, but I don't want to." He cupped his hand to her cheek. "You're the most brilliant, funny, adorable, irritating, infuriating, beautiful, exciting woman I've ever known. I want to spend the rest of my life showing you how to cook and arguing with you about dumb things."

She laughed.

"When I read the letter Alana wrote to you, I remembered something important. The last time Alana was admitted to the hospital, she asked me to make a promise."

"What was it?" Everleigh asked, searching his eyes.

"She said, 'Promise me you'll find your sunshine. Don't keep your heart closed forever.'" He paused and sniffed. "That's you, Everleigh. You're my sunshine. You opened my heart, and you're the brightest light I've ever seen."

She gasped as more tears streamed down her cheeks.

"You said Alana is our guardian angel, and she had given each of us half of the inn so we could make our dreams come true. I think you got part of that right," he continued. "She's definitely our guardian angel, but *her* dream was for us to meet. She wanted to set us up because she saw something inside us that would bind us together." He swallowed, and his eyes glittered. "Don't leave me, Everleigh. I'm begging you because . . . because I love you." His voice was husky. "And if you still want to go, then please, let me go with you."

"Cade," she whispered through her tears. "I feel like I'm dreaming because I love you too."

He dipped his chin and brushed his lips over hers. Her knees buckled, and she wrapped her arms around his neck and savored the thrill of his mouth against hers. She'd imagined his kiss so many times, but her fantasies paled in comparison to reality. As she leaned deeper into him, she felt like she was floating on a cloud.

When he released her, she held on to him for balance. "Cade," she began, sounding breathy, "you've been my strength through everything, and I'm so grateful for how you literally held me up and protected me on the night of the storm." She traced her finger over his amazing jaw, then ran her hand through his sandy hair.

"I thought you'd given up on me, Cade. You acted like you didn't care that we'd sold the inn or that I was leaving. When I told you about the offer, I hoped you'd ask me to stay. But instead, you completely shut down. As if you'd retreated into the man you were when I first met you. I thought you didn't care about me."

"I'm so sorry, Everleigh. I didn't understand until earlier today that you were hoping I would reject the offer. I was trying to protect myself from getting hurt again, but I wound up hurting you instead." His eyes searched hers. "Tell me we can be together. We can stay in Coral Cove, or I'll go to Atlanta with you."

"I don't want to go to Atlanta," she said. "I want to live in Coral Cove to be near you and my family. And I want to help you grow the B&B just like you and Alana planned. She's our guardian angel, after all. She orchestrated all of this. And I'm honored to be your sunshine because you're mine too, Cade."

He smiled and moved his thumb along her cheek, making every cell in her body leap to life. "Think we can hold on to the B&B and start a nonprofit at the same time?"

"How?" She searched his eyes.

"We'll hold fundraisers. My mom has participated in them before. Artists donate their pieces, people bid on them, and the money goes to the charity. Or we can auction off vacations at the inn. My brother is in finance, and I bet he'd offer his advice. I'll sell my motorcycle if I have to. I'll sell everything I own." He took her hands in his again. "We can make this work, Everleigh. Let's turn down the Newtons' offer, keep the inn, and start the nonprofit together."

"I'd love to." She lifted her chin. "But you're not going to sell that bike."

"Why not?"

"Because I want another ride on it."

He lifted an eyebrow. "Why?"

"Because then I get to hold on to you," she said, winking playfully. "Now, kiss me again."

His grin was wolfish, sending a sizzle of electricity through her veins. "Gladly, darlin'."

She blew out a dreamy sigh. "I *love* it when you call me darlin'."

"I'll keep that in mind, darlin'." He pulled her closer and rested his hands on her lower back. She wound her arms around his neck as he kissed her. His mouth was magic, making everything around them seem blurry and soft.

When he broke the kiss, she rested her head on his shoulder and let out a happy sigh. She felt safe and protected in his arms once again.

"How come Alana knew we belonged together but it took so long for us to figure it out?" he asked, his voice rumbling in his chest.

She lifted her eyes to his. "I don't know, but I'd like to spend the rest of my life trying to figure it out."

"Now that sounds like a plan, darlin'," he said, kissing her again.

EPILOGUE

Two months later, Valentine's Day

EVERLEIGH STEERED ALANA'S Jeep down the winding driveway and smiled as she took in the cars lining either side of the road. Warm yellow lights glowed in the inn's windows, and her heart skipped a beat as her headlights swept across the large sign that read "Valentine's Day Dinner—All Proceeds Benefit Alana's Angels." Their second charity event of the year was already turning out to be a great success, thanks to Cade. Her chest clutched.

If only Alana were here to see this . . .

She found a spot on the lawn large enough for the SUV, then climbed out, shouldered her backpack purse, and draped her coat over her arm. The mid-February evening air was crisp, and her breath came out in puffs of steam. Shivering, she bolted up the porch steps, passing the beautiful planter Cade had given her. She couldn't wait to add some gerbera daisies to it in the spring.

"Meow!" Bryant sauntered out from behind the planter and nudged her leg with his head.

"Hi there, sweetie." She stroked his ear. "I bet you're hiding out here so no one steps on you, huh?"

The cat meowed again and then scrambled down the porch steps to the driveway.

Yanking open the door, Everleigh was greeted by a flurry of activity. Conversations in every room tickled her ears, and the delicious aroma of chicken parmigiana, lasagna, and garlic bread made her pause and savor the moment.

She peered above the doorway, where Cade had stenciled those beautiful words that Alana had left on the business plan:

"An angel always finds its way to you, even in your darkest moments."

Everleigh smiled as she hugged her arms to her middle, letting memories of Alana wash over her.

"We need more sparkling juice at table four," someone hollered nearby, pulling Everleigh from her thoughts.

"I got it!" someone else responded.

Everleigh set her purse and keys on the bench in the foyer and peeked in the kitchen, where Mom and Harlowe, whose baby bump was hardly a bump, balanced trays of food. Both were ambling toward the back door.

Dad was busy filling baskets with garlic bread, while Landon and Amber, whose large diamond engagement ring twinkled in the kitchen lights, pulled trays of lasagna out of the oven. Roger stood nearby mixing up salad while his sister, her boyfriend, and Declan set the bowls on trays, preparing to take them out to the guests.

Everleigh was so touched by how everyone had pulled together to get Alana's Angels off the ground. When she and Cade shared the idea of renaming the nonprofit Alana's Angels and starting it in her memory, her family members and friends were all excited to pitch in.

A newborn's cry sounded, and Everleigh stopped herself from jumping into action.

You're not at work, silly!

She padded toward the nearby sitting room, where Cade's mother sat on the love seat holding her brand-new grandson, Jake. Stephanie smiled over at her mother-in-law, and the scene made Everleigh's heart swell. She'd been so sorry when Cade shared what his mom had gone through when she'd gotten pregnant with Declan, but she was grateful Trisha was healing from her past and had embraced Declan and his little family.

Not wanting to interfere, Everleigh moved back into the hallway.

Quinn appeared beside her and handed her a can of Diet Coke. "How was your shift?"

"Long, exhausting, and wonderful." She popped it open and took a long drink. The cool carbonation was just what she needed. "Looks like the event is going well."

Quinn pointed toward the back door. "You need to see for yourself."

"I'm sorry I wasn't here to help, but when Wendi asked me to take her shift, I couldn't say no."

"We all admire how dedicated you are to your job." She started toward the back door and beckoned Everleigh to follow. "But for real. Come see how great the tent looks. The fairy lights were a great touch."

"Where's Cade?" Everleigh asked while following her friend toward the back door.

"He's around here somewhere."

They stepped out into the cold night air, and Everleigh's eyes widened as she took in the large white tent decorated with thousands of twinkling white fairy lights and hundreds of red roses. Inside the huge tent were beautiful round tables, each one seating guests who appeared to be enjoying the delicious meal. More of their friends hurried around carrying trays and delivering their orders. Heaters provided warm air, and soft instrumental music added to the romantic atmosphere. Friends and acquaintances hustled by delivering food and taking orders. All of these people had come out to support Alana's Angels, and the entire event had been Cade's idea. Her heart swelled with appreciation and love for her wonderful boyfriend.

"You okay?" Quinn asked.

"Yeah." Everleigh sniffed and then laughed. "I'm just really happy."

And she'd felt that way ever since that afternoon when Cade had insisted she stop at a rest area on the highway. After he'd declared his love for her, she returned to the inn and moved back into Alana's former suite. Later that day, they had called Maggie and Henry Newton to renege on their gracious offer. Thankfully, the older couple had been understanding. Everleigh couldn't have imagined a better outcome.

Everleigh and Cade reopened the inn for visitors, and they fell into an easy routine. She got a job working part-time in the local NICU, and they ran the inn together. Cade also put the finishing touches on his new menu, hoping to start serving suppers for guests as well as larger events for the public. Tonight's dinner was their first time hosting a public event, and the response had been incredible.

Cade also wasted no time brainstorming fundraisers for Alana's Angels. Their first event, a polar plunge at the beach in late January, had raised several thousand dollars. With the help of his brother, they'd secured one financial backer and were working to find others. Everleigh also decided to keep Alana's Jeep, sell her Trailblazer, and donate the money to the nonprofit. So far they'd assisted two families who were struggling to pay bills and care for their ill children, and Everleigh couldn't wait to help more.

It seemed all of her and Cade's dreams were coming true. She and her sister had forged a new relationship, and she was enjoying weekly coffee dates with her as well as frequent suppers together. She and Harlowe had celebrated when Harlowe found out she was pregnant, and Everleigh couldn't wait to meet her niece or nephew in the fall.

Cade and Declan were also getting closer, and Everleigh was delighted at how well Declan, Stephanie, and their new baby fit into the family. Landon had finally proposed to Amber on Christmas Eve, and they were planning a spring wedding.

And Everleigh felt herself falling more and more in love with Cade every day. She cherished how he kept her laughing, how he supported her efforts with the nonprofit, how he cooked the most delicious meals ever, and how he took such good care of their inn guests. Not to be outdone, there were those kisses . . .

"Everleigh!" Maggie Newton waved her over to their table.

"Mr. and Mrs. Newton!" She gave each of them a hug. "I wasn't expecting to see you tonight."

Maggie playfully swatted Everleigh's hand. "I told you to call us Maggie and Henry," she scolded. "We just got to town a few days ago. We bought a little house a few miles from here, and we're so happy to finally call Coral Cove our home."

"You and Cade need to come by for supper sometime," Henry said.

Everleigh beamed. "We'd love to."

Maggie pointed to her lasagna. "Your fella is quite a cook."

"Yes, he is," Everleigh agreed.

Maggie held on to Everleigh's hand. "The inn looks lovely, and this fundraiser is spectacular." Her amber eyes glistened. "Alana would be so proud of you and Cade."

Everleigh's own eyes felt wet. "Thank you," she whispered. "Enjoy your supper."

"I can't wait for dessert," Henry declared. "I love tiramisu."

Everleigh zigzagged past the tables greeting familiar faces. She continued around the tent, searching for Cade. Where on earth was her boyfriend hiding?

"Everleigh!" Quinn called from outside the tent. "Over here!"

She joined her friend, and Quinn took her by the arm. As they walked up the path to the house, Quinn nodded her head toward the sunroom. "Someone's waiting for you in there."

"Cade?"

"Of course it's Cade." Quinn rolled her eyes. "Head on in there."

Everleigh studied her. "Why are you acting so weird?"

"Please stop asking questions and just go, okay?"

Everleigh stopped on the steps and turned toward the sunroom. The blinds were drawn, but the silhouette of a tall man moved around the room. "Cade's in there?" she asked. "Why?"

"Ugh! Just go already!"

Everleigh finished the last of her can of Diet Coke, tossed it into the recycle bin outside the back door, then jogged up the stairs and into the house. A wall of warm air greeted her, along with the buzz of conversation drifting down the hallway from the kitchen.

She moved to the sunroom doorway and stopped. Cade stood in the middle of the room, dressed in khakis and a light-blue collared shirt that complemented his eyes. His face was clean-shaven, which accentuated his angular jaw. He held a single red rose while two champagne flutes full of sparkling grape juice sat on the end table beside him.

He tipped the rose toward her. "Happy Valentine's Day."

"Happy Valentine's Day." She nodded toward the windows behind him. "Shouldn't we be helping outside?"

"It's going just fine without us."

"But you're the chef." She pointed toward the hallway. "Don't they need you in the kitchen?"

He waved her off. "Your dad and Declan have it covered. The food's prepped. All they have to do is stick it in the oven."

"You really think they can handle it without you?"

He shrugged. "If not, then they'll come find me." He held his hand out to her. "Come here, darlin'."

Swoon.

She took a step toward him and then stopped to examine her clothes. She'd been wearing her purple scrubs for nearly fourteen hours now. "I'm not dressed for celebrating anything. Can you give me a few minutes to change?"

"You look beautiful, as always." His eyes seemed to plead with her. "Please."

She scrunched her nose. "Babe, I really need a shower."

His adorable puppy dog look made her smile. She allowed him to take her hand and guide her to him. She took the rose he handed her and breathed in its sweet fragrance. Then she cupped her hand to his smooth cheek. "I love you, Cade."

He swallowed, and something flared in his eyes, making her legs wobble. "Everleigh, I love you and our life here."

"I do too."

"You're the love of my life." He paused. "For a long time, I was sure I'd spend the rest of my life alone. I'd given up hope of ever falling in love, getting married, and having a family, but after I met you, I realized life hadn't passed me by. Instead, my life was just beginning."

He dropped to one knee, and she pressed her hands to her collarbone. All the air whooshed from her lungs.

"Everleigh, I know we haven't been dating very long, but when you find the love of your life, you can't let her slip through your fingers. I almost lost you once, and I can't risk that again."

Tears stung her eyes.

"I'm ready to plan a future as your partner—your *permanent* partner." He hesitated. "If you'll let me, I want to be your husband and raise a family with you. I want to spend the rest of my life with you by my side." He pulled a jewelry box from his pocket and opened it, revealing a large, round diamond solitaire ring sitting on a white-gold setting.

"Oh, Cade." Tears streamed down her face.

"Everleigh Alana Hartnett, would you do me the honor of marrying me and making me the happiest man on the planet?"

"Yes, yes!"

He slipped the ring onto her finger, and it was the perfect fit.

When he stood, she leapt into his arms. He kissed her and twirled her around.

"I love you, Everleigh, and I promise I'll love you forever." He moved his fingertips down her cheek.

"I love you too, Cade. I can't wait to be your wife." She sniffed. "I'm so grateful Alana brought us together."

"I am too," he said. "Thank you for being my sunshine, darlin'."

She brushed her lips over his, and as he deepened the kiss, the infinite possibilities of their future life sparkled in her mind. Not for the first time, Everleigh thanked her guardian angel for bringing them together.

And deep in her heart, Everleigh knew that angel was with them still.

ACKNOWLEDGMENTS

AS ALWAYS, I'M thankful for my loving family, including my mother, Lola Goebelbecker; my husband, Joe; my sons, Zac and Matt; our five spoiled indoor cats; and our outdoor cat. I'm blessed to have such an awesome, amazing, supportive, and purring family.

To my critique partner, Kathleen Fuller, thank you for your help plotting this book. I've learned so much from you, and I look forward to working together on our future projects.

Pam Agustin—I had so much fun taking you to visit Southport, North Carolina, which was my inspiration for Coral Cove. Thank you for helping me plot this book during our trip. You were instrumental in bringing Cade's character to life. I'm so grateful that we met as pen pals nearly thirty years ago. You're the best aunt and godmother to my sons. We love you!

Kris Matthies—I can't thank you enough for sharing your knowledge of nursing and motorcycles. Thank you also for introducing me to the amazing traveling nurses—Lauren, Dorothea, and Ann—who took the time to share their stories. They are blessings to their patients, and I'm so very grateful for the time they took to talk to me.

To my dear friend DeeDee Vazquetelles—your friendship is a blessing. Thank you for proofreading this book and offering your thoughts and encouragement with this story. I don't know what I'd do without your daily texts and endless emotional support. As we always say, I'm so grateful our kids brought us together. You're my ride or die!

I'm so grateful to my wonderful church family at Morning Star Lutheran in Matthews, North Carolina, for your encouragement, prayers, love, and friendship. You all mean so much to my family and me.

ACKNOWLEDGMENTS

Thank you, Zac Weikal, for your help with my social media plans, my website, my online bookstore, and all the other amazing things you do to help with marketing. I would be lost without you!

To my agent, Natasha Kern—I can't thank you enough for your guidance, advice, and friendship. You are a tremendous blessing in my life. I hope you enjoy your retirement with your family—especially your precious grandsons.

I would also like to thank my new literary agent, Nalini Akolekar, for her guidance and advice. Nalini, I look forward to working with you on future projects.

Thank you to my wonderful editor, Lizzie Poteet, for your friendship and guidance. I appreciate how you've pushed me and inspired me to dig deeper to improve both my writing and this book. I'm a better writer because of you, and I'm excited to keep learning from you.

I'm grateful to editor Jocelyn Bailey, who helped me polish and refine the story. Jocelyn, I'm thrilled that we're able to work together again. You always make my stories shine. And I love our fun conversations about the details. (Our frequent discussions about SUVs versus trucks keep me in stitches!) Your friendship is such a blessing to me. Thank you for being amazing.

I'm grateful to every person at HarperCollins Christian Publishing who helped make this book a reality.

To my readers—thank you for choosing my novels. My books are a blessing in my life for many reasons, including the special friendships I've formed with you. Thank you for your email messages, Facebook notes, and letters.

Thank you most of all to God—for giving me the inspiration and the words to glorify You. I'm grateful and humbled You've chosen this path for me.

DISCUSSION QUESTIONS

1. At the beginning of the novel, Cade is certain he'll spend the rest of his life as a bachelor. What do you think causes Cade to change his opinion about finding his own love story?

2. Everleigh is devastated that her godmother, Alana, has passed away. Have you ever lost someone close to you? If so, how did you cope?

3. Everleigh and her sister, Harlowe, have always had a rocky relationship. Everleigh tries to mend their relationship throughout the book despite her sister's constant rejection. Have you ever struggled with a relationship with one of your family members? Were you able to overcome those issues?

4. Trisha, Cade's mother, is shocked when Declan, the son she gave up for adoption when she was a teenager, appears out of the blue. At first, she can't handle seeing him since he brings back painful memories that she longs to leave in the past. By the end of the story, she realizes she does want a relationship with Declan, his wife, and their future baby. What do you think causes Trisha to change her mind?

5. Everleigh returns to Coral Cove determined to sell the Sunshine Inn and start a nonprofit in memory of her godmother, Alana. At the end of the story, she's not sure what path to take. Have you ever

DISCUSSION QUESTIONS

experienced an overwhelming change in your life? If so, how did you adapt to it?

6. Cade is stunned to find out that he has a half brother, and he's devastated when he learns that his mother kept his brother a secret for more than thirty years. Have you had your heart broken by someone close to you? If so, how did you handle that devastation, and what did you learn from it?

7. Cade loves to cook. Do you have a special hobby or interest that you have loved since childhood? If so, what is it, and why is it special to you?

8. What has Cade learned about himself by the end of the novel? How does that influence his thoughts about a future with Everleigh?

9. Declan is crushed when his biological mother, Trisha, rebuffs him. He decides to give up on having a relationship with both Trisha and Cade. In the end, his mother comes around, and he fosters the relationships with them that he longed to have. Why do you think Declan forgives Trisha for the way she repeatedly hurt him?

10. Have you ever visited a small coastal town like Coral Cove? If you could go anywhere for vacation this weekend, where would you choose to go?

ABOUT THE AUTHOR

Dan Davis Photography

AMY CLIPSTON is an award-winning bestselling author and has been writing for as long as she can remember. She's sold more than one million books, and her fiction writing "career" began in elementary school when she and a close friend wrote and shared silly stories. She has a degree in communications from Virginia Wesleyan University and is a member of the Authors Guild, American Christian Fiction Writers, and Romance Writers of America. Amy works full-time for the City of Charlotte, North Carolina, and lives in North Carolina with her husband, two sons, mother, and five spoiled-rotten cats.

✦ ✦ ✦

Visit her online at AmyClipston.com
Facebook: @AmyClipstonBooks
Instagram: @amy_clipston
BookBub: @AmyClipston